"You want me. I can ... it for a long time. Ever since we visited the bonesetter."

"I will not lie. There is nothing I want more." He pressed warm lips against her temple. "But this is wrong."

She wrapped her arms around his neck. "Is it? Unless," she faltered, "you feel I am taking advantage of you."

"Sweetheart, no one takes advantage of me." His voice was a gentle rumble. "It's just that you've had a terrible shock."

"You have no idea."

He kissed her cheek. "That is why we cannot."

She turned her face to catch his lips. She tasted his surprise. And then he nipped at her lips. Slow and sweet. Their mouths immediately adapted to each other. He held her face in his large hands. She parted her lips and their tongues touched and parted and met again. Rose had never been kissed like this. Long and unhurried, purely for the pleasure of it, and not as a hasty prelude to sex. This man knew how to kiss. *How to kiss her.*

He broke away. "Your reputation."

Is already destroyed. She nibbled his jawline. "Don't stop."

Also by Diana Quincy

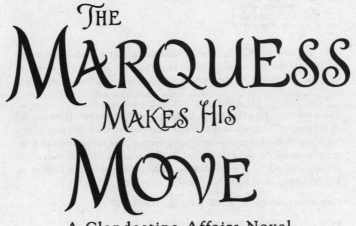

The MARQUESS MAKES HIS MOVE

A Clandestine Affairs Novel

Diana Quincy

AVONBOOKS

An Imprint of HarperCollinsPublishers

FSC
MIX
Paper from
responsible sources
www.fsc.org FSC® C021394

First Avon Books mass market printing: March 2022

Print Edition ISBN: 978-0-06-298684-9
Digital Edition ISBN: 978-0-06-298682-5

Cover design by Amy Halperin
Cover illustration by Victor Gadino

FIRST EDITION

Printed in Lithuania

22 23 24 25 26 SB 10 9 8 7 6 5 4 3 2 1

For Taoufiq—
through thick and thin.

THE MARQUESS MAKES HIS MOVE

Brandon reacted. He lunged, wrapping his arms around expensive fine wool. It took all of his strength to lug the woman back to the side pavement. She was heavier than she appeared.

"Get off of me, you lout!" She struggled in his arms.

Instead of showing gratitude, she screamed at him as if he were accosting her? Alexander Worthington, Marquess of Brandon, was not accustomed to being berated. *By anyone*.

He stiffened. "No need to thank me for saving your life."

"Let me go, you cow!" squeaked another raspy voice. A child. Brandon blinked, finally realizing why rescuing the woman took so much effort. She had her arms folded around a flailing boy of about ten or so. The coach and four thundered by on the cobblestones just as she wrestled the youth out of the way.

She relaxed her grip. "Where is your mother?"

"In Hades!" The boy took off—or at least he tried to. Brandon grabbed the urchin by his soiled collar. The boy ran in place for a second before realizing he'd been caught again.

"Bugger!" He struggled to get away. The boy was all limbs, arms and legs squirming and kicking.

"Cease this instant," Brandon ordered. "And mind your manners."

Something in his voice, perhaps the dark tone of warning, prompted the boy to go still. "I ain't done nuffin' wrong."

"I doubt that," Brandon said.

"You are scaring the child," the woman admonished.

Brandon took in the sly expression on the boy's narrow face. "He's not the sort to frighten easily."

Chapter One

$\mathscr{H}$e noticed the woman the moment before she flung herself directly into the path of a lumbering oncoming coach and four.

She was young and attractive, but it wasn't her eyes that caught Brandon's attention, although they were large and almost unnaturally blue, like robin's eggs. Nor was it her hair, which escaped its pins in long, gleaming waves the color of afternoon sunlight. No, it was her monstrous hat, an extravagant and overdone flourish of colorful feathers. She might as well have a peacock sitting on her head.

The woman stood out on the crowded London sidewalk and was exactly the sort of female he avoided—expensively dressed and probably known to high society. Although, to be fair, Brandon stayed clear of most people.

She had launched herself into the street. Feather hat and all. As she sailed through the air, her wool periwinkle pelisse flapped like a flailing bluebird. The four matching grays startled. One whinnied as eight pairs of hooves slammed against the road surface, bearing down on the woman.

Her eyes blazed. Robin-egg blue edged in amber-red fire. "Do you make a habit of bullying young children?"

"Bullying?" Irritation simmered along the surface of Brandon's skin. "I will have you know that because I saved both you and the child from being trampled, I am late for an important appointment." A meeting that had taken weeks to arrange that would show his enemies that he had lost patience.

"Nonsense." She attempted to right the feathered eyesore on her head. "I went in after the boy to pull him to safety."

"Nice hat," he responded.

Amusement lit her eyes. "Yes, well, it was a gift from my elderly aunt. She knows I have a fondness for artistic hats, although this one is a bit outlandish." She pulled back her shoulders. "She was very happy to see me wearing her gift when I visited her today."

"What did you do to her?"

"I beg your pardon?"

"To deserve that hat?"

Her lips quirked. This woman was almost certainly a lady. Her bearing and clothing told him as much. As did her clear and precise diction. In contrast, Brandon was dressed like a member of the laboring class rather than a nobleman. And yet, she didn't speak down to him.

"You, sir," she said with a twinkle in her singular eyes, "are ungallant."

He tipped his chin. "A failing I readily admit."

"I'll have you know that I received compliments about my hat today."

"Did they have eyes?"

She swallowed a snort. "My elderly aunt's friends. It's possible that their eyesight is failing them."

"Gor!" the boy piped up. "Are you gonna 'old on to me forever?"

"It will be as the lady wishes," Brandon informed him.

"If you promise not to run," she told the child, "I will supply you with a meal and perhaps an errand for which I shall pay handsomely."

Speculation gleamed in the boy's eyes. Brandon released him. The urchin looked wily enough to be lured by the promise of food and money.

Brandon shifted his weight from one foot to the other. It was time to take his leave. "I am late to my appointment. Good day."

She finally looked at him again. "I suppose I should thank you for saving me."

"You are most welcome." He bowed his head before turning to weave his way through the crowded sidewalk.

"Although," she called after him, "I did not need saving."

ROSE FLEMING STARED out the window later that day, her thoughts on the handsome stranger who'd dragged her out of the street. His vigor left an impression.

Even though her would-be savior was tall and well formed with rugged good looks, Rose kept remembering his eyes. Cynical yet glinted with humor, and so black that it was like staring into an abyss. A tap at the door cut into her reverie.

Rose turned from the window to find the housekeeper regarding her expectantly. "Yes, Mrs. Waller?"

"The footman candidate is here. The one that the agency sent over."

"Oh, yes, of course. I'd forgotten." The appointment

slipped Rose's mind because she was too busy wool-gathering. "Has he been here long?"

"About a quarter of an hour."

"Put him in the front salon."

"Yes, madam."

A few minutes later Rose joined the footman candidate. His height struck her first. He was over six feet. Standing by the window looking out, his profile revealed a strong nose, generous forehead and precise chin.

"Good afternoon, I am—"

He faced her.

"Oh." Rose stopped short, staring at the dark-haired stranger with the cynical eyes. "It's *you*."

Surprise lit his face. "Are you—?"

"*You* are here for the footman position?" she asked at the same time. Surely, it was a mistake. How could the commanding stranger she'd encountered on the street be a *footman*? This man possessed the aloof splendor of a person accustomed to being waited upon.

"Yes." He paused. Something unreadable flashed across the stern features that somehow contrived to make him handsome. "I am here for the footman position."

His deep, gravelly voice sent a shiver through her. "I am Mrs. Fleming."

"I hardly recognized you without the hat."

She bit back a smile. "Insulting your potential employer does not do you any credit."

"I apologize."

"There's no need for that." Flustered, she looked around. She almost invited him to take a seat, which one most certainly did not do with a servant. "The agency sent you?"

"That's right."

"Do you have any experience?" This man possessed both height and looks, two highly sought-after attributes in a footman. With his appealing visage and arrogant demeanor, he could find a position in one of Mayfair's finest homes. Why settle for a merchant employer in a not-quite-fashionable neighborhood like Spring Gardens?

"I have a little experience." Thick, long lashes rimmed watchful eyes. Most women of Rose's acquaintance would kill for those lashes. Pity they were wasted on a man. "But I am a quick learner. I won't disappoint you."

What he lacked in experience, he made up for in confidence. "What work have you done in the past?"

"I was employed by an elderly bachelor who passed away."

"I see. And before that?"

"Mostly work on the family farm."

"Your father is a farmer?"

"You could say that."

That explained his athletic physique. Working on a farm would require daily physical labor. Did it also account for the golden-olive tint of his skin? She'd taken him for a Spaniard at first. Or perhaps black Irish. Yet, his accent suggested neither. He spoke very well for a manservant. "Are you aware of the work that will be required of you here?"

"I assume you will enlighten me."

He certainly didn't have a servant's deferential attitude. If he was going to work in her household, Rose needed to establish appropriate boundaries. "Let us begin with your name, shall we?" she said coolly.

"Alex, ma'am. Alex Worth."

"Very good, Alex. As a footman, you will be required to rise at seven o'clock. You will clean the knives and the lamps. Set the table for breakfast and serve Mr. Fleming and myself."

"Mr. Fleming is your—?"

"My husband and the master of the house." Not that Roger acted like much of a husband. Or master of anything. "As I was saying, you will lay the table and serve at breakfast and lunch, clearing the table afterward. At five o'clock, you will light the lamps and candles and bring them into the drawing room. You will lay the cloth for dinner at six o'clock, wait on us at dinner, clear the table and wash up. You will take the candles and the lamps down at ten-thirty when Mr. Fleming and I retire for the evening."

"I don't see any reason that should be a problem."

"In addition, you will brush out Mr. Fleming's suits, my skirt hems and our shoes. Either you or Dudley will answer the front door. You will divide these chores that I've just described and any other chores that arise on any given day."

"I'm most grateful for the opportunity." He spoke in a grave, raspy tone. His manner was perfectly correct, yet the slightest trace of irony gilded each word.

"Very good," she said crisply. "You can expect to present yourself to Mr. Fleming this evening at supper."

He dipped his chin. "Yes, madam."

"Dudley will direct you to the tailor to have a livery made up."

"I will check with him, madam."

"Very good." She hesitated. "I shall see you at supper, then."

"As you wish, madam."

Rose departed, leaving him standing in the salon. It was only after she closed the door behind her that Rose realized she'd been holding her breath.

BRANDON, NOW KNOWN as Alex—he needed to become accustomed to being addressed by his name rather than his title—surveyed the stuffy attic room he shared with Dudley, his fellow footman. He could barely stand upright without hitting his head. The room just managed to accommodate two narrow beds, the table between them and a wardrobe. Not exactly the sort of arrangements Brandon was used to. But that was of no consequence.

What mattered was that he was here, in the home of Roger Fleming, London's preeminent mapmaker. A man who thought he could use a fraudulent map to cheat Brandon out of his land and get away with it.

Fleming had crossed the wrong man.

A known recluse from high society, Brandon was not an idiot. Nor did being the half-Arab heir of the Mad Marquess make him unsophisticated. Brandon suspected at least one of his adjoining landowners had conspired with the mapmaker to cheat him. Someone who believed Brandon sullied their precious ton with his mother's foreign blood and merchant roots.

He pulled what few clothes he'd packed from his valise. At the bottom lay the rolled map drawn by Fleming. He tucked the canvas in among his things and arranged them in the wardrobe opposite Dudley's meager pile of clothing.

His thoughts drifted to Mrs. Fleming. She was a surprise. An attractive woman with a sense of humor.

And not a lady after all. She was a merchant's wife, even though the expensive clothing and regal bearing suggested otherwise. In any other situation, he might be inclined to like her. Did she know her husband was unscrupulous?

Dudley popped his head in through the narrow door frame. "We're having tea now in the servants' hall. Coming?"

Brandon shut the wardrobe door. "I wouldn't miss it." He followed his fellow footman down to the basement.

"We usually have our tea after we've served at dinner," Dudley said as they trotted down the stairs. "But Mrs. Waller called for an early tea today."

They joined the home's other servants: Bess, the maid of all work, Mrs. Waller, the cook and housekeeper, and to his surprise, the boy Mrs. Fleming rescued earlier in the day.

"You're still here?"

"In me flesh," the boy responded. Brandon saw now that the child was painfully thin, his arms like flesh-covered twigs. "Missus says I'm ter be fed while she finks of errands for me."

The housekeeper sipped her tea. "Don't you worry. I'll find plenty for you to do."

Brandon stared down into the weakest cup of tea he'd ever seen. It was certainly nothing like the strong black sage-flavored tea he was accustomed to. His mother, Lady Brandon, shed most things from her Arab past, including her name (Maryam became plain Mary) when she married his aristocratic father. But she'd held on to her tea, going so far as to instruct the gardener at High-field to plant mint and sage to flavor the *shay*.

"Why ain't you drinking yer tea?" Bess set down her chipped porcelain cup. All of the dishes were chipped and mismatched. "You'd better drink up. We only get tea twice a day."

"I prefer my tea a bit stronger."

"Well, excuse me, *Yer Grace*." Dudley smirked. "I don't expect the servants got fresh tea leaves at yer last situation."

Brandon frowned. Did all servants drink from *used* tea leaves? He had no idea what kind of tea his servants at Highfield consumed. He never thought to ask.

"I fink it's good." The boy gulped his tea down and reached for another piece of bread, the only food served with the tea.

The housekeeper, a portly woman with her hair glued back in a tight bun, gestured at Brandon's untouched ration of tea and bread. "You'd best take whatever nourishment is offered. You will need it to fuel you for your duties."

"Sound advice, I'm sure." Brandon forced himself to drink the tea and made an effort not to grimace. He made a mental note to purchase tea on his afternoon out. Whenever that was.

"Where were you last in service?" Bess asked.

"I have limited experience."

Dudley spoke around a mouthful of bread. "How limited?"

So much so that he had to bribe the employment agency to place him in Fleming's four-story terraced home. He also arranged for Fleming's previous second footman to receive an offer of employment from the

Duchess of Huntington, who happened to be Brandon's sister.

"I was previously employed by an unwed elderly gentleman who died." At least that was the story he worked out with the agency. Any gaps in his man-servant knowledge could be attributed to serving in a bachelor household with few requirements. "Before that, I worked on my father's farm."

A bell jingled. It took Brandon a moment to realize it was the servants' bell. Similar contraptions were mounted in the servant areas at Highfield, but Brandon hadn't laid eyes on them in years. He was accustomed to being on the opposite end—doing the summoning.

Bess popped up. "So much fer my tea." She looked longingly at the half-full cup and crusty bread before heading for the stairs.

"Wonder what the mistress wants," Dudley said.

Brandon set his terrible tea down. "Is Mrs. Fleming a demanding employer?"

Mrs. Waller's lips firmed. "We don't tell tales about our employers."

"Not usually," Dudley said at the same time. "Especially not during the day. She normally closes herself off in her sitting room and sketches all day."

"Every day?" Brandon pretended not to see Mrs. Waller's quelling look. "She spends the entire day drawing?"

"She takes lunch and long walks. But then goes right back to it. Has done for as long as I've worked here, which is going on three years now."

"Is Mrs. Fleming an artist?"

Dudley scoffed. "Can't say. I ain't never seen any of her drawings. Not a one."

"Tea is over." Mrs. Waller stood, her chair screeching disapprovingly across the flagstone floor. "Surely you two have something more productive to do than gossip about the mistress."

"We surely do." Dudley winked at Brandon. "I have a bill the master wants me to go and pay. Alex here can brush out the master's boots by the back door."

"Owen can help you with the boots," Mrs. Waller informed Brandon. "He needs to earn his keep."

"Who is Owen?"

"Gor, that's me," the boy piped up. "What's yer name?"

"I'm Alex."

"Are you goin' to tip me fer 'elping clean the boots?"

"Most certainly not," Brandon said, leading the boy up the stairs.

Chapter Two

"You ain't a very good footman," Owen proclaimed.

"Forgive me if I do not take a street urchin's word for it." Brandon searched the cupboards in the footman's pantry until he found what passed for a clean cloth.

"You didn't even know what a footman's pantry is." Owen sat on the counter swinging his spindly legs, the heels of his worn half boots thumping against the cabinets below. "If I 'adn't 'ave told you, you'd be cleaning them shoes by the back door."

"My former employer did not have a footman's pantry." Brandon had never heard of such a room, although he assumed there must be one at Highfield. He knew there was a butler's pantry, but he'd never actually been inside it.

"Did 'e 'ave shoes?"

"What?" Brandon craved silence but the boy was a chatterbox.

"Yer employer before. Did 'e 'ave shoes?"

Brandon rubbed the white cloth against Roger Fleming's dirty black boots. The boy's nonstop prattling added to the annoyance of cleaning his nemesis's footwear. "He did have boots."

"Like I said. You ain't no footman."

Brandon ignored him and contemplated whether wetting the boot might make it easier to clean.

"Yer supposed to scrape the dirt off the edges of the sole with a bone or wooden knife."

"Learned that while living on the streets, did you?"

"Me ma cooked in a 'ouse even grander than this. I used to 'elp 'er in the kitchens. Ran errands for the 'ousekeeper and butler sometimes, too. I seen 'ow shoes are supposed to be cleaned."

"Did you now?" Brandon studied the boy. He might be of some use after all.

"Sure did," he said proudly. "After you scrape off the dirt, yer gonna use yer hard brush to get the rest of the dirt off. Then you get yer blacking brush—"

"Where is your mother now?"

The boy's face clouded. "She took ill and died."

"When was this?"

"'Bout three months ago."

"I am sorry. And you've been on the streets since then?"

Owen shook his head. "Went to stay with Ma's brother Willie but 'e's a mean drunk so when the mistress said I could come 'ere, I decided to try it out."

"Won't this Willie be missing you?"

"'E'll be missing trying to swat me."

Brandon stilled. "He beat you?"

Owen grinned. "'E tried but 'e couldn't catch me." He puffed up his scrawny chest. "I was too fast fer 'im."

"And your father? Where is he?"

"Dunno." Owen shrugged. "Never knew 'im. Ma said

'e was no good. Any'ow, after you brush the dirt off the boot, you use blacking to make it shine."

"Where do I find the blacking to polish the boots?"

"You make it, of course."

"I *make* it?" Posing as a footman was proving far more complicated than Brandon anticipated. He'd expected to mostly serve at meals and answer the door. "Surely, it can be purchased somewhere."

Owen guffawed. "It's too expensive. Cheaper to make it."

Brandon ran an appraising look over the boy. "Do you know how to make this blacking?"

"Sure do. Seen the footman do it a 'undred times. Sometimes when 'e was busy with guests, I 'ad to do it. You mix ivory black, oil of vitriol, sweet oil, brown sugar, vinegar—"

Brandon held up a staying hand. "All right, then. I will pay you a shilling to show me how to clean boots. And that includes making the polish."

He was tempted to pay the boy to do all of his tasks, but Brandon's masquerade needed to be convincing. Everyone in the household must believe he really was a footman. Shining a few boots was a small price to pay for regaining the water meadow that Highfield's tenant farmers needed to boost their agricultural output. They had families to feed. Destroying Fleming's venerable mapping business in the process would make an example out of the brazen thief and any others who conspired against him.

"Three shillings," the boy shot back.

"Fine."

"Really?" Owen's eyes nearly popped out of his head. The amount was a small fortune to an orphaned child. "Yer gonna pay me three shillings?"

"And you have to show me how to brush out clothes, clean knives and any other duties that I don't know how to perform." Which was most of them.

The boy crossed his arms over his bony chest and pretended to contemplate the offer. "Seems ter me all that instruction is worth more 'an three shillings."

"Never mind, then."

The boy popped off the counter. "On second thought, I accept yer terms."

"More pudding?" the new footman asked Rose.

"No, this will suffice." She'd never felt odd being waited on by a manservant before, but having Alex attend to her made Rose distinctly self-conscious. She was extraordinarily aware of his presence behind her. He stood at the ready and swept in at appropriate intervals to carry her plates away or refill her drink. Dudley, stationed on the opposite end of the long table, saw to Roger's needs.

"The pudding is excellent," her husband remarked.

"Yes, it is, isn't it?" she responded.

At meals, they engaged in meaningless conversation that Rose suspected bored Roger as much as it did her. They never discussed the only real subject they had in common in front of anyone. Issues related to the family mapping and engraving concern, left to Rose by her uncle and now publicly run by her husband, were nobody's business but their own.

She scooped a spoonful of pudding. "I shall be sure to convey your compliments to Mrs. Waller."

"Oh yes, please do." Roger's polite gaze shifted from her to the man standing behind her. "Alex, isn't it? You're the new footman."

"Yes, sir." The deep voice came from behind Rose. Alex was not in her line of vision, and she resisted the urge to twist in her chair to observe him while he conversed with Roger. Doing so would be highly inappropriate dinner table behavior, especially for the mistress of the house, and Roger was a stickler for the proprieties.

Her husband's gaze moved up and down as he inspected the new manservant. "Came to us from the agency, did you?"

"I did, sir, yes."

"Dudley here looks after me. You will serve as my wife's footman."

"What?" The word escaped Rose's mouth before she could remember to be more circumspect. "That's not necessary." She still had no view of Alex, but she sensed his attention to the conversation.

"I think that it is," Roger replied pleasantly, but firmly. "Whenever you leave the house, Alex here will accompany you."

"I am hardly a society miss who requires an escort when I go out. And when I do need accompaniment, Bess goes with me."

"We are better than that." Roger sipped his wine. "It will be as I say."

Rose swallowed an angry retort. "As you like." This topic was best discussed in private. The last thing she desired was to be trailed everywhere she went.

"As my wife's footman," Roger addressed Alex, "you will attend to her needs."

Rose registered Alex shifting behind her. "Yes, sir."

"You will prepare her breakfast tray, clean her shoes, brush out the hems of her dresses and attend to anything else she requires."

"I will do my best, sir."

"See that you do. I want my wife well looked after."

Roger's brows knit when his gaze fell on Rose. "You are flushed, my dear. Are you well?"

"Abundantly so. It's a bit warm in here."

"It does feel like it is going to be a hot summer." He rose. "Shall we retire to the salon?"

Chapter Three

$\mathcal{R}$ose followed her husband into the formal front salon. He closed the doors behind them. It was their evening ritual, one of the few times they were alone during the day, and able to speak frankly.

"How is Lord Wallthorne's map coming along?" Roger inquired.

"I should have it done by next week."

"Not sooner?"

"No. It is a very involved piece and I want it to be right."

"We could double our profits if you drew more quickly."

"I draw the finest maps in all of England." Although no one knew it. Few patrons would pay top prices for a map drawn by a woman. "And that is because I take my time with them."

"We need the money."

"You might try squandering less of it."

"It's important to keep up appearances. The illusion of success invites success."

"Is that why you engaged a second footman that we do not need? If anything, we require a new maid. Bess is overworked."

"Male servants lend prestige to a household." He poured himself a glass of port. "The new footman has a fine face and form. Additionally, he is tall. He looks like he could serve at a duke's table."

"That's just it. We are tradespeople, not nobility. And I don't care to be constantly trailed by a servant. You know I enjoy my long walks."

"By all means, continue to take your daily constitutional, just do so with Alex. I am afraid I must insist on this point."

"Engaging a new footman is just as wasteful as your insistence that I frequent modistes favored by the ton. Patronizing a Bond Street dressmaker is the height of indulgence. And then there's the vacant apartment above the shop. We should be renting that space out."

He shook his head. "We don't want to appear desperate. It's all about giving the impression of prosperity. At the moment my maps are the finest in London. I'm able to command the highest prices for them."

"Don't you mean *my* maps?"

He continued as if she hadn't spoken. "Having a well-dressed wife attended by an excellent specimen of a footman lends us more consequence. And will allow me to command even higher prices for our maps. It's like driving the most expensive coach. People make assumptions about your success based on what kind of coach you drive."

But they did not own an expensive coach. "What do you do with all the money you take out of the business?"

He gave her a severe look. "It is not your place as my wife to question my spending habits. However, if you must know, I hope to secure a royal warrant."

"A royal warrant?" Her mouth dropped open. "You must be jesting."

"I most certainly am not." His soft brown eyes shone. "Imagine if I am appointed the official royal surveyor, engraver and cartographer."

Alarm bolted through her. "You realize that you are actively seeking to defraud the Prince of Wales, the very man who rules England?"

He sipped his port. "Stop overreacting."

"Everyone thinks *you* draw the maps." And that was because she signed her finished works R. Fleming. Fortunately, she and Roger shared the same first initial. "What if they discover that I am the cartographer in the family?"

Roger scoffed. "Who is going to find out?"

A noise sounded outside the door. They both stilled, listening quietly. Rose couldn't be sure but it sounded like—"Do you hear footsteps?"

She darted to the door and threw it open, but there was no one there.

"Calm down," Roger admonished. "No one is eavesdropping on us. For goodness' sakes, we are safe in our own house."

BRANDON OVERHEARD SOMETHING about a royal warrant, but beyond that, he picked up useless snippets of the Flemings' conversation through the closed door. However, he did learn one important piece of information: Roger Fleming's wife was smarter than her husband. Mrs. Fleming was innately savvy enough to sense danger. Unlike her dullard spouse. Fortunately for Brandon.

Still, it was deuced inconvenient that he had to serve the wife rather than the husband. He needed access to Fleming's private rooms, his study and bedchamber. Serving as the man's personal footman would make that easier.

He escaped to his attic room while Dudley remained in the basement cleaning up after supper. Beads of perspiration quickly gathered on his forehead in the hot and airless chamber. He spread the Fleming map over his bed. There was no denying the man's talent. Brandon was no expert but this map was beautifully detailed. Too bad it was also wrong. Not for the first time, he regretted agreeing to engage a London surveyor and mapmaker.

He'd allowed himself to be drawn in by Fleming's reputation for honesty and excellence. And the man's maps were practically pieces of art. So when it came time to draw proper boundaries to enclose their properties, Brandon and neighboring landowners engaged the cartographer to survey their properties, peruse their land papers and draw maps delineating each man's property. The final result cheated Brandon out of a critical section of his land, cutting off access to a main water source.

Owen burst in. "There you are!"

Brandon casually rolled up the map. "Do you ever knock?"

Owen's face scrunched up. "What's that?"

"What do you want?"

"Why are you up here? Yer supposed to be cleaning the glasses and knives."

"Oh, joyous day," Brandon muttered under his breath. To the boy, he said, "We'd best get to it, then."

Chapter Four

W here's the rest of breakfast?"

Dudley snorted. "Treated you like a prince at yer previous place, did they?"

"Bread and tea?" Brandon stared at the paltry ration before him. "That's it?"

His stomach rumbled. He'd been up for two hours. The boy had shown him how to clean and trim the lamps. Then he'd prepared Mrs. Fleming's breakfast tray, which she took in her sitting room. Afterward, he helped Dudley clear the table and wash the dishes, glasses and utensils.

"That's all the master allows," Bess said.

"You will find that the midday meal is heartier," Mrs. Waller assured him.

Brandon could scarcely believe the meager offerings. The Flemings weren't wealthy, but surely, they could afford to properly nourish their servants. He slathered butter on the bread and downed it with the weak tea, which went down far more easily than it had the previous day.

Mrs. Waller turned her attention to Owen, who gobbled

his bread and gulped his hot tea as though it was cold water on a sultry afternoon. "After you are done eating, you'll need to sweep the front steps."

The bell rang. Dudley looked at Brandon. "That's fer you."

"It is?" He thought Bess answered when Mrs. Fleming rang.

"Yer her footman now. When she rings, you attend to her."

Brandon rose, downing the rest of his tea and taking his unfinished bread with him. "Where is she?"

"In her sitting room," Mrs. Waller said.

Bess's eyes rounded. "You can't attend the mistress with bread in yer hand!"

"Not to worry." Brandon mounted the steps two at a time. "I'll devour it long before Mrs. Fleming sees me."

When Brandon reached Mrs. Fleming's upstairs sitting room, the private chamber where the lady of the house spent most of her time, he tapped on the door. Her muffled voice sounded through the door.

"Come in."

"You rang, madam?"

"Oh, Alex, yes." She rose from a large drawing table pushed up against the window. She wore an embroidered floral dressing grown with fringed edges. "Come in."

The sun shone through the window, encasing her slender silhouette in a warm golden glow. She'd arranged her hair in a messy bun atop her head, held in place by a pencil stabbed through the center. Wispy tendrils of hair framed her face in amber threads. Any objective observer would find Mrs. Fleming to be a striking woman. Yet, she seemed oblivious to her appeal.

Her sitting room was an inviting space furnished with dark woods and faded upholstered furniture. Papers and stacks of books littered the table surfaces. Bright scarves hung over one chair. The space was not what he expected. The house's public rooms were impeccably formal, presenting a sterile facade to the outside world. But Mrs. Fleming's private rooms were intimate, colorful and unassuming.

"I shall be going to the modiste in about an hour's time," she informed him. "Since my husband insists that you accompany me, I am alerting you in the event there are other duties you must attend to before we depart."

"Yes, Mrs. Fleming. I will be ready at your convenience."

"Thank you. You may go."

As he made to withdraw, his gaze caught on a framed map above the well-worn floral sofa. He instantly recognized it as one of Fleming's. He knew the man's work in detail. He'd studied his own Fleming map a thousand times. Brandon couldn't fathom how a colorless man like Fleming could create such beauty. He peered more closely. "It's this neighborhood. Spring Gardens."

"Yes." She came to stand next to him, their mutual attention on the map. Her fragrance reached him and he inhaled the scent of lime and flowers.

"What do you think?"

"It's remarkable."

"Truly?"

"Absolutely. Particularly the details, the trees that indicate the park, the headstones in the graveyard, the city squares. The unique flourishes that are your husband's signature."

A becoming flush painted her cheeks. His praise pleased her. Even if it was for her husband.

"In all honesty," he added, "I am stunned your husband is capable of producing something so imaginative and artistic."

Her mouth quirked. "Are you insulting your employer?"

"I meant no disrespect," he lied.

"Of course you did." But he saw that she wasn't angry. If anything, Mrs. Fleming appeared amused. "You'll need to mind your tongue around Mr. Fleming if you mean to keep your position."

"And around you?"

"I appreciate frankness. It's refreshing. Most of the servants hide their real feelings."

"I'm hardly an open book."

She gave a charming little laugh. "You're anything but. I am quite certain there is much more to your story. However, it is yours to keep private if you so choose."

He felt a stab of guilt. Ruining her husband would certainly harm Mrs. Fleming. An outcome she did not deserve *if* she was oblivious to Fleming's machinations.

"As long as no lines are crossed," she said, "I do enjoy a harmless barb every now and again."

"I shall endeavor to stay firmly on my side of the line."

"Then we should get along swimmingly." Their gazes met and something warm flowed between them. They turned from each other in unison.

"I should get back to work," she said.

Work? Brandon stepped away. "I shall be ready to depart when you are, madam."

"WELCOME, MRS. FLEMING." Madame Gisele hurried forward when Rose entered the Bond Street shop with Alex trailing her. "I have set aside several gowns with the tasteful embellishments you enjoy."

"I cannot wait to see them," she said politely.

The modiste's gaze drifted up to Rose's bonnet. "Your hat is sublime. The artistry is impeccable."

Rose touched a hand to the front edge of her new hat, a wide-rimmed bonnet with a flourish of silk red roses. "That is most kind of you to say." Behind her, Rose thought she heard Alex snicker.

She followed Madame Gisele to the fitting chamber. Despite being a regular customer, Rose still felt ill at ease whenever she visited. Even the most extravagant gown could not disguise the truth that she and Roger were tradespeople, as much as her husband longed to pretend that they weren't.

"Here we are." Madame Gisele pointed to the several gowns in the changing room. "If none of the designs are to your liking, we can always make the perfect gown for you."

"I am sure these will do." Rose always selected pre-made dresses. Custom creations cost a fortune. She had no idea whether the modiste was truly French, but her prices were certainly worthy of the finest Paris designs.

As much as Rose dreaded visiting Madame Gisele's establishment, it kept the peace with Roger. He was more likely to heed her advice on important business matters if Rose humored his silly ideas regarding enhancing their consequence. She hated having to placate her husband, but there was nothing to be done for it. As her husband, Roger had the final say over everything, even though Rose's late uncle left the print shop to her.

The first garment she tried on was a pink gown with gold embroidery trimming the sleeves and hem. She came out and stepped onto the platform before the large mirror.

"Beautiful." Madame Gisele folded her hands over her chest. "This one you must have. It highlights the length of your neck, and your beautiful porcelain skin." Rose caught sight of Alex in the mirror. He'd taken up a position near the entrance. She couldn't see his eyes, but she sensed his keen gaze fixed on her.

Madame kept the compliments coming as Rose tried on dress after dress. The deep green made Rose's skin gleam like marble. The red silk was divine and on and on. The final selection was a soft blue fringed gown that enhanced the color of her eyes.

"I shall take this one," Rose said.

"Very good. Would you also like the purple silk, madam?" asked one of the salesgirls.

"I think not." Standing before the full-length mirror in the blue gown, she turned and peered back at her reflection over her shoulder. Behind her, Alex watched quietly.

"The purple gown is a bit too much," she said to the girl, trying not to let Alex's presence fluster her. She wasn't accustomed to being followed around everywhere. "The simpler lines look best on me." Besides, the purple gown was clearly the most expensive of the lot. No need to squander even more money.

"Which ones shall it be, then?" asked the modiste.

Rose crossed one arm under her chest, resting the

opposite elbow on it as she cradled her chin, contemplating her purchases. "Definitely this one. I do like the fringe, and the pink with the embroidery. The green as well."

"Exemplary taste as usual." Madame nodded her approval. "You have an artist's eye. I would love to see which hats you will pair with these dresses."

Another smothered laugh erupted from Alex.

The modiste cast an admiring look in his direction. "Perhaps your handsome footman would like to come closer." Alex wore an old livery that Mrs. Waller had found for him until a new one could be made. It was ill-fitting and too small, stretching tight against the backs of his shoulders and clinging almost obscenely to muscular thighs and other . . . assets. "I am certain my girls would like a closer look."

Alex bit back a smile. "I am quite content where I am."

Madame Gisele surveyed him from head to foot. "Mrs. Fleming is most fortunate to have you to serve her."

"I am here to see to Mrs. Fleming's every need."

The modiste examined Alex the way a discerning cook assessed the freshness and firmness of vegetables at the market. "What woman would not want a footman such as you to tend to her needs?"

One of the salesgirls whistled while another winked at Alex. "He can take care of my needs," she said with a saucy jaunt of her head. "In fact, I have some urgent things that need attending to right this minute."

"Come to think of it," laughed another salesgirl, "so do I."

Alex's eyes twinkled. "I apologize, but you must look elsewhere. I can only look after my mistress's needs."

"I think we are through here," Rose said sharply, stepping down from the dressmaker's platform with her head held high. "My husband engaged Alex. Not I." She marched toward the dressing rooms while avoiding Alex's gaze.

Behind her, she heard Madame Gisele remark, "That husband of hers, I think he is not so smart. In fact, the man must be a complete fool." The salesgirls' laughter trailed Rose into the fitting room.

After she dressed, Rose completed her order and double-checked Madame Gisele's final calculations before approving the final bill of sale to be sent to Roger for payment.

"The dressmaker was jesting about admiring your hat, wasn't she?" Alex asked once they emerged from the shop.

"She most certainly was not. Madame Gisele is a woman of taste. She understands creative genius."

"And you are the genius?"

"Not at all. I don't design these hats. I am simply smart enough to recognize a masterpiece when I see one."

"If you say so."

"When are you getting measured for your livery?" she asked.

"I have an appointment with the tailor this afternoon." He followed after her on the paved sidewalk, keeping a step behind as any respectful servant would. Although his confident swagger overshadowed any attempt at deference.

"Very well. Until you have your new livery, I think it is best that you not accompany me in public."

"That suits me." He tugged at the shoulder of his skintight tailcoat. "This livery is at least two sizes too small."

She'd noticed. The ill-fitting costume embraced Alex's masculine curves so completely that it was practically indecent. The livery left so little to the imagination that the broody new footman had already prompted more carnal thoughts from her than Roger had in four years. Not that Roger wanted anything from her besides more maps. He stopped coming to her bed long ago. Her husband's sudden, inexplicable defection from the marriage bed three months after they wed still smarted.

"Watch yourself," Alex warned, putting a hand on her elbow. "There's a puddle." She'd have stepped right into the muddy hole if he hadn't redirected her.

"Yes, thank you." She practically snatched her elbow away. Being touched by Alex reminded Rose of what she didn't have with her own husband. Did Roger really find her so unattractive? True, she wasn't a curvy woman. But being slender was supposed to be fashionable.

"You did that on purpose back there," she accused.

"Saved you from stepping into a puddle? Guilty as charged."

"Not that." She was perspiring under her pelisse. The day was particularly warm for so early in May. "You made insinuations at the modiste's when you talked about your duties."

"I was just having some fun with Madame Gisele and her girls." His dark eyes glittered. "It was harmless. Shall I get you a hack?"

"No." The last place Rose cared to be was in a cramped hackney with Alex. "I'd rather walk."

"As you wish."

They walked home in silence. It was quite a distance, but Rose was accustomed to walking. However, the sun was bright and by the time they reached home she suspected she was red-faced and she knew she was perspiring.

"Please set up my hip bath," Rose said to Mrs. Waller, who greeted them when they entered the front hall.

"I'll see to it, Mrs. Fleming."

Rose escaped to her bed chamber and pulled off her pelisse and fichu. She ran a hand over her décolletage; her skin was warm to the touch. She heard a masculine tread in the corridor. Followed by a tap on the door.

Alex entered with two large buckets. "I have your bath water."

Her maid usually oversaw the preparation of Rose's bath. "Where is Bess?"

"She's out on an errand." She watched him pour the water into the hip bath. Although Rose was accustomed to having manservants bring up her water, it felt strangely intimate to have Alex prepare her bath. Now, due to Roger's silly edict, she'd have to accustom herself to it.

Did Alex feel strange seeing to her bath? She shook off the ridiculous notion. Her footman's thoughts should be of no concern to her. Besides, he probably took no more notice of her than her own husband. Not that she needed Roger's, or any man's, admiration. She had her maps. The finest in London. That was admiration enough.

Except that she had to let Roger take credit for her work. For everything really, despite the reality that she also managed the business side of things, except for the accounts, which Roger insisted on maintaining.

What Roger did best was spend her money. Yet, he wasn't much of a drinker or gambler as far as she could tell. Where did the money go? Was he possibly saving it?

Alex stepped out into the corridor and returned with more buckets full of water that Dudley brought up. "Will there be anything else, Mrs. Fleming?"

"Did you leave one bucket for rinsing?"

"Erm. No." She'd caught him off guard. "Shall I go and heat more water?"

"No, this will do." She didn't want him coming back. She just wanted to get into the bath and relax.

"As you wish."

"Oh, and Alex."

"Yes, Mrs. Fleming."

"You will not need to attend me for the remainder of today. I shall be busy writing some letters after my bath. And this evening Mr. Fleming and I have a dinner engagement."

"Very good, madam." After he was gone, Rose latched the door. She normally left it unlocked for Bess to help her rinse off. But today she felt the need to be assured of complete privacy.

After shedding her clothing, she settled in the tub. The water was too hot but as she sat there, hugging her knees to her chest, her forehead resting on her knees, the bath began to cool and so did she. She felt more aware of her body. Of the delicate curve of her breasts and their pointed tips. The smoothness of her legs. The sensitivity of her most private area.

She began to feel overheated again. Her fingers slid down to the place between her legs. With a long sigh, Rose threw her head back and took care of her pleasure for the first time in many, many months.

TRYING NOT TO envision what Rose Fleming looked like in the bath, Brandon exited the tailor's shop after getting fitted for his footman's livery. Preparing a woman's bath was a surprisingly intimate experience. It prompted a man to have involuntary erotic imaginings.

The fitting hadn't taken long so rather than returning directly to New Street, Brandon detoured home to Peckham House. As he walked to Mayfair, images of Rose trying on gowns at the modiste replayed in his head.

She was given to expressing herself with her arms, holding them out and away from her body, palms up, as she studied her form in the looking glass, assessing how each gown fit her slender body. From what Brandon could tell, she had a fine arse, round and full, despite her trim form. Her breasts were not large.

She'd ordered several expensive gowns as though cost were no option. Yet allotted meager food rations to her servants. Contempt rippled through him. Maybe Rose Fleming was just like her lying, cheating bastard of a husband.

He put thoughts of Mrs. Fleming aside once he arrived home. His butler, Stokes, greeted Brandon when he entered the front hall.

"Welcome home, my lord."

"I'm only here for an hour or so. Please have a bath prepared and anything Cook can scrounge up for a meal.

I'm famished." He took the steps to his bed chamber two at a time. "And, Stokes."

"Yes, my lord?"

"Prepare a basket for me to take when I depart. Fill it with biscuits, tea, coffee, meats, cheeses. Whatever Cook has on hand."

"Consider it done, my lord."

"Also, use one of our oldest baskets. The more worn, the better."

Stokes, who by now was accustomed to odd comings and goings, as well as strange requests from his employer, merely nodded. "I will see to it, my lord."

Thirty minutes later, after a long, hot bath in which he luxuriated far too long, Brandon sat at his dining room table devouring cold chicken, *foul moudammas*, cheese, tomatoes, bread, olives and baked apples sprinkled with sugar and lemon zest.

"Stokes?"

The butler, who stood at the ready by the sideboard, stepped forward. "Yes, my lord."

"What do we feed the servants?"

"My lord?"

"For breakfast, for example. What do you all eat?"

"Sometimes porridge with bread and butter. At other times, potatoes with bread. Two or three times a week Cook will add bacon or fish." He paused. "Is his lordship concerned that the expenditures are too high?"

"No, not at all. Please see to it that a meat or fish is included with every breakfast." He sipped strong, hot tea flavored with plenty of sugar and fresh sage from his garden. "And what about ale?"

"Shall I bring you some ale, my lord?"

"No, the servants. Do we provide them with ale?"

"We do, my lord."

"Good." He tore off a piece of chicken and stuffed it into his mouth. Food had never tasted so delicious. "Please see to it that we have plenty of ale in the house. The servants are to have as much as they like."

"As you wish."

"What about tea?"

"The servants have tea twice a day. In the morning and then again in the late afternoon."

"What kind of tea leaves do you use?"

"Black tea, my lord."

"Fresh tea leaves? Not used?"

"No, my lord. His lordship is not in residence often enough to furnish the servants with used tea leaves. We could purchase them, of course. But the marchioness used to insist that the servants have fresh tea."

That sounded like Mama. She had loved her *shay*. "I'm pleased to hear it. I don't want anyone in this household drinking tea from used leaves. Ever."

"As you wish, my lord."

Something small and fast raced into the room. It took him a moment to realize it was a dark-eyed, curly-haired toddler. Leela, Duchess of Huntington, Brandon's sister, breezed in behind her daughter.

Her eyes lit up when she spotted her brother. "You *are* here. I can scarcely believe I've caught you at home."

"I was just on my way out, actually."

Stokes pulled out a chair for Leela. "I would love some tea," she said to the butler.

Brandon cut a piece of sliced apple. "You did hear me say that I need to leave soon?"

"Where are you going?"

"I have some business to attend to."

"Where have you been?"

"You can change the question but the answer remains the same."

"Still acting as mysterious as ever, I see."

"To what do I owe the pleasure of this visit?"

"I left some maps in Mama's upstairs sitting room and came to retrieve them. It's pure luck that I've found you here."

Something nudged at Brandon's knee. He stared at the little girl who blinked back at him with large, solemn brown eyes. "Up."

"What does it want?" he asked his sister.

Leela helped herself to some *foul* and olives. "*She* wants you to lift her up."

"And put her where?"

"On your lap, of course." Amusement danced in her eyes. "Don't look so alarmed. Maryam won't hurt you. Three-year-olds are generally harmless."

He gingerly lifted the child onto his lap. Leela handed the girl a piece of cheese. "I forgot you named her after Mama." Nibbling on the morsel, his niece snuggled close in Brandon's chest.

"Huh. Look at that." Leela sipped her tea. "Maryam doesn't usually take to people so quickly."

He felt an unexpected stab of pride. "Well, I am her uncle, after all."

"Maybe you should come and see her more often."

"I'm hungry." The child pointed to the rolls on the table. "I want some bwed."

"You want bread?" Suddenly, he was eager to give the child whatever she wanted. "Here you go, sweetling."

"Thank you." Maryam took the food from her uncle with remarkably small, pudgy fingers and settled contentedly against his chest.

"Your cook makes *foul*?" Leela scooped a bite of the mashed fava bean mixture with a piece of bread.

"*Citi* sent it over," he said, referring to their Arab grandmother.

"*Citi* does make the best *foul*. She always adds just the right amount of lemon and garlic."

Brandon stroked Maryam's little head. Her dark curls were baby soft. "Will you give her a brother soon?"

Leela shrugged. "It hasn't happened yet. And it never might."

"Isn't it rather early to abandon all hope in that direction?"

"I thought I couldn't have children at all. Maryam was a delightful surprise."

"Doesn't Huntington want an heir?"

"His current heir, his cousin, has several sons. The succession is assured whether or not I bear a son." She tilted her head. "Speaking of heirs. What about you? You need a son."

"I am considering the possibilities."

"You are?" She leaned closer. "Do you have someone in mind?"

"The Duke of Kingsley has an eligible daughter."

"Lady Olympia? She was the diamond of the season last year. She had many suitors from the finest families."

"Precisely."

"Do you care for her?"

"What difference does that make? She's a duke's daughter."

Understanding lit her eyes. "And you would delight in winning the most eligible young lady on the marriage mart."

"Isn't it past time that I restore respectability to the Brandon title?"

"That's not what you are doing. You want to laugh in the face of all of those people who rejected our parents."

"Would that be so terrible? Father wasn't any madder than you or me."

"Society thought he must be in order to marry the Arab daughter of foreign merchants."

"I shall have a bit of revenge. Imagine the uproar when the Mad Marquess's half-Arab son snaps up the diamond of the Season right out from under the blue-blooded sons of the fine lords and ladies who shunned our parents."

"Be careful of what you wish for."

"How cryptic." Brandon popped an olive into his mouth. "What is that dire warning supposed to convey?"

"Revenge doesn't seem like a very good foundation for a marriage. I already pity poor Lady Olympia."

"You should not. I'll shower her with gifts and intend to treat her with the utmost courtesy and respect."

Leela did not look impressed. "What of marrying for love?"

"Not all of us are meant to make grand love matches like you and your duke."

"Papa married for love, too."

"I prefer to take a more pragmatic view. Wedding Lady Olympia would be a favorable alliance."

"Are you certain she'll have you?"

He handed his niece another piece of cheese. "I can be charming when I put my mind to it. She seems pleased enough to receive roses from me."

"You sent her flowers?"

"I am having very extravagant arrangements delivered to Lady Olympia once a week."

"You do have a knack for getting whatever you go after."

"Exactly. Besides, I'm the highest-ranked title on the marriage mart at the moment. At least, the only one with all of my hair and teeth." He studied his niece's profile. "She really does look a great deal like Mama."

"But she has Papa's chin."

"I can see that." He contemplated his sister. With her family and work as an author of travelogues, Leela had found a contentment in life that eluded her brother. "Our blood family has dwindled, has it not? With Mama and Papa gone. It's just you and me and, now, this little one."

"Not entirely. We have numerous relatives on the Arab side of the family. Too many to count. You should think about meeting some of them." Leela herself had only recently become acquainted with Mama's relations. While he and Leela were growing up, their mother publicly rejected her Arab relatives in order to fit into their father's noble world. It hadn't worked. Not for Lady Brandon or her children.

"I've met the bonesetter." The daughter of Mama's sister ran a clinic at the Margate charity hospital where

Brandon sat on the board of governors. What Leela didn't know was that Brandon had also forged a strong bond years ago with *Cidi*, their late Arab grandfather, and their male cousins.

But Mama had sworn him to secrecy. *The nobility will never accept you as one of them if you consort with Arab merchants.* Lady Brandon tried to convince her children that they belonged wholeheartedly to their father's world. But it didn't take long for Alex and Leela to discover the truth—that they existed in a chasm between the two worlds.

"Hanna told me how you came to her assistance when Hunt and I were in Greece."

"I don't care to see the upper classes, people who have never known a day's work, taking advantage of laboring people."

"You can't avoid the ton forever. You *are* a marquess."

"I am aware. That is why I intend to wed Lady Olympia."

It was what his parents would have wanted. For most of his life, Brandon had avoided nobles. He hadn't grown up with them and steered clear of blue bloods at Oxford, preferring to associate with students whose parents were merchants, doctors or solicitors. It was this general absence from society—and the less-than-lily-white color of his skin—that made it possible to masquerade as a footman.

Leela scooped more *foul* with her bread. "It's a little awkward for you to hate the very station in life into which you were born."

"For the most part, noblemen are a bunch of pricks. Excuse my language."

Maryam peered up at him. "What's a pwick?"

"Never mind, darling," Leela said.

Brandon stared at the girl. "She's so clever! Look how quickly she picked up on that."

Leela rolled her eyes. "That's not exactly the sort of language I'd like her to learn."

"Why not?" Maryam piped up.

He guffawed. "Your papa would have something to say about that." From the first, Brandon and Huntington had not taken to each other.

Leela shot him a quelling look. "You would find Hunt very agreeable *if* you bothered to spend any time with us. He willingly risked his reputation to wed me. Now he even travels with me for my work. And look at Hanna's husband, Lord Griffin. He makes no qualms about his viscountess working as a bonesetter."

"I am acquainted with Griff. We serve on the hospital board together. He is tolerable." To Brandon's surprise, the two men were actually developing a friendship.

"Precisely. Not all noblemen are awful. After all, Papa was one."

"I will take my place in society once I wed. And I'll do it for our parents, to honor their memory. But I still don't see a place for myself among the ton any more than I do among Mama's Arab relations. The truth is that neither of us fully belongs in either place."

"*Citi* once told me that you and I must carve out our own place."

He rested his chin on his niece's downy head. "Which you seem to have done."

"And so shall you. Just you wait and see."

Chapter Five

"There he is," Dudley said as Brandon trotted down the steps upon his return from Peckham House. "Did you get lost on the way to the tailor?"

The servants were having supper in their basement dining hall.

"Am I late for the evening meal?"

Bess reached for her ale. "We're eating early because the master and his wife have a dinner engagement."

"Where have you been, Alex?" Mrs. Waller inquired.

"I . . . erm . . ." Unaccustomed to having to answer to anyone about his comings and goings, Brandon grappled for an answer. "I went to see my aunt."

Bess gasped. "On a Tuesday?"

Dudley chewed on a piece of beef. "Did Mrs. Fleming give you leave to take a few hours off?"

Alex took his place at the table. "Not exactly."

"Which means no," Owen said cheekily.

He glowered at the boy. "You are not being helpful."

Mrs. Waller's mouth tightened. "Mr. Worth, in this house, servants are entitled to a half day off on Sunday afternoon. And the occasional Sunday evening as well."

"Mrs. Fleming informed me that she wouldn't require my services for the rest of the day."

"You still have other duties in addition to attending the mistress. Such as cleaning Mrs. Fleming's shoes and brushing out her hems."

"Of course," he said smoothly. "I'll attend to those chores directly after supper."

"You cannot vanish whenever the urge takes you," the housekeeper added.

"I understand. It's just that my aunt sent me a note to attend to her immediately. She's ill," he added for good measure. There. That sounded convincing.

Mrs. Waller's expression soured. "I am not aware of any note for you being delivered here."

"Erm . . . Owen here brought the note to me as I was on my way to the tailor's."

"Where did Owen get the note?" Dudley asked.

Owen tucked his chin in his palm and stared at Brandon. "Why don't you tell 'em, Alex?"

"Someone delivered the note while Owen was sweeping the front steps. Since I had just departed, he thoughtfully ran after me and delivered it."

"Yes! That I did!" Owen's eyes sparkled. "And 'e tipped me fer my trouble, didn't you, Alex?"

Brandon narrowed his eyes. The scamp was going to rob him blind. "Yes, I did. Now, go and earn your tip by fetching the basket I left in the kitchen."

"Basket?" Owen popped up. "What's in it?"

"Bring it here and you'll soon find out." He hadn't looked in the hamper, but assumed it contained some of the food and drink items he'd requested. Whatever it was would be a welcome supplement to the sparse portion of beef, carrots and potatoes on the plate before him.

"It's 'eavy." Owen returned, carrying the basket that looked almost as big as the boy. "What did you put in 'ere?"

"Why don't you do the honors?" Brandon said to the boy.

Owen returned a blank stare.

Dudley snorted. "What the duke here means with those big words of his is that you can open the basket."

Owen dropped to his knees before the basket and removed the cloth covering its contents. "Gor! I fink Alex robbed the finest tea shop in all of London."

"Nonsense." Alex spoke around a mouthful of beef. "My aunt sent it."

"I thought she was sick," Bess said.

"She had her daughter prepare it for me." There. He might not be getting any better at lying, but at least he was quicker.

Owen reverently pulled out a large jar of tea, followed by a generous portion of coffee.

Dudley's eyes rounded. "Is that fer us?"

"For you all to share. For us, I mean." Brandon quickly corrected himself. He was, after all, supposed to be one of them.

Owen pulled out the packages one by one. "There's cheese and biscuits and *sponge cake*."

"Can we eat that now?" Dudley asked.

Brandon dipped his chin. "We may do as we like."

"And sausage rolls." Owen continued to unload the basket. "Strawberry tarts."

The list went on and on. Cook had clearly outdone herself.

Owen helped himself to a tart. "Yer aunt must be right rum."

"I beg your pardon?"

"Rich," Bess translated. "And if you have a rich aunt, why are you here?"

Brandon carefully chewed his meat, using the time to think of an answer. "She isn't," he said after finally swallowing. "She used to work for a lord and, although she's been pensioned off, they still send her generous baskets now and again." The lie sounded ridiculous to Brandon but they all seemed to accept his story.

Dudley bit into a sausage roll. "I really need to find a situation with a lord. One day I'll be valet fer the finest nobleman in all of Mayfair."

Bess scoffed. "What fancy lord is going to take a merchant's leavings?"

"What do you know?" Dudley shot back.

Bess lifted a shoulder. "Enough to understand that a footman doesn't go from being in service to a shop-keeper to brushing a duke's boots."

Mrs. Waller watched Owen empty the basket. "Tea and coffee are precious," she said to Brandon. "Naturally, you'll want to keep them for yourself."

"Not at all." He stuffed some potatoes and carrots into his mouth. "It's for all of us to share and enjoy."

"Very well, then." Mrs. Waller hastened over to retrieve the two items. "I shall take charge of rationing the tea and coffee to ensure we'll be able to enjoy them for a good, long while."

Owen snatched another tart. Mrs. Waller shot him a quelling look. "I'll also put up the food to ensure that it lasts as well."

"As you like," Brandon said. "As long as we don't have to drink used tea leaves."

"Well, la-dee-da to you." Dudley's eyes twinkled. "Working fer the Flemings is going to take some getting used to fer you. It's quite the comedown."

"I'll survive it." He came to his feet. "If you will all excuse me, I have duties to attend to."

Rose Fleming had small feet. Brandon marveled at how petite as he cleaned the lady's well-worn half boots with soap and water.

"Now the blacking," he said to Owen once the boots were cleaned to his satisfaction.

Owen shook his head. "You can't polish the boots till they're dry."

"Why not?" It would take hours for the leather to properly dry.

The boy shrugged. "They'll never look well if you do. And you'll need ter take out the laces or the blacking will ruin 'em."

"Very well." Brandon exhaled. There certainly were a lot of rules when it came to something as simple as cleaning muddy shoes. "I suppose I can brush out Mrs. Fleming's gown while I wait."

He laid the pale blue muslin gown out on the table and picked up a brush.

"Not that one." Owen popped a tart into his mouth. The boy had obviously pocketed a few before Mrs. Waller managed to hide them.

"Why not?" Brandon inspected the brush in his hand. "This is for clothes, isn't it?"

"That's a 'ard brush for coats and the like." He picked up a second brush and tossed it over.

Brandon caught it and started to brush the fabric.

"Nope."

Brandon heaved a heavy sigh. "What now?"

"You need ter brush in the direction of the nap."

Brandon stared down at the fabric. "What direction is that?"

"Toward the 'em of the skirt. You really ought ter be paying me more. Yer the worst footman I ever seen."

"So you've said. Repeatedly." Brandon brushed in the direction of the hem. "What do I do next?"

"Focus on the 'em."

"Owen!" Mrs. Waller's voice resonated through the footman's pantry.

Owen edged off the counter. "Gotta go." He disappeared through the door. "Old bat's got another chore fer me."

Brandon ran his hand over the thin cotton fabric as he brushed. It was soft to the touch and smelled like Rose Fleming—warm femininity with notes of lime and flowers. Brandon never imagined that cleaning a woman's things could be so . . . personal. But he could almost feel a whisper of Rose Fleming's body warmth. This cloth had slid along her bare skin, encasing her entire body. Heat crawled over his skin. It was almost like touching her.

Fleming was a fool. Brandon made a vow to himself. Once he married, no manservant would ever come within ten feet of his wife's things.

By the time he emerged from the footman's pantry, Brandon found Dudley alone in the kitchen. Mrs. Waller and Bess had retired for the evening.

Hips leaning against the worktable, Dudley yawned. "One of us has to stay awake to let in the master and Mrs. Fleming. You and I will have to take turns."

"I'll do it," Brandon promptly said. Here was the opportunity he'd been waiting for. "I'm not tired at all. You go on to bed. I'll wait up."

"If yer sure." Dudley rubbed his eyes.

"Very sure."

Dudley didn't need much convincing. "You'll need to keep lamps burning in the front hall. As well as in the hall and the staircase."

"I will see to it."

"Go ahead and put out the lamps in the drawing and dining rooms now since the master and the mistress aren't in."

"Of course. When should I expect them to return?"

"The Flemings live a quiet life. They don't stay out late." Dudley trudged up the stairs. "I'll just go and light the lamp in the master's bedchamber."

"I'll take care of that." Brandon followed the footman. "It's the least I can do since I was gone this afternoon."

"That's right sporting of you, Alex." Dudley continued up to their shared attic room while Brandon veered off in the direction of their employer's bedchamber.

Fleming maintained a separate room across the hall from his wife. Brandon pushed open the door to Roger Fleming's room. The lamp illuminated a tidy chamber with a four-poster mahogany bed. Shaving soap and tooth powder sat out on a dresser. A single stuffed chair was by the unlit hearth. The room felt sterile. There were few personal effects, no mementos of any sort. Fleming's chamber was strangely impersonal, almost like a room you'd take for the night at an inn.

It wouldn't take Brandon long to go through the man's things. He started with the drawers. Then shifted to the neatly arranged wardrobe, searching for proof Fleming had deliberately drawn faulty enclosure boundaries. He didn't know exactly what he hoped to find. A letter. Notes. A journal or ledger. Anything that contained the evidence Brandon needed to prove Fleming had cheated him.

The moment he received the map several weeks ago, Brandon had realized the extent of Fleming's duplicity. It did not take a Cambridge scholar to deduce who benefited most from the swindle. Brandon's Highfield neighbor, Charles Canning, the grandson of an earl, had likely put Fleming up to it.

But Brandon hadn't protested at first, even as the fury in him festered. He preferred to keep his enemies off guard. Let them think he was the fool they believed him to be. In the meantime he'd find proof that Fleming and Canning had cheated him.

And then he'd destroy them.

"WE SHOULD CONSIDER producing dissected maps," Rose said to Roger.

"Dissected what?"

"Jigsaw puzzles with maps on them." She walked along the shop floor. "They're an excellent tool to teach geography to children. I believe they would sell well."

Rose visited the business in the Strand once a week

on Wednesdays. She'd make the forty-five-minute walk from New Street more often if it weren't for Roger. Her husband preferred she stay away completely and absolutely forbade her from dropping in unannounced.

Rose missed being at the shop. Before her marriage, she spent several days a week with Uncle Trevor, a respected surveyor who taught her how to establish land boundaries. Her mapmaking skills she learned from Ben, the shop's cartographer. Even though Roger had replaced all of Uncle Trevor's workers, she still adored everything about the shop, its scents and sounds, the industriousness, keeping busy creating things and selling them.

"I do believe you should cease visiting the shop," Roger said. "It is unseemly for a woman to concern herself with business matters."

They were alone on the shop floor, except for Alex, who stood several feet away, pretending to be oblivious. The two shop apprentices were at work in the back room.

Rose stiffened. "You seem to have forgotten that my uncle left this shop to me. Mapmaking has been my family business for three generations. Everything about this shop is most certainly my concern."

"As your husband, all of your worldly possessions belong to me, including this shop." He spoke the damning words in a kindly manner, yet each one stung. This was *her* business, *her* family legacy, even if the law, and Roger, did not see it that way.

She diverted him by reaching into her reticule and pulling out a drawing. "The accounts are not as robust as they should be. In addition to the dissected maps, I want to put simple maps, like this one"—she handed him her design—"on tea towels. We could also print similar maps as needlepoint patterns."

His forehead wrinkled. "But we are a surveying and map-publishing concern." Roger was not the most imaginative man. In the four years since they'd wed, he hadn't come up with one innovative idea to help grow the business.

"Yes, and we will now publish maps on tea towels and for needlework patterns."

Despite his skepticism, Roger studied her drawing. Making money always interested him. "I don't know if it could work."

"Of course it will." She could feel Alex's attentiveness to their conversation even though he looked straight ahead and showed no reaction. "Why not add to the shop's income by selling items that are inexpensive to reproduce and can be sold at a sizable profit?"

Roger hesitated, but the glimmer in his eye confirmed she'd won him over. "Very well." He acted as if he were doing her a great favor, when they both knew Rose was the sole reason the shop made any money at all. "We shall start with the tea towels and the needlepoint patterns."

Satisfaction rippled through her. "I'll find the tea towels that work best with an ink transfer."

Breezing out of the shop feeling triumphant, she stepped into the sunshine, followed by Alex. His new livery still wasn't ready, but she could hardly visit her husband without his chosen footman in tow.

"There's a shop just down the street that has a nice selection of tea towels," she told him as they walked.

"You draw maps as well?" He kept a step behind her but with Alex's innate, rugged elegance she doubted anyone would take him for a servant if it weren't for the uniform.

"Very simple ones. Nothing like my husband's, of course." She tried not to choke on the words. She'd lived with the lie for years, but it was increasingly difficult to stomach.

"I hadn't realized the business came from your side of the family."

"Yes, my mother's father and then my uncle. My mother's brother. But Uncle Trevor worried people wouldn't frequent a business run by a woman."

"Yet, he still left it to you."

"On the condition that I wed Roger. He was Uncle Trevor's apprentice. Uncle said we should wed and run the business together. He agreed to leave the shop to me only after I consented to his conditions."

Alex's face darkened, making his features appear even more stern. "You were forced to wed?"

"Not forced, but my uncle was very much in favor of the match. I was thirteen when my parents died and Uncle Trevor raised me after that." Her uncle was a taciturn man who didn't show much emotion, but Rose had always felt secure in his devotion. "He was my only family, aside from my elderly aunt Hattie."

"Of the feathered hat fame?"

"Precisely."

"And her name is *Hattie*? This aunt who gives you hats? You don't have an uncle Glover somewhere, do you? Who perhaps gifts you with gloves?"

She smothered a smile. "There is no uncle Glover.

And I won't have you saying an unkind word about Aunt Hattie."

"I wouldn't dare. At least you've only the one feather today. Although that might be the largest feather I've ever seen on a hat."

"It's a turban." She adjusted her silk green-and-gold-patterned headdress with one curving ostrich feather waving in front.

They walked in companionable silence for a few moments. "Did you agree to marry Fleming at the expense of your own happiness?"

"Not at all. I found Mr. Fleming to be quite amiable. I came to know him quite well because he worked for Uncle Trevor for almost three years before we wed." Back then, her future husband had flattered and flirted with her. "And I wanted to keep the business in the family."

"That doesn't sound like much of a choice. How would you have survived without the income from the shop?"

"Uncle saw to it that I would be looked after. He never married and had no children. He managed to save enough money to keep me in modest comfort after he passed. But I could not bear to see the shop pass to someone else." How else would she be able to continue to pursue her passion? There was no other way to sell her maps. "I consented to my uncle's suggestion and Roger was agreeable."

"I'm sure he was." He paused. "And not just for the business."

Rose's neck burned. She felt overheated and it wasn't just the scorching June sun. Alex had the right of it.

Roger initially acted as besotted by Rose as he was by the idea of taking over a lucrative business concern. He'd certainly been eager on the wedding night and almost every night after that. But after a few months of active bed sport, he quit Rose's bed and hadn't visited her since.

Rose didn't love Roger, but she wanted children. Unfortunately, her husband clearly found the marriage bed disappointing. Why else would he stop coming to her at night?

"I gather you are very involved in the business," Alex remarked.

"Not as much as I'd like to be." Better to keep her answers vague. Even though she'd love nothing better than to tell him the truth. "Mr. Fleming thinks it is unseemly for a woman to be involved in trade."

"Maybe he fears you'll outshine him if you join the business full-time."

She laughed. "You really are incorrigible." But Alex's praise delighted her.

"Anyone can see you are the brains behind the business."

A chill cut through Rose. She needed to be more careful. No one could discover the truth. "Hardly," she said breezily. "People come to the shop for Roger's original maps. Without his talents, there'd be no shop."

"If you say so."

They reached their destination. "We're here." The tension in her shoulders eased. Their arrival put this conversation to an end. "This is where we find the tea towels."

She reprimanded herself for speaking so freely with

Alex. She kept forgetting that he was a servant. And servants talked. Even though Alex felt like someone she could trust, Rose knew nothing about the man's character.

"Feel free to wait outside if you prefer," she said, pushing the shop door open.

"You'd get a far better price for the towels if you order directly from the factory. You can purchase excellent quality cotton straight from the manufacturer."

She paused. "And you know this how?"

"My grandfather was in cotton exports."

"I thought you said you're from a farming family."

"My father was in land. My grandfather on my mother's side operated a cotton export enterprise in Manchester. I can make inquiries with my cousin Rafi, who now runs the business." He paused. "If you would like, that is."

"Yes, indeed, I would be most appreciative." She tilted her head. "You certainly are full of surprises, Mr. Alex Worth."

His serious gaze met hers. "Aren't we all?"

MRS. WALLER APPEARED on the threshold of the footman's pantry a few days later.

"The master has a guest," she said. "I have a tea tray that needs to go up."

Brandon looked up from the tedious task of brushing the glass jugs used at meals. First, he dipped them in warm water, applied washing powder and then resubmerged the jugs in water for a final rinse. He dried them upside down for the best results.

He'd learned a great deal since joining the Fleming

household. For instance, he now knew that far too many dishes, glasses and decanters were used at meals, resulting in more unnecessary chores for the overworked staff. "Can Dudley not do it? I'm in the middle of something."

"Dudley had to go pay a bill for the master. He should have been back by now but he's not and I am not inclined to serve cold tea."

Brandon sighed. "Very well." He reached for a cloth to dry his hands. "I'll take it up." He trailed Mrs. Waller into the kitchen just as Dudley trotted down the stairs.

The footman looked past Brandon. "Is that the tea tray? I can take it up."

"Excellent," Brandon said, eager to get back to his jugs.

"Did you remember lemonade for Mr. Canning?" Dudley scanned the tray. "He doesn't take tea."

Mrs. Waller huffed. "Of course I did. I do know what I'm about."

"I could use some lemonade myself." Dudley wiped his brow with a frayed kerchief. "It's deuced hot outside."

Mr. Canning? Brandon halted. Fleming's guest was Brandon's conniving Highfield neighbor? "Why don't you enjoy some lemonade?" Brandon reached for the tray. "I'll take the tea up."

"Are you certain?" Dudley pocketed his kerchief. "It is my duty to serve Mr. Fleming."

Bearing the tray, Brandon made for the stairs. "It's no problem at all."

Fleming and his guest were in the front salon. Brandon had never met Canning in person but he'd made it his business to know what the man looked like. He entered the salon.

"Come in, come in," Fleming said.

Brandon set the tray on the table between the two men.

"Alex is our newest footman," Fleming said to his guest.

"He's a fine specimen." *It was him.* Charles Canning, his neighbor, studied Brandon. "Where are you from? Alex, is it?"

"Born and bred in England, sir." Brandon kept his gaze on the floor. Although there was little chance Canning would recognize him. Most noble sons attended Eton, Harrow or Winchester. Brandon's parents sent their son to Shrewsbury in Shropshire.

"Where's that little bit of dark from?" Canning asked.

"Italy, sir." He rounded his shoulders. Slightly. Doing his best impression of a deferential footman. "My mother is Italian."

"I knew it." Canning snapped his fingers. "I took you for a foreigner the moment I laid eyes on you."

Brandon maintained an impassive expression. "Will there be anything else, sir?"

"You may leave us to our privacy," Fleming said grandly. "I shall ring if we need anything."

"Very good, sir."

Brandon exited but didn't go far. He positioned himself by a table directly outside the salon and quietly eavesdropped. A few minutes of conversation passed before Canning posed a question that caught Brandon's attention.

"Any word from him?" Canning asked.

"Not a peep," Fleming returned.

"As I suspected. His type harbors no true attachment to his late father's estate. Foreigners aren't capable of caring for property that's been in one family for generations. Only a proper Englishman has a genuine love of the land."

"Was he not born here?"

"So it is said. But who truly knows? The man is a recluse. I've never laid eyes on him. Rumor is that he lives in Arabia with his mother's people and a harem of women." Canning chortled. "He wouldn't be the only one."

Fleming's voice turned frigid. "Our arrangement is concluded, then."

"For now." The sounds of Canning gulping his lemonade followed. "I would never have guessed it of you. It's always the quiet types."

"A man has to feed his family."

"Without the shop, you'd be at the mercy of your eldest brother, working on your family farm."

"I abhor farmwork. That is why I worked so hard to train as a surveyor and engraver."

"And cartographer."

"Yes, of course, and cartographer. Rose's uncle trained me once I went to work for him and it was only natural for me to take over the shop when he died."

"You've carved out quite the comfortable life for yourself."

"One does as one must."

"You're a fortunate man and will remain so, as long as our deal remains in place. I have seen the mistress of this house. She's a beauty."

"We have a bargain." Fleming spoke in a warning

tone. "You keep what you've learned to yourself and, in exchange, I do your bidding. I imagine that your grandfather the earl would be most distressed to see the note you wrote to me."

"Leave him out of it." Canning's sharp retort cut through the air. "My grandfather has nothing to do with this agreement."

"He has a reputation for being an honorable man."

"Do calm yourself." Canning's abrupt laugh failed to hide his discomfort. "Your secret is safe with me."

"As is yours with me. As long as we understand each other."

Footsteps sounded behind him in the corridor, Bess carrying a brush and pail, her hair falling out of its cap. Brandon pretended to straighten the vase on the hall table before ambling over to meet her. "You look like you've been hard at work."

She blew a straggle of hair from her face. "I've been scrubbing floors."

"I understand there's lemonade to be had in the kitchens."

Bess brightened. "A cool drink would be just the thing." Brandon's mind whirled as they went down to join the other servants. He'd overheard enough to confirm his suspicions: Fleming and Canning had conspired to cheat him out of his land. He might not have absolute proof as of yet.

But he was on the right course.

Chapter Six

Rose strolled down Park Place off Saint James, side-stepping a nasty split in the side pavement. "They need to fix that before someone gets hurt." She paused to jot a few words in her notebook.

"This is a most unusual walk," Alex commented.

They reached the end of the quiet, deserted residential street. "A dead end. Just as I suspected." She spoke more to herself than to him as she wrote in her notebook.

"You deliberately went down a street that leads to nowhere?" Alex asked.

She glanced up at him. "Precisely."

He'd finally received his custom livery and it suited him. Roger insisted that their male servants wear a uniform. Rose chose the color and style of the costume Alex now wore. It wasn't indecent like the last outfit, but the understated navy blue tailcoat and deep green-striped waistcoat still emphasized the broad cut of his shoulders and long, well-formed legs.

Rose flushed. Feeling ashamed, she diverted her gaze. She had no business gaping at any man. She was married.

And Alex was a footman, a servant whose livelihood depended on his employment.

"Mrs. Fleming? Are you well?"

"Quite well." Turning back in the direction they came from, she quickened her stride. "Why do you ask?"

"Your color is high. I thought you might have a touch of sun. After all," he added in a wry voice, "we've walked at least five miles today."

"Are you tired, Alex?"

"Not at all. I'm just confused about why we're going up and down every street in London. If you're lost—"

"I'm not lost. I am gathering information."

"About every street in London?"

"I am from a mapmaking family."

Understanding lit his dark eyes. "You're going to map this area?"

"Not just this area. There is no definitive map of London, so I'm going to create one," she said briskly. "Eventually, we'll print copies to sell at the shop. No one need ever get lost in London again."

"And in order to draw this map, you literally plan to walk down every street in London?"

"Not *every* one. I've engaged a draftsman to assist me." Rose had ambitious plans for her detailed map of London. While her most expensive and ornate maps were primarily seen by the upscale clients who commissioned them—and a few in their circle—Rose's map of London could one day be in thousands of homes in the metropolis. It would be her most wide-reaching, most impactful project ever. *Except no one will know.*

"Will Mr. Fleming draw the final map?"

Rose scoffed before she could censor her honest reaction. She really was terrible at subterfuge. Alex tipped his head at her, surprise lighting his face.

She turned the scoff into a poor imitation of a cough. "Naturally. Having my husband's initials on any map enhances its consequence."

"Do you often collect the needed information for your husband's maps?"

"At times, I do assist in the data-gathering stage." It was a lie. Roger preferred to give Rose the information she needed to draw her maps. However, she roamed the property herself, whenever possible, to get a sense of the land, taking note of any walls, fences, hedge lines or any obvious markers, before re-creating the property in her sketches.

"Why do you not draw your own? You obviously know how."

She held her breath. "What do you mean?"

He strolled alongside her, his regal profile set against the bright sun. "You created the map for the tea towels."

She exhaled. "A rudimentary decorative map for a tea towel is quite different from the detailed, meticulously drawn maps that my . . . husband creates."

"How detailed must your map of London be? Is it not at least worth considering?"

Rose's toe hit something. Too late she realized it was the tear in the side pavement. She stumbled and came down hard.

"Oh!" Pain ripped through her leg.

"Mrs. Fleming!" Alex dropped down beside her. "Have you hurt yourself?"

"It's my knee," she gasped, her leg in agony. "I think I've twisted it."

"Breathe and take your time," he advised. "When you want to try to stand, I shall help you."

After a few moments Rose said, "I am ready."

"May I put my hands on you?"

"Yes, of course."

She felt his hands, strong and firm, around her waist. He lifted her gently until she stood on her good leg. "Can you put weight on the injured knee?"

She winced. "I'm almost afraid to try." She attempted it, but her leg could not bear any weight. Her knee gave way like a floppy noodle.

"Oh my." She grimaced. "I think I've torn something. I am almost afraid to look at it, but I think I should."

He guided her over to a cannon-shaped iron bollard and gently helped her lower herself to perch upon it. "I shall shield you from view as much as I can while you assess the injury."

He gave her his back, standing in a way that took up a lot of space, covering her from the street as much as possible.

Rose lifted her skirt and gasped. Her leg appeared deformed. The left knee pointed to the side rather than forward.

"What is it?" he asked without turning around.

"My knee looks completely mangled."

"Is it cut? Are you bleeding?"

"No, nothing like that. My knee looks like it is out of place. It is facing out to the left." She dropped her skirt. "You may turn around. I am decent."

He turned, concern etched in his face. "What would you like to do now?"

"I suppose we should hail a hackney and return home. We'll need to summon the doctor."

He contemplated her words. "My cousin deals with these types of injuries. She is very capable."

"First cotton exports and now a healer. You certainly have enterprising cousins."

"We could hail a hackney and go to her immediately. She runs a clinic at Margate."

"She?" Rose had never heard of a woman running a dispensary.

"Yes. Shall we go and see her now?"

Rose hesitated. Roger would want to summon their doctor, which was more respectable than going to a clinic. And Margate was a charity hospital. Roger would be aghast.

"My cousin cures people of their suffering almost immediately," Alex said. "You could very well be out of pain sooner if we go directly there."

Rose forced herself to breathe through the pain. Roger wouldn't have to know. "Very well."

He stepped into the street to hail a hackney with the easy command of a man accustomed to taking control of situations. Returning to her, he stooped down. "Now, put your arm around my neck."

She did as he asked. He effortlessly swept her off her feet and into his embrace. One strong arm supported her middle back; the other cradled her legs just above the knee. The side of her body was pressed against the hard sculpture of his torso, the warmth of his body intermingling with hers. Rose shivered at the unexpected physical intimacy. His masculine scent, notes of bergamot and cedarwood, mingled with the tang of male skin.

He settled her in the hackney. "You'll be fine." He squeezed her hand. "I promise."

ONCE THEY REACHED Margate Hospital, Alex carried Rose into the clinic. It was a welcoming space, tidy and spacious with large windows. But Rose barely noticed because she was once again pressed up against Alex. Scorched by the heat of his masculine frame, Rose's entire body flushed.

Being in his arms was an experience. She felt comforted and safe, cherished even, which was her being silly again. But the assurance and easy strength with which Alex took control of her situation made Rose feel cared for.

A lovely woman with tawny skin and gleaming dark hair helped a patient down from one of several examining tables. When they entered the clinic, she looked up, her surprise obvious, and hurried over.

"Hanna," Alex greeted his cousin.

Curiosity glittered in the woman's eyes. "This is most unexpected, my l—"

Alex cut her off, speaking in a language Rose didn't recognize. The woman's brows shot up. Her speculative gaze slid to Rose and back to the footman. The way Alex's cousin scrutinized him, from head to toe, was most peculiar. Rose couldn't understand what they were saying, but disapproval radiated from the woman.

"This is Mrs. Fleming." Alex spoke in English, punctuating each word. "She is in terrible pain. Surely, you cannot turn away someone who needs your help."

The woman shot him an angry look before responding again in the foreign language.

Rose's ears burned. "It is painfully obvious that we are not welcome," she said stiffly. "I am sorry to bother you. We shall go elsewhere."

The woman gave Rose her full attention. "*You* are most welcome. I am Mrs. Ellis. Please call me Hanna." Warmth coated her words. All of her hard edges vanished. "Let's get you looked after."

They followed her to a private room, Rose still firmly in Alex's arms, embarrassed to be carried about like an invalid, yet quietly savoring being in his embrace. He gently settled her on an examining table. Despite the warm day, the loss of Alex's body heat left Rose feeling chilled.

"My cousin tells me that you fell?" Hanna said.

"Yes, I stumbled. It was foolish really. I wasn't paying attention to the path ahead and stepped right into a break in the side pavement."

"Let's have a look, shall we?" Hanna glanced up at Alex. "Mrs. Fleming will require privacy while I examine her leg."

Alex's intense gaze was on Rose. "I'll be right outside." He lingered for a moment, seeming as reluctant to leave Rose as she was to see him go. "Call out if you need anything. Anything at all."

"I will." Her gaze trailed him as he quit the room.

Hanna raised the hem of Rose's skirt to examine the injury. Rose winced. Her knee was now also swollen and angry, in addition to veering off to the left.

"Ah, yes, I see," Hanna said.

"Do you? Why does it look like that?"

"The reason your knee looks off center is because you've put it out."

Rose cringed. "Can you put it back in?"

"Of course. If you will help me."

"Just tell me what to do."

"I am going to have to pull hard on your leg. Can you manage or shall I ask someone to help hold you down?"

Rose glanced toward the door. She wanted Alex, but she shouldn't. It was beyond wrong. "I can manage on my own."

"You must grip the sides of the table and hold firm."

She nodded grimly. "I understand."

Hanna removed Rose's boot and took hold of her leg near the ankle. "Ready?"

Rose braced herself. "Ready."

"Now," she instructed.

Rose clenched the sides of the table. Hanna tugged with what seemed like superhuman strength. Rose bit down hard to keep from screaming as agony ripped through her knee and Hanna almost pulled her off the table.

Hanna released her. "I think we shall have to call someone in to help hold you down."

"Let's ask Alex," Rose said immediately. "He can hold me down."

"As you like." Hanna lowered Rose's skirt to preserve her modesty before leaving to summon Alex.

BRANDON STRAIGHTENED WHEN Hanna appeared. "Is Mrs. Fleming well?"

"What game are you playing at?" she hissed in Arabic. "Why are you dressed like a footman?"

"It's no game."

"Does she know who you really are?"

"Absolutely not and we must keep it that way."

"*We*?" Brandon did not know his cousin well, but deceit obviously did not sit well with her. "Do not ask me to lie for you."

"I'm the one doing the lying. All I ask is that you don't get in my way." Brandon silently cursed himself for risking exposure by bringing Mrs. Fleming to the dispensary.

Hanna pressed her lips inward. "Can you assure me that no harm will come to her as a result of this ruse?"

"If I wanted Mrs. Fleming to suffer, I certainly wouldn't have brought her here." That wasn't exactly true, an inner voice reminded him. Destroying her family business would certainly hurt Mrs. Fleming. Brandon muted the unbidden thought. He had an aim to achieve and nothing could stand in his way.

Hanna hesitated. "I don't know. I don't like it."

He played the last card he had. "I am asking you to return the favor that I once did for you."

Her expression darkened. "You leave me no choice." She was deeply indebted to Brandon because he'd saved her bonesetting career not too long ago.

Brandon's posture relaxed. "Thank you."

"You didn't exactly give me the option to reject your request." She studied him. "Since when do you speak Arabic?"

He dropped his gaze. "I've picked up a few words here and there."

"It's more than that. You're not fluent, but the accent is good and you can obviously carry enough of a conversation to extort people. Why do you hide the fact that you can speak Arabic?"

Because it was no one's business but his own. And his mother's warnings against publicly embracing his Arab heritage still rang in his ears. He switched to English. "Are we going to stand out here all afternoon? Or are you going to help your patient?"

Hanna allowed him to divert her. "I need your help holding Mrs. Fleming down."

"Why?" Alarm rippled through him. "Are you inflicting so much pain that you're afraid she'll run away?"

"In my line of work, extreme discomfort often precedes the cure."

When they rejoined Mrs. Fleming, Brandon immediately went to her side. She was pale. Pain dulled her vibrant eyes. "How are you?"

"Your cousin has inhuman strength." She managed a grim smile. "She almost pulled me right off the table. You might not be a match for her."

"I'll consider myself forewarned."

Hanna's lips twitched. "Constantly pulling on people does develop a bonesetter's musculature."

"Bonesetter?" Mrs. Fleming sat up taller. "Nobody said anything about a bonesetter."

Hanna glared at Brandon. "You didn't tell her?"

But Brandon focused on Mrs. Fleming. "I told you my cousin can repair injuries like yours. She has an excellent reputation."

"But a bonesetter?" Mrs. Fleming's cheeks reddened. "No offense intended, Mrs. Ellis."

"None taken," Hanna assured her. "If it would set you at ease, I could ask my colleague, Dr. Bridges, for his opinion. But I am confident he will concur with my assessment."

Brandon bristled at the suggestion. "I'd wager that Hanna knows ten times more about healing your type of injury than Bridges or any other doctor in this building."

Mrs. Fleming's reaction wasn't unexpected. Most people viewed bonesetters as quacks and charlatans. But Brandon knew Hanna was no fraud. She just might be the most able healer in London.

"Trust me in this," Brandon said to Mrs. Fleming. "If Hanna says she can help you, I believe her." The faith in him reflected in her eyes plucked at his conscience. How would she look at him once she discovered Brandon's true identity?

Mrs. Fleming exhaled a long, shuddering breath. "Very well."

"Let's try again, shall we?" Hanna gripped Rose's ankle. Encased in stockings, Mrs. Fleming's silken ankle was slim and dainty. Brandon forced himself to look away. The lady deserved privacy. "Alex, you hold Mrs. Fleming so that I don't accidentally drag her to the floor."

Brandon took his position behind Mrs. Fleming and wrapped her hands in his. She held on to him with a surprisingly tight grip for such a slight woman. Her wrists were delicate, like her exposed ankle. Brandon's hands were massive claws surrounding Mrs. Fleming's petite fingers. They were pale and smooth, except for the faded ink stains on her fingers. Lying flat on the table, Mrs. Fleming stared up into Brandon's face.

"All right. Here we go." Hanna tugged on Mrs. Fleming's leg. Brandon held tight. Mrs. Fleming had the right of it; his cousin *was* fiendishly strong. He held Mrs. Fleming's gaze, silently reassuring her that she could do it. She maintained the eye contact like it was a lifeline, even as she winced from the pain. He gripped her hands more tightly, trying to bolster her. After a few tries, Hanna released Mrs. Fleming's ankle.

Brandon looked up. "Well? Is that it?"

At the opposite end of the table, Hanna peered under Mrs. Fleming's skirt while preserving the lady's modesty in front of Brandon.

"Sometimes, a little force is all it takes to coax the knee to slide back into place." Hanna released a breath. "Unfortunately, this is not one of those times."

Brandon suppressed a curse. Mrs. Fleming had endured more than enough pain for one afternoon.

"What do we do now?" the lady asked. "I'm almost afraid to hear the answer."

"I shall have to manipulate your knee back into place with my hand."

Mrs. Fleming grimaced. "That sounds more painful than pulling on my leg."

"Hold on to Alex." Hanna gently bent Mrs. Fleming's leg at the knee. "This will help relax the muscles in your thighs. It will be over before you know it."

It had better be. Brandon couldn't bear seeing Mrs. Fleming in pain.

"Very well," Mrs. Fleming said gamely before reclining flat on her back, breathing long and slow, her grip on Brandon's hands unbroken.

Hanna straightened Mrs. Fleming's leg, and reached up under the lady's skirt. "Done."

"Truly?" Mrs. Fleming tore her eyes away from Brandon to peer at the bonesetter. "What did you do?"

"I lifted your kneecap and slid it back into place."

Brandon helped her sit up so she could examine her knee. He turned his back as she started to lift her hem, momentarily forgetting her modesty in his presence.

"It's back in place." He heard the wonderment in Mrs. Fleming's voice. "May I try standing on it?"

"Yes." Hanna went to rinse her hands in the porcelain bowl. "You should be fine now."

Brandon stood close as Mrs. Fleming swung her feet off the table. She reached for his hand to steady her, her hand soft and warm and *trusting* in his, and slowly stood up, testing the strength of her left knee.

"I can stand on it." Her face brightened. She locked eyes with him. Electricity arced between them. *That was unexpected.* Color painted her cheeks before she blinked away.

"I do not know how to thank you," she said to Hanna.

His cousin toweled off her hands. "No thanks are necessary. I'm a bonesetter. Putting displaced joints back into place is what I do."

"WHAT WAS THAT language that you spoke to Hanna?" Rose asked once they were in a hackney cab heading home.

Brandon stilled. "I beg your pardon?"

"The language you spoke to your cousin."

Brandon rolled his tongue in his cheek. His mistakes were multiplying. All in the name of getting Mrs. Fleming immediate medical attention. He should have taken her home and called for the doctor as she suggested.

Instead, he'd risked his plan because he allowed this woman to get under his skin. Unfortunately, Brandon genuinely liked Rose Fleming. He admired her looks, of course, but also her sense of humor and how easily she laughed at herself. Her intelligence and assertiveness. Her business acumen. Her love of terrible hats.

"Alex?" Mrs. Fleming prompted. "Have I overstepped?"

"Not at all." She hadn't. *He* had. "I spoke Arabic to Hanna."

"Arabic?" She tipped her head to the side. "Your parents are Arabs?"

"My mother was. Yes."

She studied him and he wondered what she was thinking. Did she see him differently now? "How fascinating."

"Yes, there are many who think my heritage makes me exotic," he said coolly. "Not unlike an animal in a zoo."

Horror lit her face. "I did not mean to offend. I do beg your pardon."

Brandon cursed to himself. He had no right to take his own mistakes out on Rose. "No, I beg *your* pardon. I should not have snapped at you."

"I just find it so interesting because my grandfather was Arab. He came from Lebanon."

He blinked. "Truly?"

"And I've never met anyone else from the Levant. You are the first."

What were the chances that, in all of London, Rose Fleming would turn out to have Levantine roots? Had she been able to understand his conversation with Hanna? "Do you speak Arabic?"

She laughed and shook her head. "Only if you count knowing the words *yalla* and *habibti* as speaking the language."

He relaxed, regarding her with sincere interest. "Your grandfather, the mapmaker, came from Lebanon?"

"No, the mapmakers are on my mother's side of the family. *Jidu* was Papa's father. My grandfather was a student scholar who came to visit London. But he met my grandmother, the daughter of his professor, married her and never went home. He lived with us after my grandmother died. *Jidu*, my grandfather, used to call me *habibti*."

"My love," he said softly.

"I beg your pardon?"

"*Habibti* means my love, or my darling."

She smiled softly. "I miss him. And my parents. *Jidu* always used to say, '*Yalla, yalla*,' to rush Mama and me along when we were taking too long."

He returned her smile, the warmth between them palpable. They had more in common than he ever could have imagined. "I would never have guessed."

"I'm afraid I'm very uninformed about the region. I never met any of *Jidu*'s relatives. That is why I read *Travels in Arabia* with such interest. I wanted to learn more about my grandfather. Have you heard of the book? It was all the rage in London not so long ago."

My sister wrote it. "I have heard of it." The carriage turned onto New Street. They were almost home.

Rose glanced out the window. "Alex . . . I would prefer that Mr. Fleming know nothing about the events that transpired today."

"I gather he would disapprove of your visiting a bonesetter? Especially an Arab bonesetter."

Her face tightened. "He would find much about today objectionable. I prefer not to upset him."

"It will be our secret," he promised.

Concern glinted her gaze. Keeping secrets was dangerous. Especially ones that could be leveraged against her. But then she relaxed and favored him with a soft smile. "Thank you."

I'm not worthy of your trust. Her unguarded expression made his heart stutter. *Damnation.* He fought the urge to warn her off. To protect her from him. But all he said was, "It is my pleasure."

And the damnedest thing was that he meant it.

Chapter Seven

The Duke of Kingsley surveyed the feast laid out before him. "I must say, Brandon, you do set a grand table."

"I instructed my cook to spare no indulgence." Brandon gestured for a footman to offer more braised beef to his guest. The duke was a brawny man known for his love of a hearty meal.

"Your cook clearly knows what she's about," the duke said between bites of herb pie.

"My staff is among the finest in London." Brandon inclined his chin toward Lady Olympia and her mother, the duchess. "But Peckham House is in want of the skilled touch of a mistress of the house."

Kingsley bit into his beef. "Indeed."

His duchess exchanged a knowing look with her daughter. Brandon had invited the duke and duchess, as well as their eldest daughter, Lady Olympia, to supper. On Sunday, of course. His lone night off from his duties at New Street.

"Every marquess needs a marchioness," the duchess said with a gracious nod.

"Yes, I hope to be fortunate enough to secure a match soon."

Lady Olympia maintained a serene composure. Bedding her would be no hardship. The lady's auburn hair, the color of wine, glistened in the candlelight. The flickering flames illuminated even features, smooth pale skin and a generous bosom.

"Thank you for the flowers, my lord," the young lady said. "The arrangements are so very beautiful. I am the envy of my sisters."

"It is my pleasure." Yes, Lady Olympia would do very nicely. She might not heat his blood like, for example, Rose Fleming recently did, but that was of no consequence. He wasn't looking for chemistry or a love match. He wanted to avenge his parents, and that required securing a betrothal before the Season began. Lady Olympia had not accepted an offer during her first Season, but Brandon doubted she would remain unattached after a second.

"You are not often seen in society, my lord," the duchess remarked. "We were surprised to receive your invitation to supper."

He reached for his wine. "I prefer more intimate gatherings."

"Do you spend much time in the Levant?" Kingsley asked around a generous bite of spiced mushrooms.

"I have never been," Brandon said smoothly. "I have spent every day of my life in England, except for the occasional jaunt on the continent."

"I would love to travel to the continent," Lady Olympia remarked. "I should like to see Paris."

"I believe the city would suit you." He gave her his

full attention, adding just enough heat to his gaze to make his intentions clear. "Perhaps one day your future husband will take you to France on a wedding trip."

She colored prettily. "I should like that very much."

Brandon continued a light flirtation throughout the rest of the meal. Lady Olympia's blushes and stolen glances suggested his plan was falling into place. Once supper ended, the ladies retired to the front salon while the gentlemen stayed behind for port and a smoke.

Kingsley sucked on his cheroot. "You are quite the mystery in society, Brandon."

"Am I?"

"Most of us have never laid eyes on you."

"I spend most of my time at Highfield, my country estate."

"Ah, yes, I hear you've started enclosing your properties."

"It is time." Brandon briefly wondered just how much the duke knew about the attempts to determine the boundaries of his and his neighbors' lands. "I gather you are wondering why I invited you and your lovely duchess and Lady Olympia here this evening."

"Not really." The duke swallowed the last of his port. "I see where your interest lies. Olympia is a prime article."

"She is a diamond of the first water."

"Exactly. Every eligible bachelor vied for her favor last Season."

"Yet, she remains unwed."

"I may come to regret my decision to allow my daughters to choose their own matches. To her mother's growing consternation, Olympia has yet to favor a suitor."

"I should like permission to call on your daughter. Perhaps take her for a ride in the park."

"I have heard you keep a harem of wives." Kingsley leaned closer. "Is it true?"

"No." Brandon's neck burned but he lifted the corners of his mouth into the semblance of a smile. "I am unwed. There is no harem. I will take one wife and stay true to her." Brandon normally didn't entertain imbecile nobles. Or waste any effort proving his English-ness to anyone. But in this case, securing the prize required that he submit to asinine questions.

The duke assessed him. "You do speak quite well."

"I beg your pardon?"

"The rumors are that you grew up with your mother's people in Arabia. That you might not even speak English."

"As I said, I have never been to Palestine. I was born and educated in England."

"Does that mean you've never ridden a camel?"

"I'm afraid not."

"There is, of course, the unfortunate matter of your mother's inferior connections."

Brandon's fingers tightened around his glass. "Lady Brandon was a fine woman."

"If I may speak frankly?"

"By all means."

"The taint of commerce still follows the Brandon title."

"May I be forthright as well?"

Kingsley blew smoke into the air. "Of course."

"How many daughters do you have?"

"Everyone knows I have six girls and three boys."

"And each one of your girls will require a dowry." He whistled low. "It will cost you a great deal to secure matches for your daughters." Brandon had looked into the duke's finances. A few well-placed bribes revealed that Kingsley was solvent. But just barely. Keeping up appearances was costly with nine children to provide for.

The duke glowered. "Your point, Brandon?"

"I will not require a dowry. In fact, I will reject one if offered."

"What man rejects a dowry?"

"This one. Lady Olympia is the prize. If we suit, I want nothing else from you."

Speculation gleamed in Kingsley's face. "What are you about?"

"I simply want to make my position clear. I am thinking of making your daughter a marchioness. And you won't have to pay a single shilling to make it so."

"You are betting the smell of money will cover the stench of trade."

"Money, and an exalted title, can accomplish just about anything. More port?"

Kingsley pushed his empty glass forward. "I don't mind if I do."

ROSE BENT OVER her drawing desk, putting the final touches on her latest project, a detailed map of yet another nobleman's country estate.

She added a few last strokes to the whimsical details that set her maps apart. Lord Wallthorne, her current client, was both horse-mad and dog-obsessed, so she added depictions of his lordship's Dalmatians barking at thoroughbreds prancing in the paddock. These sorts of customizations were R. Fleming's signature.

Rose stepped back to examine her work. It was good. As good as anything she'd done in the past. It had to be. These were the commissions that paid most of the household bills, maintaining the lifestyle that Roger so aspired to.

But she was growing weary of vanity projects for entitled aristocrats. They didn't excite her like her planned map of London, which would be a critical tool for wide swaths of people—nobles and commoners alike—rather than an expensive ornament to be hung on some lord's wall. Unfortunately, Rose could only afford to work on her London map in between the more lucrative projects.

Fortunately, she sometimes received a commission of consequence that engaged her interest as well as her talents. Like the series of maps she recently created delineating new boundaries surrounding a countryside village for landowners who decided to enclose their properties.

She'd painstakingly examined the papers and notes of other obvious land markers before establishing permanent property lines. The resulting land deeds would last for decades and perhaps even longer. Rose had mixed feelings about the project. The central client, the Marquess of Brandon, probably gave no thought at all to the people who would suffer due to enclosure. Commoners who lived off the land would be cut off from the right to hunt game to feed their families, collect firewood to warm their homes and allow their cattle to graze land once available for common use. They'd no longer be able to do small-scale planting or even pick fruit from the trees.

Brandon probably didn't care about that. Not that she'd met the marquess. Rose rarely interacted with clients. As the face of the business, that was Roger's role. But even her husband hadn't met the reclusive marquess. They communicated in writing and through emissaries.

Rose startled at the sound of a tap at her door. "Yes?"

"It's Alex, Mrs. Fleming."

"Just a moment." She hurriedly drew some papers over her map before facing the door. "Come in."

"Good morning." The footman entered with her breakfast, looking like a walking advertisement for the tailor shop that made the uniform. She really should have chosen something that didn't accentuate a man's body quite so . . . vividly.

"Is it already time for breakfast?" Time passed so quickly when she worked. She always ate in her sitting room, while Roger breakfasted in the dining room. Her husband insisted on the practice because it was "the way of the quality."

"It is. Mrs. Waller added an extra sweet bun because she says you are partial to them."

Rose's pensive mood brightened. He'd been off yesterday afternoon, Sunday, and she missed his frank insights and caustic retorts. "She needs to stop doing that or I am liable to outgrow my new gowns."

He set the tray at the small round table. "There is nothing wrong with a woman who fully fills out her dresses."

She chortled. The man never did know how to affect

the deferential demeanor of a servant. Not that Rose wanted him to. It was refreshing to have a genuine conversation with someone.

He shot her a quizzical look. "Was I being too familiar?"

"I might take issue if another footman uttered such a comment." She took a seat at the table. "But I think you and I are past that now that you've seen me at my worst."

His dark brows came together. "Have I?"

"Surely, you haven't already forgotten how I stumbled in the street like a drunken sailor."

"Anyone can take a fall." He poured her chocolate with long and elegant fingers, the backs of his hands lightly dusted with hair, just like *Jidu*'s used to be. "But not all people would keep their wits about them as you did when faced with tremendous pain."

"Having you there helped a great deal. I haven't thanked you."

"No thanks are necessary." His eyes met hers. Heat prickled her skin. Something had shifted between them after their visit to the bonesetter. She didn't dare delve into exactly what that meant. "I am here to look after you, to see to your every need."

She reached for her chocolate with trembling hands, grateful for the excuse to look away. What would it be like if a man like Alex really could see to her every need? She imagined those capable fingers touching her in places no one else had in such a long time.

Longing panged through her. Rose missed having true physical contact with another person. Even just to embrace. Perhaps a child, a tiny person to shower with love and affection, to cuddle endlessly, would cure the ache in her. But Roger hadn't come to her bed in years. And she might not be able to have children. She hadn't gotten pregnant during those few months when he'd visited her bed almost daily.

"How was your afternoon off?" She changed the subject, her easy tone designed to neutralize the charged atmosphere between them. She needed to stop having indecent imaginings about a servant, a man in her employ. She was a married woman. A person of morals. "Did you do anything of interest?"

"Not particularly. How is your knee?"

"It feels fine. Your cousin is a miracle worker."

"I have been told as much."

She wanted him to stay and talk. Since moving to New Street after marrying four years ago, she'd made few new friends. She had almost no one to converse with and she very much enjoyed chatting with Alex. Their friendly sparring challenged and delighted her.

"Thank you." She was reluctant to dismiss him. "I seem to have everything I need here."

He hesitated. "I was wondering if I might ask your permission."

She sipped her chocolate. "For what?"

"I would like to plant a small herb garden off the kitchen."

"Plant a garden?" She remembered then that he was a farmer's son. "What sorts of herbs?"

"I will check with Mrs. Waller to see what she needs. But I'm interested in planting sage and possibly mint."

"May I ask what for?"

He smiled ruefully. "I'm rather partial to having my

black tea flavored with fresh sage whenever possible. And I take dried sage when fresh is not available."

"My grandfather used to like mint in his tea. But I've never heard of sage with tea."

"My mother was partial to it. And I grew accustomed to drinking my tea with *maramia*."

She loved the way the foreign word rolled off his tongue. Sharp yet smooth. "Is it an Arab custom, then? Flavoring tea with sage?"

"That and mint, like your *Jidu*. With an abundance of sugar."

Rose listened with interest. Sugar was dear. Yet, his farming family could apparently afford it.

"I should like to plant both. With your leave, of course."

"You have it."

He bowed. "Thank you." His gaze skittered over to her drafting table, where a cloth hid her map for Lord Wallthorne. "Do you sketch?"

"Now and again."

"I'd like to see your work sometime."

"I draw for myself. It's not nearly good enough to show anyone."

"Somehow I doubt that."

She changed the subject. "I hope you will share some of that sage once it is grown. I should like to sample the herb in my tea."

"As you wish. Will that be all . . . ma'am?"

She suppressed a smile. He noticed.

"Have I amused you?"

"Adding the *ma'am* never seems to come easily or naturally to you. I gather farmers are very independent minded."

"We can be." His eyes twinkled. "But I think I can be expected to come around. *Ma'am*."

She was tempted to invite Alex to join her and to share her extra sweet bun. She'd never thought of herself as lonely, but something about this man's company dented that notion, making Rose dread being left on her own for so many hours at a time.

Still, she forced herself to say, "Thank you, Alex. That will be all."

"I WANT A baby."

Roger had barely shut the double doors to the formal salon behind them after supper before Rose blurted out the words. She'd meant to use a little more finesse, acclimating her husband to the idea of starting their family before coming straight to the point. But Rose wasn't skilled at dissembling or prevaricating.

"I see." Roger crossed over to pour two ports, their evening ritual.

Rose couldn't see his expression. He took his time making the drinks. The clinking of the glasses exacerbated the tension winding through her. "Well?"

He turned to face her. "And what brought this on?"

"What do you mean? I am a woman. You are my husband. The traditional next step is a family."

He handed her a glass. "We never discussed having children."

His placid expression riled her. "It's a natural assumption on my part. Every married couple wants to have children."

"I do not."

"What?" Her stomach slipped.

"I don't want children."

"Why not?"

"This cannot be a surprise to you." He sipped his drink. "Surely, you noticed that whenever I visited your bed, I took measures to prevent you from increasing."

She faltered. He had? "I did . . . not."

"But it is not a foolproof method, which is why I stopped visiting your bed. To ensure that we don't make that mistake."

Mistake. "Why don't you want a family?"

"I see no need for children. I prefer an orderly life."

Orderly? Surely, he meant cold and sterile, absent of affection or joy, or any real happiness or contentment. All of the things she would never get from him. She clenched her teeth. "You should have told me before we wed."

"You never asked."

"It's not something a person would ask and you know it." Her voice trembled with anger. "It was your duty to inform me that by wedding you I was consigning myself to a life without children." And, more importantly, to an existence devoid of love and companionship.

"You have your maps."

"And nothing else. I don't even have friends."

"Surely, you do not blame me for that."

"I'm a terrible liar. I'm afraid that if I truly befriend anyone, I might end up blurting out the truth about the maps."

"As far as I can see, you've made a sound decision. You can hardly censure me for your lack of discretion."

She stared at Roger. For the first time Rose allowed herself to acknowledge how much she disliked the man. And probably had for a very long time. But now? She might actually detest him. She watched her husband pour himself another drink.

Roger used to have needs. He'd come to her room almost every night in the first few months after they wed. Could his appetite for the carnal side of marriage truly have died so completely? Did he not miss having true companionship, not just in bed but out of it?

Then it struck her. If she wasn't so innocent to the ways of men, she'd have realized the likely truth long ago. Roger must be sating his needs elsewhere. What else could explain his absence from her bed?

But she batted the idea away almost immediately. Her husband went to the shop every day and came home each night. When would he have time to visit a mistress? Maybe some men did not yearn for connection and intimacy.

"Will you reconsider?" She forced a civil tone. "Having children is important to me." She needed something or someone to fill the hole in her life. *Before Alex does*, the voice in her head warned.

"No, I am quite firm on this point." Roger set his drink down. "Now, if you will excuse me, I think I shall retire a bit early tonight."

It was all Rose could do to keep from tossing her glass at him. Here was yet another decision that Roger had stolen from her. Giving him the final say at the shop was excruciating enough. But this betrayal? Fury and loss churned in her chest as her husband took his leave.

Roger quietly, but firmly, closed the doors to the salon, and on any expectation that Rose's future could be any different than her present.

Chapter Eight

$\mathcal{T}$hese turned out beautifully." Her face glowing with pleasure, Rose arranged the tea towels printed with the map motif. "They will sell well."

"We shall see." Fleming watched his wife organize the display table at the front of the shop. "I hope we haven't thrown good money after bad."

"We haven't." Rose's voice cooled. She didn't look at her husband as she patted the satchel at her side. "I also brought the final drawings for the needlepoint pattern."

Brandon admired her confidence. Most women with her looks would trade on that alone. But not Rose. Her formidable business mind might be even more spectacular than her considerable beauty. And her maps, while nowhere near as accomplished as her husband's, had a unique whimsy to them. The charming towels would sell quickly.

She backed up to examine her display. "And thanks to Alex, we'll make an even larger profit on the next batch of towels."

"How so?" Fleming asked.

"His cousin owns a cotton concern in Manchester. He will supply the towels from here forward."

Fleming's lip twisted. "We shall have to discuss the matter before any final decisions are made."

"There's no need to consult each other over every decision, is there?" She straightened a towel. "I've already placed the order."

Roger turned an eye on Brandon. "Is that so?"

He nodded. "Yes, sir." Rose had finalized the order that morning.

"Your people are in cotton?"

"They are, sir." Brandon cursed himself. Once again he'd allowed his desire to help Rose, this time to develop her business idea, overshadow his main reason for establishing himself in her household. Hopefully, Fleming had no inkling that the mother of the Marquess of Brandon came from a family of Arab cotton traders in Manchester.

Fortunately, the bell over the door sounded, redirecting Fleming's attention to the new arrival.

Brandon remained staring straight ahead until a familiar voice said, "Good day. Are you Mr. Fleming, the mapmaker?"

"I am," Fleming responded. "How may I be of service?"

Brandon's heart jumped as his gaze landed on his sister. What the devil was Leela doing here? Did she know what he was up to? Fortunately, his sister didn't appear to notice him. He edged away, silently slipping into the back of the shop, where the two workers looked up at the interruption.

"The master has a customer," Brandon explained as

he peered onto the shop floor. "I think he would prefer for me to stay out of the way."

The two men went back to their work. Brandon wasn't accustomed to being dismissed so quickly, but it hadn't taken him long to learn that livery rendered him practically invisible. People tended to overlook servants as if they didn't exist. Except, of course, when something needed serving or cleaning up. While he had noted some appreciative feminine looks when he was out and about with Rose, most people, especially other men and older women, took no notice of him.

"Oh, these are adorable." Leela surveyed the tea towels. "What a delightful map."

"My wife's handiwork." A touch of disdain edged Fleming's words. As if his wife's charming maps were beneath the notice of a man of his extraordinary skill and talent. "May I present Mrs. Fleming?"

"How do you do?" Leela said to Rose. "I am absolutely enchanted by your maps."

Rose beamed. "It's just something simple that I drew up for the towels."

Leela reached for a tea towel to examine it more closely. "It is deceptively simple. There's something endearing about this map. It seems to have a sense of humor. Does that sound silly?"

"Not at all." Delight stamped Rose's face. "That is precisely what I hoped to convey."

"Do you draw other maps?"

"Very simple ones. If you would like a more thorough and elaborate map, you will want to consult with Mr. Fleming."

Fleming stepped forward, his gaze taking in Leela's finely tailored gown. "It would be my pleasure to help you, madam."

Leela flashed him a cursory smile before returning her attention to Rose. "May I see more examples of *your* work, Mrs. Fleming?"

"Oh." Rose flushed. "Certainly." She opened her satchel and withdrew her drawings. "These are maps I've created for needlepoint patterns."

Leela examined the drawings while Rose pulled another sketch out of her bag. "And these are for dissected maps for children."

"How delightful!" Leela exclaimed. "My daughter Maryam will enjoy these."

"We have not made the puzzles as of yet." But then Rose added quickly, "But we soon shall."

Fleming interjected. "Yes, I have directed that the puzzles be made post haste."

Leela darted a glance at the man. "When you do, I shall be your first customer." Leela cast an appraising look at Rose. "Do you think you might find time to call on me, Mrs. Fleming?" She withdrew a calling card from her reticule.

Rose stared at the card before lifting her disbelieving gaze to Leela. "You are the Duchess of Huntington?"

Leela smiled. "Guilty, I am afraid."

"I love your travel books," Rose said impulsively. "Especially *Travels in Arabia*."

"You are very kind."

"Your Grace"—Fleming edged ever so slightly in front of his wife—"it would be my pleasure to service you."

"That is most accommodating of you, Mr. Fleming."

Leela spoke in a friendly but firm manner. "But it is your wife with whom I should like to confer. If, that is, Mrs. Fleming will consent to call on me."

"Of course," Rose blurted out. "It would be my pleasure."

"Excellent. I shall be at home to callers on Tuesday next. If that is convenient?"

Rose visibly swallowed. "Most convenient, Your Grace. I shall be honored to call on you."

Leela beamed. "I look forward to it." She turned to Rose's husband. "And now, Mr. Fleming."

"Yes, Your Grace?" he replied eagerly.

"I should like to take six of these tea towels. Could you please see to it?"

"SHE SEEMS VERY agreeable, don't you think?" Rose posed the question as they left the shop, still buoyant after her encounter with one of her favorite writers.

Alex pulled the door closed before stepping onto the side pavement. "Who?"

"The Duchess of Huntington. Who else?"

"Oh." Alex paused, the sun dropping shadows across the severe cut of his cheekbones. "I suppose."

"Why do you think she wants me to call?"

"I cannot say."

"I quite liked her."

"She's obviously smart. She liked your maps."

Rose suppressed a smile. She should not have enjoyed the surprised look on Roger's face when Her Grace dismissed his work in favor of Rose's quite so much. It was even more ironic considering that all of the work in question was Rose's.

For the first time it struck her just how much her husband enjoyed taking credit for her work. He basked in the acclaim that should be hers, further depriving Rose of any hope of filling the yawning emptiness in her life. But she couldn't blame him because she allowed it.

Her giddiness at having met the Duchess of Huntington ebbed away. "Do you ride, Alex?"

"Ride?" He paused again. He'd been unusually quiet since leaving the shop.

"Yes, ride." Pondering her situation made her feel constrained. It was hard to breathe through the smothering sensation in her chest. "I presumed since you grew up on a farm, you might know how to mount a horse."

"Yes," he said quickly, after seeming to struggle with the question. "I *did* learn to ride on the farm."

"Excellent." She needed to escape the harsh truths in her life, if only for a few hours. "We shall ride this afternoon. You'll need to see about renting some horses."

"Renting?"

"Yes, Mr. Leigh on Mount Street rents his animals out." Rose and Roger kept a carriage and two horses, but carriage horses weren't suitable for riding.

Two hours later they were riding out of London, nearing Richmond. They'd made their way slowly at first, wading through the city's crowded streets. Along the way Rose's conversation with Roger replayed in her mind. *I don't want children.* He deprived Rose not only of a family, but also of a husband's love and companionship. Even if Roger could not love her, a true friendship might have sufficed. Perhaps working together in the business would supply the fulfillment Rose craved.

But Roger all but banned her from the shop. *Her shop.*

And he very happily took credit for her work. Meanwhile, at home they barely spoke. The truth was that Rose felt most alone when her husband was in the room. He'd closed himself off to her long ago.

A lump swelled in Rose's throat at the colorless future that stretched before her. Her husband was neither lover, nor friend or companion. No children. No family. Few friends. She had her work, but her maps were no longer enough. She wanted more, but had no idea how to go about getting it. Had one bad choice, consenting to marry Roger, locked her forever into a life that was increasingly impossible to bear?

Panic rose into her chest. She spurred her mare on, into the wide-open fields that finally stretched before them. Desperate to feel free and unencumbered, she leaned forward over the mount's neck, her seat hitting the saddle with each downward stride, moving in tandem with her mount. She could hear Alex's mount behind her keeping pace, the horses' hooves pounding the grass in hard, rhythmic clunks.

The wind slapped her face, robbing her of breath. She gasped in gulps of air, feeling alive. Present. And not just a bystander in her own life.

Then she was laughing and didn't realize she was crying until the wind whipped her damp cheeks. Her vision blurred, a watery landscape stretched before her.

"Mrs. Fleming." Alex rode up next to her. He sat a horse well. Elegant. In command. Like everything else he did. "Rose! Stop! You're going too fast in this terrain, especially riding sidesaddle!" he called out, the words full of urgent warning. "There are trees up ahead. It's dangerous."

But she didn't stop. She was tired of being told what to do. Instead, she went faster, as if she could outrun her problems.

"Rose!" Alex came closer and reached over to grab her reins. She jerked her mount away. Just a few more strides. This was one thing in her life she could control at the moment. Of course, she wasn't foolish enough to race into an unfamiliar tree line.

Tears blinding her, she pulled her mount to an abrupt stop and dismounted. She dropped the reins and strode away on the grass, tearing off her bonnet and tossing it aside. Embarrassed by her tears, she inhaled lungs full of air to calm herself. She didn't want Alex to see her in such a state.

"Mrs. Fleming." Alex ran up beside her, his tone stern. "What was that? You could have seriously injured yourself." He searched her face when he reached her. His tone changed. "What's wrong?" She heard the care in his voice and registered his distress at her current state.

She shook her head.

"What is it?"

"Nothing." She kept walking. "I'm just overwrought."

"A woman like you does not become agitated for no reason. Won't you tell me?" He laid a gentle hand on her arm. "Maybe I can help."

The warmth of his touch spiraled up her arm. "You cannot. No one can."

"Let me try."

"Only I can help myself." She finally halted and faced him. "My husband doesn't want children." It was all she dared reveal even though there was so much more to it. *My husband doesn't love me. I think I might despise him. He steals my work and I am complicit in the deception.* She longed to confide in Alex, but didn't dare.

Tenderness softened the roughness of his features. She stood with her arms hanging by her sides. She didn't move. She couldn't trust herself. Alex took the responsibility from her, stepping forward and folding her into his arms.

She sank into the hard planes of his body, curling into the warmth and solace he offered, into the scent of shaving soap, leather and horses. "I'm sorry. I am behaving like a hysterical woman."

"Shhh." He rubbed her back in comforting circles. With her cheek against his chest, she could feel his heart beating strong and fast. "A man would have to be a fool not to want a family with you."

"He doesn't want anything from me." Except the maps that brought him money and glory. Roger took everything and gave nothing.

"I don't think that's true," he said.

"What?" she sniffled, her nose stuffy.

Still embracing her with one arm, he produced a handkerchief with the other. "He clearly is interested in you the way a man is interested in a woman."

She almost snorted. Alex couldn't be more wrong. She blew her nose and allowed herself a few more moments to savor the comfort he offered. When was the last time anyone had embraced her? "I think Mr. Fleming is bored with me."

"He is not."

Alex spoke so firmly, so plainly, that Rose pulled

back to examine his face. "Why do you say that? I am his wife. I am in a position to know."

"And I am a man." His hand still rubbed her back. "I know when another man desires a woman. I can see it in the way he watches you when he thinks you aren't looking."

She shook her head. Alex had no idea. She gave him a watery smile. "What you must think of me. I have a roof over my head, plenty to eat, a comfortable life and yet here I am—"

"I think you are extraordinary." Eyes like black onyx glittered, enveloping Rose in the sweetest heat. "Mr. Fleming is to be envied for having you as his wife."

"You shouldn't say such things."

He cupped her face in his large, warm hands. "No, I should not." He lowered his face to press his lips against her forehead. It was chaste, yet yearning spiraled through her.

"Alex," she whispered. Her hands came up to cover his as he caressed her cheeks. "Thank you for comforting me."

"Rose." Her name on his lips sounded like an intimacy. A shiver went down her back. His hands were rough. Rougher than they used to be. His breathing, deep and rhythmic, vibrated through her. This encounter was more intimate than anything she'd ever shared with her husband. She didn't want to move.

If only the moment could last forever. But honor dictated that it could not. They both stepped away at the same time, almost like synchronized dancers.

Because Rose was still married, even if she didn't have a husband.

OWEN LINGERED BY the back door. "Whatcha doing?"

"What does it look like?" Brandon dug out the last planting hole, savoring the feel of the damp soil beneath his fingers. It had been too long since he'd worked the earth. "I'm putting in a small herb garden."

"That ain't a footman's duties."

"I'm aware. But I want some sage for my tea." He pulled the small plant he'd brought from Peckham House from its pot and lowered it into the hole. He probably would not be around to truly enjoy the fruits of his labors, but working in the garden was its own reward.

"Sage?" The boy scrunched up his face. "What's that?"

"An herb."

The boy shrugged a bony shoulder. "Never 'eard of it." He watched Brandon drop the rest of the small plants into the holes he dug. "What else is there?"

"Some mint. Parsley, coriander and a few other things Mrs. Waller asked for." All of which he'd brought over from his garden at Peckham House.

"Are you sure you weren't a gardener at yer last position?"

"Quite sure."

"Cuz yer a much better gardener than you are a footman. You couldn't be a more terrible footman if you tried."

"No one asked for your opinion." He unpotted some parsley.

"Owen, that is rather unkind, don't you think?" Rose's amused voice startled the boy out of his slouch.

He straightened up. "Apologies, ma'am."

Rose appeared in the doorway. "It seems to me

that you should make your apologies to Alex and not to me."

"Beggin' yer pardon, Alex," he mumbled while staring down at his shoes.

"That's better," Rose said. "Now, don't you have some lessons to attend to?"

"Yes, ma'am." The boy slipped past Rose and slinked back into the house.

"Lessons?" Brandon asked.

"There's a clergyman who runs a school for children like Owen. The boy will go three times a week for four hours."

She sat on the steps looking fresh and lovely in a striped pink-and-white dress with a ruffled neck. Meanwhile, he was sweating like a stevedore and probably reeked like one. His sleeves were rolled up, baring his forearms, an indecent display in front of the lady of the house.

But she'd come to him. He was surprised to see her. Rose had avoided him since their ride in the country two days ago. She barely turned away from her drafting table when he brought in her meals.

She watched him work. "Is this your sage garden?"

"It is." Her gaze followed his hands as he rolled his sleeves down, covering forearms that were liberally dusted with dark hair. "I've added a few other herbs that Mrs. Waller requested."

She blinked away from his arms and eyed the small pots. "Where did you get the plants? I don't recall seeing a charge for them on the household accounts."

"From a friend. He works for a grand lord who has an extensive garden."

"I must say I agree with Owen."

He paused to look at her, holding one soiled hand over his eyes to shield them from the sun's glare. "That I'm a terrible footman?"

Her eyes sparkled. "That you're a natural gardener. I suppose that's to be expected of a farmer's son."

"I have had my hands in the soil for as long as I can remember." That much was true. Brandon preferred to be outside, either in his own garden or glasshouse, or working with his tenants on their farms, experimenting with new growing techniques. But even the best planting was for naught without a nearby water source, which Fleming's map had put out of the reach of a wide swath of Highfield's tenants.

But it was safest to steer clear of his past when speaking with Rose. "You arranged for Owen to go to school?"

"Yes. The boy is very clever. If he learns to read, he could make something of himself." She paused. "You needn't look so surprised to find that I'm not a complete ogre."

"I just assumed all those feathers in your hats consumed most of the household budget."

She smiled. "You really are a ghastly man to be so unkind about my hats. But I suppose not everyone can understand art."

"That's for certain." He grinned and resumed his work. Rose Fleming was a woman of many surprises. She spent extravagantly on her gowns and fed her servants the barest minimum rations, yet she'd gone to the trouble to help secure a better future for an orphan.

"I wanted a word with you," she said after a moment, "about what occurred the other day."

He didn't look up from the herbs. "What occurred the other day?"

"I apologize that you had to see me that way. But thank you for your care of me."

He paused, raising his eyes to meet hers. "You don't ever need to apologize to me. It was my pleasure."

She flushed and looked away. "Tomorrow, I'd like to call on the Duchess of Huntington directly after lunch."

"I shall be ready." He should get Dudley to go in his place. If Leela spotted Brandon, his masquerade would be over, as would any chance of finding evidence he'd been cheated. He blew out a breath. He'd searched everywhere he could think of in the house without any luck thus far.

Here he was, his hands red and chapped from washing dishes, and fingernails blackened by the daily shoe cleaning. The soreness in his muscles never went away, and he was perpetually hungry thanks to the meager meals allotted to servants. But none of that mattered. Brandon was willing to do whatever it took to expose Fleming.

The last thing he needed was for his sister to ruin everything.

Chapter Nine

*I*t's practically a palace." Rose gazed up at Weston House, the Duke of Huntington's mammoth home. "I don't know what I am doing here."

Neither did Brandon. What was Leela up to? "I'll wait here outside until you are ready to depart."

"Nonsense." Rose scoffed. "You'll burn up out here."

She wasn't wrong. The unseasonable heat did make his livery even more scratchy and stuffy. He was perspiring heavily but couldn't risk going inside. Not even for a cool ale or lemonade. "The fresh air will do me well," he lied.

She chuckled. "I suppose even in the city, one remains a farm boy."

"Yes, that's it." He eagerly latched on to her assumption. "I do miss the country air." But he didn't miss being outdoors on hot and sweaty afternoons such as this one.

He escorted her to Weston House's shiny black door. Huntington's servants would show Rose in, while Brandon remained behind, outside and out of sight.

The door opened almost immediately. "Good day."

It was Huntington's butler. Brandon kept his eyes on the man's shoes and roughened his voice. "Mrs. Fleming to see the Duchess of Huntington." Keeping his chin tucked, he hoped the rim of his hat would shield his face from view.

"Her Grace is expecting Mrs. Fleming. This way, madam." As Rose entered his sister's house, Brandon spun on his heels and returned to the side pavement to wait. He pulled at his neck cloth. It was deuced hot. Whatever Leela wanted, he fervently hoped she wouldn't keep Rose too long.

"You want me to draw maps for your upcoming book?" Rose could hardly believe her ears. She was obviously up to the task but the Duchess of Huntington had no way of knowing that. "I am flattered, Your Grace, but we are barely acquainted. You know so little about my true abilities."

"I've seen enough." The duchess was uncommonly handsome with luminous olive skin, dark eyes and hair that cascaded in riotous curls about her shoulders. "And you must call me Leela."

Rose could hardly believe this unexpected stroke of luck. "Only if you will consent to call me Rose."

"Rose, it is." Leela reached for her tea. "I did engage a draftsman while we were in Greece. But I should like for you to use his information to create the final maps to appear in *Travels to Greece*, my forthcoming publication."

Excitement pulsed through Rose. "I shall have to use a different initial to sign my name on your maps of Greece."

Leela sipped her tea. "Whatever for?"

"My husband Roger signs his maps with the initial R."

"Why don't you sign your maps with your full name?"

"Because people consider maps drawn by a woman to be inferior."

Mischief sparkled in the duchess's eyes. "They also once considered travelogues written by women to be inferior." Leela caused a minor scandal not so long ago when she publicly revealed herself to be D. L. Chambers, authoress of the immensely popular book volumes *Travels in Arabia*.

"Your obvious talent, along with my name and title, will lend consequence to you and your maps once my volume is published," the duchess continued. "Before long, people will begin to commission maps from you in your own right."

"I can barely imagine that." What would it be like to have customers consult directly with her rather than go through Roger? "It would be something to be able to take credit for my work."

"From my experience, I can assure you that public recognition can be quite nice," Leela declared. "I cannot wait for all of London to become acquainted with your talents."

"You are very kind."

"We women must stick together. The men in charge have made rules to their advantage, which happen to be to our great disadvantage. Women must make our own rules." She nibbled on a biscuit. "Now, tell me all about yourself."

Rose smoothed her skirts. "There's very little to tell, I'm afraid. I am an only child. I have not had an adventurous life." Certainly nothing like Leela's. "My parents died when I was young, leaving me in the care of my uncle. He was a surveyor and owned an engraving concern. I practically grew up in his shop."

"That's where you learned to make maps."

"Yes." Rose reached for her tea. "That's how I met my husband. He worked for my uncle." She rather liked Leela and never dreamed a duchess could be so easy to talk to. "What about you?" she dared to ask. One was not supposed to question a duchess but Rose didn't think Leela would mind. "I understand your mother was Arab?"

"Yes, from Palestine. I went there after my first husband passed to meet Mama's family. And then I decided to write about my travels."

"My grandfather was also Arab."

Leela's brows lifted. "Was he?"

"Yes, from Lebanon. That is why I read *Travels in Arabia* with such interest. To learn more about where he came from. I really know almost nothing about the language or the culture."

"I learned a great deal about the Levant when I traveled there."

"You've led such a fascinating life." Rose sipped her tea. It was sweet, aromatic and slightly astringent. "Is there sage in the tea?"

"Yes, Arabic tea is often served with sage or mint. I honestly prefer mint but my brother just sent over fresh sage from his garden."

"This is how my footman likes to take his tea," Rose said. "He is Arab as well and has just planted sage, mint and other herbs in our garden."

"Really? There aren't a great many Arabs in London. And you say he is handy in the garden?"

"Yes, he's from a farming family. But his mother's people are cotton merchants in Manchester."

Leela went still. "Is that so?"

"Yes. He secured an excellent deal for the tea towels with the maps on them. The ones you purchased."

"Did he?" An expression that Rose could not interpret crossed Leela's face.

"Is everything all right?"

"Just fine," Leela responded cheerily. "Would you care to have a look at the draftsman's notes and sketches to see if they're what you need?"

Rose scooted forward. "Oh yes, I would like that very much."

BRANDON STARED UP at his sister's house. How much longer was Rose going to be? If she took too much longer, he'd be nothing but a puddle of perspiration by the time she returned. He was overheated all the time these days. His attic room was unbearably stifling at night. Was this what his servants suffered through?

He drew off his hat. Wearing it just made him hotter. At least he'd found a bit of shade and an iron bollard to sit on.

Someone thunked him hard on the back of his head. "Ouch!" He jumped up and found himself staring into his sister's glaring face.

"What the devil are you doing, *hamar*?"

"I am not a jackass, thank you very much," he snapped. "Where is Mrs. Fleming?"

"Busy looking at some notes and sketches from my

Greece trip. Why are you pretending to be Rose Fleming's footman? What are you up to?"

"All you need to know"—he drew a handkerchief from his pocket and mopped his perspiring face—"is that I have no intention of hurting her."

"This is why you've been so absent of late, is it not? It's the reason no one can find you? *Citi* is concerned. She came looking for you."

"She did?" He didn't like to worry his grandmother.

"She said you normally visit her every month."

"I was busy."

She raked a scornful look down his body. "Busy impersonating a footman for who knows what foolish reason."

He kept his gaze trained on Weston House. "I might be many things, but you know better than most that being a fool is not one of them."

She harrumphed. "I don't know about that. You're a marquess wearing a footman's livery, roasting in the sun."

He pulled at his neckcloth. "I really am going to have to see to it that my footmen have lighter-weight uniforms to wear in the summer."

"You still haven't explained why you're having your own private masquerade in the middle of the day in the middle of Mayfair."

"I have my reasons."

She rolled her eyes. "You always do. You just don't bother to share them with anyone. And since when do you visit Mama's family in Manchester?"

"I go from time to time."

"Since when? I thought you wanted nothing to do with our Arab relations."

He switched to Arabic. "That's not exactly true."

The way Leela's mouth dropped open was almost comical. "You speak Arabic?" she answered in their mother's native tongue, which she'd learned on her travels. "How? When?"

"I picked up the language long ago. During the summers I never came straight home from school. I went to Manchester first and spent time with *Cidi* and our male cousins at the cotton concern. Later, after university, I also engaged an Arabic tutor."

"I never knew."

"Mama insisted that I not tell you. She wanted you to be as English as could be." Lady Brandon believed the ton would be more accepting if she erased all outward traces of her children's Arab blood.

"Why did she let *you* go? *You're* the marquess."

"I didn't leave our parents much choice. When I was fifteen, I demanded to meet Mama's relatives. I knew she used to sneak off to visit them."

"You did? How?" She flattened a hand against her chest. "I just found out recently."

"I overheard her and Papa talking about it. I confronted them and demanded to be allowed to meet our Arab relations." It hadn't been easy to convince Mama. Lady Brandon did everything in her power to shed her Arab past so that the ton would find her worthy of Papa and her title. She changed her name from Maryam to Mary and never talked to her children in Arabic. Instead, she insisted they learn French, the language of the nobility.

Leela stared at her brother. "All of this time you've been seeing our cousins?"

"The male ones anyway. Can we speak about this later?" He stole a look at Weston House. "Mrs. Fleming would be very surprised to see the Duchess of Huntington speaking to her footman."

"Imagine how shocked she'd be to find me in conversation with the Marquess of Brandon."

"What is the purpose of Rose Fleming's visit to Weston House? Why did you invite her to call on you?"

"It's hardly a footman's business to know what his mistress is getting up to." Leela folded her arms over her chest. Not a good sign. "Now, either you tell me what's going on, or I march right inside to tell Rose exactly who you are."

"Leela, you have to trust me. This has nothing to do with Rose Fleming. Her husband cheated me out of my land and access to water that our tenants need."

She frowned. "What water?"

"The stream we used to play in as children that leads to the water meadow."

"How could they swindle you? That water meadow has always belonged to Highfield."

"You're aware that we are enclosing all of the properties surrounding the village?"

"Yes, and?"

"Roger Fleming drew the maps. He gave the water meadow to Canning."

"Canning?" She twisted her lips. "That prig with the property bordering ours?"

"Exactly. I need to find evidence that those two conspired to steal my land."

"And being a footman in the Fleming house is how you intend to achieve that?"

"It's the only way I could think of to get inside so I could search the entire house."

She contemplated his words. "Do you think Rose knows what her husband did?"

He shook his head. "No, and I have no intention of harming her." He paused. "It's complicated."

"I can see that."

"My dilemma is that I originally intended to completely destroy Roger Fleming. But now I cannot, because it would leave Rose with nothing but a scandal and a ruined business."

Understanding animated her face. "You *care* about her?"

Too much. He shrugged. "We are friends of a sort."

"What about Lady Olympia?"

"What about her?"

"Where does she fit in?"

"I've spoken to her father, the duke, and have signaled my interest in possibly making Lady Olympia my marchioness."

"And Rose?"

"Is a married woman. I have to make certain that holding her husband to account doesn't destroy her life."

"I've only been acquainted with Rose Fleming for a short time, but she strikes me as a woman who can look after herself."

"Does this mean you'll keep my secret?"

"For now." With a flip of her hair, she started to cross the street back to her house.

"And Leela?"

She paused. "Yes?"

"Let's dispense with your flicking me in the head. We are adults now."

She skewered him with a skeptical look. "And yet, here you are still playing dress-up."

"I HOPE I haven't kept you too long." Leela sailed back into the cavernous library to find Rose immersed in the Greece drawings.

"Not at all." She tore her gaze away from the papers littering the library table. "I trust all is well."

"Oh, yes," the duchess said breezily. "I just needed a moment to speak with my brother."

"Am I intruding? I do beg your pardon." Maybe Rose had outstayed her welcome. She swept a hand over the cluttered table. "I'm afraid I lost myself in all of this."

"Don't be silly. You must stay as long as you'd like."

"I don't want to keep you from your brother."

"You are not." Her gaze fell on the papers. "Are the materials satisfactory?"

"More than satisfactory," Rose said. "Your Greek draftsman is very competent."

"I trust this means you will accept my offer to provide the maps for my next volume?"

"It would truly be my honor." Only an idiot would refuse. Having her work associated with Leela and her bestselling books offered a means of getting out from under Roger's thumb. Of establishing herself as a cartographer in her own right.

"Excellent," Leela said. "More tea? I can have a warm pot brought in."

"You are very kind, but I could not eat or drink another thing."

"I suppose you shall have sage in your tea whenever you please now that this Arab footman of yours has planted some in your garden."

"His name is Alex, and I've no doubt I shall soon be enjoying the herbs."

"Alex, is it? How long has this Alex been in your employ?"

"Not very long. Only a few weeks."

"And is he good at his job?"

"He is learning." The duchess's interest in Alex was odd. Was it because Leela and the footman shared Arab blood? "Alex doesn't have much experience as a footman. He grew up on a farm."

"A farm? Interesting."

"To be honest, I have to brush out my skirts after he does."

"He brushes out your clothes." Leela's eyes twinkled. "Why do you keep this Alex around if he cannot execute the most basic duties required of a footman?"

"He works hard and shows true promise. Alex has improved considerably since he first started. He's become quite proficient at cleaning our boots."

Leela pressed her lips inward. "I see."

"Besides, he is good company. My husband insists I have a footman accompany me every time I leave the house."

"Good company? Alex?"

"I am sure you would find him insolent. But I am just a merchant's wife—"

"And a mapmaker," Leela interjected.

"Yes, and a mapmaker." How glorious to be able to say it out loud.

"Please continue," Leela urged. "You were saying?"

Rose momentarily lost track of their conversation. "Oh yes, I'm just a merchant's wife so I have no airs to put on with my servants. Alex makes me laugh. In truth, I've experienced some . . . challenges of late . . . and he's been a stalwart by my side."

Surprise chased across Leela's face. "Has he?"

Rose flushed. "I'm sure you find it terribly inappropriate to befriend my footman."

"Not at all." A gentle expression softened the duchess's features. "I think it is truly remarkable."

Chapter Ten

$\mathcal{T}$he following Sunday afternoon, Brandon took Lady Olympia for a ride in his black-topped burgundy barouche.

"Do you not care for Hyde Park, my lord?" she inquired as the carriage entered Green Park. Her maid rode up ahead with Brandon's driver.

"I thought this might be a nice change." He'd deliberately instructed his coachman to avoid fashionable Hyde Park where they were certain to be spotted by the ton's prying eyes. Brandon intended to secure the prize before flaunting his victory. "Do you mind?"

"Not at all." She fluttered her lashes. The diamond of the season knew how to flirt. She wore a becoming embroidered white gown. The pink ribbons on her bonnet matched the sash on her dress. "Thank you for the ribbons you sent over for my sisters and me." She fingered the ribbon on her bonnet. "They are lovely."

"Not nearly as lovely as the lady who wears them." He forced the gallantry expected of a man who intended to court a lady. He'd sent enough fripperies to furnish a haberdashery, sufficient for all six of Kingsley's daughters, so that his gift could not be deemed too personal for an unwed girl to accept from a gentleman.

She smiled graciously, accepting his compliment as if it were her due.

He cleared his throat. "I wanted to speak with you about my intentions."

"My father mentioned that you might be interested in courting me."

"But only if such a development is agreeable to you."

"I assure you that it is." She regarded him through her lashes. "Most agreeable."

She was direct. Brandon appreciated that. But his blood did not warm as it might had Rose favored him with such an inviting look. Not that it mattered. He was looking for a suitable wife, and Lady Olympia met all of his requirements. She was lovely and of excellent family. The perfect instrument to exact revenge on the ton's favored sons.

Maybe he'd even give his children Arabic names, just to watch exacting noble matrons sputter over the unthinkable idea of a Lord Laith or Lady Samira. "And you are aware of my mother's origins?"

A firm nod of her chin. "I am, my lord."

"Excellent. I want all interactions between us to be completely transparent."

"It's not as though you are a heathen, as the rumors suggest," she said brightly. "To the contrary, with your manner of dress and speech, you're as English as anyone I know."

He bit back a sarcastic retort. She clearly meant it as a compliment, a stamp of approval. His parents would be thrilled their quest to carve him into the perfect English nobleman hadn't been a complete failure. Brandon had learned their lessons all too well.

"I truly enjoyed visiting Peckham House," Lady Olympia continued. "It's a perfect home for entertaining."

Nothing interested Brandon less than talk of ton gatherings, except perhaps the parties themselves, but he gamely took her lead. "Do you think so?"

"Oh yes, my grandmama says your grandparents used to hold the most marvelous entertainments."

"They did?" Brandon had little recollection of his father's parents, who died when he was a boy. But he doubted his parents attended many of his grandparents' entertainments. Mama and Papa had preferred the country, rarely venturing into Town. Did they stay away from Brandon's noble grandparents by choice? Or had they been unwelcome?

"Do you attend many parties?" he forced himself to ask.

"Oh yes." Her face shone. "We are out practically every afternoon and evening during the Season."

"That sounds . . . tiring."

"Not at all," she chirped. "I adore seeing people. Being sociable is so very invigorating. Do you not agree?" She looked up at him with large, inquisitive green eyes.

"I am afraid that I rarely entertain."

She patted his hand with her gloved fingers. "Men cannot be expected to manage gatherings. Once you take a wife, your marchioness will no doubt see to everything."

Brandon's bountiful lunch, consumed barely an hour earlier, curdled in his gut. Although it shouldn't. He'd deliberately pursued a creature of the ton. He could hardly find fault with Lady Olympia for personifying the society he reviled.

"I am certain you will make a very fine hostess," he offered.

"I do hope so. I cannot wait to try my hand at it. Mama has spent a great deal of time training me in the running of the finest houses and planning the very best routs."

"I can well imagine it." The idea of throwing fabulous parties to flaunt his victory had sounded appealing in theory. But the reality of it, embodied by the ton darling at his side, caused dread to bubble up inside him. His sister's words came back to him.

Be careful what you wish for.

ROSE WAS SO immersed in her work that she didn't turn around when Alex appeared with her breakfast tray on Monday morning.

"Hard at work?" he asked.

Rose turned to face him. "How was your afternoon off?" She hated how much she missed his company on Sundays.

"Uneventful." He set her tray down.

She had no idea where he went during his time off. "Do you have family in Town or are most still on the farm?"

"I have some family here. They have a place near Red Lion Square."

"Red Lion Square?" It was a respectable address. Home to solicitors, doctors and merchants. Solidly middle class.

His gaze went to her drafting table. Panic rose. She'd neglected to cover it. And then she remembered she had nothing to hide. At least not with this assignment. "You're working on maps."

"Yes, for the Duchess of Huntington. She wants me to provide the maps for her next book, *Travels in Greece*."

A speculative expression came over his face. "Does she?"

"She apparently liked the tea towels a great deal."

"May I have a closer look?"

She again had to tamp down the urge to hide her work. "Of course. But I've just begun. It's very rough."

Her heart pounded as he crossed over to examine her efforts. It was silly to be nervous. Her maps were widely acknowledged to be among the finest in London. But this was the first time her work was assessed by someone who knew she, and not Roger, was the cartographer.

For Leela's project, Rose had to push herself way beyond her usual area of comfort. People needed to believe Rose Fleming's maps were drawn by a different hand than R. Fleming's. The details, techniques and strokes all had to be uniquely different than anything she'd created before.

"These are very good." He moved the top sketch aside to look at the next one. "I don't know anything about maps, but the level of craftsmanship is impressive."

Delight streaked through her. Alex's praise meant more to her than it should. "Must you sound so surprised?"

"I had no idea at all that your talents were at this level." He shot her a sidelong glance with those dark, enigmatic eyes. "You've been working on maps all along, haven't you?"

Rose's mouth went dry. "What do you mean?"

"Dudley says you spend all day sketching. But you've been drawing maps."

She straightened. "The servants gossip about how I pass my days?"

He gave her a solemn look. "I do not. Anything discussed between us stays private."

"And the other servants?"

"Of course they gossip about you. They've got to have something to entertain themselves with beyond scrubbing dishes and brushing mud from shoes."

"You *do* know that servants are not supposed to gossip about their employers."

His attention returned to her sketches. "This is why the servants haven't seen any of your drawings. Because you are making maps." Comprehension lit his face. "That's it!" He snapped his fingers. "I now know precisely why you are hiding your talent at mapmaking."

"I do not know what you are talking about." She backed away. "I think you should leave now. My breakfast is getting cold."

"You hide your talents—"

"I said *please leave.*"

"—because you don't want to upstage your husband."

"That is not—" She halted. "What?"

"You are a mapmaker, too. It makes perfect sense. You grew up in your uncle's shop. It's no wonder that you learned cartography."

"A bit perhaps," she hedged.

"A *bit*, my horse's behind."

"Alex!" she half-exclaimed, half-laughed. "A footman should not talk to his employer in that manner."

"If you'd allow yourself to fully explore your talents,

I think you'll find that you are at least as talented as Mr. Fleming. Perhaps even more so."

"More talented?" She bit back a smile. "I am rather certain that is not possible."

"Don't hide your abilities in order to please a man," he said urgently. He gripped her arm, sending a charge up to her shoulder. "My sister did that and—" He stopped abruptly.

"And what?" she asked, breathless. "What did your sister do?" This was the first she'd heard of any sister.

He released her arm with a disarming smile that sizzled through her. "As you said, I should leave you before your breakfast gets cold."

"But I'd like to hear about your sister."

"Another time, perhaps." He was already at the door. "Enjoy your breakfast."

"ARE YOU TRULY going to wed a duke's daughter?" Brandon's cousin Rafi asked before biting into a nectarine.

"*Inshallah.*" Brandon reached for a date-filled *maamoul* cookie. "God willing. That is my intention." Conversations with his Arab relatives were usually spoken in a mix of Arabic and English.

"*Willah?*" Their grandmother sucked on her hookah, percolating the water in her pipe and engulfing herself in a cloud of smoke. "Who else is he going to wed?"

Brandon had taken a detour while running an errand for Rose to stop by the house near Red Lion Square owned by his Arab relatives. In addition to *Citi,* he found his cousins Rafi and Elias, Hanna's brothers, nestled in the front salon of the modest terraced home.

"I'm surprised to find you two in Town." His cousins spent most of their time in Manchester at the family trading business. A revolving set of his Arab relations stayed at the London house whenever they were in Town.

"We had business in London," Rafi said. "We also brought the order of tea towels for your friend with us. We delivered them to Mrs. Fleming's shop today."

"Excellent. She'll be very pleased."

"About your duke's daughter," Rafi said. "Will she have you, this diamond of the ton?"

"Of course she'll have him," Elias interjected. "He's got a title after all."

"I have other charms."

Rafi chewed on his nectarine. "Like wagons full of money."

"And a huge town house in Mayfair," Elias put in. "That cancels the fact that he's related to Arab traders."

Brandon's mouth twitched. "Exactly." He was accustomed to his cousins' raillery. They'd grown close during the summers when he'd visited *Cidi* at the trading house in Manchester, where both cousins had worked since their teens.

"This *maamoul* is delicious," Brandon said to his grandmother.

"*Sahtain, habibi.* Eat them in good health." The date cookies were a favorite that *Citi* often sent over to Peckham House when she was in Town, although she never came herself. Growing up, *Citi* had only ever visited them at Highfield in the country. Away from prying ton eyes.

Elias's eyes twinkled. "Instead of this duke's daughter,

Brandon could marry a nice Arabic girl, like we're expected to."

"*Malaya minuk*. Don't be silly. He'll wed a noble girl." Steel coated *Citi*'s words. "His own kind."

"But you are my own kind, too," Brandon reminded her, "as are Arab girls."

Citi tsked her disapproval. "Your mother sacrificed a lot so that your father's people would accept you and Leela. Your sister was smart enough to marry a duke. Now you must take this duke's daughter."

Unwittingly, Rose's face flashed before him. What would it be like to have a wife with a quick mind and ready sense of humor? With a passion for creating that exceeded her interest in hosting lavish entertainments?

"*Ismah*. Listen to me, *Citi*." His grandmother exhaled, fortifying the tent of smoke around her. Having his grandmother call him *Citi* had taken some getting used to. It was a term of endearment that served to define the relationship between him and his grandmother.

"What if I choose to marry neither an Arabic girl from the community nor a noble lady?"

Citi clamped her lips together and blew out, making a noise of flatulence to signify her derision. "Then you wouldn't be truly accepted anywhere. You'd be even more out of place than you feel now. Listen to me, *habibi*, stay with your own kind."

He quashed any thoughts of Rose. Obviously, he couldn't marry her. She was already wed. But what if he actually found another woman whose company he enjoyed as much? "What if one of *my own kind*, as you call it, doesn't appeal to me?"

Citi's lip curled. "It makes no difference. You do it for

your children. So that they will never feel out of place the way you did."

Brandon couldn't argue with that. Although he'd grown up with almost every advantage, he'd never truly belonged anywhere. He did not want that sense of isolation for his children.

Rafi leaned forward in his chair. "Do you have a particular lady in mind who is not, as you say, one of your kind?"

He pushed the image of Rose out of his mind. *What the devil was wrong with him*? "No." He stuffed the rest of the *maamoul* into his mouth.

"Are you certain? *Akeed*?" Rafi wiggled his eyebrows. "Maybe you're thinking of this Mrs. Fleming. You were so very eager to help with her hand towel purchase."

"*Bi sharafak*? Seriously?" Brandon asked. "Don't be ridiculous. Mrs. Fleming is married."

"*Khallas*," *Citi* proclaimed. "Enough. Alexander will do as his parents would have expected. He already told you he plans to take the duke's daughter."

"Precisely," Brandon said with a sharp nod. His course was set, his carefully laid plans about to come to fruition. Soon, he'd have his land, Lady Olympia and his revenge. But instead of a sense of triumph, unease rippled through him. He shook it off and reached for another *maamoul*.

"*Yalla*, I have time for one more cup of tea before I go."

"CALM DOWN, I'M coming," Brandon muttered under his breath at the insistent knocking on the Flemings' front door. It was late Sunday morning and he was about to leave for his afternoon off.

The woman on the doorstep was in her early thirties with sandy-colored hair and a smattering of freckles dusting her nose and cheeks. She wore a cape that matched her hair and a worried expression.

"How may I help you?"

"I must see Mr. Fleming immediately."

"And you are?" The woman's clothing and manner suggested she was of the laboring class.

"Mrs. . . ." She paused. "Tell Roger that it's Irene and that it's urgent."

This woman was on such familiar terms with Fleming that she referred to him by his Christian name? Brandon stepped aside to allow the woman entry. "I shall see if Mr. Fleming is home to callers."

She tiptoed inside, hiding her hands in her skirts, stealing a furtive glance around the front hall. "Thank you."

"Please wait here." Brandon climbed the stairs. As with most Sunday mornings after breakfast, Fleming was in his study.

"Who?" he asked when Brandon announced the name of his visitor.

"She said her name is Irene," Brandon repeated, "and that she is here on an urgent matter."

The blood rushed from Fleming's face. "Where is she?" He shot to his feet. "Where did you put her?"

"In the front hall, sir."

"Damnation." He rubbed the back of his neck. "Where is Mrs. Fleming?"

"I believe she is in her sitting room."

Fleming rushed from the room and hustled down the stairs. "Irene?"

"Roger." The woman looked up, relief etched on her face. "There you are."

"For lord's sake, Irene." He took her by the elbow and pulled her into the front salon. "What are you doing here?"

"I had to come. It's Reginald."

"What about him?"

"He's ill."

"What's wrong with him?"

"He's feverish."

Fleming turned to Brandon, as if suddenly remembering his presence. "Not a word of this to Mrs. Fleming."

"As you wish, sir."

The words were barely out of his mouth when Fleming pushed the door closed, although it stayed slightly ajar. The low, urgent murmurings of a clearly distressed Irene were followed by the reassuring tones of Roger Fleming.

After a few moments the door swung back open and Fleming barged out of the room.

His eyes narrowed when he spotted Brandon. "What the devil are you doing out here?"

"Standing by, sir, in case you are in need of assistance." Brandon grappled to come up with a plausible reason for his presence. "I thought you might wish for me to divert Mrs. Fleming were she to appear and inquire as to your whereabouts."

Fleming's expression relaxed. "I'm going out. My sister is very distressed. I have a family matter to attend to."

"Very good, sir."

"And say nothing to Mrs. Fleming. I don't want to upset her needlessly."

As if the whoreson cared about his wife. "As you wish."

Fleming bustled Irene out the door. From a front window, Brandon watched them flag down a hackney cab and bundle inside. He resisted an impulse to follow them. He had plans for his day off. Even though he dreaded the afternoon ahead, he could not cry off from a scheduled tea with Lady Olympia and her parents.

Turning from the window, he headed up to Rose's sitting room. He never left for his day off without saying goodbye.

"How are the maps coming?" he asked after she answered his knock by bidding him to enter.

"Well enough, I suppose." She pivoted from the drawing table to face him. Her hair was adorably askew as it usually was when she worked. Her thick amber strands of hair were again held up by one of her drawing pencils. "I'm awfully nervous."

"Don't be. I'm certain the duchess will love your maps."

"Do you really have so much faith in my abilities?" She tucked a wayward strand of hair behind her ear.

"Of course. That, and we must consider the fact that the duchess liked your very simple tea towel maps."

A smothered laugh escaped her throat. He loved to see her smile. "Are you suggesting that my tea towels are so rudimentary that Her Grace won't expect much more from me?"

He shrugged his answer.

She shook her head, her gaze dropping down his body. "You're wearing your jacket."

"It's Sunday. I'm about to leave for my afternoon off."

"I see." Her smile was soft with regret, as if she would miss him even if it was just for the day. "Do you have something interesting planned?"

"No, I—" He decided against lying to her. He'd already done enough of that. Some lies were necessary. But when he could, Brandon preferred to be truthful with Rose. "Nothing particularly special. Will you work all day?"

"Most likely. I've little else to occupy my time." She paused. "Did I hear Mr. Fleming go out?"

"Yes, just a few minutes ago."

"Oh? He didn't mention any plans for today. Roger isn't one to be spontaneous. Do you know where he went?"

"He didn't say."

She lifted a shoulder. "Well, that gives me more time to attend to my maps without worrying that he'll come in and discover what I'm working on."

"You haven't told him about your commission from the duchess?"

"Not as of yet." She cast her eyes downward. "I am delaying because I'm not sure how he'll react."

"Will he be angry? Or jealous?"

"He won't be pleased. I would rather postpone any unpleasantness for as long as possible."

"He won't forbid it, will he?"

Her eyes glittered. "He could *try*."

"I would place my bet on you any day."

Their gazes held. Longing pulsed between them. He

looked away. This woman had begun to disorder everything in him. His heart. His mind. His cock.

"I guess I shall be on my way."

"Enjoy your day." She forced a cheerful note into her farewell as he closed the door behind him.

But Brandon still registered the underlying sadness in her voice. And the ache in his own throat.

Chapter Eleven

"We'll stop at the end of this street," Rose said after she and Alex had covered about four miles. She was collecting information for her map of London. "We are so close to the shop. I would stop in if Roger did not object so to my visiting on any day other than Wednesday."

"Speaking of the shop," Alex said as he walked a couple of steps behind her. "I saw my cousin last week and he said he'd delivered the tea towels."

"He did?" She halted. "Roger didn't mention it." She pondered for a moment. "Let's stop by the shop very quickly. I am willing to risk my husband's wrath in order to see what the new tea towels look like."

Five minutes later they entered the shop. "Good day," Rose said to Paul, the clerk. She didn't know any of Roger's workers particularly well, not after he'd replaced Ben and Uncle Trevor's other workers.

"Mrs. Fleming." Paul's eyes rounded. "This is an unexpected visit."

"I thought I'd stop in briefly to see the new towels from Manchester."

"Certainly." He pointed out a front table. "There they are."

"Oh, some of them have already been printed up?" She reached for one, running a hand over the fabric and her map.

Alex came up beside her. "What do you think?"

"They're an excellent quality. Particularly for the price." She set it down and arranged the rest of the cloths in a more pleasing arrangement. Irritation shot through her. If Roger allowed her to come to the shop more often, she could ensure the displays always looked their best.

"Will there be anything else, Mrs. Fleming?" Paul asked.

"Where is my husband?" She shifted over to the next table to arrange some of the boxed puzzles that were finally ready for sale. "I should like to speak with him about the displays."

Paul's forehead scrunched up. "Mr. Fleming went home."

"What?" Rose looked up. "Why? Is he ill?"

"No, he went home for lunch as he does every day but Wednesday. Because, of course," Paul added helpfully, "on Wednesdays, you come to him here at the shop."

Rose's hands dropped away from the puzzle boxes. "He went home for lunch?"

"As he does every day."

"Every day?" Rose repeated dumbly.

"Except Wednesday," Paul said.

Rose's ears started ringing. "Except Wednesday."

Paul's smile slipped. "Unless . . . erm . . . I am some-how mistaken."

Rose forced a cheerful tone. "No, there is no mistake." Her voice sounded high and whiny. She tried to lower it. "Is he due back soon?"

"Let's see . . ." Paul looked at the clock on a shelf closest to the counter. "He's usually gone for three hours. As you know."

"Naturally." She plastered a polite smile on her face, even though the floor rocked beneath her feet. "Three hours. Every day. But Wednesday."

"Which means Mr. Fleming should return at any moment. Would you care to wait for him?"

Rose's eyes stung. "No, I shall just see him at home this evening." She needed to escape. *Where was Roger? Who was he with?* "Please don't mention my visit to Mr. Fleming. It would just upset him. You know how he prefers that I only visit on Wednesdays."

His eyes grew bigger. "But surely . . . you are not asking me to lie to my employer?"

I am your employer! she wanted to snap.

Alex approached Paul. "Mrs. Fleming is planning a surprise for her husband and if he learns of this visit, the surprise will be ruined. You would not want that, would you?" He pressed something into Paul's hands. "For your trouble. And your discretion."

Paul stared at the money in his palm. "Of course." He slipped the coins into his pocket. "You may count on my discretion."

Through her watery gaze, Rose tried to pull the door open to make her escape. Alex came to her side and opened it for her. "Thank you, Paul," she said faintly before rushing out onto the side pavement.

"Mrs. Fleming." Alex's hand brushed her elbow. "Are you all right?"

She pressed a hand hard against her stomach, trying to dull the pain there. "Where does he go?" She looked wildly at the footman. "What does he do?"

"I have no idea."

"You said that servants talk. Have you ever heard any gossip that would explain where Roger goes *every* day while he pretends to be at the shop?"

"Nothing. I give you my word as a ge— . . . I give you my word. I have heard nothing about this. I am as surprised as you are."

"I doubt that. You are not married to the man."

"Mr. Fleming could have a perfectly reasonable explanation for where he spends his afternoons."

"How likely do you think that is?"

"What would you like to do?" he asked, grim faced. "I am at your service. Do you want me to follow Mr. Fleming to see where he goes?"

"No."

"What, then? Tell me how I can help."

She tried to collect her thoughts. "Tomorrow we are both going to follow my husband."

Alarm flickered across his face. "I don't think that's a good idea. Whatever we discover could be very upsetting to you."

"Precisely. Today we established that my husband is a liar. Tomorrow I intend to find out if he's also a cheater."

"THERE HE IS," Alex murmured.

Rose stared at the thatch-roofed cottage as the front door opened. The entire afternoon felt like a dream.

Or a nightmare.

She and Alex had followed Roger from the shop to

Walham Green, a village about twenty minutes outside London that she'd never heard of. Her husband had disappeared into the stone cottage almost two hours ago. The sun was broiling, not that she noticed, but Alex insisted they take shelter in the shade of an old oak tree while waiting for Roger to reappear. The massive trunk hid them, while also providing a clear view of the cottage.

The door opened and three children streamed out into the front yard. Roger followed with a sandy-haired woman, their arms wrapped around each other. Two of the children had their mother's hair color. The third had brown hair. The two tallest boys sprinted around the yard yelling and chasing each other. A much smaller boy toddled over to Roger and tugged on the fabric of his pantaloons. Roger released the woman and bent over to pick up the child.

"Papa, Papa," one of the older boys yelled, "come and play with us."

The woman slipped her hand into Roger's. "Papa must go back to Town, boys." *Papa.* Rose swayed on her feet. *Papa.*

A warm breeze blew over her. She felt Alex's firm arm slip around her waist. "Steady there." His voice was calming, reassuring. The only solid thing in a world that suddenly didn't make any sense.

"Unfortunately, I cannot stay." Roger nuzzled the neck of the child in his arms. The boy squirmed and giggled. "Papa must get back to the shop."

"At least Reginald is feeling better," the woman said.

Roger ruffled the hair of the child in his arms. "He'll

be back playing with his brothers in no time at all, won't you, my big boy?"

The tallest boy, who looked to be five or six years old, bounced a ball in Roger's direction. He caught it one-handed and tossed it back. "Excellent catch!"

"Reggie lost my marbles, Papa," one of the boys called out. "Will you buy me new marbles?"

"Perhaps. If you behave and attend to your studies, I shall think about it."

"He has children." Rose's stomach churned. How could this be real? Her husband's words came back to her. *I see no need for children. I prefer an orderly life.* "He told me he didn't want them."

"Rose, I'm so sorry." Alex's arm remained braced around her. Offering support. Keeping her from collapsing. From falling apart.

Tears blurred her vision. "What he really meant was that he doesn't want *more* children." She swallowed down the acid that rose up into her throat. "At least not with me."

"We should leave." Alex gently tugged on her waist. "You've seen what you came here for."

"How could he?" The unfathomable extent of her husband's betrayal spiraled through her.

"*Haywan*," Alex growled. "He's an animal, a beast."

Rose couldn't move. Her gaze remained locked on her husband as he played with his children. This Roger was a stranger to her. Her Roger was courteous, remote and cold. The man before her openly displayed his affection. He smiled easily. He tenderly embraced his child and his mistress.

She couldn't bear it. But she also couldn't look away. "He has everything. Children. A woman he obviously loves. My shop." *The significant earnings from my maps.* "And he thinks he can leave me with nothing."

"Rose." Alex put an arm around her. "*Yalla*. You've seen enough."

Yalla. How long had it been since anyone had said that to her? Images of *Jidu* flashed in her mind. And of Mother and Father. And Uncle Trevor. And Aunt Hattie, whose health was failing. They were the only real family she'd ever had. The rest of her relatives were scattered throughout England. She barely saw them. Even her husband had his own family.

How alone she was.

She blindly allowed Alex to lead her away. They'd paid the hackney driver to wait for them across the meadow. She stumbled over a mound of grass. Alex caught her, steadied her, urged her on, while her mind struggled to accept what she'd seen with her own eyes.

And yet, behind the shock, deep down inside her, fury kindled in Rose's belly.

"DID YOU SEE the oldest boy?" Rose asked Alex that evening when he brought in her supper.

Brandon set down the tray, pleased to see the color had returned to her cheeks.

"You seem better." He was relieved. All afternoon she'd been like a ghost of herself, her eyes hollow. She hadn't spoken on the way home and vanished into her bedchamber as soon as they arrived.

"I could not bear the idea of sitting at the table with Roger."

Pleading a headache, Rose had ordered a tray brought to her room. Dudley waited on Fleming in the dining room while Brandon attended to Rose. Which was just as well. It would be difficult to keep from slamming Fleming's face into the soup and holding it there while he choked.

"The oldest boy is at least five or six." Dark shadows smudged her eyes. "Roger has been with that woman longer than he's been married to me."

"That does appear to be the case." Canning had mentioned something about Fleming having his own harem. Was this what he meant? Brandon shook his head. Irene was pretty enough, but Rose was spectacular. Beautiful and smart. What kind of fool would look elsewhere when he had a diamond like Rose to warm his bed?

"And the smallest one was what, three or four? Do you know what that means?"

He nodded grimly. "Fleming had a child with this woman while he was married to you."

Her eyes snapped with anger. "I've been supporting that woman and his children since Roger married me."

He looked startled. "Excuse me?"

She looked away. "My shop. I meant he has been using my shop to support his family. It's why he married me."

"I doubt that's the only reason." Brandon detected palpable masculine interest on Fleming's part whenever his wife was around. "He's obviously taken by your charms as well."

She laughed. But it was absent of any trace of amusement. "You have no idea." She slipped into a chair at the table. "Join me."

"That wouldn't . . . erm . . . I should not."

She looked at him, her blue eyes catching the light. "At this moment I need you to be my friend, not my footman."

He relented, taking the seat opposite her, even though he wasn't much of a friend. He'd lied to her from the first. Whatever happened, he intended to make certain he did nothing to add to Rose's pain.

"Here." She pushed the plate of mutton and vegetable pie toward him.

He shook his head. "I'm not going to eat your food."

"I'm not hungry."

"You need to eat. How about we make a bargain? I'll sit with you on the condition that you eat your supper."

"I'll share it with you."

"Agreed." He cut the meat. Leaving the fork for her, he speared the mutton pieces with a knife. "I need to tell you something."

"What is it? Am I in for another shock?"

"It would be difficult to surpass what happened today." He set the knife down. "The name of your husband's mistress is Irene."

Her eyes widened. "You've known about her. You lied?"

"No, I did not lie." *At least not about Irene.* Guilt knotted his gut. "The truth is I had no idea who she was when she came here about a week ago."

"Here?" Her voice rose. "To this house? When?"

"One week ago Sunday." He told her everything he remembered about the woman's visit.

"Roger said this woman was his sister?"

"He did."

She rose. She was trembling. "Excuse me."

He stood as well. "Rose. Mrs. Fleming. What can I do?"

"Just give me a moment." She vanished into her adjoining bedchamber.

Brandon sat back down, unsure of what to do. Should he follow Rose and try to comfort her? Agitated, he tapped his foot hard against the wooden floor. What he should do is march straight into the dining room and bash Fleming's head in.

He forced himself to calm down. He was too emotionally involved. He needed to remember his mission and focus on finding the evidence that Fleming had purposely cheated him. If he were in his right mind, today's discovery would thrill him.

The proof he needed could very well be hidden in Irene's cottage. He'd return to the cottage soon. A thorough search was required in order to discover whether Irene's cottage concealed more than Roger Fleming's secret family.

Rose reappeared after several minutes. She looked refreshed. As if she'd washed her face and tidied her hair. "Thank you for telling me about Irene." She crossed over to the door and pulled it open.

"Where are you going?"

"To speak with my husband. Please ask him to join me in the drawing room."

ROGER CLOSED THE double doors to the salon before facing Rose. "Are you ill, my dear? You were missed at supper."

"I am feeling a little sick to my stomach."

"I trust you are better." He crossed over to the drinks tray to pour the port. "Lord Wallthorne was well pleased with his map."

"Was he?"

"Yes, indeed." He handed her a glass. "I'll send someone from the shop to collect payment this week. And he is interested in having me map his property in Sussex next. I think I can demand more money for my services this time."

"Don't you mean *my* services?" Cold fury enveloped her. She marveled at how smoothly Roger lied to her while carrying on a double life. As if he hadn't a care in the world while he used her money to do as he pleased and kept Rose tethered to her drafting table.

"Yes, yes, of course. Your services."

"I don't have time for Lord Wallthorne."

His forehead puckered. "Since when do you turn down work? This is a very lucrative commission. We cannot afford to turn this opportunity down."

"I'm working on another project."

"What project?" His glass froze in midair. "We don't have any current commissions."

"We don't." She sipped her port. "But I do."

"What the devil are you talking about?"

"I am doing the map illustrations for the Duchess of Huntington's newest volume."

"If Her Grace is interested in my services, why didn't she come to me?"

"Because she isn't interested in engaging R. Fleming. She has commissioned *me*, Rose Fleming."

His face twisted. "That's preposterous. I won't have my wife engaged in trade."

"Is that so?" She gave him a mocking smile. "Who's going to draw your precious maps if I don't engage in trade?"

She watched him grapple for a response, while her mind searched for ways to take control of the business. After all, she was the mapmaker in the family. The breadwinner. Her days of doing Roger's bidding were over. She owed him nothing.

"Is the duchess paying you well?" he asked.

"Her terms are very generous."

He crossed his arms and tapped his fingers against them. "Naturally, you will turn the money over to me once you've been paid."

"Why? So you can buy new marbles for your son?"

"Because I'm—" He froze. "M-my what?"

"Your son. Or maybe you can purchase a new bauble for your mistress. Is it just the three boys? Or are there more children hidden away in the cottage at Walham Green?"

They locked eyes. She watched the shock in his gaze dissolve into a fixed stare that unnerved her.

"So." He ambled away to pour himself another drink. "You finally know."

She fought to keep her voice steady. "Did you think I wouldn't find out?"

"I had hoped for that. All in all, I thought it would be easier on you if I carried the burden alone."

"The burden of lying and sneaking around? Of pretending to be at the shop while spending most afternoons with that woman?"

He faced her, appearing remarkably calm for a man whose world was about to come crashing down on him. "This situation does not need to be messy."

"That's where all the money is going, isn't it? To your strumpet."

He stepped toward her. "Watch your tongue. I won't have you insulting Irene."

She gave a mirthless laugh. "Forgive me for insulting your mistress."

"Sarcasm doesn't serve either of us."

"This is why you changed, isn't it? Those first few months we were somewhat content. And then you withdrew from me completely."

"You're a beguiling woman and a pleasure to bed. I enjoyed the early days of our marriage a great deal." His eyes roamed over her with more hunger than he'd displayed in the past three and a half years. "Perhaps too much. It made Irene very unhappy."

"Bedding your wife upset your mistress? But she is more than happy to take my money, isn't she?"

"I wanted to continue as we were, but Irene wouldn't hear of it. She demanded that I stop bedding you. I couldn't risk getting you with child. There's no telling what Irene would have done if you'd had a baby."

Disbelief bubbled up inside her. "You allowed your whore to dictate what happens in our family?"

"Stop calling her that," he warned.

"And in the meantime, I've been supporting your mistress and your bastards."

"My children are not bastards."

"I don't know what else to call the children of your mistress."

His jaw twitched. "Irene is not my mistress."

"What do you prefer to call her?" Her voice rose. "Your paramour? Your lightskirt?"

"*My wife*. Irene is my wife. You, my dear Rose, are my mistress."

Chapter Twelve

"*Y*our what?" She huffed an incredulous laugh. "Have you taken complete leave of your senses?"

"It's the truth." Roger spoke in a quiet voice. "Irene and I have been wed for almost seven years now."

"You really are a bedlamite." Her voice rose. "We—*you and I*—were married in St. Andrews in Holborn four years ago, three weeks after Uncle Trevor died. Or have you very conveniently forgotten that?" They'd moved up their plans, wedding quickly and quietly, after her uncle's sudden death.

"I haven't forgotten," he said gently, taking her elbow. "Why don't we sit?"

She jerked her arm away. "Why don't you admit that you have a mistress and that you've been lying to me for all of these years?"

"I was lying," he admitted, "but I am being truthful now. Irene and the boys are my true family."

The words stung. "But I am still your wife. To my everlasting regret."

"No, you are not." He shook his head sadly. "Rose, dear, please do sit down. What I must tell you will be difficult to hear."

She backed away, her mind reeling. "Do you think I am an idiot? That I would believe anything you say? All you have done is lie to me from the first."

"I acknowledge that I haven't been completely honest in the past. But I am trying to be so now."

"Then why don't you start with the fact that you and I were married in Holborn."

"Yes," he said placatingly, "we were. But because I was already wed to Irene, the second marriage, my marriage to you, is invalid."

Rose closed her eyes and massaged her temples. "I cannot believe this. All you do is lie."

"I am not lying."

She bit the inside of her cheek. He had to be. But then she remembered Roger's insistence they marry by special license in a church that was unfamiliar to them both. She'd been so caught up in her grief over Uncle Trevor's death that she hadn't thought to question any of the hasty wedding arrangements.

"You didn't want the banns read at either of our parishes where people know us." Her voice sounded like it was coming from very far away. "That's why you obtained a special license and arranged for us to marry at a church where no one knew us."

"Yes." He dipped his chin. "It would have been impossible to read the banns at my parish church because that is where I married Irene."

Her legs felt watery. She slid into the nearest chair. "When you came to work for Uncle Trevor you told him you were unmarried."

"I was at the time, but I was already keen on Irene. Everyone in Walham Green expected us to marry."

"And yet you still flirted with and flattered me at every opportunity."

"Once I met you, I started to envision a different future. One that meant I didn't have to toil away on the family farm while never having anything for myself."

"You saw a more profitable future."

"I'll admit that the shop was a big part of the appeal. Your uncle trained me to be a surveyor and engraver and I discovered I had a talent for both. Owning the shop meant I'd never have to sully my hands with dirt again. I despise toiling out in the elements, perspiring in the hot sun." He paused. "But you were equally as appealing."

"Yet, you still wed Irene."

"I got her with child. It was an accident, but I was obliged to marry her. Our families knew each other. Everyone expected it of us. I couldn't cry off."

She massaged the back of her neck. "And you conveniently neglected to share your happy news with me and my uncle."

"It was wrong, but I couldn't let go of my dream. I still wanted you and the life of a merchant rather than that of a farmworker who wouldn't even own the land he poured his sweat and labor into. And I had a family to provide for."

She stared at him. "That's bigamy. You'll go to jail."

"I would," he agreed, "if there were proof of our marriage."

"What are you saying?"

"If you check, you'll find that our names are not in the marriage register at St. Andrews."

Rose's mind felt fuzzy. "But we signed our names."

"For a small fee, I was able to wipe our marriage from the books."

"You erased all proof that we are wed?"

"All public proof, yes. I had to. I couldn't put myself in a position of being a bigamist. But nothing has to change. No one ever need know. We can continue as we are."

"Continue as we are?" She snickered. "With me and my maps supporting you and your family?"

He watched her closely. "Once you calm down and view the situation more reasonably, you will see it is the only path forward."

"If you believe that, you have truly lost your wits." She fought to order her thoughts, to try to comprehend what he was telling her.

"Drink your port," he advised. "It will help settle you."

"Wait . . . if we are not married, the business is mine."

She spoke more to herself than to him. This meant Roger had no claim on anything. Not her. Not the shop. Could she really build her own future? Choose a true husband? An image of Alex, his fathomless ebony eyes and sardonic smile, flashed in her mind, brightening her heart.

"If we aren't married"—she spoke slowly, her mind filtering through the ramifications of Roger's deception—"then I have no husband."

Roger's mouth twitched. "We've lived here together as man and wife for four years. If it were to be known that we are not truly wed, you would be ruined," he said tightly. "No respectable person will frequent a map and engraving business run by a disgraced woman, even if she does make the finest maps in all of England."

"You thought you could cheat me out of everything."

Anger kindled in her belly, burning through the initial shock. "My business. A true husband. Children."

"I couldn't resist. It was so perfect. You were young, innocent and alone. And so beautiful. You had no family to stand up for you. The more I thought about it, the more I realized my plan could work. I could have both you and Irene, as well as the business."

She came to her feet. "There is one thing you failed to consider."

He rose as well. "Is there?" he asked patiently, in a tone of voice that suggested he was humoring her. "What would that be?"

"That the young, sheltered girl you swindled would one day grow up. I'm no longer innocent. You saw to that. And while I might not have family to stand up for me, I am quite capable of standing up for myself." She strode toward the door, struggling to keep her balance. The floor seemed to rattle beneath her feet.

Roger came up behind her. "Now there, I know this is devastating news but—"

"Devastated?" Rose rounded on him with a ferocious smile. She would never give Roger the satisfaction of seeing her fall apart. "You think I am upset? Put your mind at ease. The truth is that, despite being a debaucher of women and a swindler of the very worst sort, you have done me a great service."

He regarded her warily. "How so?"

"Learning that I am not married to you makes this the best day of my life."

THE FRONT HALL spun, light from the candle chandelier arcing streaks of gold in the air. Rose teetered for a moment, her head bombarded with thoughts she couldn't make sense of. Only sheer will kept her from falling apart. Her world had just collapsed, and she was about to follow suit.

But not here. She gritted her teeth, forcing herself to stay upright and not shatter into a million pieces. She couldn't allow Roger to witness her utter devastation.

Her sitting room. She could go there and crumble. She blinked hard. The staircase throbbed. It seemed so very far away. She needed to get to the stairs. She reached out toward them but her legs wouldn't move. They were disintegrating beneath her. Nothing to hold her up. She was sinking, the patterned marble of the front hall floor coming up to meet her.

"Mrs. Fleming!" Strong arms scooped her up. Alex. "Mrs. Fleming, shall I call a doctor?"

She gave a weak laugh. "Mrs. Fleming." Who is Mrs. Fleming? *Irene is Mrs. Fleming.* She was still Miss Rose Kanaan. Her father's name. *Jidu's* name. She belonged to them, but they were gone. She didn't belong to Roger. *She never had.* She didn't belong anywhere.

"You're shaking."

Rose was perspiring, yet she shivered. "It's so cold," she whispered.

"Let's get you to your sitting room, where you can lie down." They were moving up the stairs. Alex's shoulder was warm and firm against her cheek. She peered up at his black eyes and confident nose, absorbing his naturally severe-looking visage, one that softened when he gazed down at her.

"You are carrying me again," she said faintly. "Always saving me." But this time she couldn't be rescued.

What Roger had done to her could not be wrenched into place by Alex's bonesetter cousin. Or anyone else.

"Here we are." He kicked open the door to her sitting room and carried her across the room to settle her on the sofa. He left her momentarily; she heard the tread of his footsteps before he reappeared with her embroidered red shawl and wrapped her in it. She gathered the warm wool around her and blankly stared at her drafting table. She last left this room as Mrs. Fleming. Only it was all a lie. She'd never been Rose Fleming.

Alex stoked the fire. The logs crackled and settled. Then he was back, hovering over her, concern lining his forehead. He put a hand against her forehead. Gentle and reassuring. Warm. "You don't have a fever. It must be the shock of learning about Mr. Fleming's mistress."

"Undoubtedly." She almost laughed. Irene isn't Roger's mistress. *I am.* Her heart raced.

Mistress.

Whore.

Ruined.

She was an unrespectable woman.

She wretched; her body convulsed. Alex went away to retrieve her porcelain washing bowl and then sat beside her. He held the bowl for her in one hand while rubbing her back in small, comforting circles. "That's it. Just let it go."

She heaved a few times. Even though her stomach was empty, her body continued to gag, as though desperate to rid itself of the truth. Roger had not only deceived and betrayed her. He'd wholly ruined her. Destroyed her life. Left her nothing. Not even her reputation. Or her self-respect.

She curled up into a ball away from Alex. Her muscles ached. Pain streaked through her shoulders and arms. Up her legs. She was sore all over.

Alex stood up. "Who can I call? Let me send for someone who can come and be with you."

"No. No one," she croaked. As if she could confide the unspeakable truth to anyone. "Just need to sleep." Fatigue overwhelmed her. Her eyelids were too heavy. She was sinking away from Alex. From the world.

It was almost bliss.

THREE MORNINGS LATER Alex brought in Rose's breakfast. To his relief, he found her on the sofa in her sitting room. It was her first time out of bed since confronting Fleming about Irene. During that time Mrs. Waller carried the food trays into Rose's bedchamber, but they came back practically untouched.

"It's a relief to see you out of bed."

She regarded him with a blank look on her face. He could barely make out her expression. It was dark; the curtains were still drawn. The room was humid and stuffy.

"Where shall I put your tray?" He forced cheer into the words. "The table by the window as usual?"

"I'm not hungry."

"Nonetheless, you have to eat." He set the tray down on the low table before the sofa. He crossed over to pull back the curtains and throw the window open.

"No." She held up a hand to shield her squinting eyes from the brightness. "Close the curtains. I don't want to see—"

"What don't you want to see?"

"Anything." She shrank back into the sofa, curling her legs beneath her. Alarm rippled through him. She seemed to have a complete disregard for everything. Mostly herself. Rose never sat in such a relaxed manner in his presence. "The world."

She wore one of her feathered dressing gowns, this one in purple paisley. The cheerful garment looked incongruous with her face, which was pale except for the dark smudges ringing her eyes.

"You cannot sit alone in the dark in an airless room," he said sharply. "Are you trying to make yourself ill?"

She barely lifted a shoulder. As if a full shrug took too much effort. "It won't make any difference."

He left the window open. "You have to eat something. I'm not leaving you until you do."

"I cannot." She bit her lip. It was rough and chapped, as if she'd been worrying it for the past three days. "My stomach won't keep anything down."

"I've brought you tea with sage from the garden. It'll soothe your stomach." He poured for her. "And Mrs. Waller was up early making sweet buns. She knows they're your favorite."

"I see you intend to make a pest of yourself."

He grinned, relieved to see a spark of her old self. "As only I can."

She accepted the tea from him.

"Now you actually drink it," he urged. She took one sip and then another. He pushed the plate of sweet buns closer to her. "And some food."

Looking too drained to argue with him, she nibbled on a sweet bun. He watched her consume about a third of it.

"Are you certain there isn't someone I can call for you? Someone you can confide in?"

"What should I tell them?" she asked wearily. "That my hus—that Roger has another family? How is my darling *husband*?"

"Carrying on as usual." Fleming didn't seem particularly concerned about how the revelation affected his wife. While Rose remained confined in her room, her husband continued with his daily routine. Breakfast, leaving for the shop, returning for supper and then port in the salon. As if he hadn't a care in the world.

"Of course he is. And why not?" Bitterness edged the words. "His life is unchanged. He has everything he wants. Irene. Children. My shop."

"You cannot allow him to break you."

She gave a wan smile. "Some things are completely out of my control."

"But you alone control yourself."

She gave a bitter laugh. "If only that were true. *Men* have dominion over themselves. Women's lives, their reputations, are subject to the whims of men."

Brandon didn't know how to deal with this defeated version of Rose. Not when he was accustomed to her vitality and determination. "You have your life apart from him. For instance, your project for Lee—for the Duchess of Huntington."

She glanced at her drafting table. "I haven't had the energy to work on that."

"Is there a deadline, a particular time, that the maps need to be completed by?"

"In a month's time. There are several I need to complete. I am already so behind. I cannot concentrate on anything but—" Her voice trailed off.

"After you are done eating, why not spend some time working?" He couldn't bear to see her so dejected. "It might take your mind off unpleasant matters. Do not let your husband take this success from you."

An acid laugh emerged from her throat. "My husband."

"I gather it went poorly when you confronted Fleming about Irene." Alex was stunned to see Rose laid so slow. "Was he particularly cruel?"

"Cruel?" She closed her eyes. Her face crumbled a little and he feared she was going to cry. "Roger tends to deliver his deepest betrayals coated in equal doses of courtesy and empathy."

"He didn't deny it?"

She shook her head. "Irene and the boys are his true family."

"*You* are his lawfully wedded wife."

She dropped the remainder of her sweet bun on her plate. "I'm awfully tired." She curled up on the couch, wrapping her dressing gown more tightly around her and closing her eyes. "I need to rest."

He watched her for about a minute, as her breathing deepened. He didn't want to leave her alone but his absence would be noted and there were chores to do. At breakfast, Mrs. Waller had pointed out that the footman's pantry needed sweeping and mopping. It took Alex a minute to realize she'd directed her comment at him and that he'd neglected one of his duties.

He had to go. After covering Rose with one of her

fringed shawls, he turned to depart. As Brandon reached the door, her weak voice sounded behind him.

"Draw the curtains before you leave."

ROSE DRAGGED HERSELF out of bed the following morning. She got up slowly because her head was pounding and had been for three days. Any movement made it worse. She didn't know how she was going to cope with her new situation, but she needed to face the new realities of her life. She couldn't stay in bed forever and just wish it away.

There was a knock on the door and Alex came in with her breakfast.

"Good morning. Would you like to eat by the window or on the sofa?"

"Let's try the table this time." Her voice was rough from disuse.

"That's progress." He set the tray down and poured for her.

She sat at the table. "Is there sage in the tea?"

"There is. My grandmother always says sage will settle any stomach."

"Your Arab grandmother?"

"The very one."

She reached for the tea. Everything was such an effort. Her arms felt like there were boulders attached to them. She would start slow. Today, at least, she'd manage breakfast. The tea was hot, strong, sweet and flavorful. It was the first time she could actually taste anything in days. She picked up a piece of toast.

"You seem better today," Alex remarked.

"I cannot stay in bed forever. Unfortunately." She had no idea where to go from here. If people discovered she and Roger weren't legally wed, her reputation would be in tatters, and any hope of continuing her mapmaking would be over. Just thinking about her dilemma was enough to send her back to bed.

He paused. "If there is anything I can do for you, please tell me."

"There is nothing you or anyone else can do." No one must know the truth. At least not until Rose could begin to contemplate her path forward. If she wasn't Rose Fleming, then who was she? What was her role in the world if she wasn't Roger's wife? She wasn't even a respectable spinster.

The door opened. Roger appeared. "Alex, please leave us."

Alex paused, as if reluctant to leave them alone.

"Alex?" Roger said sharply. "I asked you to withdraw."

Alex stared down at Rose. Nausea swirling in her belly, she dipped her chin, signaling for him to obey Roger's command. "If you need me—"

"My wife will not have need of you," Roger interrupted. "If she requires anything, I will see to it."

Alex favored Roger with a cold stare. "Yes, sir."

Roger watched after the footman as he departed. "The insolence!" he said after Alex was gone. "I've a mind to let him go without reference."

Rose set her tea down. "No."

"What?"

"Alex stays."

"I am still the master of this house—"

She brought her fist down hard, slamming the table, rattling the porcelain dishes. "I said he stays." Her voice, high-pitched and loud, sounded unhinged to her own ears.

Roger startled. "I know you are overwrought—"

"Overwrought? I don't think the word for how I feel exists." Her voice rose at the end of the sentence. Fury roiled through her. How dare he act as if nothing had changed? As if he hadn't deceived her in the worst possible way, robbing her of her future.

She wanted to tear his face off. To beat him with her fists until he was bruised and bloody. She'd never felt more powerless and full of rage. Leaping to her feet, she hurled her half-full teacup at him. It slammed into his chest, staining his waistcoat.

He jumped back. "Dammit, Rose, I insist that you get a hold of yourself." He produced a crisp white kerchief and started patting his gray waistcoat.

"Do you really? Insist I get a hold of myself?" She snatched up a plate and dropped in on the floor. It hit the faded Axminster carpet with an unsatisfying thump.

"Stop this at once."

She reached for the saucer and flung it at the hearth with all of her strength. The plate shattered on impact, shards dropping to the ground in a series of desolate clinks.

Roger looked truly alarmed. "This is not going to make anything better."

"I don't know about that. I actually feel a little better." She was out of breath and exhausted, but also strangely exhilarated. "Why are you here, Roger?"

"I was concerned about you."

"It's a little late for that, don't you think?"

"You haven't appeared for supper for four days in a row."

"I will never, ever have supper with you again," she snarled, her contempt energizing her. "I will never again sit at the same table as you."

"I understand that you are upset. And I acknowledge that I have treated you shabbily."

"*Shabbily*? Is that the correct word for a swindler who stole a respectable girl's virtue and destroyed her life? Who used treachery of the worst kind to try and purloin her business?"

He shifted his feet. "I have come to you with a concession that will no doubt improve your spirits considerably."

"Truly? And what's that?"

"I have spoken to Irene and we both agree that it is only fair to you that we resume carnal relations."

She blinked. "What?"

"You have always wanted a family and now I am prepared to give you one."

She gaped at him. "You have taken a complete leave of your senses."

"Not at all. I look forward to it. I welcome resuming relations with you."

"And in exchange, I am to show my gratitude by creating maps that will support you, Irene and the children. And, of course, our by-blows."

"It's a fair exchange."

She started laughing.

He frowned. "This is a serious matter."

She sank back in her chair, laughing so hard that

she had to hold her stomach. Her eyes teared up. "Oh, Roger," she managed between gasps of uncontrollable laughter, "you truly are an imbecile."

His face tightened. "You are not in any position to jeer at me." He snapped his fingers. "Your shame can be made public just like that."

"*My shame*?" Fury zipped through her. "What about *your* shame? You deceived me. Have you no decency?"

"You lay with a married man."

"I thought you were my husband!"

"Did you? I begin to wonder. Maybe whoring is in your nature. You always welcomed me to your bed."

"I wanted children!"

"I can easily claim you were a party to this deception all along and happily agreed to be my mistress." He paused, drawing a calming breath. "But come now, there is no need to resort to ugliness."

"As long as I continue to draw my maps."

"The fee from Lord Wallthorne should be forthcoming any day now. It's a very generous amount. It'll keep us until you can take on another project."

"Get out of my rooms." She couldn't stand the sight of him.

"Now, see here—"

She snatched up the nearest plate. "Get. Out. Of. My. Rooms."

Alarm glinted his eyes. "Get a hold of yourself."

She curled the hand holding the plate back toward her body. "I am warning you."

He warily watched the movement of her wrist. "We are not done discussing this matter."

"That is not for you to decide." Extending her arm,

she flicked her wrist in a springlike motion, releasing the plate. It spun through the air toward Roger's head.

"What the devil!" He ducked and the porcelain flew over his head, shattering against the wall.

Roger backed up away from her. "Clearly, you are not ready to discuss this matter."

She pitched a fork at him. "I will never be ready. Get out!"

The fork bounced off Roger's arm. "I shall return when your hysteria has ceased." He reached the door and fled through it just as a spoon flew over his head.

Breathing hard, Rose collapsed back into her chair.

Alex reappeared a minute later. He took in the broken plate and overturned teacup on the Axminster. "Are you all right?"

"Were you listening?" she asked. Had he overheard the truth?

"No, I was waiting by the stairs in case you had need of me."

"Please prepare my bath."

"Now?"

"Yes, now." She paused. "What day is it?"

"It's Sunday."

"Why are you here? It's your day off."

"I didn't want to leave you alone."

"You only get one afternoon off a week," she protested. "You should not waste it on looking after me."

"I am exactly where I want to be. I'll see to the bath."

"We're going out." Roger was about to discover that he wasn't as in control as he thought.

"Where are we going?"

"To Lord Wallthorne's residence on Berkeley Square."

Chapter Thirteen

$\mathcal{N}$ow what do we do?" Alex asked.

He and Rose stared up at Lord Wallthorne's Berkeley Square mansion.

Rose drew a fortifying breath. "Now, you go and lift the knocker. And you tell them that Mrs. Fleming is here for Lord Wallthorne's secretary. Or man of business." Panic bubbled up inside her. "I have no idea. Who pays the bills for a lordship?"

"Do you have the bill?" he asked.

"No. I-I assumed Roger had already sent it over." Her shoulders sagged; the fatigue and dejection that had gripped her for days started setting in again. "This was probably a very bad idea."

"Mr. Fleming doesn't know that you intend to collect the fee for his map, does he?"

My map. "He might," she hedged.

"You will anger him."

"It's nothing he doesn't deserve."

"If you are set on this course, then I shall take care of it." He escorted her across the street and into the park. "Wait here."

He crossed back over and headed down into the servants' entrance. Rose leaned against the trunk of a mature tree, breathing in the sensation of fresh air on her face after so many days locked up in her room. She scanned the square. It was empty except for the milkmaids making their deliveries and servants sweeping the front stairs of elegant town homes. Only the laboring people were out. It was too early in the day for the fashionable people to put themselves on view.

Around her, everyone's life continued as normal while Rose no longer knew what normal was. Her life before, when she'd believed herself to be Mrs. Rose Fleming, had been frustrating and inadequate. But at least she'd had a solid understanding of her place in the world. Now she couldn't envision the future, or her place in it. The only thing clear to her was the precariousness of her situation. Her reputation teetered on the precipice of catastrophe.

"Here you go." Alex was slightly out of breath, his sable eyes glittering. "Paid in full."

She stared at the pouch in his hands. "Truly?"

"I would not lie about this." He grinned, flashing pearly teeth. "You were right. They had the bill."

"How? Who did you get it from?"

"It was a stroke of luck, really. I told them at the servants' entrance that I'd been sent to collect the money. The earl's secretary had the amount ready. Mr. Fleming is sending one of his clerks to collect his fee this afternoon."

For the first time in days, excitement bubbled up inside Rose. "Let me see." She loosened the strings and peered inside. It was the first time she'd ever seen the money her maps earned. It was a heady feeling. "I don't think I've ever seen a more beautiful sight."

"It's all there. I checked the amount in the pouch against the bill of sale."

She gazed up at him, feeling triumphant, giddy. Relief rushed through her. Impulsively, she launched herself into his arms. "I don't know how to thank you."

She startled him, momentarily threatening his balance, but then he steadied himself and strong arms closed around her. "The pleasure was all mine," he murmured into her cheek.

The sensation of being up against Alex's strong body sent a tremor through her. She nuzzled the crook of his neck.

He stiffened. "Mrs. Fleming."

"Don't call me that." She shook her head into his neck. "Don't ever call me that. I'm Rose."

"Rose," he said, whisper soft. "Stop. You are not yourself."

She pushed herself more firmly against him. Rose was more aware than ever of Alex physically as a man. She wasn't married. Appreciating Alex's masculine appeal no longer left her guilt ridden. He was still a servant, but he never seemed to be at her mercy. "You want me. I can feel it. I've felt it for a long time. Ever since we visited the bonesetter."

"I will not lie. There is nothing I want more." He pressed warm lips against her temple. "But this is wrong."

She wrapped her arms around his neck. "Is it? Unless," she faltered, "you feel I am taking advantage of you."

"Sweetheart, no one takes advantage of me." His voice was a gentle rumble. "It's just that you've had a terrible shock."

"You have no idea."

He kissed her cheek. "That is why we cannot."

She turned her face to catch his lips. She tasted his surprise. And then he nipped at her lips. Slow and sweet. Their mouths immediately adapted to each other. He held her face in his large hands. She parted her lips and their tongues touched and parted and met again. Rose had never been kissed like this. Long and unhurried, purely for the pleasure of it, and not as a hasty prelude to sex. This man knew how to kiss. *How to kiss her.*

He broke away. "Your reputation."

Is already destroyed. She nibbled his jawline. "Don't stop."

"We must. First, because we are in the middle of Berkeley Square." He smiled down at her. "And second, we want to be far from here when Fleming's clerk comes to pick up the fee you've already collected."

"Oh. That." Still dazed by the drugging impact of kissing her footman, Rose allowed Alex to lead her away.

"WHERE IS IT?" Roger burst into Rose's sitting room later that afternoon.

"Where is what?" Rose turned from her drawing table. Not that she was getting any work done. She was too busy replaying the kiss in Berkeley Square over and over in her mind.

"You know exactly what I'm speaking of." A vein

throbbed in his temple. "You sent your footman to collect my fee from Lord Wallthorne."

"Don't you mean *my* fee?"

"Do you deny it?"

"No."

"Do not test me." His spittle sprayed into the air. He stepped closer. "Give me the money."

She brushed imaginary lint from the sleeve of her bright floral dressing gown. "No."

"Do not force me to behave in an uncivil manner. I will tear up every part of your private rooms if I have to." His gaze slid to the maps on her drawing table. "Starting with the sketches you are drawing for the Duchess of Huntington."

"You are welcome to look anywhere you like, but I don't have the money. It is in safekeeping."

"You're lying."

She was. "I'm not. But if you wish to search my rooms, I cannot stop you. You've already plundered my life. Ransacking my rooms will make little difference."

"I have tried to remain courteous with you."

"Have you?" She crossed her arms. "You *do* like to keep your secrets. Imagine my surprise when I discovered that Lord Wallthorne paid twenty percent more than you said you intended to charge him."

"The accounts are not your concern."

"They are when you hide the fact that you are collecting an extra twenty percent for my maps. And I don't have to guess where that money went."

"I knew this was a grave mistake." He stared at her, red mottling his cheeks. "I told Irene I should get you with child."

"What a favor she did me by forbidding it," she snapped.

"You would be far more biddable if children were involved. You would not risk having your sons and daughters called bastards."

"You truly would have done that to me? To *your* own offspring?" Her stomach roiled. "You are the very definition of loathsome."

"Your opinion of me is of no matter. Ours is a business relationship now and I expect you to do your part. Make your maps and we'll divide the fee."

"You've forgotten something very important. I'm not your wife. When I catered to your foolish whims in the past it was because I felt obligated to as your wife. But I no longer answer to you."

Trepidation crossed his face. "What are you planning?"

"What is the matter, Roger?" she mocked. "Are you afraid if I stop drawing my maps that you'll be reduced to toiling on your family farm?"

He stiffened. "I will never work in the fields again. I'm an accomplished surveyor and engraver. I will always find work."

"Then you have nothing to be concerned about, do you?"

"What are you planning?"

She had no idea, but Rose would never admit that to him. "I intend to act in my own best interest with no concern for others. Just as you have."

LATER THAT EVENING Brandon knocked on Rose's door. "Mrs. Fleming, I thought I'd say good-night and see if you require anything."

He didn't normally check on her once she retired for the evening. But these days, aside from today's visit to Berkeley Square, Rose barely left her private rooms. He was worried about her. He also couldn't get the sublime sensation of kissing her out of his head.

"Mrs. Fleming?" It took a moment to adjust to the poor lighting. He spotted her still figure by the window, standing in semidarkness. "Are you well?"

She flinched at his words. Any fight in her from earlier in the day vanished. He approached her. She shook her head, holding up a hand, signaling for him to stay away. Moonlight slanted across her face, revealing glistening cheeks.

She was crying. "Have I offended you? Is it about what happened . . . between us this afternoon?"

She put her hand over her mouth to stifle a sob. "I feel so much shame."

"You were overwrought after learning about your husband." Guilt slashed at him. He should not have allowed any contact this afternoon. "You cannot blame yourself. I take full responsibility."

"No, that's not it." Tears streamed down her face.

He went to her. "Then tell me what it is. Let me help you."

"You cannot. No one can. Roger has made a harlot of me."

"Do not talk of yourself that way," he said sharply. "You are an honorable woman."

"I thought I was, but I am not."

Brandon cursed himself. He'd known Rose wasn't in her right mind in Berkeley Square. Yes, she'd initiated the intimacy between them, but he'd participated fully and *most* enthusiastically. In doing so, he'd made things immeasurably worse for her. "If anyone behaved badly it was me. I took advantage of you when you were in a most vulnerable state. I will resign immediately if you'd like."

"No!" She grabbed his arm. "Don't leave me. I could not bear it."

"But if what happened between us is so upsetting to you—"

She interrupted. "I need a trustworthy friend now more than ever."

Trustworthy. He was hardly that. Fleming might be the bigger bastard, but they were both liars. Brandon was still deceiving her, but he was also beginning to realize that he'd do just about anything to protect her.

"Alex." She ran her hand up his arm. His skin prickled. "Thank you for being here." She stepped into his arms. She was trembling. He closed his arms around her and held her close.

"You're going to be all right," he whispered. "Don't let him destroy you."

"I need you so much."

"I am here. As your friend."

She pressed herself against him. "Alex."

His body tensed. He wanted nothing more than to take what she offered. But it was wrong. "Sweet Rose." He feathered a hand across her cheek. "You don't really want this. You are looking for comfort."

"Only from you." She lifted her face. "Please."

He looked into her pleading eyes, soft and warm, desperate. How could he deny her anything when she looked at him like that? He lowered his head, kissing her in tender nips, relishing the soft firmness of her lips under his. Her moan scalded his blood. She opened her mouth. Their tongues met.

They sank to the ground. He kissed her jaw, nibbled on her earlobe; his hand caressed her neck, and went lower still. Until he reached the sweet, soft swell of her breast.

Alarm lightninged through him. *What was he doing*? He pulled back. "We have to stop."

"Do you want to stop?"

"No. *God, no.*"

She practically climbed into his lap. She unbelted her dressing gown and shrugged it off. She wore a thin white night rail. "Touch me." She took his hand and placed it over her breast. He immediately cupped it. Only a thin fabric barrier kept him from feeling her fully. "I need to be touched."

He was hard and heavy. He'd never wanted to make love to a woman as much as he wanted Rose in this moment. She pulled down her night rail, exposing her breasts. They were as beautiful as the rest of her. He circled her erect nipple with his finger, first one and then the other. He lowered his head to do the same with his tongue, circling that perfect tip, tasting her.

"Oh *yes.*" She threw her head back. "Don't stop."

He mouthed her breast; his tongue touched her nipple, flicking back and forth over the tender point. Indulging in both breasts, he nipped and sucked while running his hands up her soft back. He traced her collarbone and neck with his hands before doing the same with his mouth, kissed her neck and her collarbone, delighting in the scent and taste of her.

Their lips met again in a desperate and reckless kiss. She kissed him with abandon, like she was starved; her body was a delicious weight on his cock. He wanted nothing more than to flip her over onto the floor and drive all of her troubles and unhappiness away. Leaving only pure physical pleasure.

A tread in the corridor sliced through the room. Alarmed, Brandon broke away, moving quickly to restore Rose's clothes. She uttered a sound of protest.

"Someone's coming," he whispered, breathing heavily.

"It's just Roger going to his room. He won't come in here."

How could Fleming resist? If Rose were Brandon's he'd be in her bed every night. He drew her dressing gown over her shoulders. "We cannot be sure of that."

His body still broiling, he stood and offered his hand, helping her to her feet.

"I am positive he won't come to my room," she said as he tied the belt of her dressing gown. "I know because he hasn't visited my bed in years."

He froze. "That's not possible."

"I assure you that it is. He doesn't want me that way."

"He's a damned fool. If you were mine, I wouldn't be able to resist you."

She put her hands over his where he was tying her belt. "Come to me this evening. After everyone is abed."

He wanted to. With *everything* in him. Brandon stared into her glittering eyes. Her hair was tousled, her cheeks flushed. He took a breath and then did the hardest thing he'd ever done in his life.

"I cannot. I do not bed married women. It would dishonor us both. You would regret it. And I would regret your regretting it."

Before she could speak, before she could change his mind—because it wouldn't take much—Brandon spun on his heel and retreated, racing for the door as if rabid dogs were after him.

ROSE INSISTED THAT Brandon take the following day off since he'd missed his usual Sunday. He took the opportunity to visit Walham Green, the little village twenty minutes outside London where Fleming's mistress lived.

He needed to acquaint himself with the woman's comings and goings in order to determine when to search the house for the evidence that he'd been cheated out of his land. Sunday would be a natural choice, *if* Irene took her children to church. But they were by-blows, bastards, and she a fallen woman. Would she dare show her face in church?

He arrived at the home of Roger Fleming's mistress just as the woman in question departed with a basket in hand. His pulse quickened. Irene was leaving? If the children were in school, that left a clear field for him to search the cottage. But then an older woman appeared in the doorway, holding the youngest child.

"Say goodbye to Mama," the woman directed the child. The boy waved a chubby hand.

Irene blew the boy a kiss. "I won't be long."

"Take your time," the older woman responded before closing the door.

Because he couldn't search a cottage occupied by a

woman and toddler, Brandon followed Irene to the village. Learning a thing or two about her habits might prove helpful to his search.

She went into a butcher shop and exited a short time later, adjusting some paper-wrapped items in her basket. As she strolled, Irene paused to speak to some older ladies she encountered. The women treated Irene with courtesy. Did they accept her role as Fleming's mistress? Or were they in the dark about it?

When she stepped into the bake shop, Brandon followed. He stood back while she made her purchases. "I'll take a loaf of bread. And some of the usual sweetmeats for the children."

"How are those little rascals?" the proprietress, a red-faced woman with round cheeks, asked. "Has Reggie recovered from his bout with fevers?"

"Oh yes. He's right as rain." Irene wrapped the bread in a cloth before carefully adding the purchase to her basket. "Mama is looking after him while I run my errands."

"And how is Mr. Fleming?"

"As busy as ever with the shop, but he'll be home for lunch shortly so I must make haste."

"Of course, dear." The baker handed the wrapped sweets to Irene. "Do send my regards to your husband."

Her husband. The villagers thought she and Fleming were husband and wife? That explained how Irene retained the sheen of respectability.

"I will tell him. Thank you, Mrs. Miller." Brandon turned his back, pretending to study something on a shelf while Irene exited. He couldn't risk her recognizing the Flemings' footman.

"May I help you, sir?"

Brandon faced her. "I'd like some bread, please." He surveyed the baked goods stacked behind her. "And a couple of pies."

"Very good, sir."

"And perhaps some of the sweetmeats the prior customer ordered."

"Oh, you mean Mrs. Fleming? She's such a dear. She and her husband are raising three boys. They're a delight."

"Are you so well acquainted with all of your customers?"

"We're a small village. I've known both Irene and Roger, that's Mr. Fleming, since they were children. They were sweet on each other for as long as I can remember. We all knew they'd wed one day."

"Did they marry here in the village?"

Wariness flickered across the baker's face. "What is your interest in Irene? She is a happily married woman. I have not seen you before today."

"That is because I've never been here before," he said smoothly. "I am just passing through on my way to London."

"I see."

He added two more loaves of bread to his pile of purchases. "I noticed a charming stone church and wondered if all of the villagers wed there."

She eyed his stack of baked goods. She stood to make a tidy profit off him. "Yes, that is where Mr. and Mrs. Fleming were wed."

"I think I'll need to add a couple of tarts. How long ago were they wed?"

"At least seven or eight years ago now." She placed the tarts with his other items. "Will that be all?"

"Yes." He drew his leather wallet from his pocket. "You've been most helpful."

Leaving the shop with his baked goods in a basket, provided by the baker at a not-quite-fair price, Brandon strode toward the church.

Could it be? Was Roger Fleming married to both Rose and Irene? His neck burned. Irene clearly knew about Rose. But Rose still thought she was Roger Fleming's only wife.

There was only one way to find out if Fleming was an even worse scapegrace than Brandon imagined. He reached the stone church, pulled the door open and went inside.

Chapter Fourteen

"Mrs. Fleming, do come in."

Nerves taut, Rose entered the barrister's office. Andrew Fulke kept a set of chambers at Gray's Inn, the ancient lodging quarters at the intersection High Holborn and Gray's Inn Road. The area, near St. Paul's Cathedral, was frequented by barristers, students of law and literary-minded men.

"I have pulled your uncle's will, as your note requested. And how is Mr. Fleming?"

She forced a smile. "He is well." It felt strange to be out in a world where everyone still viewed her as a respectably married woman.

The barrister, a small-framed man who exuded energy and intelligence, was an old friend of Uncle Trevor's. They'd met years ago when Fulke stopped by the shop to make a purchase. As the man who drew up her uncle's will, Mr. Fulke had the answers that could help determine Rose's future.

"Mr. Fleming treats you well?" He regarded her with a solemn gaze. "I have wanted to check in on you, but your husband has discouraged it."

"He has?" She had no idea.

"Mr. Fleming said you do not welcome visitors at the house."

"I don't know why he would say that." She would have enjoyed reminiscing with her uncle's old friend. "As a family friend from before my marriage, you are most welcome to call."

"I was worried for you." Compassion etched his lined face. "You seemed somewhat isolated."

Rose had always assumed her solitary state was the natural outcome of marrying and moving to a new neighborhood. It had never occurred to her that Roger had engineered it. Why? To keep her alone and dependent upon him? To keep her malleable?

"I was disappointed that I could not attend the wedding," he continued. "I would have liked to. I felt it was my duty to my old friend."

"Roger asked you not to attend our nuptials?"

"He said you were still in mourning and wished to have no guests present."

"But why would he—" Her voice trailed off. Of course. If there'd been witnesses to their nuptials, it would be hard for Roger to claim the marriage never took place. The full extent of his betrayal burned through her for the hundredth time.

"I am sorry you were not there," she said. "It would have meant a great deal to see a friendly face."

Fulke placed his interlaced fingers on the desk in front of him. "Now, I gather you have sought me out for a reason. Something about the will, I presume."

"Yes." Rose shifted in her seat. "Uncle Trevor left the shop to me, did he not?"

"He did."

"Were there any conditions attached to my acquiring the property?"

Lines formed between his brows. "Such as?"

"My uncle wanted me to wed Mr. Fleming. I wonder whether he made that a condition in the will." Rose held herself painfully still, preparing herself for an answer that could destroy her last hope.

Fulke set his spectacles on the bridge of his nose to peruse the document on his desk. "No, it isn't here in the will. Trevor left the property to you outright."

Rose finally released the breath she'd been holding. "So"—she spoke slowly and deliberately—"if I were not married to Mr. Fleming, I would have complete control over the property and all business relating to the shop?"

"That is correct. However, since you are a married woman, all of your property, all of your assets, became Mr. Fleming's the moment you wed."

"I see. Thank you, Mr. Fulke." Rose clasped her fingers together to keep her hands from shaking. "You have been most helpful."

"It is my pleasure." He paused. "I hope you know that you will always have a friend in me."

"You are very kind." She rose, every muscle stretched tight. "Your friendship means a great deal."

He escorted her to the door. "Trevor used to say you wanted many children. May I hope you have been so blessed?"

"No, I have no children."

"I am sorry."

She smiled. "Do not be. It is for the best." She paused. "May I ask you another question in complete confidence?"

"Of course."

"If a man is legally wed and then takes a second wife, is that second marriage valid?"

"It is not. The man would be a scoundrel and a bigamist, which the law frowns upon. The first woman, whoever he married first, is the sole true and legal wife."

"And the second wife, even if she were to have proof of her marriage lines, is not legally married? The husband has no dominion over her?"

"Absolutely not. In the eyes of the law, she remains an unmarried woman." Concern filled Fulke's face. "I don't mean to overstep, but you seem troubled. Is all well?"

"Thank you for your concern." She pulled her shoulders back and took a deep breath. "I . . . I will be fine."

And for the first time in many days, she actually believed that might be true.

"Bread and sweetmeats and pies?" Mrs. Waller emptied the basket as the rest of the staff watched with wide eyes. "And tarts, too."

"Who'd you get it from this time?" Owen asked around a mouthful of sweetmeats. "Yer aunt again?"

"Erm . . . my cousin." The startling revelations about Rose's true marital status consumed Brandon's thoughts so thoroughly that he forgot to invent a plausible reason for returning to New Street with enough food to open his own bakeshop. "She . . . erm . . . enjoys cooking."

Dudley's mouth twisted. "She baked all of this for her enjoyment?"

"She has a bake shop," Brandon added.

"You sure do have some interestin' relations," Owen observed.

"Ah, that explains all of the baked goods." Mrs. Waller uncovered a pie. "We shall each have a piece with our tea."

They gathered around the servants' table. Brandon was grateful for the rich, dark tea flavored with *maramia*, although he swallowed the herb pie without really tasting it. Discovering Fleming's gross betrayal of Rose sickened him. The bastard had played a trusting and honorable woman false in the worst way imaginable. And now it was up to Brandon to reveal the truth. He could not allow her to remain ignorant of what that snake had done to her.

He gulped his tea, hardly noticing when it scalded his tongue. Regret clawed at him. Rose didn't deserve Brandon's deceit, either. That he'd kissed her, touched her intimately, made his duplicity even worse.

Rose was entitled to know everything, and that included the truth about Brandon. About who he was and why he'd masqueraded as a footman. If being honest with Rose jeopardized his plan to take his revenge on Fleming, so be it.

"What do you think?" Dudley's voice penetrated his thoughts. Brandon blinked and looked up from his pie. Everyone at the table was staring at him.

"About?"

"Mrs. Fleming." Dudley forked a large bite of pie. "She gave you the day off and then went out."

"She did?"

"She wouldn't say where she was going and insisted on going alone. She just returned not fifteen minutes ago."

"She does seem very upset," Bess put in. "She's not herself. Hasn't been for days."

Dudley reached for more pie. "You think she found out about her husband's doxy?"

Mrs. Waller tsked. "This talk is most inappropriate."

Brandon stared at Dudley. "You know about Irene?"

"I am his footman, ain't I? I've had occasion to deliver some money or Mrs. Waller's fine bread pudding to the doxy."

"You take food that Mrs. Waller cooks to Irene?" Brandon asked, incredulous.

Dudley stuffed a generous bite of pie into his mouth. "It's a favorite of his doxy."

"But ain't Mrs. Flemin' a pretty woman?" Owen asked. "Why does Mr. Flemin' need a doxy?"

Dudley smirked. "Sometimes a man likes variety."

"Is Irene as pretty as the mistress?" Bess asked.

"Enough!" Mrs. Waller set her teacup in its saucer with a clatter. "I won't have this indecent talk at tea."

Brandon fixed his cold gaze her. "Is it decent to send food baked in Mrs. Fleming's kitchen to Mr. Fleming's mistress?" He didn't bother to strip the contempt from his voice.

She flushed. "Well, pardon me, *Your Grace*. You have much to learn if you intend to keep your position. If I defy the master, I will be released from my position without recommendation. And who would hire me then?" The words dripped with acid. "Or would you rather I starve in the gutter? People in our position cannot afford to stand on principle."

Shame swept through Brandon. He wasn't morally superior to anyone at this table. He'd lied to Rose, too. Also, it had never occurred to him just how precarious a servant's life could be. Mrs. Waller might be a commanding presence at the servants' table, but in truth, she and all of the people at this table were powerless. And each one of them faced the daily prospect of destitution.

The bell rang. They all looked up. Brandon's blood iced. The summons came from Rose's sitting room. He pushed to his feet. There was no putting it off.

It was time to tell Rose the truth. All of it, including his own deception. He could only hope she would not hate him.

"YOU WENT OUT today. Alone."

"I did." Rose stood by the window, wearing a gown featuring bold blue-and-white vertical stripes that ran the length of her skirt. She hadn't yet removed her hat since returning from her mysterious outing. The wide-brimmed contraption was liberally trimmed with artificial fruit including strawberries and grapes.

"Nice hat."

Her lips quirked. It was the closest she'd come to a smile in many days. "Roger will hate it. He'll also dislike my gown. He equates tastefulness with quiet colors and an absence of pattern."

"And you clearly do not." Her outfit certainly drew attention, but she managed to carry it off with effortless style. "Are you dressed like that in order to draw your husband's ire?"

"Not at all. What Roger thinks is no longer relevant to me. It will be such a relief to quit frequenting Bond Street modistes."

"You don't enjoy shopping on Bond Street?"

"I abhor it, but Roger insisted."

"Why?" He'd thought her frivolous when she purchased gown after gown at the dressmaker's shop.

"He is convinced it added to our consequence to frequent the same merchants as the ton. It is beyond foolishness." She waved a hand as if swatting a fly. "Roger has always been imprudent."

"And now you intend to do as you please?"

"Exactly. And that begins with my clothing. I prefer bright shades and interesting patterns." She touched the rim of her hat. "And I enjoy the artistry of elaborately trimmed bonnets."

"Obviously."

"From now on, I shall dress as I please. I am done muting myself, my person, my abilities, in order to make a man more comfortable."

"Bravo." He clapped his hands twice. "I am fully in support."

"Thank you."

"And if you want to look like you have a fruit bowl sitting on your head, that is your right."

A laugh erupted from her throat. "You truly are insolent. It is no wonder that Roger wants to replace you."

"And how about you?" He'd always known his time in this house was limited, but the thought of leaving New Street and never seeing Rose again knocked the wind out of him. "Do you also wish for me to leave?"

She lifted her chin. "I am foolishly inclined to keep you around. Despite your impertinence."

"I am pleased to see that your spirits have lifted." Finally. Uncertainty gripped him. He hated the idea of bringing Rose low again after she'd finally emerged from days of melancholy.

He gentled his voice. "May we sit for a moment?"

"You and I?"

"I have something that I must tell you and it will be difficult for you to hear."

"Are you leaving?" Alarm shadowed her face. "Have you found new employment? I did not think a man like you would remain a footman for long."

"No, it is nothing like that." He took a deep breath. "I went to Irene's cottage today."

"Why would you do that?"

"I'll explain everything." He gestured to the sofa. "Will you sit? Please."

She removed her hat pins and lifted the bonnet from her head. After carefully setting it on her round eating table, Rose joined him.

Dread coiling in his gut, Brandon took Rose's hand in his. "If there was any way I could avoid hurting you, I would do it. I would take a bullet to avoid harming you."

She stared down at their clasped hands. "You are frightening me."

"What I discovered today in Walham Green is very distressing, but you deserve to know the truth and it would be wrong of me to keep it from you."

The cords of her throat moved. "I see."

"I want you to know that I even visited the local church and looked at the registry myself. I needed to confirm the truth before I burdened you with such grievous news."

Rose paled. "You've learned the truth about Roger and Irene."

He gaped at her. "You know?"

"That Roger is married to her?" She swallowed. "Yes, I am aware."

"How long have you known?"

"Roger told me the night I confronted him in the salon."

His clasp on her hand loosened. "That is why you've been so upset, so overwrought." Her behavior over the past few days began to make more sense. "It wasn't just discovering that your husband has a mistress and a family."

"Precisely. I learned that Roger isn't my husband at all. It has all been a detestable lie."

His fist clenched. "Fleming is as contemptible as they come. He ought to be called out for his reprehensible behavior."

"Called out?" She gave him a strange look. "You have very aristocratic notions for a footman."

Brandon flushed. Now was the time to reveal his true identity. But something stopped him. A warning deep within him. *Not yet.* Rose had been through enough already.

"Thrashed, then," he said instead. "Beaten to within an inch of his life. He should suffer the consequences of what he's done to you."

"But he will not." She looked away. "Now you know the truth. I am a fallen woman. I am not respectable nor decent in the eyes of society. I am utterly ruined. Roger saw to that."

He gently turned her chin back to him. "You have nothing to be ashamed of. You are the most decent and admirable woman that I have ever met. It is Fleming who should bow his head in shame. Not you. Never you."

"But society will not see it that way. Roger has erased all trace of our marriage. It would be my word against his. He made certain there were no witnesses to our nuptials." She looked down at her lap. "Either way, I am still a woman who allowed herself to be bedded by a man who is not her husband. I have lived in sin here with him for these last few years."

"You are not at fault. You believed him to be your husband."

"But he wasn't. There is no way for me to emerge from this situation with my reputation intact." She looked up. "Whenever I walk down the street, people will whisper and point and say, 'There is the foolish woman who bedded a man she thought was her husband.' To some, I will be an object of pity. To the rest, a laughingstock."

"There *must* be a way forward for you. Send Fleming back to his village. Style yourself a widow and remarry quickly."

"If only it were that simple." She sighed. "Roger isn't going anywhere. He has made it clear he intends to inform all of London that I am a whore—if I do not continue with this charade."

"You are not a—" He could not even bring himself to utter the word in connection with Rose's name. "You are a woman full of talent, generosity and grace."

"That is good of you to say. But the London gossips and the clients at my shop will not see it that way. Roger holds all of the cards and I hold none."

"That is not exactly true."

"What do you mean?"

"Roger and Irene appear to be very well established in Walham Green. News that he has presented himself as a man married to you would cause a scandal in his village. He has much to lose."

She brightened. "I had not considered that. I thought I was all alone with no—"

He reached for her hand. "You are not alone." His serious gaze held hers. "I shall stand by your side for as long as you need me."

He lowered his face to touch his lips to hers. He was soft and gentle at first. Her mouth was soft and yielding beneath his. And hungry and eager. He deepened the kiss and she responded even more enthusiastically. But it wasn't right to take what she offered. "This is wrong."

"Why?" She touched the tips of her fingers to her swollen pink lips. "Are you spoken for?"

He swallowed. "I am not. But you've been through a terrible upheaval."

"You just learned the truth today. I have known about it for a while now. I know my mind."

"Still, I don't want to take advantage of you."

"When I asked you to come to me the other evening, why did you decline?"

"Because I believed you to be wed."

"But I am not wed. Nor am I an innocent virgin." She looked straight into his eyes so that there was no mistaking her meaning. "I would like this specific kind of comfort that only you can offer."

Heat pooled in his groin. "Are you certain?"

She stood and held out her hand. "I am."

BRANDON KISSED HER. He could hardly believe his good fortune. He folded her into his arms, melding her body to his. What had he done to deserve the attentions of this lovely, brilliant woman?

He deepened the kiss, savoring every sensation. She hadn't been bedded in a long time, so he devoted himself to seeing to her pleasure.

Her moans and seeking hands, her eager mouth, suggested she approved of his efforts. Rose's fingers slid down his back and squeezed his buttocks. Desire rocketed through him. She wasn't missish about lovemaking. Her enthusiasm fired his blood.

He pulled back. "Will you undress for me?"

"Since you asked so nicely." She stepped back and untied the ribbon high on her waist. Her heated gaze holding his, she pulled the loosened gown over her head. It was broad daylight and she stood before him in a thin chemise that barely disguised the bounty that lay beneath—the shadows of pert breasts and the hair at the juncture of her thighs.

"More." His voice was hoarse. "I want to see all of you."

Her cheeks bright with color, she pushed the chemise off her shoulders and let it slide to the floor. Naked, she stood straight and proud, unabashedly allowing him to look his full.

"God," he breathed. "You are perfection."

"Now you."

"With pleasure." He quickly divested himself of his clothing. "Not that you have to ask."

She didn't bother to disguise her interest in his body.

"Oh my." Her attention slid to his cock, which was long, thick and eager to be inside her. She licked her bottom lip and he almost spent right there.

He surged forward. Hauling her naked body against his, he lifted her up against him, relishing the skin-on-skin contact. She wrapped her legs around his waist.

Surprised, but delighted, he murmured into her ear. "You certainly are not shy about what you want." He nipped the delicate lobe and went down with her onto the bed. His mouth closed over her breast, his tongue tasting and teasing the erect nipple. Her arms fell to her sides. He missed the feel of them roaming his skin. Turning his attention to her other breast, Brandon glanced up at Rose's face. Her eyes were closed and she was biting her lip.

"Is this all right?" he asked, mouthing her breast.

"Yes." But her eyes remained scrunched together. His hand slid down her belly to the place between her legs. She was wet. Very wet. The tension in his muscles increased. He fought the urge to mount her and plunge deep, instead mustering all of his self-control to force himself to take his time, to make sure she was ready for him—in both body and spirit.

"Are you certain?" he asked.

"Yes." Her voice was strained, as if speaking was an effort.

He paused. Although her body was responding, maybe she did not care for the attention he lavished on her breasts. He slid down her beautiful form, ready to put his mouth on her, to bring her off. But she stopped him as he kissed and tasted his way over the slope of her belly.

She opened her eyes and looked straight into his. "Please." She was breathless, her cheeks flushed. "Just finish it."

He'd intended to go slow this first time, but he wanted to give her whatever she needed. He positioned himself over her, kissing her deeply. She kissed him back, but her ardor no longer matched his.

Confused, he broke the kiss. "Are you certain that you are ready, my beautiful Rose? We can stop."

"No, don't stop." She widened her thighs to receive him. "I am ready. Please, Alex."

He could not deny her, especially not when he wanted her so badly. He entered her slowly, until he was fully seated, giving her body time to adjust around him. Her insides clutched his cock. She felt like heaven, even as she remained completely still.

He searched her face, uncertain about whether he should continue. "Rose?"

"Go on," she encouraged, pressing a kiss against his lips. "I am fine."

He didn't want her to be fine. He wanted her breathless with pleasure. He began to stroke into her, moving steadily and with all the care he could muster, even though his body wanted to take her hard and fast.

She'd been so eager at first, as eager as Brandon. But now she lay passive beneath him, not cold exactly, because he felt her body softening to him. He took his time and she at last began to move to his rhythm.

"That's it, my love." Now that she was here with him, he began to move faster, getting caught up in the pleasure of it. He reached between them, to where they were joined, and touched her. She arched under him, but her hands were still not on his body. They clutched the bed-clothes so tightly that her fingers were white.

"No." She squirmed as if trying to move away from the touch of his fingers, but the word was caught on a whimper as the tension in her body released and she cried out. Brandon finally let himself go, barely pulling out in time to spend all over her belly. He stilled and shivered atop her, spent yet somehow bereft, feeling disconnected from Rose even though their unclothed bodies were pressed up against each other. But then, at last, soft, warm arms tightened around him.

He relaxed into her with a contented sigh.

ROSE COULDN'T RESIST wrapping her arms around Alex after the most glorious physical experience of her life.

She welcomed his delicious weight and heat, the hard planes of his body pressed into hers and the ability to hold him so close that she could feel his heart beating in tandem with hers. She fought to regain her breath. They were both flushed, their skin damp.

Holding herself back while making love had been agonizing.

Now that she finally had him in her arms, Rose wanted to hold on to Alex forever. But when he stirred, she immediately released him. He shifted to his side, propping his weight up on one elbow, his head in his hand.

He leaned in and kissed her so tenderly that Rose's throat ached. Pulling back, he regarded her with a solemn gaze. "Are you all right?"

"Of course." She'd never felt better.

"And"—he cleared his throat—"it was satisfactory?"

"It was lovely." Superb. Sublime. She didn't have the

vocabulary to accurately describe what it was like to be with a man as loving and generous as Alex.

With Roger, she'd had to focus her efforts to achieve any satisfaction for herself. But with Alex, her body had a mind of its own, responding fiercely, almost savagely, to his passionate embraces. Roger had never cared for her pleasure, but Rose had taken it anyway. Sexual congress with Roger had been a purely physical encounter. With Alex, it was excruciatingly intimate, and didn't feel remotely like the same act she'd engaged in with Roger.

"What of you?" she asked. "Did you enjoy it?"

"That goes without saying." He pressed his lips against her shoulder. "I should think it was obvious."

Yet, he seemed perturbed. Roger had accused Rose of being too forward in bed. Perhaps following one's carnal impulses was wrong. She had no mother to advise her in such matters. Uncle Trevor certainly never broached the subject and Aunt Hattie was a spinster. Had Alex thought her too eager? He'd seemed shocked when Rose wrapped her legs around his waist. It was a natural instinct but she restrained herself after that. Not that it was easy, especially not with Alex using his talented mouth and fingers to draw a response from her.

"Why that frown?" Alex feathered his fingers along her forehead. "I hope you don't regret what we've just done."

"No. Never. It was"—she searched for a word that didn't make her sound overly enthusiastic—"very enjoyable."

His face fell. "I see."

She hated to think that she'd disappointed him. "You

have been very kind to me." She reached for his hand. "I cannot begin to imagine how much more difficult this would have been without your support."

Alex entwined his fingers with hers. "I have only just begun to offer my assistance. Fleming is not going to get away with debasing you."

"He thinks he already has."

"He's a fool." He pressed his lips against the back of her hand. "This fight hasn't even started yet."

Chapter Fifteen

 $\mathcal{T}$hat evening before supper Rose finally returned to her drawing desk to work on designs for the Duchess of Huntington. She forced herself to concentrate because she was terribly behind. These maps presented the beginning of an independent life. She had to make sure they were her best creations yet.

She poured all of herself into her work, using the joy and passion she'd experienced with Alex to fuel her creativity. Losing herself in the Greek landscapes even allowed Rose to forget about Roger's treachery—at least for a few minutes at a time.

There was a sound at the door, probably Alex bringing in her dinner. Rose brightened. Maybe he could sit and talk to her while she ate. Maybe he'd care to repeat this afternoon's tryst. But she didn't dare initiate for fear he'd find her far too forward for a respectable woman. He wasn't only a remarkable lover, he was also a good friend. She increasingly relied on both his counsel and companionship. She didn't want to risk doing anything that might turn Alex away from her.

"There you are." She turned from her maps. "I'm famished."

"Are you?" Roger stood in the doorway. "It is good to see that your appetite has returned." He looked beyond her, his interested gaze settling on her maps. "And you have returned to work. Excellent. I have a new commission for you."

Acid rose in her throat. She could barely stomach the sight of the man. "You cannot believe that I will ever allow you to take credit for my maps again."

"You have always been a woman of uncommon good sense. I had hoped you would be able to put your emotions aside by now." He sighed as he turned to close the door behind him. "But I see that is not to be."

"I am working on my maps for the Duchess of Huntington." She sat up straighter. "From now on, I will secure my own commissions."

He shot her a look of pure disdain. "Just because that heathen duchess has seen fit to engage your services, you cannot imagine that the rest of good society will follow suit. The duchess is hardly respectable. Her mother came from a family of tradespeople." He sniffed. "True, her father was a marquess, but everyone says the man was a bedlamite. He'd have to be in order to sully his family lines with the blood of an Arab merchant's daughter."

Rose's fingers tightened around her pencil. "My grandfather was an Arab. Or have you forgotten?"

"Fortunately, your fair hair and blue eyes betray no evidence of your tainted blood. Also, it's not as if I truly took you to wife."

The barb stung, as he'd intended, but Rose wasn't ashamed of who she was.

"Arab coloring is beautiful," she retorted. In fact, she wished she looked a little more like *Jidu*. She'd feel closer to him. "Look at Alex. You said yourself that he is a fine specimen."

"Alex is Italian. He is certainly not Arabian."

"Who told you that?"

"He did."

"You must be mistaken." Why would Alex lie about that?

"In any case, one cannot compare a footman to a marquess. A peer is obligated to keep pure bloodlines. Brandon violated that rule."

"Brandon? Are you speaking of the man I drew the map for a few months ago?"

"I'm referring to his father. The younger Brandon, who commissioned the map from me, is even more of a recluse than his late father. He is probably ashamed of his background. The rumor is that he intends to pursue a duke's daughter. I suppose he thinks her pure blood will cleanse his own tainted line."

"As if you have any standing at all to pass judgment on anyone."

"And his sister, the Duchess of Huntington, writes those travelogues of hers. No respectable lady works."

"Would you rather her husband lie about her work and claim it as his own?" she asked sweetly. "Do you find taking credit for your wife's work to be honorable?"

"As you know, you are not my wife."

This time she didn't flinch. "Yes, I am aware, which means you have no claim at all to my shop."

He cackled. "You think you can run the shop on your own?"

"I know I can."

"You have always had an inflated sense of your abilities. Even your uncle knew you weren't capable of managing the enterprise. That's why Trevor practically begged me to marry you. He knew *I* was needed to keep the shop successful."

"He thought what was between your legs was required to make the shop profitable." She tossed the pencil onto her drafting table. "But I intend to prove you both wrong."

"I should like to see you try. I possess the only key to the shop. You are not to step foot into my business."

"You don't own it."

"I do in the eyes of the community. The only way to prove otherwise is to tell the world that we are not wed. That we pretended you were my wife when, in reality, you are just my mistress."

This time he struck a nerve. She clenched her fists. "You will pay for what you've done."

"When will you understand that you are completely powerless to do anything about this situation?"

"Never underestimate the determination of a wronged woman."

They were interrupted by Alex, who finally appeared with her supper.

"Not now," Roger barked. "Your mistress and I do not wish to be disturbed."

"Please do come in, Alex." Rose crossed over to sit at the table. "I am famished and Mr. Fleming and I are quite through."

"As you wish, madam." Ignoring Roger, Alex came over with her tray.

"I will no longer stand for your insolence." Roger spoke sharply to Alex. "Consider yourself released from your position."

"No." Rose reached for her fork. "He stays. Alex, I am now your employer. I will pay your wages and you will answer only to me."

Roger's face reddened. "You go too far, Rose. Do not push me. You will not like what happens."

"As if you have not already done your worst." She scooped a bite of partridge with bread sauce. For the first time in days, Rose had an appetite. She was feeling more and more like herself again. Not the Rose who was Roger's wife, but the imitable young woman she was before Uncle Trevor died.

Roger scowled at Alex. "If you value your position, you will not take this woman's direction over mine."

"I do value my position," Alex returned, his gaze cold and steady. "I serve at madam's pleasure and will continue to do so."

"She does not have the money to pay your wages."

"Of course I do." Rose spoke between bites. "The generous fee from Lord Wallthorne should last me a good while."

Roger advanced on her. "Why, you—"

Alex stepped in his path. "I wouldn't try it if I were you."

Apprehension washed over Roger's face. "This does not concern you. You are just a servant. You have forgotten your place."

"My place is to see to my employer's needs. And you are no longer my employer."

Roger stepped back. "You had better come to your senses soon, Rose. Do not test me. I can destroy you."

"You should leave." Alex practically butted chests with Roger. "Now."

"You think your guard dog can protect you from ruin?" Roger shot another look of pure malice at Rose. "Don't be a fool!" He spun on his heels and departed, slamming the door shut behind him.

Rose set down her fork, suddenly feeling very drained. These days any encounter with Roger had that effect.

Alex set a hand on her shoulder. "Are you all right?"

The weight of his hand felt good. "I will be if you'll sit with me for a moment."

"As long as you continue to eat. You'll get too thin. You need your strength."

Had he found her displeasingly thin when she'd disrobed? "Is that a complaint about this afternoon?"

"Never." His hand slid over to cup her jaw. "I have no complaints at all about this afternoon. Everything about it was marvelous and you are a marvel."

She looked up as his face came down to meet hers. He kissed her thoroughly. His hand slid into her dress to cup her breast.

"Alex." Desire rampaged through her. "I need you."

"I'm here," he murmured against her lips.

She reached for the placket of his breeches and started to unbutton his trousers.

She felt his smile against her lips. "You're a very demanding mistress."

She froze. Had she overstepped again?

"Don't stop," he urged.

"It's not appropriate." She dropped her hands. "I am your employer."

"Then I resign." He swept her up into his arms and half tossed her onto the sofa. "Effective immediately."

"Oh!" His easy strength took her breath away. "What a shame. I'll have to hire a new footman."

He frowned. "I don't care for the idea of any other man tending to your needs. I might have to withdraw my resignation in the morning."

She smiled up at him. "Thank goodness."

He came down on top of her, pressing her deep into the sofa, melding his mouth to hers. The kiss was hot and intense. He paused. "Is this all right?"

"More than all right." She reached up to kiss him heatedly, and relished the hot press of his erection against her skirts. "Extremely, extremely all right."

A jumble of activity followed. Between kisses and touches, her skirt was pulled up and he'd unbuttoned his breeches, freeing himself. She reached for his hardness, wrapping her fingers around him. She'd never touched Roger like this, had never wanted to. With Alex, she couldn't resist. He was so beautiful. But then she caught herself. She shouldn't be too forward. She released him and dropped her hands to her sides.

"Don't stop," he murmured.

She dropped her knees open, welcoming him. "Hurry," she whispered into his ear. "I want to feel you inside me."

She needed him to rush before she lost all control and allowed her hands to roam, to stroke his member, to feel the weight of his balls in her hand, to squeeze his buttocks in both of her hands. She wanted to run her mouth all over him, to suck his nipples, to taste everything.

Maybe she was unnatural. Maybe decent women didn't desire such things.

Alex plunged inside her, stroking hard and fast. The push and drag, the sensations of him grinding into her, sent tingling shivers through her. Reaching between them, he fingered the bundle of nerves that made her crazy with excitement. She couldn't stand not touching him, so she gripped his clothed shoulders, which was safer than bare skin.

His face was serious and intent as he stroked into her. Rose could stare at him forever. He held her gaze as he made love to her. Emotion welled in her chest. The unexpected intimacy of the moment provoked her to tears. The tension within her body continued to spiral upward until it finally broke and she cried out, shuddering as waves of pleasure rolled over her.

He kissed her hard and continued to slide into her, until he froze and released into her, flooding her body with his seed. He buried his face in her neck, breathing heavily, his exhales sweetly humid against her skin. She felt sublime. Free and light, floating on pleasure. They lay there for a few minutes, enjoying each other—the intermingled heat, the sensation of skin-on-skin contact.

"Are you well?" He pressed a kiss against her cheek. Her stomach growled and he laughed. "I guess there's my answer." He lifted himself off her.

"Don't go," she protested.

"You have to eat. You've practically starved yourself these past several days."

He stood and went into her bedchamber. She heard the splash of water before he returned with a damp cloth. He'd put himself back to sorts; his breeches were buttoned. His hair was still ruffled, though, and his jaw darkened already because his beard grew in so rapidly.

She took the cloth from him and went into her bedchamber to clean herself in privacy. She hummed to herself, the delightful aftereffects of their lovemaking still rippling through her. When she rejoined him, he pointed to the food-laden table.

"Now you eat."

She sat and reached for her fork. "You are very demanding."

He took the chair opposite her. "I am when it comes to looking after you."

"That was . . . wonderful." She felt herself blush.

His eyes twinkled. "I think I'll rescind my resignation now. Or perhaps I should wait. In case you'd like me to come to you tonight, once the household is abed?"

Rose wanted nothing more, but would he think her unnaturally forward if she invited him to come to her bed this evening? Was she expected to be coy? Unsure of how to respond, she changed the subject. "To be completely honest, I do not know how long I can continue to pay you. The duchess's fees should help. But after that I cannot guarantee your wages."

He flashed his teeth. "I shall have to take my chances."

"Shouldn't you be more concerned about the potential loss of your livelihood?"

He shrugged. "As you've said, I look well enough to find a position in a noble house."

"Ha. What a braggart you are. But that is the truth. With your fine form and face, you should be able to find a position."

His eyes heated. "You think I possess a fine form and face?"

"Isn't it obvious?" Did he think she'd lie with just anyone? She shivered as a sudden chill assaulted her. "Why did you tell Roger that you are Italian?"

"To keep my position." He briefly looked away. "Not every employer cares to engage an Arab."

"I rather see it as a point in your favor."

"That is very fortunate for me."

She sliced off a bite of partridge. "I saw my solicitor today."

"Did you? Why? To ask about your options regarding your marriage?"

"Hardly. I accept that I am not wed. But I wanted to know if I own the shop outright."

"And do you?"

She nodded. "Uncle Trevor left it to me with no pre-conditions."

"Isn't that excellent news? Why do you look so glum?"

"How can I claim ownership? How do I dislodge him from my shop? If I summon the authorities, I'll have to admit that I am not married to Roger."

"Ah." He stroked his jaw. "I see the problem."

"Precisely. In order to claim what is rightfully mine, I would have to publicly ruin my reputation."

He pondered her words, then a gleam lit his eye. "Maybe not."

"What do you mean?"

"Finish your supper." He rose, a small smile on his lips. "I have something to see to."

"Where are you going?" She didn't want to lose his

company so soon. "If you're still my footman, shouldn't you be seeing to what I tell you to see to?"

"Enjoy your meal." He disappeared through the door. "I shall return for the tray later."

Rose smiled after him. Alex was so wonderful. She could hardly believe her good fortune. Her gaze fell upon dessert. Mrs. Waller's bread pudding was one of her favorites. She slid the plate closer to her. Scooping up a mouthful of the sweet dessert, she wondered what Alex was up to.

THAT SUNDAY ALEX informed Rose that he had a surprise for her.

"What sort of surprise?" she asked as he led the way on the side pavement. No one had surprised her with anything in years. At least not anything pleasant. "I'm not sure I can survive another unexpected occurrence."

"This is nothing like what Fleming put you through. You will like this."

"How can you be so certain?"

"I know you, Rose." He winked. "I know what you like."

Heat rose on her cheeks. "You certainly do."

"Here we are."

"Why are we at the shop?" She stared up at the storefront. "It's Sunday. We're closed today."

He produced something from his pocket that glimmered in the sun. "Not if you have the key."

She stared at the skeleton key in his hand. "That is not the key to the shop." She ought to know. She'd used it often enough back when Uncle Trevor allowed her to come and go as she pleased.

"Isn't it?" He placed it in her palm. "Why don't you give it a try?"

What was he up to? Then it hit her. The lock was different. "What have you done?"

His eyes twinkled. "Open it."

She put the key in and turned it. "You changed the locks?"

"I had them changed, yes."

"But that must have been expensive."

"My cousin is a locksmith. He owed me a favor."

She pushed the door open and stepped inside. Entering the shop never failed to delight her. It was like coming home. She took in the maps laid out on tables, her puzzles and tea towels. Nostalgia waved over her. This was the first time in years that she'd been in the shop alone, without Roger or the strangers he'd hired after Uncle Trevor died. She inhaled the scent of paper and ink. How she'd missed this place. Exhilaration waved over her. Now, at last, she could finally spend as much time here as she pleased.

Brandon peered up the stairwell. "Where does this lead?"

"There's a vacant apartment up there. I always urged Roger to rent it but he said doing so would make us appear less prosperous." She wandered past him into the back area, her hand lingering over the engraver's table.

Alex motioned to the mirror on an easel. "What is that for?"

"Once the maps are drawn, the engraver props up the drawing so that he can view it in the mirror so he can reverse the image. The etching on the engraving plate has to be drawn in reverse for the print to come out correctly."

"So Fleming draws the maps, your man here engraves them on a plate and then Fleming colors them in?"

"That is how it works." Except for the Fleming part. Roger could barely draw a stick figure. "Once the map drawing is engraved, it is colored in by hand."

"That's a painstaking process. I can see why Wallthorne paid so dearly for the map. I hope you are charging the duchess a small fortune for *your* maps."

"Probably not as much as I should." Especially when she considered how much Roger charged Wallthorne. "But that is of no account. If this volume is as successful as Her Grace's other travelogues, the publicity will be priceless."

"You do know that you can do it."

"What do you mean?"

"You don't need Fleming. You can run this shop. You have a talent for maps. Perhaps as much of a talent as Fleming. More importantly, you clearly have a head for business."

The conviction in his voice moved her. Alex believed in her. The past couple of weeks had shaken everything in Rose's world. Even, momentarily, her belief in herself and her abilities.

"You have the right of it." She turned in a small circle, surveying her shop. *Her domain.* "This is all mine and I intend to make it work." She would begin by bringing back the surveyor and master engravers who used to work for Uncle Trevor. If she could find them.

"And you will make this shop more prosperous than

ever," he said. "The tea towels and dissected maps were your idea. I cannot wait to see what you do next."

"One of my first official decisions will be to rent out the upstairs apartment. That will be a very nice source of income. And I have so many more concepts I'd like to test. I was forced to introduce them to Roger slowly. He is not good with change and innovation."

"And now you have the *only* key to your shop."

For the first time in weeks, hope for the future surged within her. Maybe there was a path forward after all, one that was not necessarily cloaked in ruin and despair.

She stared at the key in the palm of her hand. "This might just be the most incredible thing anyone has ever done for me."

"There is nothing I would not do to secure your happiness."

Their eyes met. Heat arced between them. They both stepped forward at the same time and surged into each other's arms. His mouth came down over hers. Tender and sweet. He kissed her carefully as if she might break. But she did not want him to be careful. She pressed herself against him. Their lips parted. His tongue touched hers lightly. She was dissolving into a million warm little pieces of pleasure.

"Well, well, well. This certainly explains everything."

Rose broke apart from Alex, her breathing heavy, her body heated, to find herself staring into Roger's ruddy face. "What are you doing here?"

"A neighbor sent word that someone was tampering with the locks. That is what I am doing here. I obviously do not need to ask you the same thing."

"You have no business here," Alex said. "State your

piece and leave Miss—?" He stumbled. He didn't know her name.

"Kanaan. Rose Kanaan," she answered. It was exhilarating to say it out loud. Taking back her name made her feel another step closer to reclaiming her old self, discarding the colorless, obedient wife who smothered her wants and needs by putting her husband's desires above her own. Gone were the days of subjecting herself to the whims of a mate who was not only less talented than she, but also less intelligent.

"As I was saying," Alex said, "state your business and then leave Miss Kanaan alone."

Roger's eyes widened. "You've told your footman of your shame?"

"The shame is yours," Alex growled, "and you are trespassing here."

"*My* shame? As you well know, Rose is no innocent." He faced Rose. "You never were an honorable woman. Now that I think back on it, you behaved more like a mistress rather than a wife between the sheets. You *claim* you were welcoming because you wanted children but—"

Alex's arm jerked back and he punched Roger hard in the mouth. Roger went down, grasping at the easel to ease his fall, but it gave way, tilting over, the mirror slamming to the ground and shattering into heavy shards.

Alex hovered over Roger, his arm cocked to deliver another blow. "Apologize to the lady."

Rose stepped forward to prevent Alex from hitting Roger again. "It is over," she told Roger. "We've changed the locks. You are trespassing here."

Roger glared at her. "Do you think it is that easy?

I will make certain everyone knows that you are a ruined woman." He fingered the blood coming from his nose. "I will shout it from the rooftops if I have to. No one will frequent the shop of a fallen woman."

"Married woman," Rose blurted out.

Roger's brows drew together. "What the devil are you talking about?"

"Alex and I are betrothed." She straightened her spine. "We shall be married by the end of the month."

Chapter Sixteen

$\mathcal{B}$randon spun around to stare at Rose. She was deathly pale except for the bright red spots high on each cheek and the glittering blue of her incomparable eyes.

"What?" Roger sputtered. "You're lying!"

Rose's unrelenting gaze held Brandon's. He registered the unspoken apology in the look they exchanged. As well as her desperation.

"Am I?" Her gaze remained steady on Brandon. "You may ask Alex if I am lying."

Brandon's face heated. A part of him rejoiced at the idea of having Rose by his side until the end of his days. But his situation wasn't simple. Nothing about their current predicament was uncomplicated. Rose didn't even know who he really was.

"Ha!" Roger barked a contemptuous laugh. "Even a lowly footman won't marry a woman as dishonorable as you."

Brandon's chest clenched when Rose's face fell. No matter how Brandon answered, he would end up hurting her. The deceitful web he and Fleming had spun around

Rose, each for his own purpose, ensnared her in a trap from which there was no true escape.

"You're a laughingstock, my dear," Roger gloated. "Maybe you should reconsider the business arrangement I offered you."

Anger scalded Brandon's blood. He grabbed Fleming by the collar and hauled him to his feet. "It will be the honor of my life to take Miss Kanaan to wife. Insult my future bride and I will pummel you so badly you'll forget who you are."

Fleming stumbled back. "You cannot have my shop! You think I'd allow a servant to steal my establishment?"

"This enterprise belongs to Miss Kanaan." Brandon reached his arm out behind him. Rose stepped forward to slip her hand in his. He clasped it tightly, enjoying the pressure of her fingers gripping his. "And, as her husband, I will do everything in my power to protect her property from interlopers and scapegraces such as yourself."

Fleming gaped at Rose. "Do you not see what he is doing? He looks at this shop and knows it can all be his if he can fool you into wedding him."

"As you did?" She interlinked her fingers with Brandon's. "Alex is nothing like you."

"Is that so? How well do you know your footman, Rose? You know nothing about who he really is."

"I know that I can trust him." The words were strong and firm.

She believed in him. The words were like a knife to Brandon's gut. He didn't deserve her faith.

"He's going to steal it all from you."

"Get out." Brandon shoved Fleming hard enough for the man to stumble backward. "If you dare to trespass on this property again, you'll regret the day you were born."

"Marrying a servant won't make you an honorable woman," Fleming shot back at Rose as he backed away toward the exit. "Nothing can."

Fleming slammed the door shut behind him. Through the store's bow windows, Brandon watched the man stomp away. He contemplated Fleming's parting words. Unfortunately, the whoreson was right. Nothing could erase the stain on Rose's reputation.

Except, perhaps, marrying a marquess.

"I won't hold you to it." Rose locked the shop door with shaky hands after Roger's departure. "I don't know what came over me. It was so wrong of me to put you on the spot like that. I hope you can forgive me."

"Rose."

She was trembling and couldn't meet his eyes. "I don't know what to say. I am so sorry." She was babbling but couldn't stop herself. "Truly, I don't know—"

"Rose." He took hold of her shoulders. "Stop."

She forced her gaze up to meet his. "You must resent me so."

"Any man would be thrilled to receive a proposal from a woman as unique and special as you."

"You seemed horrified."

"I was surprised."

There was more to it. He was in turmoil. She could see it. Was it because he secretly agreed with Roger?

Did he believe her to be the sort of woman a man dallied with but did not take to wife? "Would it really be so horrible?"

"It would be glorious, beyond anything I could have expected for my life." His face darkened. "But . . . there are things you don't know about me."

"Have you killed anyone? Stolen from or cheated anyone? Do you intend to cheat me?"

"No. Never."

"You could be a merchant, a shop owner, rather than a servant."

He clamped his jaw shut. "This is your shop. I will never take control of it."

"But we could work together. And you don't seem indifferent to me," she stammered. "There is a certain warmth between us."

"Making love with you has been the most moving experience of my life. No woman has ever appealed to me more." He struggled to find the words. "But my life is complicated."

"Forgive me." She looked away. "It is completely understandable if you aren't interested in wedding a woman bedded by a man who is not her husband."

"Stop that. I view you as you are. As a respectable woman. I don't care about your past."

"And I do not care about yours," she said. "I believe we could make a go of it."

"You've been through a terrible shock." He interlocked his fingers behind his neck, stretching his elbows wide. "You are not in the right mind to make a life-altering decision."

"I don't have the luxury of taking my time. Roger

will do all he can to ruin my reputation. I need to be a married woman in earnest before he starts spreading his stories."

"Damnation." He paced away from her. "I should break his neck. That will shut him up."

He seemed so conflicted, but the more Rose thought about wedding Alex, the more sense it made. Marrying would help save her reputation and she would finally be wed to a man she actually cared for.

"When you say your situation is complicated," she ventured to ask, "does that mean you are promised to another?"

"No." He spoke sharply. "I am not committed to anyone."

Still, he hesitated. "I release you unequivocally. You are under no obligation to me."

"Maybe I want to be obligated to you."

Now he was just being generous. "You must take at least a few days to consider your decision."

"We both know you don't have the luxury of time."

"My proposal was a rash one. Your answer should not be."

He took a long breath. "I will at least take a few hours to think on your offer."

"You mustn't rush. I don't want you to feel forced into wedding me."

"I am not a man who does anything I don't care to. I can guarantee you this much—if I ask you to be my wife, it will be because there is nothing I want more."

"WHAT ARE YOU going to do?" Leela asked.

Her husband, the duke, popped a stuffed, wrapped

grape leaf into his mouth. "I thought you said your brother was interested in Kingsley's daughter."

Brandon glared at his sister. "Have you shared my private business with everyone?"

"Of course not." Leela flashed an adoring look at the duke. "Huntington is my husband. He's *not* everyone."

They were attending a family dinner at the Zayman family house off Red Lion Square. *Citi* often supervised the cooking of a Sunday meal for any family members who were in Town. At the moment it seemed to Brandon that every single one of his mother's relations was packed into the narrow town house. The raucous chatter, a mixture of English and Arabic, was so noisy that he could barely hear his own thoughts. Many stood while they ate due to a lack of sufficient seating. To Brandon's surprise, Leela's haughty duke did not seem bothered to be standing while eating.

"What are you all talking about?" Hanna wandered up with her husband, Viscount Griffin.

Hunt picked another grape leaf off his plate. "Brandon here is courting the Duke of Kingsley's daughter, but he's gone and gotten himself betrothed to a tradeswoman."

Brandon scowled. "I am not betrothed to anyone. As of yet."

"Kingsley's daughter?" Griff eyed the food on his wife's plate. "Lady Olympia was the diamond of the season. Are you certain she'll have you?"

Hanna followed her husband's gaze. "You may have my *sfeeha* if you'd like."

"Much obliged, my darling." Griff helped himself to the open-faced meat pie.

Brandon exhaled through his nostrils. "In answer to your question, yes, I have reason to believe Lady Olympia welcomes my suit and no, I am not betrothed to anyone at the moment. Does no one here keep any confidences?"

Leela grinned. "This family's idea of keeping a secret is to tell it to only one person."

"Who then reveals it to one person," Hanna put in.

"And before you know it," Griff said, "everyone knows your business."

Brandon stretched his neck from side to side. "I see I'll receive no sound advice from this lot." He'd come directly to Red Lion Square after escorting Rose back to New Street. His thoughts were tangled. He'd had a plan for the way his life was supposed to go, but now his carefully laid-out future was about to unravel.

"I need more *sfeeha*," Griff announced.

"And I could use another helping of grape leaves," the duke said. "We shall leave you to the ladies' counsel, Brandon."

The duke and the viscount wandered off, threading their way through the crowd toward the food laid out on the dining room table.

"I shall go as well," Hanna said, "so that you might speak to your sister in private."

"Actually, I would appreciate it if you could stay, at least for a moment," Brandon surprised himself by saying. "Your perspective would be welcome."

"Would it? My outlook as someone from the laboring class? Or as a viscountess? Because there is very little I could tell you about being a lady."

"Both actually. And you are very much a lady."

"Well, thank you for saying so but the ton continues to be scandalized because I haven't given up bonesetting."

"And they don't think much of me," Leela contributed, "because I am still writing about my travels."

"If I wed Rose, she'll be elevated in much the same way as Hanna was."

"How can you wed Mrs. Fleming?" Hanna gaped at him. "Is her husband deceased?"

"Something like that." Brandon was unwilling to share the details of Rose's situation. "Wedding her would save her from scandal."

One of Leela's brows arched. "A scandal you are responsible for?"

He bristled. "No, I had nothing to do with it. Must you assume the worst?"

"You *were* deceiving her about your identity."

"How did she react when she learned who you really are?" Hanna bit into an olive. "It must be shocking to discover your footman is actually a marquess."

"Well, about that—" He allowed his voice to trail off.

"What about that?" Leela gave him a pointed look. "You did tell her who you are before you proposed?"

"Not exactly." He wasn't about to reveal that Rose had done the proposing. Some might condemn Rose for being too forward but not Brandon. He cherished her boldness.

Hanna blinked. "She might not care to marry you when she learns the truth."

"Why wouldn't she be thrilled?" Brandon tried to convince himself of the truth of his words. "Any woman would rather wed a marquess than a penniless footman. She'd become a marchioness."

Hanna and Leela exchanged disbelieving looks. "Men." They both uttered the word at the same time.

"What?" His gaze flicked between his sister and cousin. "What am I missing?"

"You have lied to her and deceived her," his sister informed him. "Most women do not take kindly to that."

Hanna waved at someone behind Griff. "Obviously, you must tell Rose the truth before you wed. *If* you decide to actually marry her."

"How have you coped with becoming a viscountess?"

She shrugged. "We are not much in with the ton. I continue my work and we mostly keep to a small circle of friends whose society we enjoy."

"Do you ever have moments when you regret your choice?"

Her eyes softened. "Not for a moment." She looked past him again. "*Citi* is giving me the eye, *Yalla*, excuse me. I must see what she needs."

"Of course." Brandon stepped aside to allow his cousin to pass.

"Now that we're alone," Leela said, "are you going to share the full story?"

"I don't know. Can you be relied upon not to whisper a word of this to anyone? It involves Rose's reputation."

"I promise," Leela said. "I quite like Rose and would do nothing to harm her." Brandon shared the most basic details to give his sister some insight into the situation.

"What a complete scoundrel Mr. Fleming is!" Leela exclaimed when he was done. "Poor Rose! I see why you felt obligated to accept her proposal of marriage."

"She has offered to release me from the obligation."

"Do you wish to be released?" She scrutinized his

face as if she could find the truth written there. "Or do you care for her?"

"I have indicated an interest in courting Lady Olympia, as you well know."

"The question is a simple one, really. What do you care most about? Rose? Or your scheme to laugh in society's face by wedding the diamond of the season?"

"It is not that simple."

"Isn't it? Are you certain you're not the one complicating matters?"

"It is up to me to avenge our parents. To return our family to its rightful place in society. It's what Mother and Father would want."

"Perhaps. But what do *you* want?"

Rose. The answer swooped into his thoughts before he could think about it. "I've always wanted nothing more than to tweak those nobles who rejected our parents. Winning the jewel of the season out from under the noses of their precious sons would be the perfect way to exact my revenge."

"But will that make you happy?"

"What difference does that make?"

She smiled softly. "Every difference once you've found someone to love."

He huffed. "Father married for love and look what happened to him."

"What happened to him? He was rejected by the ton, which he couldn't care less about and was happily wed for more than twenty years. Father was so heartbroken by Mama's death that he followed her to the grave within the year."

Emotion constricted his chest. "I do not want my children to experience the rejection that we did."

"Granted, it hasn't always been easy, but I would not change anything about my life. I am grateful for the perspective our background has afforded us. We are the richer for it."

"Do you not worry about the slights your daughter will receive?"

"I do, but she is the daughter of a duke and the granddaughter of a marquess. Whether anyone likes it or not, we are here. We have just as much of a right to be here as anyone else. Our children, yours, mine and Hanna's, will grow up together. They will have each other."

"If only I could see things as clearly as you do."

"The first question you must ask yourself is, do you love Rose?"

"Who is Rose?" *Citi* seemed to appear out of nowhere.

"Now you've done it," Brandon mumbled to his sister.

Their grandmother spoke to them in Arabic. "Rose is not the name of the duke's daughter, is it?"

"No, Kingsley's daughter is Lady Olympia," Brandon said. "I am considering wedding a mapmaker instead."

"A merchant?" *Citi* blew out her lips, making the sound of flatulence. "You should marry your own kind."

"Rose's grandfather was Arab." His grandmother's approval mattered to Brandon. "From Lebanon."

"*Yanee*?" *Citi*'s perpetual frown softened. "*Yalla*, if she's *Arabiya*, that's better. At least she's one of us."

Brandon bent to kiss her cheek. "Thank you, *Citi*."

Citi harrumphed. "But I still think you're a donkey for not marrying the duke's daughter."

AFTER DINNER WITH his Arab relations, Brandon went home to Peckham House. He dispatched a boy to inform Rose that he would be away for the night. He needed time to think, to consider his options, although he didn't really have any alternatives. Abandoning Rose to face scandal and ruin alone was unthinkable.

In the bath that evening, he thought about his parents. Would Father be disappointed in the direction his life was taking? Would Mama? Both of them had married for love and never regretted their choice. They'd tried to launch both Brandon and Leela into the upper reaches of society, even though they'd both rejected the ton in favor of a quiet country life.

If Brandon married Rose, would he be marrying for love as Papa had? He liked her immensely and enjoyed her company. He was certainly attracted to her. Having the privilege of bedding Rose with great regularity was one of the supreme advantages of the union.

He ruminated over that question before he fell asleep that night. What a difference his feather mattress and fine, fresh linens were compared to the lumpy hay mattress and rough blanket in his shared attic room on New Street. He fell asleep almost immediately.

The following morning at breakfast, he envisioned waking up with Rose every morning, the sunlight cutting across the bluest gaze he'd ever seen. And then having Rose seated across from him, discussing their day or some story in the latest broadsheet. The images brought a smile to his lips. What would it be like to have someone he genuinely cared for to go through the years with—having children, celebrating holidays, enjoying meals and long country walks? He hadn't anticipated having simple everyday pleasures to look forward to.

But wedding Rose meant cutting all ties with Lady Olympia. The young lady wouldn't be heartbroken, she hardly knew him, but she might lament not becoming a marchioness. Brandon wasn't terribly concerned about Lady Olympia's prospects. As a duke's daughter, she enjoyed numerous options and opportunities. Unlike Rose.

If he decided to wed Rose, Brandon must immediately inform Lady Olympia and her father that he would not be making an offer of marriage. Instead of regretting the potential loss of the duke's daughter—and the attainment of a long-held goal—Brandon felt lighter, freer.

Was it possible that Rose had inadvertently released Brandon from a future he'd never truly wanted? Had his parents even needed avenging? They'd never seemed bitter, just eager for their children to have a place in society.

Releasing himself from the burden of having to right the wrong done to his parents freed Brandon to follow his own path. What *did* he want? Rose's face appeared before him. He finally acknowledged what his heart had known for weeks. He loved Rose beyond measure and would do everything in his power to be with her.

Maybe he was a fool after all.

Or maybe he was just his father's son.

Chapter Seventeen

"*Y*ou are rejecting *my* daughter?" Kingsley barked. "Of all of the insults I've been dealt, this is surely the worst."

Brandon paid a call on the duke directly after breakfast at Peckham House.

"I mean no disrespect, Your Grace," he said solicitously, "but I do not think your daughter and I will suit. I cannot make Lady Olympia happy. She enjoys society. I prefer a quiet life. She can make a better match elsewhere."

"You've got the right of it," the duke fumed. "She most definitely deserves far better than you. I must have been touched in the head to consider your suit."

Brandon stared at the man's red face and puffed-out cheeks. Kingsley was far more upset than he'd anticipated. But why? Lady Olympia had her pick of suitors.

"If that is all," Brandon said as he rose, "I would like to speak to Lady Olympia myself to explain the situation to her."

"She's in the garden." The duke gestured toward the

double glass doors that led to the outside. "What exactly do you intend to say to her?"

"That we do not suit. That I do not intend to ask for her hand in marriage." Through the glass, Brandon spied Lady Olympia strolling among the summer flowers. Dressed in white, she carried a parasol to shelter her face from the sun. "And that it is for the best that we end our acquaintance before taking matters any further." He moved toward the doors.

"I should have known." Kingsley's derisive tone sounded behind him. "Blood will always tell. Beneath those fine manners, your mother's foreign merchant blood runs too strong for you to be a true noble."

Brandon's grip on the door handle tightened. "I understand you are upset."

"Why should I be upset?" Kingsley retorted. "Not only does Arab merchant blood run in your veins, but there is the madness from your father's side. Only a bedlamite would taint his line by mixing with laboring class foreigners. It was a narrow escape for our family. I am grateful for this turn of events."

"As am I." Brandon let himself out to join Lady Olympia.

He paused for a moment, watching her kneel to pluck a pink rose and bring it to her nose. She spotted him then. "Lord Brandon."

He went to her. "Lady Olympia." He bowed.

"My lord." She curtsied. "This is a pleasant surprise. You usually visit on Sundays."

"I have come to tell you of a decision I have come to."

She plucked a petal from the flower. "About the future?"

"Indeed." He cleared his throat. "You are, of course, a diamond of the first water."

She looked up from the bloom in her hand. "But?"

"I do not think that we suit. You deserve a husband who will devote himself to your happiness."

"And you will not?"

"I am incapable of being the companion you deserve."

She pulled another petal. "Have you met someone that you would rather wed?"

He did not want to lie to her. "There is a woman who finds herself in dire circumstances. Wedding her will secure her future and her reputation."

"Are you the reason she is in dire circumstances?"

"No, I am not."

"And yet you are determined to come to her rescue." The words were tepid. "How gallant."

"I offer my sincerest apologies if you feel that I have misled you. But I don't believe I can make you happy."

She tossed the rose away. "Imagine a man of your connections thinking to throw over a duke's daughter."

"We never officially courted," he reminded her. "I haven't thrown anyone over. It is my hope that we can part as friends."

"I wanted to be a marchioness," she said tightly. "It's the highest title available on the marriage mart. Have you never asked yourself why the Season's incomparable would accept the suit of the son of the Mad Marquess and his Arab merchant wife?"

"I assumed it was because you wanted the title so badly that you were willing to overlook my *inferior* connections."

She seemed to miss the sarcasm in his words. "Precisely. So you see, whether or not we suit is immaterial. It is the title I want to marry, not you."

"Unfortunately for you, the title and I are inextricably connected."

Lady Olympia's expression hardened. "You should be grateful I am willing to overlook your tainted blood-lines."

He studied the tight lines of her lovely face. How had he ever envisioned spending his life with a woman who, except for the title, disdained everything about him? "Consider yourself fortunate that you won't have to lower yourself."

She lifted her chin. "It is important that you know your place and not get above yourself."

He huffed a laugh. He had to see the humor in it. It wasn't as if his motives were pure. The two of them had been playing at their own game with no concern for the other's welfare.

"We've both had a narrow escape." He bowed to take his leave. "It sounds to me as if we are well rid of each other."

ROSE SPENT ALL morning at her draft table trying to work, but she wasn't able to drive Alex from her thoughts. Shame burned through her at the memory of his shocked face after she'd blurted out that they were betrothed. Roger's contemptuous expression when Alex hesitated before confirming her claim made it all im-measurably worse.

Rose knuckled her tired eyes. She couldn't remember the last time she'd eaten, and sleep had eluded her last night. When she finally managed to doze off, she dreamt of Alex and Roger. In her jagged dreams, they both laughed at her. Obviously, Alex couldn't even bear to stay in the same house with her now. He'd slept elsewhere last night.

She'd miscalculated. Badly, it seemed. She and Alex were friends, and there was no denying the strong physical attraction between them, yet the idea of marriage caused him to flail about. Most footmen would be overjoyed to acquire their own business enterprise. But not Alex.

She threw down her pencil, cursing the societal strictures that required her to replace her fake husband with a genuine one. The laws and norms were obviously constructed to keep a woman in her place.

A soft tap at the door cut into her thoughts. "Come in."

Alex entered, dressed in street clothes rather than his livery. He took up all the space in the room with his masculine presence. Why wasn't he in uniform?

"Why are you dressed like that?" Panic welled within her. "Are you leaving?"

"No, let's go for a walk."

"We don't need to go anywhere. If you intend to let me down—"

"Please," he said gently. "I'd like to show you something." She reluctantly reached for a bonnet and shawl, and a few minutes later they were walking in the direction of Mayfair. It was an almost unbearably hot afternoon. Rose crossed to the shady side of the street, with Alex quietly following behind her. It was easily the hottest day of the year and having the sun drilling down on her felt even worse.

"Where are we going?"

"To Grosvenor Square."

It was one of the toniest sections of Mayfair. "But why?"

"You will see when we get there. Shall we get a hack?"

She preferred to work off the nervous energy. "No, let's walk."

They trod in relative silence for the next long while. Rose's nerves were a mess. Long walks normally did not bother her but she was overheated, light-headed and impatient to hear his decision.

"I've spent the last twenty-four hours contemplating your proposal," he said as they turned onto Curzon Street.

Her leg cramped. "How much farther are we going?"

"It's just up the street."

Thank goodness. Her head started to pound. "You must understand that I do not need you to rescue me." The words burst out of her. "I will find a way to manage on my own. A marriage must be a union that you truly want, not something gallantry has forced you into."

"You must know that I find you enormously appealing. No one else sets me in my place quite like you." His heated gaze dropped to her lips. "We suit in many ways."

"But you seemed horrified when I told Roger we were betrothed."

"That had nothing to do with you. You must believe me. No woman has ever captured my interest as you have." His gaze was intent on her face. "Are you all right?"

"It's a little warm." Her face was broiling.

"Not that warm. When was the last time you ate any-thing?"

"This morning." But she'd barely touched the breakfast tray. And she'd sent her supper tray back untouched last evening. She might have missed lunch as well.

"Rose?"

His voice was an echo. "Hmm?" The world spun. His strong arm slipped around her waist.

"Come on, this way."

He half carried her up some steps of one of the grand houses. "What are you doing? Where are we going?"

"I know the people here."

"The servants?"

"Yes."

"Shouldn't we be using the servants' entrance?"

"No." The door opened immediately.

"Good afternoon, my—"

"Hello, Stokes. Miss Kanaan has had too much sun. Which guest chamber is closest?"

"I'll show you there . . . erm . . . Alex."

Rose shook her head. "This is unnecessary." But it was a relief to be out of the sun.

They entered a stunning foyer with marbled floors and high ceilings covered in paintings.

"What is this place?" Rose had never been inside any house as grand. "Who does it belong to?"

"I'll explain everything momentarily." He directed her toward the stairs. "For now, we need to cool you down and get some food into you."

The butler watched them from the base of the wide, carpeted staircase. "Shall I bring up some food, my . . . erm . . . Alex?"

"Yes, and cool water and lemonade."

"Oh, I couldn't eat." She could barely muster the strength to make it up the stairs.

"You will eat," he said firmly. "Lack of nourishment is why you're swooning right now."

"I am *not* swooning." She was a woman who worked, who supported herself and her entire household. "I am not some fainthearted, weak-minded lady who *swoons*."

They turned down a long corridor. "No, you are a strong woman who almost faints because she hasn't properly nourished herself for weeks now. Here we are."

He guided her into a large bedchamber where floral silks adorned the canopied four-poster bed. Cheerful curtains matched the sumptuous bed coverings. "This is a guest chamber?" It was the most finely appointed room she'd ever been in.

"Why don't you lie down?"

She halted. "Absolutely not. We cannot just make ourselves at home in a stranger's bedchamber."

"This pile does not belong to a stranger. We are most welcome here. I'll explain everything but at the moment, your face is alarmingly pale and we need to make sure you are well."

She eyed the comfortable-looking stuffed chair by the window. "I'll sit there. I'm not going to lie down in a stranger's home."

"You are so stubborn."

"You were hard to manage as a footman," she retorted. "Maybe you'll be too insufferable as a husband."

"You will have to put me in my place as needed. You are very good at that."

Somewhere in her foggy mind, she registered that Alex talked as if he intended to linger in her life. Hope blossomed in her chest. "Will you be around for me to do so?"

He settled her in the chair. She sank into the fluffy feathered cushion. "I certainly hope so." He put a hand to her cheek. His touch felt cool and comforting against her hot skin. "Are you feeling any cooler? Stay here and rest. I'll return shortly."

"What? Where are you going? You cannot mean to leave me alone in a strange place."

"I'm just stepping out into the corridor. And then you will eat and drink even if it takes until midnight to get your strength back."

She uttered a faint protest as he departed, but then set her head back against the soft chair. Alex was right. She hadn't had much of an appetite since learning of Roger's betrayal and even forewent her long walks. Physically, she truly wasn't at her best. Roger had wreaked havoc on both her mind and body.

It was past time she stopped giving him so much power over her. She'd taken back her shop and now it was time to fully exorcise him from her life. She didn't know how yet, but she'd find a way. It was past time she ceased being Roger's, or any man's, victim. Taking control of her life began with looking after her health, eating well and taking walks in order to regain her usual strength and vigor.

Alex reappeared several minutes later, but returned empty-handed. "I thought you were bringing me something to eat?" She realized she was hungry. "I'm ravenous."

"The food is being prepared, but let's cool you down first." He came over to help her stand.

"I am not an invalid," she grumbled, irritated at herself for her weakened condition. They stepped into an adjoining room with a huge bathtub up against the far wall. "What in the world?"

"You're flushed and need to cool down. We've set up a cool bath for you."

"I cannot bathe in a stranger's house."

"Why not? I'll be right here with you, if you'd like."

"You'd like that, wouldn't you?"

His eyes twinkled. "I certainly would. And I promise to look my fill." His expression grew more serious. "You've been under a great deal of strain. Can you not just relax and allow your obedient footman to tend to you?"

The bath did look inviting. The idea of immersing herself in cool water sounded heavenly. "Maybe just for a few minutes."

"Allow me to undress you."

"Those are hardly a footman's duties."

"But they are a husband's," he murmured in a low, deep voice that made her shiver.

"Are you saying—?"

"Let's get you in the bath first and then we'll talk." She stood still while he removed her hat, dress, chemise and stockings. His efficient hands did not linger or seduce. It was such a relief to feel the air on her bare skin.

"Now, in you go," he commanded once she was undressed.

She stepped into the tub and sank into the blissfully cool water. "This is paradise."

He dipped a washcloth into the water and ran it over her cheeks and forehead to cool her down.

It was heaven. She closed her eyes. "You are spoiling me."

"It is well past time that someone did." He ran the wet cloth over her shoulders. "And, if you will allow it, I should like to continue to do so. As your husband."

Her eyes shot open. "What?"

He smiled, his eyes bright and warm. "I'd like to accept your proposal if the offer to wed still stands." He produced something from his pocket that glimmered as it caught the light. "Miss Rose Kanaan, will you do me the great honor of becoming my wife?"

"Are you certain?" Rose's heart pounded against her ribs. "I do not want you to feel forced into this."

"As I have said, no one forces me to do anything." He reached for her damp hand. "Will you accept this betrothal gift as a token of the promise we intend to make to one another?"

Rose stared down at the ring in his hand. It was the color of gold and featured a floral design. Tiny pearls surrounded the modest diamond at the center, like the petals of a sunflower. How had he managed to purchase the ring on a footman's salary? The band looked like gold but maybe it was made of pinchbeck, a brass that resembled the precious metal. Whatever it was made of, it was invaluable to her. "It's beautiful."

"Beautiful enough for you to accept?" He looked into her eyes, his expression somber. And . . . was that a touch of nerves in his voice?

"You won't be sorry," she said breathlessly. "The shop is very profitable."

"I am not wedding the shop. I am marrying you, Rose Kanaan."

"You do understand that I do not need you to rescue me? I will find a way to manage on my own. This marriage must be a union that you truly want, not something chivalry has forced you into."

He ran his hand over her bare shoulder. "You must know that I am completely taken with you." His heated gaze dropped to her lips. "We suit in every way."

Warmth flowed in her belly. "But you seemed so uncertain before."

"The only truth that matters now is that you are in my heart. We were meant to meet. It was written."

"Written?"

"Fate." His gaze was intent on her face. "Please say you will wear my ring."

She held out her hand. "Will you put it on me?"

He pushed the ring onto her finger before leaning in for a long kiss. Suddenly, the bath didn't feel cool. He broke the kiss. "There are important matters for us to discuss before we go any further. I want there to be no secrets between us."

Rose looked away. She was hiding certain truths from him. She'd wanted to confide in him but Alex already seemed wary of aligning himself with a woman of business. He was a footman, a servant and too honorable a man to be a fortune hunter.

Would he be completely put off to discover his future wife was London's preeminent mapmaker? Rose commanded higher fees for her maps than any of her male counterparts, a sum that was certainly higher than Alex's footman's wages.

She peered into his warm, confident gaze. He was as self-assured a man as she'd ever met, but learning just how lopsided their earning capacity was might puncture that confidence. Yet, she had no choice. He had to hear the truth. They couldn't marry without Alex knowing everything.

She swallowed. "I have something that I must tell you as well."

"I look forward to hearing everything. But first, let's get you back to rights." He stood and stepped into the bedchamber, returning with a tray of food. "You need to eat and finish your bath. And then we'll talk."

"Yes." She ran her fingertip over the ring on her finger. "We do need to have a discussion before going forward." She was proud of her work and would never apologize for it. She was done lying about being the finest mapmaker in London, perhaps all of England. Rose was prepared to step out of the shadows and accept any accolades that were due her. If Alex had any qualms about that, it was best that they both knew it before wedding.

He broke off a piece of cold chicken and fed it to her. "Delicious." She chewed slowly, savoring the bite. "But that might have something to do with the hand that feeds me."

"If I have to prepare every bite to make you better, I will happily do so."

She accepted another morsel, this time allowing her lips to linger on his fingers. "I could become very accustomed to being spoiled."

He sucked in his breath. "Behave. You need to eat."

"Maybe I have other needs as well."

"The faster you eat, the more quickly I can tend to your other needs." She allowed him to feed her several more bites and she drank a glass of lemonade. She felt much better. The food and drink gave her strength.

After she'd eaten all of the chicken, he fed her a

strawberry. It was red, plump and juicy. She sucked his finger into her mouth. Coming back to herself meant reclaiming everything. She enjoyed sexual congress and wouldn't hide it from her future husband.

He groaned as she drew his finger deeper into her mouth. "Rose."

"The water is getting a little too cold."

"I thought you were in a rush to get out of the bath in a strange house."

"Now I'm eager for you to get into the bath." She dipped her chin and regarded him through her lashes. "I've never made love in a bathtub before."

"Dammit!" He surged to his feet, kicking his boots off, tugging and pulling until his feet were bare. "You are impossible to resist." His clothes followed. Rose watched unabashedly, desire pounding in her veins. He tore off his shirt, baring his glorious chest, and pushed his breeches off.

He jumped into the bath with her, splashing water all over the floor. Laughing, she embraced him. "You're making a mess."

"By the time we are through, it'll be much worse." His lips latched on to hers. She kissed him hungrily, not holding back. She wanted him to know all of her before they fully committed to each other. He slid down to suckle her breast. She moaned.

"Do you like that?" he asked.

"I *love* it."

He maneuvered her around until his back was against the tub and she was straddling him. His hand dipped to between her legs. "How about this?"

She arched her back. "That's even better."

His mouth latched on to her breast again. "You are a goddess."

Her hand slipped under the water to grasp his hard length. "Is this all right?"

He grimaced with pleasure. "A little firmer. It won't break."

"I should hope not." She tightened her grip. "I need my husband to be in full working order."

He reached up to kiss her while they explored each other's bodies; water sloshed over the sides. Their hands ran urgently over each other.

"Come here." He lifted her, positioning her so that she sat on the edge of the tub. "Hold on tight."

"What are you doing?"

He pushed her legs apart. "I'm going to taste you."

"Oh." Curiosity flared as she watched him position his face so that he was staring directly into the most intimate part of her. "Are you certain?"

"Oh, *yes*." He put his mouth on her. His tongue flat against her, he lapped long strokes up and down her private area, teasing the bundle of nerves where sensation was centered.

She spread her legs wider as a shiver of pleasure rolled through her.

"Good girl." He rewarded her using his fingers to part her, to allow him better access. Then he flexed his tongue against the excruciatingly sensitive nub. She almost crumbled from the impact. Thank goodness there was a wall behind her to hold Rose up.

His breath hot against her, he increased the pressure, kissing and licking until she could barely stand it. She watched him through half-closed eyes, the sight of his head between her legs unbearably erotic. She ran her hands through his hair and pulled him closer. With a murmur of approval, he started to suck on her. All of that sensitivity in his mouth sent her over the edge. She lost all control and cried out, collapsing into the tub with a splash.

"Hold on to the sides of the tub." He positioned her over him and Rose sank down onto him. "Yes, just like that."

Gripping the sides of the tub, Rose began to move over him, deep strokes followed by more shallow ones, letting the sensations guide her body. She began to move in circular motions; everything was magnificently sensitive and the tension in her body started to tighten again.

Alex moaned. "Damnation." He held on to the sides of the tub as if his life depended upon it, letting her have her way with him. He gave Rose full control, allowing her to explore, which she'd never done with Roger, who'd insisted on always manipulating every part of their interactions in bed.

Alex thrust himself into her, firm and determined, like he couldn't get enough. Bracing one hand on the tub, he slipped the other between her legs. It was all too much and exactly what she needed. The tension in her broke, pleasure overflowing. She collapsed into Alex as he pumped vigorously into her a few more times before finding his release.

Chapter Eighteen

*A*fterward, Brandon wrapped his arms around Rose as she lay back against him in the tub. His heart beat hard, his body still shimmering with the aftereffects of their lovemaking. He relished the feel of her body against his, unable to recall ever feeling more content and hopeful about the future.

This time Rose hadn't held back. She proved to be a full partner in their lovemaking, taking what she wanted without waiting for him to take the lead. The effect was intoxicating. He nuzzled her neck. "Being with you like that was beyond anything I could have imagined."

She smiled, pressing her lips against his forearm, which wrapped across her upper chest. "I am not too bold for you?"

"Is there such a thing?" He nipped her shoulder. "But I must say you surprised me. The previous times we lay together, it was wonderful, but you were more . . ."

"I held myself back."

"Did you? But why?"

"Roger said I was too forward when it came to bed sport. I feared you would think the same."

He stiffened. The thought of that whoreson laying his hands on Rose was bad enough. To think that he'd shamed her for enjoying herself made him want to pummel the man. "He's a bastard who never deserved you. I want you as you are. The real you. I want no artifice or untruths between us."

She paused. "Should we have that talk now?"

He didn't want this moment to end. But it was time. After all, revealing his true identity was the purpose of this visit to Peckham House. "I think we should get out of the bath and be fully dressed to have a proper conversation." He cupped her breast and ran his thumb over her nipple. "There are far too many distractions in this tub."

She turned her head for a long, leisurely kiss. "Not to mention that the owner of this mansion could come in and find us."

"I told you there is no danger of that."

She rose, the water rushing from her body. "You certainly are being mysterious about your connection to the man this house belongs to."

"All in good time." He wanted to sit back and fully enjoy the view but forced himself to stand. They rubbed each other dry with the towels, stealing kisses and love bites as they did so. They'd just dressed when an urgent knock sounded at the door.

"Sir . . . erm . . . Alex." Stokes's muffled voice sounded through the door. Why the devil was his butler interrupting? He was supposed to have the afternoon off, along with the rest of the staff. Once Rose's bath and food were prepared, Brandon had dismissed all the servants for the day. He wanted them out of the house so he and

Rose could have complete privacy. He imagined telling her the truth, addressing any of her lingering concerns, and then, if he was very fortunate, making love anywhere in his house that struck their fancy.

"Why don't you return to the bedchamber?" he suggested to Rose. "I'll join you shortly."

"Is something wrong?"

"Not that I am aware of." Once she went through and closed the door behind her, Brandon pulled open the door. "What is it, Stokes? I told you I didn't want to be interrupted."

The butler presented a note. "It's from your steward at Highfield. There's been a fire."

Brandon's alarm rose as he read the note. The West Wing, the guest wing, had been damaged. More importantly, two of the grooms were badly injured trying to fight the blaze. The staff awaited Brandon's instructions on how to proceed. "Send word to Highfield that I shall come immediately."

"Very good, my lord. Shall I pack your bag?"

Brandon didn't employ a valet so certain tasks fell to Stokes. "Yes, please see to it."

After the butler departed, Brandon joined Rose in the marchioness's bed chamber. He'd told her it was a guest chamber when in truth, it would be her room once they wed and she became mistress of both Peckham House and Highfield.

He found her examining a painting, a landscape that had been one of his mother's favorites. "This is beautiful."

"Rose, an urgent matter has come up."

She faced him. "Is everything all right?"

"There's been a fire at my family property."

"At the farm?"

"And people have been injured. I must go."

Concern flashed in her face. "Is your family well? Were they hurt?"

"My family is safe, but I must see to the others."

"Of course. I understand completely."

"I'll escort you home in a hackney. When I return, we will hash everything out." He pressed a kiss against her lips. "And then we shall be married as soon as possible."

ROSE MISSED ALEX terribly. She couldn't wait to begin a life with him, to live and love and work together at the shop. The prospect of waking up with him every morning seemed like a marvelous dream. She received one note from Alex about ten days after he left London, telling her that matters at home were taking longer than he expected and that he missed her.

She slowly regained her strength by eating and sleeping well, and resumed her long walks. Although she still felt fatigued and sometimes took an afternoon nap, Rose's creativity and productivity returned, allowing her to produce some of her best work ever.

Fortunately, the shop also occupied much of her time, which kept her from pining too terribly for her betrothed. Uncle Trevor's former workers, the ones Roger had replaced, all agreed to come back and work for her. She spent a few hours at the shop each day and hoped that Alex would agree to take over most of the day-to-day operations when he returned. She wanted to focus on her maps and product development.

Three weeks after Alex's departure, Rose paid a call on the Duchess of Huntington and was immediately shown to the library. She'd finally completed the Greece maps for the duchess's book. They were slated to be printed in black-and-white in the duchess's book rather than the colorful creations Rose normally produced for clients by hand once they'd been engraved. She'd added new flourishes to make the black-and-white maps more special. She hoped the duchess approved. Leela joined her in the library, trailed by a young girl with enormous chocolate eyes and curling hair of the same shade.

"My dear Rose." To her surprise, Leela pulled her in for a warm hug. Rose hugged her back somewhat awkwardly. She hadn't realized the duchess was such an effusive person. "What wonderful news."

"I'm pleased to inform you that I've completed the project." She withdrew the maps from her worn leather satchel and spread them over the library table. "I can make any changes you require."

Leela's eyes twinkled. "Straight to business, I see."

Rose resisted the urge to pace while Leela examined her work. Her first major independent project needed to be well received in order for her future solo endeavors to prosper. The child clutched a handful of her mother's skirts while she peered up at Rose.

The duchess took her time studying each map. "These are remarkable. The little embellishments are wonderful, the hills, the trees. The details in your replica of the Parthenon are exceptional, especially considering how small it is."

Relief and pride cascaded through Rose. "I experimented with some new techniques to make these maps special on their own since they will not be in color."

"You did a magnificent job."

"If you have any suggested modifications, I'd be happy to address them."

"I have none that I can think of. I trust your judgment. After all, you are the expert mapmaker here." She smiled brightly. "And besides," Leela said meaningfully, "you wouldn't cheat a family member."

Rose tilted her head. "Pardon?"

Leela paused, a tiny frown marring her lovely face. "Erm. Forgive me." She gave an uneasy laugh. "I was up all night writing and I'm half-delirious from the lack of sleep."

"Of course," Rose said. "So you do find the maps acceptable?"

"Without question."

The child finally spoke. "Your eyes are very blue."

Rose smiled down at her. "People have told me that since I was a very little girl."

The girl looked to her mother. "Is the map lady with the bright eyes going to be my new auntie?"

Rose shot a puzzled look at Leela.

The duchess reddened. "Darling, why don't you go and find Nurse. See if she'll give you a treat."

"Are you?" The girl stared up at Rose. "Are you going to marry Uncle Alex and be my new auntie?"

"Maryam!" Leela spoke rapidly to the girl in Arabic.

"Why not?" the girl responded to her obviously agitated mother. "Uncle Alex told me he is going to marry a lady who draws pretty maps."

Panic flashed in Leela's eyes as she darted a look at Rose. "Children!" she said with a forced smile.

"Alex?" Rose looked from Leela to the child and back again. "Do you know Alex?"

"He's my uncle." Maryam lifted her chin. "He's going to give me a horse."

"Are you referring to my footman?" Unease slithered through Rose's stomach. "What is going on here?"

Leela pressed her lips inward. "Oh, Rose, I am so sorry."

Rose fought off a rising sense of dread. "For what?"

Leela took a deep breath. "I assumed Alex told you the truth before he left for his country estate. Obviously, I was mistaken."

"What truth?"

"That you're my new auntie!" the child interjected with a happy smile.

Leela set a gentle hand on the girl's head but kept her attention on Rose. "I stopped by Peckham House a few days ago and Stokes said Alex brought you by the house. I assumed he took you there to show you your future home after telling you the truth."

"My future home?" Rose couldn't make sense of Leela's words. "I think there's been some mistake."

"I shouldn't say anything more. Brandon . . . erm . . . Alex, I mean . . . should be the one to explain everything."

Rose shook her head. "But I don't know when Alex will return." What did Alex have to do with the Marquess of Brandon?

Leela squeezed her arm. "Just know that he cares deeply for you."

"Who does?" It didn't seem possible.

"My brother Alex, the Marquess of Brandon."

"Alex is Brandon?" She finally managed to form the thought in her mind. "But he's a footman."

"Come and sit, dear." Leela gently ushered Rose over to a sofa. "This is no doubt a great shock."

"Mama, I'm going to get my treat from Nurse," Maryam announced before skipping out of the room.

Rose sat in a daze. "Of late, my life seems to have become one big shock after another."

"Brandon should be the person to tell you everything, but it is also not fair to leave you dangling." Leela went to pour a glass of water. "The truth is that Alex, your footman, is Alexander Worthington, the Marquess of Brandon. My brother."

"Your brother? That's why your daughter called him Uncle Alex?" Rose felt like she'd been struck with a hammer. "Alex isn't a footman?"

"You must have noticed that he seemed out of place in the servants' hall."

"Oh." Snippets of their time together rushed back as the truth fell into place. Of course Alex wasn't a footman. Rose had sensed that something was off with him from the very first. Alex's innate arrogance, the lack of deference and his terrible footman skills, why he'd never truly fit in as household staff, made perfectly awful sense.

Rose hadn't bothered to follow the obvious clues because she'd been too busy ogling the man. And cherishing their friendship. A knife twisted in her chest. There was no Alex. It was all a lie. "Why would he pretend to be a footman?"

"He has his reasons, but that is for him to tell you." Leela pressed the glass into Rose's hand. "Drink this."

She stared at the duchess. "You knew about this? *You*

are a part of this?" What kind of scheme was this? "Is that why you engaged me to draw your maps?"

"No, absolutely not! I wanted you to create my maps because I was absolutely charmed by your work the day I walked into the shop. That is the sole reason I decided to hire you instead of Mr. Fleming. I only learned of Brandon's plan after I asked you to create the maps for my book."

"His plan?"

Leela pursed her lips. "He's a scoundrel of the first order for not telling you everything before he left for Highfield."

"Was there really even a fire?" The inside of her mouth was as dry as sandpaper. "Or was that a lie, too?"

"That much is true. There was a terrible fire that injured two of his staff and did some damage to the West Wing of the house."

Alex possessed a house large enough to have *separate wings*? "But he lied about everything else." The future she managed to rebuild for herself after Roger's betrayal crumbled. Alex the footman didn't exist. He was just a mirage. Part of someone's scheme to do . . . what?

"Alex should explain everything to you himself. I've put my foot in it already." Leela squeezed Rose's hand. "But please do not doubt that he cares very, very deeply for you."

A harsh laugh erupted from her throat. "He certainly has a devastating way of showing it."

"You have every reason to be angry and upset," Leela said sympathetically, "but I honestly believe my brother holds you in the highest esteem."

"Your brother is a stranger to me." She set her jaw. "The Alex I thought I knew doesn't exist."

"YOU CHANGED THE locks at home as well?" Roger barked at Rose the moment he barged into the shop. "You had no right to do that! *My name* is on that lease."

"Hello, Roger."

Ben, who'd been her uncle's most able employee, appeared from the back of the shop. "Is this man giving you trouble, Mrs. Fleming?"

"No, everything is all right, Ben. Thank you." Ben shot Roger a contemptuous look before vanishing into the back.

"*Mrs. Fleming?*" Roger smirked. "I see you are still using my name to give you the shine of respectability."

Rose had anticipated this visit ever since two locksmiths appeared and changed the locks in the house the day after Alex's . . . no . . . *Brandon's* departure to his country estate. Rose insisted on thinking of that scapegrace as Brandon to remind herself that the Alex who was dear to her had never really existed. By changing the locks, his lordship—she still couldn't quite believe a marquess had scrubbed her dirty shoes and brushed out her clothes—was obviously trying to be protective, but he'd neglected to shield Rose from the greatest danger— Brandon himself.

"Alex changed the locks," she informed Roger, feeling no compunction at all to protect the marquess. "You may take up any concerns you have with him."

"The footman?" His eyes bulged. "How dare he? You must have directed him to do so. He *is* your betrothed."

Rose returned to straightening the shop shelves. "I was as surprised as you."

Roger's appearance at the shop came three days after Leela's shocking revelation. Rose still reeled from the truth about Brandon and she had a million questions for the reprobate once he deigned to return to Town.

But she wouldn't allow him to destroy her. She'd drawn on all of her strength to survive Roger's treachery. She refused to allow another man to break her down again. She still had her shop and her talents and could very well forge her own future alone. Rose would never again give any man the opportunity to betray her.

"Why don't you take your concerns to Mr. Henry, the landlord?" she asked Roger.

"I already have. Henry refused to see me. All his servant would say is that Henry was aware of the change. It makes no sense at all!"

It made perfect sense. The marquess had obviously exerted his power and influence over Mr. Henry. He'd probably shown his appreciation in gold.

"This needs to be over now, Rose," Roger snapped. "I have reached the end of my patience."

"As have I," she retorted. "You have no idea."

"I will tell the world that you are not Mrs. Fleming. Will a publisher produce the duchess's book if it is known that a woman of questionable reputation drew the maps? Think of the scandal."

"How will your fellow villagers react once they know how you deceived me? You will not emerge unscathed if you reveal the truth about our marriage."

"Not unscathed, perhaps, but a man can survive scandal with just a dent to his reputation. A woman, on the other hand, is never again acknowledged by decent people."

Frustration roiled her insides. He was right. "You are contemptible. Get out of my store."

"Just give me my shop back, Rose. That's all I ask."

"Why don't you go and find another position? You're a surveyor and an engraver."

"I have tried but no one will engage me at the moment. Give me the shop back. You continue drawing maps. We'll view it as a business arrangement," he cajoled. "You can even continue your liaison with the footman, as long as you are discreet."

She gritted her teeth. "I said get out of my shop. And don't come back."

"One week." He pointed a finger at her. "I shall give you seven more days to come to your senses. And then I shall make the truth known. I'll start with every shop owner on this street and I'll go from there."

Rose clenched her fists. Roger was so certain he had her cornered. She was fed up with duplicitous men throwing her life off course. It was time to deal with Roger in her own way.

And then she'd decide what to do about Brandon.

Chapter Nineteen

*R*ose stepped into the vestibule at St. Andrews in Holborn.

She'd married Roger, or thought she had, in this church four years ago. Her memories of the day were fuzzy. She hadn't yet recovered from the shock of Uncle Trevor's sudden death. She vaguely recalled shifting her gaze from the red-faced rector to stare up at the coffered ceiling while exchanging vows at the altar.

Her gaze landed on notices posted on the wall. Among them were several banns, legal notices that proclaimed a couple's intention to wed. Roger had gotten a special license to avoid posting the banns, so that he could more easily erase all traces of their nuptials.

But how careful was he? If Roger made even one slipup, Rose would find it. She'd use proof of Roger's bigamy as leverage to stop him from ruining her reputation. And then she'd be able to tell Alex . . . Brandon . . . to go to the devil. She'd save her reputation and her business on her own. She was done with men who let her down.

"May I help you?" asked a compassionate voice. Rose turned to greet a full-faced man with a ruddy complexion.

"Are you the rector?"

There was a welcoming smile in his kind eyes. "I am."

He looked vaguely familiar. "I believe you performed the marriage ceremony for my husband and me."

He blinked. "Did I?"

"It was on July 16, 1813."

He studied her for a moment. Then his face lit up. "I believe I do recall. I remember thinking that the bride possessed the bluest eyes I've ever seen."

The tightness between her shoulder blades eased. He *remembered*. Thank goodness her eyes made a lasting impression. "I was hoping to look at the registry that we signed."

If she found their names, she'd have proof that she and Roger were married. It also helped that the rector recalled performing the ceremony. She prayed Roger hadn't been as careful as he'd thought. Hopefully, he assumed Rose would be too embarrassed or ashamed to visit the church to verify his story.

"Very well. If you will follow me." The church kept the old registries in a special room off the altar. There were dozens of them, a testament to the church's long-time roots in the community.

"Ah, here it is. This is the register that should contain your marriage lines." The older man opened the book and leafed through. He paused and frowned. "Hmmm. It should be right here."

Rose's stomach sank. "You cannot find evidence of our marriage."

"It looks like the page containing your marriage lines was torn out." Consternation crossed his face. "But who would do such a thing?"

Someone who'd been well paid to do it. "Would there be any other record of our marriage?"

"The special license."

Which Roger had either disposed of or hidden away. *There's no public proof of our marriage*, Roger had said. Public proof. Which meant what? That he'd kept private proof?

"And the banns, of course," the rector added.

"The banns? But Mr. Fleming obtained a special license."

"Even so, in this church we require that the banns be posted."

"What happens to the banns certificate after the marriage has been conducted?"

"The couple will often keep them. We store the ones that are left behind as part of our records."

Rose vaguely recalled seeing the special license. But she'd never laid eyes on the certificate of the banns. Her pulse leaped. "Could it be here?"

"Let me look," the rector said. "We normally keep them in a box, sorted by year." He pulled a box from a nearby shelf and looked through it. "Ah, here is your year. Here's the month of July."

Rose held her breath. Did the box contain the key to saving her reputation and her business, thus freeing her from a forced marriage to a lying cheat?

The rector shook his head. "Unfortunately, it's not here. I am sorry, Mrs. Fleming. But there is no proof of your marriage here at the church."

BRANDON PEERED OUT the window as the carriage turned onto New Street. He'd rushed back to London the moment he received Leela's note. *Rose knew the truth.* He had to see her immediately, to explain himself. He needed to smooth everything over and set matters to rights between them. Surely, Rose would be understanding once he explained why he'd pretended to be a footman.

They pulled up to find Owen sweeping the front steps. The boy's eyes rounded as Brandon emerged from his shiny black-and-yellow conveyance. "Gor, guv! Where'd you get that coach?"

"Owen," he asked impatiently, "is Mrs. Fleming at home?"

Owen's owlish eyes took in Brandon's snowy cravat, fine tailcoat and fawn leather breeches. In his haste to reach Rose, he'd neglected to don his usual workman-like clothing. But it no longer mattered since Rose knew the truth.

The boy stared at Brandon's gleaming Hessians. "Where'd you get them boots?"

"I must see Mrs. Fleming." He set up the stairs.

"Yer not using the servants' entrance?"

"I don't think Mrs. Fleming will mind."

"She might. Seein' that she gave away all of yer clothes. Said somethin' about never seein' you again."

That didn't bode well. "Where is she?"

Owen clamped his mouth shut and held out his open palm. Brandon dropped a few coins into it. "Well?"

"She's in 'er sitting room."

He passed the boy and went inside, taking the steps two at a time. He almost bumped into Bess as he rounded the corner to Rose's rooms.

"Alex!" She stared at him. "You look like a lord!"

"Hello, Bess. I am in a hurry to see Mrs. Fleming."

"I thought you were gone. Mrs. Fleming gave me one of yer coats for my brother."

"That was generous," he called back over his shoulder. "He is welcome to keep it."

When he reached Rose's door, he knocked before going in. She was at her desk, working. His eye caught on the map laid out on the sofa table. It was the one he'd hidden in his attic room.

"Just leave the tea tray on the table, if you please, Mrs. Waller."

"It's not Mrs. Waller."

Her sketching hand stilled. She drew back her shoulders and took a long inhale before standing. She finally turned to face him. She was a vision, with vivid eyes and long and loose golden hair. She wore an asymmetrical green tunic with fringed edges over her pale yellow gown. "It's you," she said coolly. "What are you doing here?"

"I see you found my map."

Her icy-blue gaze met his. "That map belongs to the Marquess of Brandon."

"Yes," he said gently, "it does."

Her eyes dropped down his body. "I see you are no longer bothering to assume your humble laboring-man disguise."

"I am sorry you had to learn the truth the way you did. You deserve better."

"I certainly do. But I'm apparently destined to be associated with men who commit unforgivable acts of treachery and betrayal."

His heart turned over. "I never intended to hurt you. I tried to tell you."

"Was that before or after you bedded me?"

"What happened between us, the intimacy, was very real."

"I agree. It just didn't mean what I thought it did."

"I have deep feelings for you. I might have lied. But my care for you, my ardent desire to marry you, is genuine."

Her laugh was bitter. "You really are no better than Roger. He enjoyed bedding me as well. And both of you did so under false pretenses."

"I am nothing like him."

"You would like to believe that, wouldn't you?"

"I came here because of Roger Fleming. I know he cheated me and I was desperate to prove it. I needed an excuse to get into this house and search for evidence."

"Did you bed me so you could search my rooms?"

"No! I bedded you because you found your way into my heart. I searched your chambers when you were out with Fleming."

"Did you find what you were looking for?"

"No, but I did find something far rarer and precious. A wife of my own heart."

"We are not wed yet."

"Regardless, when I look at you, I see my future." He was desperate for her to understand. "Fleming drew that map that cheated me out of my land. His borders have cut access to an important source of water for my tenant farmers."

She flushed. "That's impossible. Those maps are very carefully laid out. Roger understands how important it is for the maps to be precise. Our reputation depends upon it. If word spread that we produced an inaccurate survey, our reputation would be destroyed."

"There is an ancient stone fence that has always served as the dividing line between my property and that of my neighbor, Charles Canning. I believe Canning paid Roger to ignore the fence in order to alter the property lines in his favor."

"But that is madness!" She lost all aloofness. "Our maps draw top prices. One imprecision like the one you describe could do irreversible damage to our enterprise."

"Maybe Canning made Fleming an offer he felt he could not refuse."

She took a deep breath and looked directly into his eyes. "Roger did not draw that map."

"*You did.*"

Somehow, he'd known it all along. The exquisite details, the charm and creativity. Fleming had neither the talent nor the imagination to create such extraordinary masterpieces. But the woman standing before Brandon did.

"You draw all of the maps." Admiration pulsed through him. "Fleming was just a cover."

"Clients will not pay a woman what her talents are worth. Men can demand a much higher wage."

"What an extraordinary talent you are. Does Fleming even know how to draw a map?"

"Very rudimentary ones. No one would pay good money for them."

"Did Leela discover the truth about you? Is that why she engaged you to create the maps for her book?"

"No one knows the truth about my maps except me and Roger. And now, you."

He didn't doubt her. The maps were like the woman, vibrant and unique. "But you never came out to survey my property."

Anger flashed in her eyes. "Roger insisted that he would do it. He never mentioned any stone fence. A marker like that is an obvious dividing line between two properties."

"Does he always do all of the surveying for your maps?"

"No, I prefer to see the property myself. It allows the topography in my maps to be more detailed and personalized. But Roger said the Marquess of Brandon didn't want a female surveyor on his land."

He stepped forward. "He's lying. He never asked permission for you to visit Highfield. I never met the man before I began working here. Fleming came to Highfield when I was away."

"And you believe he purposely recorded the wrong information and omitted the stone fence."

"Either that, or he got the correct information and disregarded it when Canning showed up and bribed him. I've found no evidence in this house. I intend to search Irene Fleming's cottage next."

"You believe Roger might hide important documents there?"

"It's possible. Fleming is in possession of a damning note that Canning wrote that I believe is related to their plan to cheat me."

"How do you know that?"

"I overheard them talking. I know the note exists. I just have to find it." He stepped toward her. She stepped back. "You must understand, this was all about correcting an injustice."

"No matter who was harmed in the process?"

"I never intended to hurt you," he said ardently, "especially not after I met you. I resolved to do nothing that would harm you."

Her pink mouth twisted. "That worked out rather well, didn't it?"

"The reason I took you to Peckham House was to tell you the truth. But then you were overcome by the heat and one thing led to the next and then we got word of the fire at Highfield."

"Even if you had told me then, it would have already been too late. In any case, it no longer matters."

"Of course it does. I still want to marry you."

"Everything about our association was built on a lie."

"That's not so. You might not have known my true name and circumstances, but Alex the footman and the Marquess of Brandon are the same man."

"And that man deceived me," she said sadly. "You cannot imagine that I would ever give you the opportunity to hurt me again. What a fool I would be."

"I will spend the rest of my life making it up to you. Please allow me to give you the protection of my name. *Stay with me.* I missed you madly when I was away. I am not certain I could bear a life without you."

Her eyes glistened. "And I am not certain that I could bear a life with you."

"TELL ME WHAT I can do," Alex pleaded.

It was almost like talking to a different man. Rose couldn't stop seeing Alex's resemblance to his sister. He and Leela shared the same eyes.

How had she not seen it earlier?

His tailcoat was expensive and well fitted; his boots gleamed. He'd finally donned clothing that matched his innate arrogance. Alex slipped into the role of titled aristocrat like a fitted glove. Alex the footman had been slightly awkward and unsure, despite his lack of deference and ready confidence. The Marquess of Brandon radiated cool self-assurance. Except for the urgency in his voice.

"Please, Rose, just tell me what I can do to fix this and I shall do it."

She wanted to tell him to go straight to hades. To rage at him for deceiving her and obliterating any trust she had in him.

But she could not. She hadn't found the necessary proof to save herself. Rose knew, even before Alex arrived, that she had to go forward with their marriage. Like Roger, this man had taken away all of her options.

"I will not give up my mapmaking."

Surprise lit his face. "I would never ask you to."

"I won't give up the shop, either."

"Agreed." His puzzled gaze searched hers. "Are we discussing the terms of our marriage?"

"And I refuse to conceal the fact that I am a mapmaker."

"You should shout it from the rooftops. I would if I possessed your talents."

She narrowed her eyes at him. "Why do you want to marry me? You're a marquess."

"With you I don't have to dream. You *are* the dream."

"Wedding a laboring woman would be an embarrassment to any nobleman."

"I want you, Rose. Ultimately, it's as simple as that. As the Arabs say, I have seen many eyes, but I only get lost in yours."

Her heart clenched but she immediately hardened herself against sentimentality. Softening gave Alex the power to hurt her again.

"Very well. You are a grown man who has made his bed." Now he could lie in it. Just not with her. "I want a separate bedchamber."

"The chamber you saw at Peckham House is the marchioness's room. The door opposite the bathing room connects to my rooms."

"I insist that you not make use of that door." She crossed her arms over her chest and tried not to wince at the tenderness in her breasts. Her courses were overdue. "Unless you are invited."

He turned his head slightly, regarding her with a sideways glance. "Am I to understand that such an invitation will not be forthcoming any time in the near future?"

"You may assume that."

"Very well. I certainly don't intend to force myself on you. I'll win you back."

"We shall live separate lives."

"Absolutely not." He set his jaw. "I am not getting married to be alone. I agree not to visit your bedchamber until you invite me, but we shall take our meals together."

Her neck muscles rigidified. "I prefer breakfast in my rooms, as you well know. It is the way of married women."

"Supper, then. And tea in the afternoon."

"I take my tea alone while I work."

"I shall join you for tea." His voice was firm. "Wherever you choose to take it."

She saw he would not budge. "You will not limit my time at the shop. I shall come and go as I please."

"Agreed. However, as my marchioness, you will be expected to visit the tenants now and again."

"I think I can manage to mingle with the common people," she said drily. "After all, they are my people."

"And mine," he pointed out. "My mother's family is in trade. Also, there is nothing common about you."

"I am already negotiating the terms of our marriage. There's no need to flatter me in order to sway my decision."

"The words are sincerely felt and said." He paused. "But I must warn you—"

"Shall I brace myself for more dark secrets?"

"You should know that, although you will want for nothing, it will not always be easy to be wed to the son of the Mad Marquess and his foreign-born, merchant-class wife. There will be challenges. Not everyone will accept our union and invite us into their homes."

"I hardly view that as a downside. I have maps to create and a business to oversee. Not being able to make small talk with snobbish nobles will not hurt my feelings."

"There are our future children to consider."

"How so?"

"They will face some social hardships. Leela and I were not always welcomed in certain quarters of the ton. Our offspring can expect to face the same lack of warmth."

"I see." She hadn't thought of that.

"However, they shall find camaraderie with Leela's children, as well as any offspring my cousin Hanna will have. She is wed to a viscount."

Her mouth dropped open. "And he allows her to continue bonesetting?"

"I suspect Griffin couldn't stop Hanna even if he tried."

Queasiness stirred in her stomach. "Very well. How soon can we be married?"

"I've obtained a special license."

"I see you have thought of everything."

"I know you are only consenting to marry me in order to ward off scandal and to save your reputation. But I vow to work every day to earn your forgiveness and your trust."

She wondered if that was possible. "We are agreed, then. Shall we marry next week?"

"Yes." Hope shone in his face. "Absolutely."

Nausea swirled in her chest. Her mouth watered. She hadn't expected such a strong physical reaction to yet another upheaval in her life. "Send word about the arrangements. Until then, I prefer that you refrain from visiting me."

His face fell. "Rose. I know I've hurt you—"

"Good day." The urge to cast her accounts bubbled up into the base of her throat. "I shall see you next week."

"Very well." He reluctantly accepted her decision. "I shall send word about the timing of the wedding."

He'd barely closed the door behind him before Rose rushed into her bedchamber and fell to the floor before her chamber pot. She retched and emptied the contents of her stomach. Afterward, she rinsed the sour taste out of her mouth and pressed a cool, damp cloth against her face.

Feeling very tired, she rose and climbed into bed. And fell into a deep, dreamless sleep.

UNSETTLED, BRANDON TROTTED down the stairs. He'd gotten the result he wanted but it felt like a hollow victory. Rose would be his wife in name only. The last thing he wanted was a cold marriage.

Still, he had hope. Rose was a naturally warm woman with a good heart. He'd win her back. As his wife, she'd be in close proximity. He'd find ways to apologize to her over and over, to eventually persuade her to give him another chance to prove himself worthy.

The household staff suddenly materialized when he reached the front hall. They immediately pelted him with questions.

"What are you about?" Dudley eyed him suspiciously. "Owen here told us you were dressed like a duke."

"The mistress said you are no longer employed here," Mrs. Waller added.

"I told you 'e ain't no footman." Owen tossed the coin Brandon had given him earlier in the air. "A servant don't tip nobody like this."

"Why *are* you dressed like a nob, Alex?" Bess asked.

To Brandon's surprise he'd missed this group. Their meals belowstairs, shared cramped attic quarters and executing certain tedious chores in tandem, had built a friendship of sorts. "I do owe you all the truth."

"What truth?" Dudley growled. "Are you saying you've been lying to us?"

"Of course 'e's lying." Owen pocketed his coin.

"''E ain't no footman any more than I'm the king of England. 'E didn't even know what a footman's pantry was when 'e got 'ere."

Brandon pretended to frown at the boy. "I ought to demand all of my money back from you for being an incessant chatterbox."

"He paid you money?" Mrs. Waller's disapproving gaze drilled into Owen. "For what?"

"To show 'im 'ow to be a footman."

"Owen is correct," Brandon told them. "I am not a footman."

"The boy says you showed up in a fine carriage," Bess said. "Where'd you get it?"

"It belongs to me."

Dudley snorted. "Balderdash!"

"There was fancy writing on 'is carriage," Owen reported to his rapt audience, describing the Brandon insignia. "Like the toffs 'ave. Maybe 'e *is* a toff."

Four sets of eyes swung to Brandon. "Are you?" Mrs. Waller half whispered. "Is your father a lord?"

"He was. But his title passed to me upon his death."

"What are you?" Dudley demanded to know. "Are you some sort of baron?"

"I'm a marquess."

They froze, staring at him. Then they all burst out laughing. "That's a good one," Dudley guffawed.

"I'll say!" Mrs. Waller bent over, racked with mirth, pressing her hand to her stomach. "Imagine a marquess cleaning mud off a tradesman's shoes."

Bess wiped tears from her eyes. "Or a lord sitting down to meals with the likes of us!"

Only Owen maintained a serious expression. "I knowed

it from the first. 'E talked too fancy even when 'e tried not to."

"Owen has the right of it. I am the Marquess of Brandon. Mrs. Fleming is going to be my wife. We shall be wed before the month is out."

The laughter subsided. The three adult servants exchanged uneasy looks.

"Did something happen to Mr. Fleming?" Mrs. Waller's mouth dropped open. "Is Mr. Fleming dead?"

"The marriage is being . . . has been annulled," he said.

"Annulled?" they all said together.

"Indeed. It was not a legitimate marriage."

Bess elbowed Dudley. "I told you. The master always kept to his chamber. And the mistress always to hers."

"It explains why there ain't no children," Dudley replied.

"I know you ain't no footman," Owen said, "but are you truly a marquess?"

"I am."

Owen slapped his thigh. "I always known it. 'E didn't know nothing about cleaning boots. What footman doesn't know 'ow to make blacking?"

"But why would a marquess go into service?" Dudley asked.

"I have my reasons, which shall remain private." He drew a breath. "But I do owe you an apology for not being truthful."

"Maybe 'e ain't a marquess after all," Owen muttered. "I ain't never 'eard of the quality beggin' the servants' pardon."

Concern lined Mrs. Waller's forehead. "What is going to happen to the house?"

"I imagine that it will be shut down, emptied and returned to its owner even though the lease isn't up yet."

Bess's chin quivered. "But what's going to become of us?"

Dudley twisted his lips. "He showed up lying about who he is and now yer leaving all of us without a situation?"

"About that," Brandon said to him. "You've said you'd like to be a gentleman's valet and I find myself in need of one."

Dudley sputtered. "Truly, Alex . . . erm . . . your lordship?"

"Truly." He turned to Mrs. Waller. "I am also in need of a housekeeper. Because I am rarely in London, I have kept a skeleton staff in Town. But now that I am to be married, I expect my future wife will want to spend a great deal of time in London. Consequently, we shall need sufficient staff."

Mrs. Waller flushed. "It would be an honor, my lord."

"And you, Bess, I'm certain we shall be in need of a parlor maid."

"Oh! Thank you, sir! Erm . . . my lord! I never imagined I'd be a parlor maid in the home of a marquess."

Owen cleared his throat. "And what about me?"

Brandon resisted the urge to smile. "What about you?"

Alarm flitted across the boy's face. "Yer not just goin' to leave me 'ere, are you?"

"How would you like to be my tiger?"

His scrawny face lit up. "That'd be real fine, Alex. Real fine."

"Show some respect, child." Mrs. Waller swatted at

him but Owen ducked out of the way. "His name isn't Alex. You must refer to him as my lord or his lordship."

Brandon smiled as they all erupted into excited chatter. But he noticed they now lowered their eyes rather than looking directly at him, and they spoke to Brandon with a newfound deference. Alex the footman was truly gone. Brandon would never be one of them again. And for a moment he experienced a fleeting sense of loss.

Chapter Twenty

They married on a Saturday morning. At her first wedding, a grief-stricken Rose was in a fog over Uncle Trevor's sudden death. Her second time at the altar, she fought waves of nausea as she bound herself to a man who'd deceived her.

But there was no denying that Alex looked exceptionally handsome in his dark suit and snowy cravat. His gaze holding hers, he repeated the vows that bound them together with solemn earnestness. His ebony eyes shone with such intense tenderness that Rose had to look away. How easy it would be for her to fall under his spell again. She must always stay on her guard.

Afterward, Leela hugged her hard while her husband, the duke, heartily shook Alex's hand. They parted ways on the steps of the church because Rose declined to have a celebratory wedding breakfast. Theirs was a marriage of necessity and convenience. She just wanted to get on with it.

"Are you well?" Alex asked after handing her up in the carriage. He sat next to her rather than in the opposite seat. As her husband, it was now his prerogative to sit close to her if he pleased. "You look rather pale."

She peered out the window rather than at him. "My stomach is a bit unsettled."

He reached for her gloved hand. "There have been a great many changes in your life."

"And not a one of them of my own making." If only she'd found proof of her marriage to Roger. She could be at the shop right now navigating her own future.

He squeezed her hand. "You will not regret your decision. I shall devote myself to making you happy."

She slid her hand away. "Will the staff be awaiting our arrival?"

"Yes, they are most eager to meet the new Marchioness of Brandon."

Marchioness. Everything happened so fast and Rose had been so preoccupied with finding a way to stand on her own that she hadn't given new title much thought. "They will think me a strange mistress. A mapmaker who goes to the shop most days of the week."

"They will see what I see, my beautiful bride who is a formidable woman. But mostly, they will just stare at your hat."

Rose resisted the urge to smile. For her wedding day, she'd chosen the much-remarked-upon hat with blue feathers from their first meeting. But she'd redesigned it a bit to make it more to her liking. "You noticed."

"How could I not? I must say I am growing fond of your hats. Anyone who doesn't appear to have an animal or an orchard sitting on their head looks positively boring."

"You spoke to the owner of the house on New Street?"

"I did. He understands that the property will be emptied by the end of the month."

"I'll have to supervise the packing." There was so much to do. "The staff will require letters of recommendation. Everything happened so quickly that I haven't spoken to them yet. I intend to pay them at least three months' wages to see them through until they secure a new situation."

His lip twitched. "That sounds reasonable."

She saw out the window that they were approaching Peckham House, its imposing stone facade bright in the sun. "You are aware that I know nothing about managing a grand house."

"I have hired a new housekeeper to look after things. You must occupy yourself with the running of the house only if it pleases you. We have a small staff at the moment as I was rarely in Town before."

"Do you prefer the country?" There were so many things about her new husband that she knew nothing about. He was practically a stranger.

"I do. But there are now delightful enticements to keep me in the city."

"You should stay at Highfield if you prefer country life." It might be easier to guard her heart that way.

"But my bride prefers the city and I prefer to be with my bride."

"Brandon, I—"

"My name is still Alex. Won't you call me by my name, Rose?"

Her eyes stung. "No, I cannot." She feared being

drawn back into her infatuation with him. "The Alex I knew does not exist. Referring to you as Brandon helps me remember that."

Hurt crossed his face, but he quickly masked it. "I pray you will not always feel that way."

She fervently hoped that she would. How else could she protect herself?

THE STAFF ASSEMBLED in the front hall to greet the marquess and his new bride. Rose resisted the impulse to dash back to the carriage. Steeling her spine, she allowed her husband to lead her into the fray.

"Well, Stokes," he said to the butler as Rose stood stiffly by his side, "here is the new mistress you've been longing for."

The butler stepped forward. Rose recognized him from her previous visit, when she could never have envisioned returning as lady of this grand house. "Welcome home, my lord, my lady. On behalf of the staff, please accept our most heartfelt congratulations on your nuptials."

"Thank you," Alex said. "Now, if you will introduce the staff."

Taking a deep breath, Rose lifted her chin and tried to quell the jitters in her belly.

"Of course, my lord," the butler said. "The marchioness will find she is already acquainted with the housekeeper."

"Am I?" Rose's eyes widened as the woman stepped forward, the full set of keys at her waist jingling. "Mrs. Waller! What are you doing here?"

The woman beamed. "Welcome home, my lady."

Alex removed his beaver hat, handing if off to the nearest footman. "I couldn't be the reason your entire staff lost their positions."

"We can discuss the week's menu when you are ready, my lady," Mrs. Waller said.

"Thank you, Mrs. Waller." Relief blossomed in her chest. She'd secretly worried Alex's housekeeper would be a supercilious woman who looked down her nose at a laboring-class mistress.

Mrs. Waller's voice wavered. "I haven't looked after such a grand house before but I shall do my best."

Rose leaned closer to the older woman. "And I have never been mistress of such a grand house," she murmured to the housekeeper. "We shall have to learn together."

"I am sure you will do an excellent job," Alex reassured the housekeeper. "Stokes here will help you adjust."

The butler dipped his chin. "Certainly, my lord."

Alex ushered Rose down the line. "I hope you are pleased." His breath was warm in her ear. "I thought you might be more comfortable in your new home with some familiar faces about."

"That was most considerate." His kindness moved her.

They paused. "And here is someone else you will recognize."

"Dudley," she exclaimed. "You are here, too?"

He puffed his chest. "I am his lordship's valet." He executed a very distinguished bow.

Another familiar face stepped forward next to him.

"And here is Bess," Alex said. "I thought perhaps Bess could tend to you until you engage an experienced lady's maid."

"Oh." She hadn't stopped to consider that most ladies

of her station were attended by a personal lady's maid. She shot Alex a grateful look. "Bess will do very nicely until I settle in."

"Owen is here, too. But he's enamored of the horses and has spent most of his time in the mews with the grooms since his arrival."

"You have engaged my entire staff?"

"I have. My existing staff is very small. Now that I am wed, Peckham House will require more servants. I thought you'd want me to engage the New Street staff."

There were more introductions, but not many given the modest size of Alex's staff, which was a good thing since they were all becoming a blur. It would take time for Rose to learn all of their names.

Bess hurried up behind her, grinning from ear to ear. "Shall I show you to yer bedchamber, my lady?"

"I shall take care of it." Alex led Rose past the group. "After I give her a short tour of the rest of the house."

"It was very good of you to engage the New Street staff," Rose said once they were out of earshot. "I'm sure they never expected to be in service to a marquess. Especially not after coming from a merchant household."

"They will need to acquire a bit of polish, but that will come with time."

He showed her his home. Her home now. They passed through eight reception rooms, a gallery featuring paintings of Worthington ancestors, including a portrait of his mother and father. Both Alex and Leela took their looks from their mother, a lovely woman with dark, intelligent eyes that seemed to have seen a great deal.

They went up a wide, winding, cantilevered stone

staircase, which led to more rooms, most of which featured high ceilings and ornate cornicing. Rose's favorite chamber was a light-filled formal sitting room that was rarely used, according to Alex. She didn't care for the weighty, old-fashioned furniture, but she loved the parquet floors and the two generous floor-to-ceiling windows overlooking the square.

They finally came to the last room. "You will remember this place," Alex said to her when they entered the marchioness's rooms. *Her* bedchamber. It was all so dizzying.

She turned in a little circle, a wondering expression on her face. "The last time we were here, I could never have imagined I would return as mistress."

"You must redecorate this space to your tastes. I can only imagine how many feathers and tassels that will entail."

She smiled wanly, overwhelmed by it all. The thought of redoing anything in this grand house was daunting.

"You look tired," he added. "Would you like to rest before luncheon?"

"Oh yes." She embraced the opportunity to be left alone, to be quiet with herself as she processed all of the changes in her life. "I think I shall."

"Very well. If you need anything, anything at all—"

"I shall ring for Bess. Thank you for bringing her here. It's such a comfort to have some familiar faces about."

"I hope I, too, can provide comfort and solace. That I can be your friend, and perhaps, one day, more."

She faltered. "I cannot promise anything."

"I can be patient. I might not be able to anticipate an

eventful wedding night, but you and I are now bound together until death parts us. And forever with you, in whatever form it takes, is a gift for which I am profoundly grateful."

LATER THAT DAY Brandon dressed for supper with care. This evening would be their initial meal together as husband and wife, and his first real opportunity to begin regaining Rose's trust. To demonstrate to her that a life with him could be happy. That she could learn to believe in him again.

"The missus is going to think you look right rum," Dudley said approvingly as he helped Brandon into his snug tailcoat.

"Mind that you refer to her as Lady Brandon or my lady or her ladyship," Brandon corrected. "Especially when we are in company and have guests."

"Right you are, Alex . . . erm . . . sir . . . my lord."

Brandon suppressed a smile as Dudley fuddled about for the correct manner of address. "Not to worry. You'll get it right soon enough." He was feeling charitable and buoyant this evening, eager to dine with his bride for the first time.

There was a tap at the adjoining door. Brandon perked up. Was Rose coming to him?

But it was Bess. After stepping into Brandon's chamber, she carefully closed the door behind her.

"What is it, Bess?" Brandon asked cheerfully.

"Her *lay-dee-ship*"—the maid took great pleasure in emphasizing each syllable of the honorific—"is unwell and begs yer lordship's pardon."

Brandon's bright mood dimmed. "Begs my pardon?"

"She wishes to take a light meal in her bedchamber and retire early."

"On 'er wedding night?" Dudley exclaimed before thinking better of it.

Based on the terms of their agreement, Brandon had every right to barge into his wife's bedchamber with his own supper plate in hand. She had agreed to have all meals together except for breakfast.

The problem was that she hadn't looked well earlier. She was pale and sickly. Marrying him hadn't had the effect Brandon hoped for. When he'd left her after his abbreviated house tour, he'd wanted nothing more than to stay with her, to talk to her, to know her impressions of their wedding. But she'd leaped at the chance to be rid of him.

He'd had high hopes for their life together after the wedding. But rather than helping to bridge the gap between them, their nuptials seemed to drive Rose further inside herself. Further from him. She seemed overwhelmed and it was lowering to realize she wasn't inclined to lean on him for support.

He tore off his cravat. "Very well. Please send my wife my very best wishes for a swift recovery."

Bess hurried back into Rose's room. Dudley regarded Brandon dubiously.

"What?" Brandon snapped.

"Mrs. Fleming . . . erm . . . my lady must not 'ave liked what she sampled so far to cry off on 'er wedding night."

"Get out." His valet needed to learn not to voice everything that was on his mind. "And mind that you understand that a valet's job is to give his master comfort and ease. Not to insult him."

"If yer in need of some instruction about how ter please a woman, I ain't never had any complaints in that area . . ."

"I don't require any advice," he barked. "And not a word of this to anyone."

"Yer secret is safe with me, Alex . . . erm . . . my lord."

"If I learn that you've gossiped about what happens in the privacy of my bedchamber, you'll find yourself out on your arse without a letter of recommendation."

"But nothing is happening in yer bedchamber—"

Brandon barely restrained his temper. "Do you take my meaning?"

"Yes, my lord. I'm yer man through and through. I know what you've done for me, how you've raised me in life. So if there's anything I can do for you . . ." He raised his eyebrows meaningfully.

"You can go and tell Cook that I'll take supper in my rooms as well." He never ate in his chambers. Eating alone in his dining room had never bothered Brandon before. But the thought of doing so this evening, when Rose should be sitting opposite him, made his mood all the blacker.

"ROSE?" BRANDON SET his coffee down and shot to his feet the following morning. After their marriage negotiations, he hadn't expected her to join him for Sunday breakfast in the garden. "This is a pleasant surprise. Are you feeling better?"

"Yes, thank you. Am I intruding?" She wore ropes

of necklaces and a bonnet crowned with a profusion of flowers.

"You could no more intrude upon me than the sun could intrude on a fine spring day. You are mistress here now."

All last evening, on their wedding night, he'd stared at their adjoining bedchamber door and wondered what she was doing. Had she thought of him? He imagined her sleeping in the large plush bed and hoped she might have dreamed of him.

He took in her outfit, the morning dress and pelisse. "Are you going out?"

"That depends."

"Upon what?"

"You, actually."

"How intriguing. Why don't we eat and you can tell me all about it?"

"Breakfast is not part of our marriage contract."

"But supper is and you denied me the pleasure last evening," he reminded her.

She stiffened. "I was unwell."

"I'll take your word for it. As to breakfast, as a gentleman, I can hardly continue my meal if you refuse to join me. I cannot eat while a lady stands."

"Very well. Perhaps a cup of chocolate."

"Stokes will see to it." Brandon nodded to his butler, who inclined his chin and stepped away. Brandon pulled out a chair for Rose. "Let us hope a hive of bees doesn't decide to pollinate your hat."

"The flowers are rather realistic," she agreed. "The hat maker who trimmed this bonnet is truly an artist."

"If you say so." He settled back in his seat. "How was your first night in your new home?"

"This is a beautiful house."

"But?"

"I was quite attached to my little sitting room on New Street. I shall miss being surrounded by my own things."

"You must make any changes that will make you more comfortable."

She paused. "You mentioned yesterday that you intend to search Irene Fleming's cottage."

"That is correct."

"And I presumed you might be inclined to go today."

"Why would you assume that?"

"Because it is Sunday and the entire family is likely to be at church."

He sipped his coffee. "You are very clever."

"I want to go with you."

He almost spit out his coffee. "I beg your pardon? Breaking into someone's house uninvited is not exactly an ideal activity for a lady."

"Neither is mapmaking, but there you have it."

"Why do you want to accompany me?"

"I have my reasons."

"I am going to need to hear them if you intend to go with me."

She relented. "I want to see if Roger kept any proof of our marriage."

"I thought he told you he destroyed all evidence of your union."

"He did. But then I thought about it. What if something had happened to me during the time we lived together as man and wife? What if Roger was called upon to present proof that he was indeed my husband when it came to matters of who should inherit the shop?"

"That's a rather macabre thought." His expression sharpened. "Or has Fleming given you reason to fear for your life?"

"Roger is many things but I don't think he's a murderer. It's something he said. He told me that there was no public proof of our marriage. Why put it like that? Why say *public proof* rather than just *proof*? Is it because he has private proof of our marriage in that cottage? If so, I mean to find it." Stokes appeared with her chocolate and poured it for Rose.

"You and I are wed," Brandon said once they were alone again. "You have nothing to fear from him. You have the protection of my name."

"How long do you think it will take Roger to learn that I've married the Marquess of Brandon? And how soon after that do you think he will turn up on your doorstep—"

"*Our* doorstep."

"How soon before he turns up on *our* doorstep demanding to be compensated for staying quiet about bedding me before my wedding to the Marquess of Brandon?"

The coffee in Brandon's mouth tasted like acid. "I see your point."

"I thought you might." Rose sipped her chocolate. "What do you say about us going to Walham Green today?"

He saw there'd be no dissuading her. And knowing Rose, if he didn't agree to take her along, she might try to breach the Fleming cottage without him. "Drink up. It looks as if our first official outing as a married couple will entail breaking into someone's house."

Chapter Twenty-One

$\mathcal{A}$lex strolled into the Flemings' cozy bedchamber with Rose close behind. "Let us hope finding what we're looking for proves as easy as breaking into the cottage."

"The front door was unlocked." Rose opened the wardrobe. "I think we can expect the search to be more of a challenge."

"True. I'll check the other bedchamber."

Their quick tour of the Fleming cottage revealed it comprised just three rooms. The center room for cooking, eating and a sitting area for the family. A few toys were strewn across the floors. It appeared that the children slept in one room and their parents in the other.

Rose went through the wardrobe, through both Irene's dresses and Roger's jackets and trousers. Their bedchamber was very much a shared room. Roger's tooth powder and shaving implements shared a surface with Irene's hairbrush and pins. It was a stark contrast to the way she and Roger had lived, each in their own room, their clothes and personal-care items distinctly separate. Being inside this cottage crystallized how much of a home and family Roger had created with Irene and their children.

They searched for several minutes. Rose looked every-where she could think of. "Anything?" she called out after finding nothing of interest.

"Not a thing." They met in the main room. Alex tossed something onto the nearest chair. "Except for this."

"What is that?" Rose asked.

"It looks like a map Roger drew for his sons. I wouldn't have noticed it except that it was tucked away on a high shelf. Do you think he was hiding it?"

All maps interested Rose, even Roger's. And why tuck it away? She reached for the canvas to examine the rudimentary drawing. "It's of the cottage and the sur-rounding area." She noted that Roger had added flowers, trees and streams and other landmarks. Crude imita-tions of Rose's signature flourishes. "Where did you find this?"

"On a shelf in the children's room. The top shelf."

"Could the children reach that shelf?"

"It's probably too tall for them."

She studied the map. "Something about this isn't quite right."

"Besides the fact that it looks like it was drawn by a schoolboy? Maybe one of the children drew it."

She shook her head. "Technically, it's very exact." A little too precise for child's play. "And although he's noted certain landmarks as expected—" Her sentence trailed off as she strode across the room and out the door.

"Wha—" Alex hurried after her. "Where are you going?"

She studied the map as she walked. "Here is the hill that he's marked. And the spring." She resumed walking. "What we're looking for is beside a big rock formation."

"Why? What are you seeing in the map?"

"Some sort of hidden treasure."

"Hidden treasure? You cannot think it's real. He probably drew that map for his children."

"Then we've nothing to lose. But I don't think so." She picked up the pace.

"How big of a rock are we supposed to be looking for?"

"That, I'm not sure of. Roger is a terrible cartographer. His scale is always off. Which means the rock could be taller than you or might just reach my waist."

He took the map from her. "Where does it indicate treasure? I see no coins or pots of gold."

She paused to point to the symbol of a rectangle with a black circle inside it "That suggests something buried in a box."

"Does it?" He studied it more closely.

"There are different symbols for gold or treasure. Some are known only to the mapmaker. Pirates used particular symbols depending on what part of the world they came from."

"There's the rock."

She looked ahead at a rock formation that came to Alex's shoulder. Excitement swept through her. "Yes, that must be it."

"We don't have a shovel."

"We have our hands."

"I am going back to find a shovel." He jogged away and returned a few minutes later. "Where do I start?"

She took the shovel and posted it into the ground on the far side of the rock. "Here."

He began to shovel. "We could very well find nothing but child's nonsense."

"Possibly. But that map was, in all likelihood, drawn recently."

He tossed away a shovel full of dirt. "How do you know that?"

She surveyed the map again. "Roger has drawn irises and sunflowers, which bloom in July. What if he felt challenged after learning we'd discovered the cottage? What if he decided to hide his most precious documents away from the house?"

Alex continued to shovel. After several minutes Rose's enthusiasm began to ebb. What if she had it all wrong? Maybe there was nothing here. But the measurements were too precise for a map drawn for children. The clink of the shovel cut into her musings. "What was that?"

Alex grinned. "I think I've hit something." He started shoveling faster, tossing shovels of dirt at a fast clip. Throwing the shovel down, he sank to his knees and uncovered the rest of the tin with his hands.

Rose sank down next to him. "Do you think—?"

"Maybe," he answered. "This just might be our lucky day." He unearthed a rectangular tin container.

Her breath caught. "It's a box." Reaching into the dirt, he pulled it out and opened the hinged top. Something was wrapped in cloth. Rose reached for it and unwrapped the package. It was a collection of papers—a folded letter, a familiar-looking certificate.

Her skin prickled as she picked up the document. "This is it." Rose stared at the names. *Roger Fleming.*

Rose Kanaan. Followed by the dates the banns were read at the church in Holborn.

> *First time, Sunday: June 27, 1813*
> *Second time, Sunday: July 4, 1813*
> *Third time, Sunday: July 11, 1813*

Alex peered over her shoulder. "What is that?"

"The banns certificate. Proof of our marriage. The rector who performed the ceremony remembers marrying us. That, along with this document, prove that Roger is a bigamist. Now, he also has something to lose if he tries to claim that we were never wed."

He reached for the folded letter. She noted the slight tremor in his hand as he unfolded it. "My God."

"Is it Canning's letter?"

He nodded. "Canning is very clear on his instructions about where to draw the property line to deprive me of the water meadow."

Their eyes met in triumph. "This is it! And it's thanks to you that I found it." He shifted toward Rose as if to embrace her. Alarmed, she shot to her feet, backing away. She could never let him in again. She might not survive a second betrayal from Alex, especially not after what Roger had put her through.

He stared at the ground for a moment before rising to join her. "Rose," he asked softly. "Do you think you will ever forgive me?"

"Even if I wanted to"—she struggled to keep her voice from trembling—"I do not believe I am capable of ever placing my complete trust in you again."

She turned back toward the Fleming cottage with the banns certificate in her hand. Shoving Canning's note into his pocket, Alex followed.

"WHAT THE DEVIL are you two doing here?" Fleming strode out of his cottage. It was all Brandon could do to keep from pummeling the man on the spot.

Rose waved the paper in her hand. "I am here to retrieve what's mine."

Alarm filled his eyes. "How—? You *trespassed* into my home?"

"Shocking, isn't it?"

"Give me that." He tried to snatch the paper from her.

Rose whipped her arm away just as Brandon stepped between them. "I would not try it if I were you."

"This has nothing to do with you, you ingrate." Roger glared at him. "I should never have given you a position in my house. You are the least competent footman I've ever laid eyes on."

A laugh escaped Rose's lips. "Oh, Roger, you really have no idea what you've gotten yourself into."

That laugh tingled through Brandon. They were a team, he and Rose, and a darn good one. One day she would believe it again.

Fleming ignored Rose. "You trespassed into my house," he snarled at Brandon. "If you do not return my property to me, I shall call the magistrate."

"Oh, you should call him," Rose called out merrily. "*Please* do it."

"Yes, why don't you, Fleming?" Brandon's voice was a low warning. "And while you are at it, tell him the Marquess of Brandon would like to have a word."

Fleming's eyes bulged. "Brandon sent you?"

"In a manner of speaking."

Rose giggled. It had been too long since he'd seen her express any amusement. And it was worth everything.

"The marquess sent you to what?" Fleming planted his fists on his hips. "Infiltrate my home? For what purpose?"

"To find proof that you cheated me."

"Cheated you? I don't even know who you are. How could I possibly cheat you?"

Rose sauntered over. "I don't believe the proper introductions have been made. Roger Fleming, meet Alexander Worthington, the Marquess of Brandon."

Fleming stared at Brandon. "You?" He swallowed hard. "The . . . the . . . marquess?"

"In the flesh."

He repeated the words as if he couldn't quite believe it. "*You* are the Marquess of Brandon."

"Indeed. You see, Fleming, people of my sort, Arabs, *do* have a love of the land. In fact, my love for my land runs so deep that I intend to destroy you for trying to take it from me."

"She drew the map." Fleming pointed to Rose. "I had nothing to do with it."

Rose shook her head. "I vow I cannot think of a word that accurately describes just how much of a worm you truly are."

"I speak the truth," Fleming said to Brandon. "Ask her yourself. Rose is the true mapmaker."

"I know you gave Rose faulty information when she created the map." Brandon withdrew Canning's letter. "I have here a missive from Canning congratulating you on redrawing my property lines at his request."

Fleming ran a hand over the back of his neck. "I cannot believe you found the buried box."

Rose smirked. "Despite your terrible drawing, you do always insist that map coordinates be extraordinarily precise. And it worked. I found your buried treasure."

"And now," Brandon growled, "you will pay for what you have done. I shall leave no stone unturned in my quest to completely ruin you."

The door to the cottage flew open and Irene dashed out. "Please don't hurt him." She came to a halt beside her husband. "He didn't mean to lie. He had no choice."

"Mrs. Fleming." Brandon was taken aback by the woman's distress. "This conversation is most unpleasant. Perhaps you'd prefer to wait in the cottage."

"You must understand," she pleaded. "Roger had no choice. Mr. Canning found out about me and the children. He threatened to tell Rose everything. And then where would we be?"

"Exactly where you are now," Rose replied.

"We have young children." Tears ran down her face. "If you destroy their father, how will they eat?"

"If only you'd shown the same concern when you and your husband decided to deceive me in the worst way possible," Rose retorted.

"Exactly." Brandon's jaw worked. "Fleming should have considered Rose before he lied and cheated. As should you have. You did go along with his unspeakable deception regarding my wife."

She frowned. "Your wife?"

"We don't even know your wife," Roger put in. "Do you hide her in one of your harems? No one has heard that the Marquess of Brandon has taken a wife."

"Just yesterday, Miss Kanaan made me the happiest man in England." Rose stepped closer and put her hand on his arm. "Meet my marchioness."

Roger gaped. "You married Rose? Even though she's a merchant? She wasn't even pure."

Brandon snatched Roger up by the collar. "She is all that is good and honest. Unlike the treacherous snake who stole her innocence. Rose is purer than anyone I know. Pure of heart. Pure of soul."

The Fleming children streamed out into the yard. Brandon resisted the urge to snap at them to return to the house. He dropped his hands. Roger stumbled back.

"Do we have company, Papa?" the tallest boy asked.

"Are they coming in for tea?" asked another, his curious gaze running over the two strangers in his front garden.

Brandon stepped closer to Fleming, who flinched and reflexively moved back. Brandon gripped the man's shoulder to keep him still. "If anyone asks, your union with Rose was annulled," he murmured. "Do you understand?"

Fleming nodded shakily. "Yes."

"If you dare to sully her reputation," he warned, "you will pay a heavy price."

Fleming darted a look at his children, who'd wandered off to play nearby. "As you wish."

"You are not to show your face in London again."

"That's not possible," Roger protested. "I am a trained surveyor and cartographer. I must find work."

"No one in London will give you employment." Brandon bared his teeth. "I've seen to that. I have made it my mission to destroy any business that dares to employ you. I have already put out the word."

"*You* are the reason I haven't been able to find a position? I have children! Surely, you will not let them go hungry." He turned his pleading gaze to Rose. "You are not a cruel woman. You wouldn't let my children suffer."

"Of course not." Rose smiled. "I hear that farm life can be healthy for children, with all of that fresh air and plenty of room to run."

His face lost all color. "You would condemn me to a life working on my father's farm? When he passes on, the farm will belong to my brother, and I will have nothing to show for all of my efforts."

"All of your efforts have led you to this place." She stepped closer. "And now you shall finally live the life you so richly deserve."

ROSE SLIPPED HER hand out of Alex's as they strode away from the cottage to where his coach awaited them. For a fleeting moment he tightened his fingers, reflexively resisting the loss of the physical connection, but then immediately released her.

"We make an excellent team, you and I," he remarked. "It was good to see you laugh."

"I haven't had much to laugh about recently." But finding the proof of her marriage left her feeling giddy, and more optimistic than she had in a long while.

"You now have the evidence you need to keep Fleming at bay."

"That I do." She'd stood up for herself and beaten

Roger at his own game. "I've taken back at least a tiny bit of control over my life."

His expression was grave. "A day too late."

"How so?"

"If you'd found that certificate before yesterday, you would not have been forced to marry me to save your reputation."

"I wasn't forced into anything."

"But would you have married me if you'd had that certificate? Do you now feel you were trapped into this marriage?" He paused. "If you want an annulment, I will grant it."

"No, I made a decision and I intend to stand by it." Her choices were even more limited than Alex knew.

He released a breath, looking tremendously relieved. Rose resisted the urge to slide a protective hand over her belly. She'd missed her courses. The nausea, tender breasts and unrelenting fatigue suddenly all made sense.

But she couldn't be completely sure. Her life had been in a state of upheaval for several weeks. Her body could be reacting to an overabundance of emotional turmoil. She needed to wait a few more weeks. Once she knew for certain that she was increasing, Rose would tell Alex.

But until then, she'd keep her suspicions to herself.

Chapter Twenty-Two

"Let's clear a space by the window," Rose directed. "I'll need the light."

"Yes, my lady." Dudley, assisted by one of Alex's footmen, moved furniture around in Rose's bedchamber to accommodate her request.

Alex popped his head in from the corridor. "What is going on?"

"We are trying to decide the best position for my drawing table." Her stomach dropped at the dubious expression on his face. "Should I not move anything?"

The marchioness's rooms had probably remained untouched for decades, possibly since Alex's mother last resided here. And here Rose was changing everything around on her second full day in residence. She still felt like an interloper. She certainly didn't feel like a wife.

"This afternoon I am going to New Street to supervise the move," she explained. "I'll need room for my drawing table but I should have checked with you before changing anything."

"Nonsense. These are your rooms now. You must do as you please." He surveyed her bedchamber. Rose felt a little warm. Having Alex in her rooms made the generous space feel so much smaller. "Won't it be a little too crowded in here if you add your drawing table?"

"Crowded? This chamber is enormous."

"Still, I think I have a better idea." He offered his arm. "Shall we?"

She was hesitant to touch him, but reluctantly took his arm and pretended not to notice the electricity that arced between them. "Where are we going?"

A secretive smile curved his lips. "You shall see."

She eyed him suspiciously. "You seem awfully pleased with yourself. What are you about?"

He escorted her down the corridor to the sunny sitting room with an abundance of excellent light that she'd admired. He pushed the door open. "After you, my lady."

Rose stepped inside, still wondering why he was being so mysterious. But then she caught sight of the room and her breath hitched.

It was as if she'd entered a completely different chamber, yet one that was utterly familiar. He'd transformed the sitting room, replacing the stiff, formal furniture with Rose's faded sofa from her own sitting room at New Street. In addition, her side tables, eating table and other furnishings, including her books and scarves, were all in place. And, best of all, her drawing table stood against the windows.

She hadn't thought it possible, but she instantly felt more at home. "Oh, Brandon."

"Do you like it? You seemed to appreciate this room above all others when you toured the house."

"When did you have this done?"

"I put Mrs. Waller and Stokes in charge yesterday

while we went to Walham Green. They supervised the move. You mentioned that you missed your things. I thought this might help."

She gazed at the map mounted on the wall behind her sofa. "You even have the map I drew of the New Street neighborhood."

"Maybe one day you'll replace it with a map of your new home and neighborhood."

Tears stung her eyes. "I do believe this is the most thoughtful thing anyone has ever done for me." On impulse, she hugged him. "Thank you ever so much."

He seemed surprised for a moment, but then his arms closed around her. "I don't want you to want, Rose," he whispered into her hair, "not for anything."

She let him hold her. Allowed herself this momentary lapse to indulge herself in him. She missed his warmth, the feel of his body, the intimacy they once shared. With him holding her like this, she could close her eyes and pretend, just for a moment, that he was still Alex from before.

"I want desperately to make you happy," he said.

She breathed in the scent of his shaving soap. "I miss the way it was with us on New Street."

"I know." Alex didn't rush to his own defense. He just held her, allowing Rose to soak in the moment and sort through her emotions. "I do as well. I still care for you. That has never changed. Dare I hope that you still have feelings for me?"

"It would be easy to give in to the full force of your magnetism." But their troubled past kept her from embracing a shared future.

"Can you not allow yourself to do so? You are my

wife now. I would protect you with my life. Perhaps when you are done punishing me for my deception—"

"I am not trying to punish you. I wish I could put the past behind me. I hate that it's keeping me from fully seizing my life now." She thought of the baby she might be carrying. She couldn't resent her child's father. No child should grow up with that.

She gently disengaged, feeling his reluctance to release her. "I knew, or I thought I knew, who Alex was. You must now give me time to learn who the Marquess of Brandon is. He is still a stranger to me."

"You might not have known my true name or station in life, but you do know who I am. The man I am has not changed."

"I must learn that for myself." Before she could entrust her heart to him. "What is real and what isn't? Is an attachment built on a massive fraud still genuine? Or is it a lie, too?"

"I know it is real. And once you realize the truth, I am hopeful that we can create new memories. Even better ones."

"We shall see." She wandered over to gaze out the window by her drawing table. She looked back at him. "Thank you for arranging this room. Everything is perfect. This light is excellent."

"It certainly is." Unabashed admiration gleamed in his sable eyes. "You are practically glowing."

HE JOINED HER later that day for tea in her new studio.

"Right on time," she remarked when he entered, casually covering up what she was working on before joining him on the sofa.

"I was counting the minutes." He spoke the words lightly but it was the truth. Mealtimes and afternoon tea were the only periods he could be guaranteed time alone with her. "What are you working on?"

"Your sister's maps."

"I thought you'd completed those."

"Almost. I am just putting the finishing touches on them." She poured the tea with grace and surety, her movements concise and purposeful. "What are those?" she asked when he bypassed the still-warm Bath buns and tartlets in favor of round patterned cookies dusted with powdered sugar.

"*Maamoul*. It's a date-filled cookie. My grandmother sent some over this morning in celebration of our wedding."

Rose reached for one. "Is she angry that she wasn't invited to the ceremony?"

"I think *Citi* has attended enough weddings in her time." One or another of his cousins always seemed to be getting engaged or married. "Besides, I don't believe she ever expected to attend my nuptials."

"Why ever not?"

"*Citi* has always felt that Leela and I should keep ourselves separate from the rest of the family."

"But why?"

"Because of who our father was. And she feels that way now, more than ever, given that Leela is wed to a duke. She is adamant that we should make our place with our father's people."

"With noblemen and women? And have you?"

"As I've told you, we never quite belonged in either

place. But I insisted on knowing my cousins on my mother's side and we have since become close."

She bit into the cookie. "Oh, this is quite nice."

"You'll be happy to know that we'll always have a steady supply. Whenever she is in Town, *Citi* sends *maamoul* over. She knows these are my favorites."

"It sounds as if she spoils you."

He drank his tea. "She does."

"I suppose I shall meet her soon?"

"Very soon. Leela insists on hosting a supper to welcome you to the family. All of our Arab relatives, who are in Town, will be there to gawk at you."

"Another event to be nervous about." She broke off a piece of cookie. "They can hardly be pleased that you've married a laboring-class mapmaker."

"Nonsense. They approve of you because your grandfather was Lebanese."

"They do?"

"Yes, as long as we can trace at least a few drops of Arab blood in you, then *Citi* will regard you as one of us."

"I barely know three words in Arabic!"

"Blood is thicker than vocabulary." He polished off his *maamoul*. "And if you'd like, I can teach you the language. For example, there is the word *hayati*."

Her face lit up. "*Jidu* used to call me that."

"It's a term of endearment. It means my life, or my love."

She flushed and focused on her cookie. "I see."

He knew he should not push his flirtation too far. She had asked him for time and he must give it to her.

It was the least he could do. "There is a matter that I should like to discuss with you."

"Yes?"

"I'd like to travel to Highfield, my country estate, as soon as you are willing. I realize that you have the shop to tend to but I must deal with Canning."

"The neighbor who cheated you?"

"Exactly. I need to see about recovering the land he stole from me."

"What will you do if he denies any wrongdoing?"

"I have his note, proof that he extorted Fleming in order to cheat me. It needs to be handled immediately because my tenant farmers must have water access by the time the winter crops are planted in mid-September."

"I'd like to go and see the land for myself."

"Excellent." His spirits lifted. He'd expected her to resist or to ask him to go to the country without her. "I shall make plans for us to depart the morning after Leela's supper party. If that is agreeable."

"Most agreeable." She smiled into her teacup. And he caught a glimpse of a fleeting expression on her face that he could not quite interpret. "I cannot wait to reach Highfield."

"So you are the woman who thawed our chilly marquess," said Alex's cousin Rafi, whose handsome classical features contrasted with Alex's more rough-hewn good looks. A mischievous expression on his face, Alex's cousin bent over Rose's hand, lingering a tad longer than necessary. "*Zay il umar.*"

"That's quite enough." Alex reached over to separate their hands. "Watch yourself."

"Oh ho." Rafi's eyes twinkled. "The lady has not only captivated my cousin, she even has the power to provoke him to jealousy."

Alex settled Rose's hand firmly on his arm. "The only provoking person here is you, *ibn khaltee*."

"Translation?" Rose asked for at least the fifth time since they'd arrived at the family supper party the Duchess of Huntington hosted in honor of their marriage. Alex had numerous relations and it was impossible to keep track of them all.

"I said you are as beautiful as the moon," Rafi informed her. "One of the highest compliments that can be paid to a woman of superior looks."

Rafi's gentle teasing amused her. "I see you are a flatterer."

Rafi set a hand upon his chest. "I speak the honest truth."

"And what did Brandon just call you?"

"*Ibn khaltee* means cousin."

"But," Alex interjected, "the literal translation is 'son of my maternal aunt.' In Arabic, we are very specific about which side of the family our cousins hail from. Speaking of family, I have many other relations for you to meet. We must leave Rafi to practice his wiles on someone else."

"You allowed him to goad you," Rose remarked as Alex led her away, "when he is harmless."

"Rafi has a way with women. And you seemed charmed enough."

Rose bit back a smile. Alex *was* jealous, even though he must know the encounter with Rafi was utterly innocent. He seemed on edge, but he was still a vision to her in his fine dark clothes, his natural arrogance on full display in the way he carried himself, shoulders back and spine straight as if daring the world to deny him anything. No one would ever believe this man had masqueraded as a footman, going so far as to clean shoes and wash dishes. It spoke of how far Alex would go to accomplish whatever he wanted.

At the moment he clearly wanted her. Rose longed for him physically. But she needed to sort out her feelings without allowing bed sport to color her judgment. Once he was back in her bed, Rose couldn't be trusted to think clearly.

As they went in to supper, Alex introduced Rose to his grandmother. She was a plumpish woman with shrewd eyes set deep in a scowling, prune-like face. Although small in stature, *Citi* was an indomitable presence and presided over the party like a queenly matriarch.

"You are pretty," *Citi* proclaimed in a heavy Arabic accent that reminded Rose of her *Jidu*'s. "But too skinny. You need to eat."

Something about *Citi* made Rose feel at home. She immediately warmed to the fearsome woman. "My *Jidu* used to always tell me that."

"Because it's true." *Citi* patted the chair next to her. "*Warada* will sit with me."

At Rose's confused look, Alex explained. "*Warada* is Rose in Arabic."

Rose flushed with pleasure. "Oh, how lovely." Being

assigned an Arabic version of her name made her feel more included.

"Maybe you two can speak more after supper," Alex interjected after seeing there was only one available seat next to his grandmother.

"*Malaya minuk.* Nonsense." *Citi*'s natural frown deepened. "Don't be so eager for your bride that you cannot be without her for one meal."

"Go on, Brandon." Rose slipped into the seat beside the old woman. "*Citi* and I shall become better acquainted."

Alex reluctantly wandered away, taking a seat near some of his uncles and aunts that he'd introduced her to earlier. They greeted him in a jumble of Arabic and English. He responded with good humor and deference to his elders, even though in English society he far outranked them all.

In normal circumstances, tradesmen were beneath a nobleman's notice and certainly would never share the same supper table. This evening was a revelation, allowing her to discover a new side of Alex—the dutiful, respectful nephew who did not use his rank as a buffer between him and his laboring-class relations.

Maybe Brandon and Alex weren't so vastly different after all.

Citi proceeded to insist that Rose fill her plate. Many of the dishes were unfamiliar to her—rolled cabbage, stuffed grape leaves, what appeared to be meatballs with two pointed corners. But then she spotted a familiar beige-colored spread sprinkled with olive oil.

"Is that *hummus*?" The chickpea and sesame paste

spread used to be *Jidu*'s favorite, the only dish her grandfather had ever prepared.

"Yes, yes, it's good, *Citi*, very good." Alex's grandmother immediately added a big dollop to Rose's already heaping plate.

Memories of *Jidu* rushed back when Alex's grandmother referred to Rose as *Citi*. Her grandfather also used to address her as *Jidu*. It was strange to English ears, but the term of endearment was a show of affection on *Citi*'s part.

Rose dipped her bread into the *hummus* and savored the taste and the memories it evoked. She could almost feel *Jidu*'s presence at the table. She had the fleeting thought that maybe her grandfather had sent these people— including Alex—to her so she wouldn't be alone.

"Eat more, eat more," *Citi* prodded. "You have to be healthy so you can give Brandon a son."

Rose thought of the child she increasingly believed was growing inside her and reached for more food.

"HERE WE ARE." Alex led Rose into what seemed like the one hundredth room at Highfield. Stumbling after him, Rose gulped in the fresh country air whenever they passed an open window during the tour.

"Are you certain you're not ill?" he asked for at least the fifth time since they departed London.

She plastered a serene smile on her face. "Quite sure." She'd never been prone to carriage sickness before, but the urge to cast her accounts had hit her several times on the journey.

His brows furrowed. "Your skin has a greenish tint. It's almost as colorful as your bonnet."

"I am sometimes prone to carriage sickness," she lied. Rose wasn't purposely hiding the truth; she just wanted to be absolutely certain there was something to tell before she said anything. Once she'd missed her courses for a second month, she'd inform Alex she was increasing.

"At least you are now on *terra firma*," he said. "Hopefully, the country air will do you good. You have been rather unwell."

"I am certain it will." She strolled closer to an open window in the high-ceilinged chamber.

"At least you seemed to have regained a little of the weight you lost after the debacle with Fleming."

"I am trying." She forced herself to eat now that there might be a child to nourish. A thrill went through her. Could it be true? Would she at last be a mother?

"What do you think?" he asked.

"Of Highfield?" She inhaled another lungful of air, which seemed to help, as did being out of a moving carriage. "It's stunning."

The white-stone manor house seemed to glow in the sun. And its rooms were gracious and somehow still comfortable and welcoming.

"I'm pleased you approve. This is where Leela and I spent most of our childhood." He did seem more relaxed and less burdened here in the country. "But what I meant was, what do you think of this room?"

Her stomach finally feeling more settled, she took in the high ceilings and large windows overlooking the garden. "It's beautiful."

"Is the light satisfactory?"

"Satisfactory for what?" She tilted her head. "Is this to be my studio?"

"If you would like it to be."

"It's perfect."

"I have ordered a drafting table for you, custom made with a tilting surface. I'd hoped it would be delivered before our arrival."

"You had a drawing board made especially for me? You have thought of everything."

"I am trying. I want you to be happy. I don't want you ever to regret your choice of a husband."

"I am trying, too." She took his hand. He immediately interlocked his fingers with hers. "Thank you for being patient with me."

"It is I who should be thanking you for giving me a chance, despite our less than auspicious beginnings."

They stood there, eyes locked, the physical attraction leaping like flames between them. The wisest course was to step away to break the moment. But she didn't move.

"Rose," he murmured, whisper soft. "My beautiful Rose."

She closed her eyes as the force of their shared chemistry pounded through her. "Oh, Brandon," she said when she opened her eyes again. "You don't make it easy to keep my distance."

His dark gaze drilled into her. "I said I would give you time to learn to trust me again. But I never agreed to make it easy for you to leave me." He lowered his face. "And I never will."

Being the center of his intense focus thrilled her senses. Alex made Rose feel like she was the only woman in the world worth noticing. She closed her eyes and waited to feel his lips against hers. He was gentle and warm, his hunger tempered by a sweetness that twisted through her. He widened his mouth over hers, kissing her soulfully. His movements, tender but posses-sive, stamped her as his, ruining her for any other man.

He kissed his way down her neck, his hands coming up to cup her sore and overly sensitive breasts. She wore her stays looser these days to accommodate her swelling bosom, which made it easy for him to lift them out.

"They have never been large," she said, wondering if he preferred well-endowed women.

"I have had the privilege of seeing them previously and I find all of you to be enchanting." He fondled her as he kissed the tip of one breast and then the other. "Let me assure you that men love all breasts no matter their size." She'd always been small, but pregnancy made her more voluptuous. "I see you have gained a little weight here as well."

She stiffened, his comments bringing her back to the reality of their situation. They were married, yes. But this man wasn't Alex. She mustn't allow sexual desire to muddle her thinking. She couldn't give herself to a stranger even if he was her husband. They must learn each other again. And they couldn't do that by pawing each other in the middle of the day.

"I think that's enough." She slipped away, restoring her breasts to their rightful place inside her dress.

He groaned. "That was not nearly enough."

"You agreed to give me time to become acquainted with Brandon."

"How long do you think it will take? I'm not that

interesting." He followed her, pulling her into his arms. "I'm truly a little boring. You probably already know all there is to know."

She maneuvered out of his embrace. "You are anything but boring."

He gave her a slow smile. "Is that so?"

"In fact," she said honestly, "it's possible that you are the most interesting man I've ever met. A marquess who pretends to be a footman. It's truly fascinating."

"Two people can learn a great deal about each other by going to bed together." He playfully reached for her again. "There are all sorts of interesting things you could discover about me while I pleasure you."

"No doubt." She dodged his arms. If she allowed him to catch her, she'd be tempted to test his carnal promises. "When are we going to visit Charles Canning?"

He halted. "Well, you certainly know how to kill a man's amorous mood. Canning is away from home at the moment, but should return in a few days' time." He paused. "And what do you mean, *we*? I am going to see Canning."

"I want to go with you."

His eyes flashed. "Canning cheated *me*. I shall deal with him. The very last thing I care to do is subject you to that man's odious presence."

"You are not the only person he cheated," she retorted. "My signature is on that map. Canning and Roger put my reputation as a mapmaker at risk when they decided to steal from you. If it were to be known that I made faulty maps, I would be ruined before I even truly started."

He stared at her, but behind the frustration, she registered his admiration. "Life with you is never going to be dull. Exasperating, perhaps. But never dull."

"So it is settled? You agree to take me with you."

"As if I could forbid you from going. You pretend to ask for my blessing, but we both know you'd see Canning without me if I refused to give it."

"Naturally." She smiled brightly. "But I'd much prefer to go with you."

Chapter Twenty-Three

Owen," Rose called to the boy when she spotted him exercising horses with a stable groom near the paddock. "Have you seen Lord Brandon?"

She'd come down after breakfast eager to hear more about how Alex intended to deal with Mr. Canning. Their discussion was cut short the previous afternoon after Alex was called away to resolve a crop dispute between two of his tenant farmers. He stayed gone past supper and, to Rose's surprise, she'd missed his company. This morning Rose wandered the massive house, checking the rooms she was familiar with, his bedchamber and study, the library and dining room, even her studio, but he was nowhere to be found. That was when she tried the stables.

"Yes, Mrs. Fle—erm . . . my lady." The boy trotted over. "'E said 'e was going to eat an orange."

"An orange?"

The groom followed Owen. "His lordship didn't say he was eating an orange. He said he was going to the orangery."

Owen's face twisted. "What's an orange jury?"

"An orangery is a glasshouse for the growing of plants." Rose turned to the groom. "Could you direct me?"

"Certainly, my lady. Go along the path beyond the stables and you'll come to it."

Rose thanked him and followed the gravel walkway as directed. She hadn't realized there was an orangery at Highfield. She'd never been inside one. Glasshouses were an indulgence few could afford.

She came to a handsome, tall, rectangular building with a wall of windows that went up two stories high. She entered to find several long rows of potted trees with tufts of soft green leaves. A gardener in worn clothing and shirtsleeves was on his knees at the far end, repotting a tree. As she grew closer, the man looked up at her approach.

"You're not a gardener!"

Alex's face lit up. "No, indeed." He straightened, looking more like the Alex she remembered in his work clothes. The V-neck of his shirt revealed tufts of dark chest hair. "This is a pleasant surprise."

"I looked everywhere for you."

"Is that so? Perhaps I should make myself scarce more often if it is going to compel you to give chase."

"I am not chasing you." She looked at his soiled hands and perspiration-dampened brow. "I see you were sincere when you told me you like to work in the garden."

"I find it soothing to be alone with my thoughts, working with my hands."

"Should I leave you to your thoughts?"

"Don't you dare. My thoughts are full of you these days so you might as well stay and be here in fact as well as in my thoughts."

"Please continue what you were doing." She gestured to the tree. "I don't want to interrupt your work."

"So long as you stay and talk to me."

"Very well." She wandered a little, taking in the scenery. "What an enchanting space." She came upon a charming bench with pillows tucked away among the plants.

"I see you've found my secret lair." He came up behind her. "If I want to hide away where no one will find me, I settle on that bench."

"It is very inviting." She fingered a leaf of the nearest plant. "What kinds of trees are these? I thought people grew oranges and lemons in orangeries."

"Some do." He wiped his brow with the back of a soiled hand. "But Mediterranean plants also grow well in glasshouses. These are olive trees."

"Olive trees?" She examined them more closely. The leaves were two-toned: deep green on one side and silvery gray on the other. "I don't believe I've ever seen an olive tree."

"My mother was partial to them." They circled back together and he knelt to repot the tree. "They reminded her of the land of her birth. I've also planted some of these trees along the wall on the southern end of the property."

She enjoyed watching him at his task, his deft hands working in the dirt. "Can olive trees grow outdoors here in England?"

He nodded. "Olive trees are hardy. They grow with little water in Palestine."

"Did your mother enjoy gardening?"

"No, but she did enjoy the results. Father did everything in his power to please her. He built this orangery for Mama so that he could have olive trees brought in."

How utterly romantic. "He must have loved her very much."

"I am beginning to think it is a Worthington trait." He glanced up from his task as he finished repotting the plant. "That when we Worthington men love a woman, we do everything in our power to please her."

"Is that a proclamation?" She asked it lightly, in a teasing manner, but the more earnest part of her longed to know the truth. A child's father should love its mother.

He stood, his gaze intent on her face. "When you are ready to hear the truth, I shall tell you."

Her heart beat hard. "How will you know when I am ready?"

"Uncle Alex!" Something whizzed by Rose's skirt and practically propelled itself into Alex's arms.

Laughing, he knelt to scoop Leela's daughter up into his arms. "If it isn't my favorite niece."

The dark-haired child wrapped her arms around Alex's neck. "I am your only niece." Rose watched as he easily chatted with the child, showing her easy warmth and affection. For the first time she envisioned him as a father. Her child would have a loving papa.

"I have a surprise for you. There is a new foal, a baby horse in the stables that you might like to meet."

"Horsey! I want to see!"

"I hope we are not interrupting." Leela came up behind Rose. "But we thought we'd take advantage of your hospitality for an afternoon."

Rose hugged her. "This is a delightful surprise."

"You are just staying for the afternoon?" Alex asked.

"You must stay longer," Rose insisted.

"Maryam and I are joining Hunt at a house party not far from here. I took advantage of the proximity to drop in for a short visit with my favorite brother and my new sister."

The child stared at Rose. "Hello."

"This is your aunt Rose," Alex explained to the child. "She is my wife."

"You're my aunt now?"

"Hello, Maryam. I am delighted to see you again."

The child squirmed out of Alex's arms. Once he put her down, she tugged on Rose's hand. "Come see Bissa."

She looked to Leela. "What is that?"

"Her new kitten," Leela explained. "Maybe Auntie Rose doesn't care for cats."

The girl frowned. "But everyone likes cats."

The animals made Rose sneeze but she wasn't going to allow that inconvenience to get in the way of becoming acquainted with her new niece. "I would love to meet your kitten, if it's all right with your mother."

"If you're certain?" Leela said. "She can be a handful."

"I have not spent much time with children." Rose allowed the girl to lead her away. "Perhaps I should become better acquainted with them."

LEELA'S GAZE TRAILED them. "How is Rose? She seems a bit pale."

"She is adjusting, I think." Brushing off his hands, Brandon watched his niece lead his wife away. "I am giving her all of the time she needs to come to the conclusion that I am not a cad and deceiver by nature."

"Maryam seems to be taken with her. As taken as her uncle."

He considered her words. He hadn't anticipated falling in love. "It's certainly an unexpected development."

"Do you have any regrets about not taking Lady Olympia to wife?"

"Lady Olympia might make some man a fine wife one day. But for me, no woman compares to Rose. That is why I am willing to be patient. There can be no other option."

Leela's eyes widened. "Now you are beginning to sound like Papa. Perhaps you are more like him than either of us ever imagined."

"Maybe I am. This glasshouse is our parents' Taj Mahal. A physical testament of Father's love for Mama."

She ran a hand over a narrow tree trunk. "Olive trees do remind me so of Mama. What will you build for Rose to show your devotion?"

He chuckled. "Nothing quite so grand as this, I'm afraid. Although I have ordered a drafting table and other furnishings to help her with her work. I've had the music room changed into a studio where she can create her maps."

"Once I got over the shock, I realized that it's not terribly surprising that Rose is the real R. Fleming."

"You saw through the ruse before the rest of us. You did hire her to create the maps for your book."

"She did a beautiful job."

"Hopefully, once her drafting table arrives, she'll be able to complete your maps."

"Rose has already finished my maps. They're at the typesetter."

"Are they?" He frowned. "I thought Rose said she was still working on them. I must have misunderstood."

IN THE AFTERNOON, they had tea in the garden with Leela and Maryam.

"Another sandwich, darling?" Leela asked the girl.

Maryam gazed worshipfully at Rose. "I want Auntie to put it for me."

"Someone is enchanted," Alex remarked.

Leela's eyes twinkled. "She is not the only one," she murmured.

"Which sandwich would you like, sweeting?" Rose didn't know a lot about children, but she was equally drawn to Maryam. Would her child share the girl's beautiful round, dark eyes and thick curls?

The girl pointed out her choice and Rose dutifully delivered it to her plate. "Here you go."

Leela turned to her brother. "Isn't there a new foal in the stables that you wanted to show Maryam?"

Alex swallowed some tea. "There is."

"Perhaps you'd like to take her to see it now because we must be leaving soon."

"Already?" Rose protested. "But you just arrived."

"We have to be back at the house party for supper or the hostess will have my head." Her gaze darted meaningfully between Rose and her brother. "Besides, you two are still newly wed and must have your privacy."

Rose flushed. She could feel Alex's warm gaze on her.

Munching on her food, the child turned to Alex. "When can we go see the new horsey, Uncle?"

"As soon as you'd like," he responded.

Maryam scooted off her chair. "Now, now."

"You are just as impatient as your mother," he said laughingly before rising.

Leela watched Alex lead her daughter away before turning her attention to Rose. "I finally have you alone for a few minutes."

Rose took in Leela's intent gaze. "Should I be worried?" she asked, only half in jest.

"How are you doing? Truly?"

"I am adjusting. Brandon has been most accommodating."

"You've changed him, you know."

"I have? How?"

"He never expected to marry for love."

Rose flushed. Had Alex not shared the circumstances that precipitated their marriage? "We've . . . as you know . . . ours was something of a marriage of convenience."

"Anyone can see that he cares a great deal for you." Leela sipped her tea. "He abandoned very carefully laid plans to make you his wife."

He did? "What sorts of plans?"

"He was going to wed the Duke of Kingsley's daughter, Lady Olympia. She was easily the diamond of the season."

Rose's stomach sank. "I had no idea he had an attachment to another woman."

"Oh, there was no attachment. At least not to Lady Olympia."

"Do you mean to say there was *another* woman?"

"No, nothing like that." Leela chuckled. "Brandon and I grew up in unusual circumstances. Society has not always welcomed us. Our mother was the daughter of a foreign merchant and the ton prides itself on its mythical blue blood."

"Which your mother did not possess." She paused. "And neither do I."

"Precisely. He viewed Lady Olympia as a prize because she would help restore the family position in the eyes of society. And because, by winning her, he would best all of the sons of the men and women who had looked down at my parents."

"He wanted to avenge your parents?"

"Yes. But then he met you."

Rose couldn't stop thinking about the woman Alex had wanted to marry. "What happened to Lady Olympia?"

"He broke things off with her. He'd just begun courting her and never officially asked for her hand, but he had every reason to believe she would have welcomed an offer of marriage."

Rose gasped. "Brandon broke with the daughter of a duke to marry me?" Rose was just a laboring woman, a girl from the merchant class, just like Alex's mother. "But why? When he could have had the most coveted bride of the season?" Why had he set aside all of his dreams and ambitions to take a wife of common blood?

Leela smiled. "Isn't it obvious? He's more like our father than either of us ever thought."

"I am afraid that I don't understand."

"My brother is a driven and determined man. Nothing can deter him from his goals once he sets his mind to something."

"And yet he abandoned his plans to take a noble bride."

"He didn't abandon his goals. His goals changed. You became his goal. He wanted to win you. He still does."

"But why?"

"I think it is obvious, don't you?"

"I'm afraid nothing is obvious to me. I still am staggered that Brandon was supposed to marry the daughter of a duke."

"He is obviously entranced by you. I've never seen my brother this happy. He's as content with himself and his place in life as I've ever seen him." She put her hand over Rose's. "My brother married you because he wanted to. Not because he felt forced into it. I hope you realize that."

"I suppose I am beginning to."

"Good." Leela rose. "Now I have to go and retrieve my daughter so we can be on our way."

Still dazed, Rose stood up. "I'll go and ask Mrs. Waller to pack the sandwiches for Maryam in case she gets hungry later."

Rose smiled to herself on her way to the kitchen. Alex had chosen her over the daughter of a duke. It was unthinkable! He'd abandoned plans to avenge his parents' memories for her. How could she continue to question his devotion to her and their marriage? It was time to become husband and wife in earnest. And that meant no more secrets.

It was time to tell Alex about the baby.

Chapter Twenty-Four

*F*inally." Brandon examined the new drafting table and accompanying desk he'd ordered for Rose. "Put them by the window," he directed the workmen who delivered the pieces.

Rose was seeing Leela and Maryam off while Brandon supervised the delivery. She'd no doubt take her afternoon nap directly after Leela's departure.

His wife's continuing fatigue puzzled and concerned him. The country invigorated Brandon. The open spaces, trees, streams and natural elements calmed his mind while energizing his body. He'd hoped it would do the same for his wife, but Rose napped far more at Highfield than she ever had at New Street.

After what Fleming put her through, Brandon knew enough about Rose to understand that she took to her bed whenever she was upset or overwhelmed. Even though they were growing closer, Rose continued to take to her bed every afternoon. Was it an excuse to avoid him? Was she still having trouble coping with her new situation?

Once the workmen departed, Brandon set about un-
packing the work things Rose had brought from Peckham House. Maybe she'd want to get right to work now
that her drafting table had arrived.

If so, he'd surprise her by helping to set up her workspace. He pulled out the papers, the charcoal, the pencils and paints she used for her mapmaking. He set a
few things up on the flat table next to the drafting paper.

There were all sorts of sketches and notes. He stacked
them neatly, save for one that floated to the floor. He
bent to retrieve it when a drawing caught his eye. It was
the old stone gating near the western edge of his property, the proper boundary outside the water table. Rose's
original map of the Highfield estate completely omitted
the stone gating.

She claimed not to know of the stone fence's existence.
It was an obvious boundary marker, she'd said. And yet,
here it was. He studied the accompanying notes. He
didn't recognize the handwriting, but the intent was
easy to decipher. *Omit the stone fence. Add the water
table to C. Canning's property.* So bold faced. So plain
to understand.

Rose knew about the fence.

"There you are," Rose's cheerful voice sounded
behind him. "Leela and Maryam are off. I shall miss
them." She advanced and examined the drafting table.
"This is perfect. It allows me to draw at a number of
convenient angles. Thank you so much."

He blinked. "You are welcome."

"I cannot wait to get to work."

"On Leela's maps."

"Yes. They are almost complete." As she spoke, she slid a rolled map away from him. "What are you doing in here?"

He watched her casually cover the rolled map up with other papers. "I thought I'd surprise you by helping set up your workspace."

"That is very thoughtful of you but there's no need. I am very particular about how my supplies are organized."

"Is there something you'd like to tell me?"

She stiffened. His heart sank when she avoided meeting his gaze. "Such as?"

"Like why you're lying about Leela's maps. I know you already completed them."

"I don't know what you think is going on but—"

"Why do you feel compelled to hide what you are really working on?" he continued, handing her the paper. "And why claim you didn't know about the stone fence dividing my property from Canning's when this paper that I found with your notes very clearly suggests you did know but eliminated it after being told to do so?"

"What?" She snatched the paper away from him and examined its contents. "What is this? I've never seen this before."

"Are you certain?" He hated to ask. But it was plain as day that she was hiding something. "It was among your things."

"That's not possible. Where exactly did you find it?"

"It was with the things you packed up from your studio at Peckham House to bring here."

Her eyes snapped with anger. "I told you I've never seen that paper."

"I want to believe you."

"But you don't. You are calling me a liar."

"I am not." He struggled to remain calm, to avoid jumping to any rash conclusions. The Rose he knew wasn't capable of this kind of deception. "I am simply asking you for an explanation. You would do the same if the situation was reversed."

"Yes, I would. Because you have lied to me and deceived me during most of our acquaintance. You have given me reason to doubt your word." She pressed a hand against her chest. "I, on the other hand, have never given you reason to doubt my word. I revealed that I drew the map of your estate the very minute you told me of your interest in it."

"Yes, you did," he acknowledged. "But in regards to this matter, can you blame me for wondering how this note came to be here?"

"I blame you for believing that I could cheat you. I blame you for believing that integrity in my work means nothing to me." She threw down the paper. "I thought we were truly beginning to know one another. But the truth is that we don't trust each other."

"Rose, I—"

"I've heard enough." Rose snatched up the rolled map she'd tried to hide from him earlier and walked out of the studio with it tucked under her arm. Unbidden, suspicion flared. What was she so intent on hiding from him that she wanted to keep it on her person?

"Stokes!" Brandon strode out of the room, calling for his butler.

"My lord."

"Who has access to Lady Brandon's studio?"

"Who, my lord?"

"Yes, who besides the servants can come and go at will?"

"No one. Except for the men who delivered the desk and table for the marchioness today but they were never alone."

"Thank you." Brandon ran upstairs to find Dudley supervising the housemaids as they cleaned the master's chambers.

"Have a care with that and with that," Dudley barked.

"Dudley. A moment." He stepped back into the corridor.

"My lord." Dudley joined him, closing the door. "How may I be of service?"

"An unauthorized person has been in the marchioness's studio. They left a note. I want you to find out who it was."

"What was in the note?"

"A valet isn't supposed to ask questions."

"If I ain't asking no questions, how am I supposed ter find the answers?"

"You are supposed to question other people. *Not me.*" Closing his eyes, he pinched the bridge of his nose. "This is of utmost importance. If there is a malefactor among the staff, I want to root him or her out immediately."

"A male what?"

"Malefactor. Someone who commits a wrongdoing. A villain. The other staff will talk to you and Bess and Mrs. Waller more readily than they'll speak to me."

"You got it, guv . . . erm . . . my lord. I'll see to it immediately."

"PLEASE SADDLE A horse for me," Rose instructed the groom at the stables.

"Now, my lady?" He peered up at the gathering clouds. "It looks like rain."

"I won't be long." She needed to see the stone fence for herself. To understand just how inaccurate her map was.

"Shall I send a groom with you? You don't know the estate very well and it's rather large."

"I know it better than you think." After all, she'd mapped out every inch of the property. "I won't require a groom."

Owen climbed out of one of the horse stalls. "I'll go with you Mrs. Fl— . . . erm . . . my lady."

"You get back to mucking out the stalls," the groom ordered.

Owen turned a pleading expression Rose's way. "But 'er ladyship likes me to accompany 'er when she goes riding on account of me being 'is lordship's tiger and all."

"Very well." Rose decided to rescue the boy from an afternoon of cleaning horse droppings. "Owen may accompany me."

"As you wish, my lady." The groom cast a dark look at the boy.

Owen smiled brightly in response.

Before long they were riding toward the western edge of Alex's property. "When did you learn how to sit a horse?" she asked the boy.

"Used to exercise the 'orseflesh sometimes at the grand 'ouse where my ma worked afore she took sick."

"Do you enjoy working in the stables?"

"I love 'orses. One day I'm goin' to be 'is lordship's stable master."

"If you work hard and attend to your lessons, I am sure you can make that happen."

He beamed in response. "Do you know where we're goin'? Or are we lost?"

"We are not lost. I have mapped this property so I know exactly where we're going."

"Is it true that you drew all those maps and not Mr. Fleming?"

"Yes, it's true."

"I'm glad yer not married to Mr. Fleming anymore. Alex is way better than 'im. And 'e has much better 'orseflesh and we eat a lot better."

"Were you hungry when we lived at New Street?"

"Mr. Fleming used to take food for his doxy and 'er brats so there was less fer us." He blushed. "Beggin' yer pardon."

She'd never realized the servants had gone without in order for Roger to feed his family. "Do you have enough to eat now?"

"Oh yes. Alex says we can 'ave tea twice a day and not with used tea leaves. And we get all the ale we want and at breakfast we're ter 'ave meat at least three times a week. We never 'ad meat fer breakfast at New Street."

A rumble of thunder sounded from above and a light sprinkle wet her face. They should turn back but then she spotted it. "There's the fence."

"What fence?" Owen asked.

"This is what I came to see."

He scrunched up his face. "What's so important about an old falling-down fence?"   .

"In this case, it is very significant." They came to a stop. Sitting atop her mount, Rose pulled out the map she'd brought with her and examined it, comparing what she'd drawn previously to the reality before her. The gray stone barrier was crumbling in some areas but it was long and solid and, for a cartographer, told an important story. It was a perfect marker for a boundary on a map. And Roger knew it. That was why he hid it from Rose and hadn't let her travel to Highfield to see the property.

Thunder roared overhead and lightning lit up the sky. Rose's mount whinnied and reared, catching her off guard. She dropped the map and grabbed for the horse's mane, but it was too late and she tumbled to the ground.

"Mrs. Fleming! Erm . . . my lady!" Owen scrambled off his mount and sprinted over just as Rose was getting to her feet. "Are you 'urt?"

"I am fine." Rose tried to stand but her left knee twinged. "Help me over to sit on the fence." She tried not to put too much weight on the injured leg as she limped over to sit down.

"Is yer knee gone bad?"

"I hurt it not too long ago. I think maybe I've reinjured it." Her heart thumped. Her knee was sore but that was nothing. What if she'd hurt the child that she was now convinced she carried? How could she have been so careless? "It doesn't hurt too terribly, but I don't think I should ride back."

"Should I go and get 'elp?"

"Yes, tell Brandon to send a gig for me." That should be safer for the baby than riding back on the horse. "But reassure him that I am well and uninjured. I just wish to be prudent."

"Yes, my lady. Should I just leave you 'ere alone?"

"I shall be perfectly safe. A sprinkle of rain never hurt anyone. Now run along."

Once Owen mounted and rode away, Rose slipped her hand over her belly. "I hope you are well, little one. I am sorry if I scared you. I cannot wait to meet you."

She yawned as she surveyed the property around her. A bird flew overhead. The trees rustled in the slight breeze. Her eyelids grew heavy. This baby left her feeling tired all the time. She slipped off the fence and into the grass. Yawning again, she curled up into a ball, closed her eyes and fell asleep.

"Rose! Rose!" the urgent voice cut into her sleep.

"What?" she mumbled. Someone picked her up. "I can walk," she protested.

"Nonsense." Alex's voice. "You passed out."

She opened her eyes wide. "I did no such thing. I was taking a nap."

His dark eyes probed her. "You already had one nap today. You're clearly ill. I've called for a doctor." He settled her in the wagon.

"I don't need a—" But then she quieted. The doctor might be able to check on the baby. Rose wanted to tell Alex the truth. But what if there was no baby? Especially now that she'd allowed herself to be thrown from her mount by recklessly dropping the reins to study her map. First, she'd see what the doctor had to say. And then she'd tell Alex the truth.

BRANDON PACED THE corridor outside Rose's bedchamber while the doctor examined his wife. "It's taking bloody forever."

"'E's only been in a few minutes," Owen pointed out.

Brandon hadn't noticed the boy standing in the shadows. "What are you doing here?"

"Are you going ter toss me out for letting 'er ladyship take a fall?"

"What were you two doing out there?"

"'Er ladyship said she wanted to see that old stone fence fer 'erself."

Guilt clawed at him. Rose would never have been out there if it weren't for Brandon. "Why were you with her?"

"She refused to take a groom. But I made 'er feel sorry for me cuz I 'ad to sweep out the 'orse droppins so she let me go. So are you?"

"Am I what?"

"Goin' ter toss me out fer letting 'er ladyship take a fall?"

"What? No." He scrubbed a hand down his face. "Go on and get your supper."

Looking relieved, Owen scampered away just as the door to Rose's bedchamber opened and the doctor finally appeared.

"Doctor." Brandon strode over to him. "How is my wife?"

"She is well." The doctor closed the door behind him.

"And her knee?"

"Is fine. She should be able to walk on it by the morning."

"What about her overall health? She is constantly fatigued."

"Well, now, that is to be expected of a lady in her condition."

"What condition?" Alarm roiled in his gut. "What is wrong with her?"

"Women who are increasing are often fatigued."

Brandon blinked. "Women who are increasing?"

"Precisely. I daresay you should expect her ladyship to continue to need plenty of rest before she begins her confinement."

Brandon stared at the man. "Are you saying my wife is with child?"

The doctor studied his face. "You didn't know?"

He interlaced his fingers flat atop his head. He couldn't believe it. "She's with child."

"Yes, probably about two months along."

"And my wife knows she is increasing?"

"She strongly suspected and I believe the marchioness has the right of it. She exhibits all of the symptoms one expects of a woman in a delicate condition."

"Such as? What symptoms?"

"Nausea, fatigue. Tenderness in certain feminine areas."

"And you are certain?" he asked, still dazed.

"Quite sure. You, my lord, will soon be a father."

"May I go in and see her?"

"Of course. But be mindful that she must remain calm and unworried for the sake of the child."

Remorse twisted through Brandon. He'd accused Rose of being a liar and a cheat. His accusation had driven her to behave recklessly. "I shall do my best."

His heart pounding, Brandon went in to see his wife. Rose sat up in bed wearing a dressing gown, the cover pane pulled up to her waist, while Bess fussed around her.

"Please leave us," he said, not taking his eyes from his wife.

"Yes, Ale . . . erm . . . my lord." The maid's curious gaze darted between Brandon and Rose before she quit the room.

Rose held his gaze. She looked well, luminous even. "You are full of surprises, Lady Brandon."

Her hand slid over her belly. "Brandon, I—"

"Please let me speak first." He approached her. "I must beg your forgiveness. I was wrong to suggest that you might have purposely misled me about the stone gate."

"I saw the gate. It's an obvious marker," she said urgently. "That is where the boundary should be drawn."

"None of that matters now."

She frowned. "Of course it does. You must have your land back. It is of critical importance."

"Why?" he asked gently. "So that our son might inherit it one day?"

Her expression softened. "The doctor told you about the baby. You do know that it could be a girl."

"I should love a little girl who looks like her mother. I could spoil her terribly."

"I can well imagine it. You certainly cosset Maryam."

"I am filled with regret that you didn't trust me enough to tell me about the child."

She reached for his hand. "It wasn't that. I suspected that I was increasing before we married but there is no way of knowing for certain until a few months have passed."

"The doctor seems rather sure that you are carrying." He paused. "Is the baby why you consented to marry me?"

"Yes. I couldn't risk having this child born out of wedlock."

His heart contracted. "So you did feel trapped into marriage. Just not for the reason I thought."

"I made a decision that I do not regret. I think perhaps I was relieved to be forced into marriage."

He looked up from their clasped hands. "Relieved?"

"I think I've always known that Alex was the man for me. That I wanted him no matter what."

"Dare I hope you still feel that way?"

"We still have much to learn about each other but I do so want to try to make a go of this marriage."

"As do I." He exhaled a shaky breath. "All of this time, the fatigue, the feeling sick to your stomach, I thought those were reactions to being forced into a marriage you did not want. When, in truth, it's the best possible news. You are with child."

"Are you pleased?"

"Very much so. We are already a family, you and I. But the idea that we have now created a child together is a remarkable bond that will forever connect us." He brought her hand to his lips. "Rosie. My beautiful *Warada*. You had me so worried."

"I am fine, truly. But before we can get on with our lives, we must settle the matter of your land."

He waved a dismissive hand. "I don't want to talk about that."

"I will not rest until we right the wrong that was done to you." Her lips firmed. "I drew that map. My reputation is at risk."

"The doctor says you must stay calm."

"At the moment nothing is more upsetting to me than knowing my inaccurate maps are out there in the world. I will not be able to rest until we change the boundaries in fact and in my maps. And I want to know how that note about the false boundaries came to be in my studio."

"I looked into it and we found the culprit rather quickly."

"You did? Who is it?"

"One of the maids, a new hire, admitted she was paid to put the note in your studio."

"By whom? Who paid her to do that?"

"She didn't know his identity, but I would venture to guess that it was either Canning or Fleming. I intend to get to the bottom of the matter. And then we shall find a way to restore my land and your professional reputation."

"Excellent. If we work together as a team, who could stop us?"

He grinned. "No one. But now you must rest."

"I will if you promise that we can return to Town soon."

"In a few days, perhaps, after you've recovered. In the meantime I will go to London in the morning and set things in motion. And then I shall return here to you."

"What do you have planned?"

"I'm going to call on Canning's grandfather, the Earl of Blaine. Once we know where he stands, we can set our course. If our plan requires our return to Town, so be it. As long as you promise to rest until then. Starting now."

She yawned. "I am tired. Will you stay with me until I fall asleep?"

He squeezed her hand. "It would be my pleasure."

"But you are sitting entirely too far away." She smiled shyly. "Will you come closer?"

Warmth rippled through him. "With pleasure." He gently stretched out beside her on the bed, taking care not to jostle her. Then he did something he'd longed to do for quite some time. He took his wife into his arms. Rose came willingly, cuddling against his chest.

"Did you really jilt a duke's daughter?" she whispered.

"I see my sister the chatterbox has been at work again."

"Is it true?"

He pulled her closer. "I didn't jilt her. I never officially asked for her hand."

"But you chose me, a tradeswoman, over the most desirable woman in London?"

"Wrong." He pressed a kiss against her smooth forehead. "The most alluring woman in all of England is here in my arms."

She yawned. Her breathing gradually became deeper and more rhythmic, her body soft and warm as it pressed up against his. He savored it all, a keen sense of calm coming over him.

He closed his eyes and gave in to the profound pleasure of sleeping with his wife.

Chapter Twenty-Five

𝒯he Marquess of Brandon?" The Earl of Blaine peered at Brandon over the top rims of his spectacles. "So you do exist."

"It would appear so." Brandon hoped Canning's grandfather, the head of the family, would live up to his reputation as an honorable man. He called on Blaine at his London residence on St. James Square and was shown to an upstairs sitting room where he found the old man settled in a stuffed chair, reading a book.

"I appreciate your taking the time to see me, Blaine."

"How could I pass up the opportunity to meet London's most reclusive noble?" Gray eyes twinkled in a weathered face. "There are all sorts of interesting rumors about you."

"I doubt I could live up to them."

"If even a quarter of the stories are accurate, I will not be disappointed." He closed the book in his lap. "Is it true that you grow olive trees in your glasshouse?"

Brandon blinked. "That is true."

"See there? You are of interest already. I would love to see them one day." The earl put the book aside.

"I have longed to visit the Levant. I devoured your sister's travelogues."

"Delilah would be very pleased to hear that."

"I suppose the rumors about your harem in Palestine are too shockingly delicious to be real."

"I am sorry to let you down but I have never been there. And I have yet to meet anyone who actually maintains a harem."

"I am crestfallen. Another preconceived notion shot to smithereens. Do you at least speak Arabic?"

"A bit. I learned the language from my mother's relations. More recently, I engaged a tutor."

"It's a fascinating culture. I've read a great deal about the Levant. We have your ancestors to thank for algebra and trigonometry."

"I imagine there are students the world over who aren't especially grateful to the Arabs for those particular contributions."

The earl chuckled. "True." His rheumy eyes settled on Brandon. "Come and sit. Tell me why you are here."

Brandon found himself liking the older man. He hated to burden him. "I regret that I bring distressing news."

"Unfortunately, bad news is part of life, especially when one has lived to see his seventieth year."

"It is regarding your grandson."

"Which one? I have a dozen."

"Charles Canning."

Interest glimmered in his eyes. "And what is your issue with Charles?"

"We are neighbors. He is attempting to steal my land."

Frowning, the older man removed his spectacles. "That is a serious accusation."

Brandon laid out the details of the story, explaining how Canning and Fleming plotted to mislead Rose about the property lines when she drew the map.

"And you've married this mapmaker?"

"I have."

"You are suggesting that your lady is the R. Fleming who drew Wallthorne's map?"

"She is."

"I've seen his map. It is an exquisite piece of work."

Pride flushed through him. "My marchioness is extraordinarily talented."

"Have you confronted my grandson with your accusations?"

"Not yet."

"You do realize it is my duty as the head of this family to stand by my grandson."

"What if I am able to give you proof?"

"That is a different matter. If you bring me evidence of my grandson's wrongdoing, then you may depend upon me to set matters to rights."

"I have heard you are a fair man."

"I try to be. If you can prove a relation of mine swindled you, you shall receive recompense. I will see to it personally. In the meantime I shall summon my grandson and ask him about this matter."

"What will happen to Canning if I can prove he's a cheat?"

"He will pay a dear price." The earl's amiable expression hardened. "No one tarnishes this family's honor."

Brandon considered the earl's words before speaking. "Perhaps you'd like to come and see my olive trees in person."

"IT'S MUCH SMALLER than Highfield," Rose remarked as Brandon helped her alight from the carriage in front of The Willows, Charles Canning's manor house. The three-story brick manor was larger than the New Street property, but not by much.

"That is to be expected. Highfield is the country seat of a marquess. Canning is just one of several grandsons of an earl."

"*Just?*" Amusement animated her fine eyes. "I see 'Brandon the marquess' is much higher in the instep than 'Alex the footman' ever was."

"I look down upon all liars and cheats." He tucked her hand into his elbow. "And anyone else who is deserving of my scorn, no matter their rank or wealth."

"You speak as if being the younger grandson of an earl makes Mr. Canning utterly disposable."

"He is, in society's eyes. I did not decide that. The ton did."

She surveyed the landscape around them. "How much land does Mr. Canning own?"

"Not much. The Earl of Blaine has four sons and the eldest, his heir, will get the lion's share of the money and property. The grandsons will get even less. What Canning tried to steal from me would add significantly to his very limited assets."

The circular drive was immaculate, the bushes and flowers perfectly trimmed. The house gleamed in the sun. "He certainly takes good care of his property."

"The place was a bit run-down when Canning took possession of it. No one lived here when Leela and I were growing up. The earl purchased it and gave it to Canning as a gift when he reached the age of majority."

She couldn't imagine being gifted a house. "It is in excellent condition now."

"Canning takes great pride in the manor and its grounds. He apparently pours all of his money and energy into bettering the place. He engaged London's most renowned landscape architect to design his gardens."

They approached the glossy black door. "What if the butler doesn't admit us?" Rose asked. "Mr. Canning doesn't know that we're coming."

"Oh, Canning will see us. His butler would never turn a marquess away."

He felt her eyes on him. "You truly are not an easy man to decipher."

"How so?" He was making a conscious effort to be as open as he could with her. It was not his natural state. "I am being completely frank with you."

"At times you refer to your title and the nobility in mocking terms, yet you don't hesitate to use the power that comes with rank and wealth."

"What is the point of having power if you don't use it? I do attempt to employ the privileges I've been afforded to help those who've been born without them."

"Is that what you did with Hanna? At the family supper party, your cousin mentioned that you'd stepped in to assist her."

"Precisely. The medical establishment attempted to ban Hanna from practicing bonesetting in London. I stepped in and used my rank to shield her from that injustice."

"It almost sounds as if you do not believe in the inherent superiority of the nobility," she gently teased.

"The idea that a man born to wealth and status is inherently superior to one who works to earn his keep is farcical."

"You must be the most enlightened peer in all of England. I suppose mixing with your mother's people has broadened your view of the world."

He shot her a wry look. "Being born a shade or two darker than your average nobleman educated me to the ways of the world as nothing else ever could."

She lowered her voice, nerves edging each word. "Do you think our plan will work?"

Before he could answer, the door to Canning's country manor opened and, as Brandon expected, they were immediately admitted. The inside was as pristine and immaculate as the exterior, with tasteful furnishings and polished floors.

Rose eyed a large blue-and-white porcelain vase showcased on a side table. "He has expensive tastes for a man who is not expected to inherit."

"As I understand it, The Willows is profitable."

"The Marquess of Brandon?" Canning swept into the receiving room. "When my butler informed me that my neighbor was calling, I could scarcely believe it. But here you are."

"In the flesh," Brandon said.

"What a pleasure it is to at last make your acquaintance." Canning's guarded gaze darted between Brandon and Rose. He showed no sign that he recognized Brandon as Roger Fleming's footman. "I have met all of my other neighbors. But you have remained quite the hermit."

"Hardly a hermit. Merely selective about who I include

in my social circle," Brandon said with icy courtesy. "May I present my marchioness?"

"Lady Brandon." Canning's face lit with interest. "I had not heard that Brandon has taken a wife."

"It was a private affair," Brandon said.

Canning bent over Rose's gloved hand. "Do we have Lady Brandon to thank for his lordship's sudden desire to be in company with his neighbors?"

"You could say that." Rose slipped her hand from Canning's grasp at the first opportunity.

"I am pleased to welcome you both to The Willows." Despite his outward show of ease, Canning's shoulders were rigid. "Would you like to see the gardens? They are my current pride and joy. Although, I have also installed an apple orchard that gives me great satisfaction."

"Not at the moment," Rose said. "You are correct to assume that I am partially responsible for our visit to The Willows."

He blinked several times in succession. "Is it because you wish to see my roses? I am known to grow the finest ones in the county. My rose garden is without peer."

"We have a matter to discuss with you," Brandon said.

"Oh?" He fidgeted with a cuff link at his wrist. "My grandfather has summoned me to call upon him tomorrow. He mentioned that it has something to do with you."

Rose exchanged a glance with Brandon. "He no doubt wishes to speak with you about the map I created that determined the property lines for your estate as well as Brandon's."

Canning's forehead crinkled. "I am afraid I do not

understand. As Brandon here knows, we engaged Mr. Roger Fleming, the foremost mapmaker in London."

She took a fortifying breath, her chest visibly moving in and out. "Before my most recent marriage, my name was Rose Fleming. The R. Fleming signature on your map is mine. I was wed to Roger Fleming."

"I thought you looked familiar. And what do you mean *was*?" His brows shot up. "Is Mr. Fleming deceased?"

Brandon interjected. "The marriage was annulled."

This was the story he and Rose had decided upon. An annulment was scandalous, but living with a man to whom you were not wed was far worse. Besides, being a marchioness would mitigate most societal scorn.

"Annulled?" Canning's glance flicked between Brandon and Rose. "On what grounds, may I ask?"

"You may not. Let us just say that fraud was involved."

"What is pertinent to you," Rose said, "is that I created the maps, not Roger. I now know that the maps are inaccurate and must be redrawn."

"You *are* serious." Canning stared at her. "*You* are R. Fleming? You. A woman. And not Roger?"

"That is correct. Roger led people to believe that he made the maps."

"You've cheated all of the people who believed their maps were being drawn by a man known to be the finest cartographer in London."

"You're one to speak about being a cheater," Brandon interjected.

"I am the finest cartographer in London." Rose lifted her chin. "But I am not a man. The quality of the maps speaks for itself. Whether they were drawn by a woman should have no bearing."

"It makes all of the difference." Indignation filled Canning's words. "A woman could not command the prices we all paid when we thought Roger Fleming was making those maps. I've been swindled."

"Give it up, Canning," Brandon said. "You knew before today that my wife drew your map. That is why you paid one of my maids to plant that note about the boundaries in her work studio."

The cords in Canning's throat moved. "Why would I do such a thing?"

"To make it look like those were Fleming's original notes, so that it would appear that my wife was part of the deception. I could hardly bring you down if it meant implicating my wife as well."

Canning's face darkened. "I think you should leave."

"With pleasure." Brandon removed the letter from his pocket. "But first, let's discuss this missive that you wrote to Roger Fleming that spells it all out. You told him how you wanted the map drawn to cheat me out of my water meadow."

"That paper is w-worthless," he stammered. "Those are merely the boundaries of my property as I believed them to be. I would argue that I gave specific markers. Truthful ones."

"Who do you think you are dealing with?" Brandon's voice was a low warning. "It has long been acknowledged that the dividing line between our two estates is the old stone fence, which puts the water meadow solidly on my side of the boundary."

"A marker such as that would be a natural dividing line for any cartographer," Rose added. "Mr. Fleming neglected to mention its existence to me. He knew it would be an obvious indicator of where the boundary should be drawn."

Canning's hand slid into the pocket of his tailcoat. "It is not my fault that your husband—or whatever he was, or is, to you—neglected to mention some old fence. All my letter did was indicate to him what I personally believed were my property lines. I did nothing improper."

"Except for threatening to expose Fleming as a bigamist if he didn't draw the map in a way that swindled me out of my land," Brandon said. "Your biggest mistake was underestimating me. No one steals what is mine."

"No one will believe you." His right hand still in his pocket, Canning swiped perspiration from his top lip with the back of his left. "How will you tell the story of how I chicaned you without revealing your own wife's very scandalous past? Will you tell them that before becoming your marchioness, your lovely wife lived with a man without the benefit of marriage?"

"You will leave my wife out of this," Brandon said chillingly. "Unless you would prefer that I call you out on a field of honor."

"A duel?" Rose exclaimed. "There will be no duel fought over my honor."

"And what of Lady Brandon's honor?" Canning pushed. "She *has* admitted to drawing the map. She and Fleming were clearly partners in any deception. Are you really such a fool, Brandon, that you cannot see what is in front of you?"

"That is what you wanted me to believe, isn't it?" Brandon kept his words calm and measured. He did not allow men of Canning's ilk to provoke him. "That's why you planted those notes in my wife's studio."

Canning pointed at Rose. "This *lady* has ch-cheated every client she has ever had by pretending to be a man. And now she is ba-bamboozling you by convincing you she wasn't in league with Fleming on this map."

"That," Brandon pointed out, "sounds like an acknowledgment that you provided inaccurate parameters in hopes of stealing my land."

"What if I did?" Canning burst out. "I would counsel you to think before you pursue this matter any further. You have far more to lose than I do. Given your mother's low associations and your father's eccentricity, you are already in possession of a dubious reputation. Adding a wife of questionable birth and character will not enhance your consequence."

Brandon smothered a tug of amusement. The little bastard actually thought he had him beat. He smiled coldly. "You believe I will allow you to steal my land in order to protect my wife."

"What else can you do? Yes, I admit it. I did use my knowledge of Fleming's bigamy to get what I want. I threatened to expose him if he didn't produce a map that gave me the water meadow."

"*My* water meadow. You are admitting that you stole from me."

"I'll deny it to anyone who asks. Who are you going to tell? Who will believe you?"

Brandon stepped forward. "Make no mistake. You will pay."

"Stop right there!" Canning pulled something from

his pocket, a small flintlock pistol, no bigger than six inches long.

"He has a gun!" Rose exclaimed.

Fear for Rose's safety tore through Brandon. He kept his gaze on Canning's face. "There is no need for violence."

"It is a lucky thing that I thought to bring a pistol for my p-protection." Canning waved the gun around. "I thought to myself, what is a man of Arabian extraction capable of? There is no telling what someone of your ilk might do."

"Stop this nonsense at once!" The Earl of Blaine shuffled into the room.

"Grandpapa?" Canning's mouth fell open. "What are you doing here?"

"Your butler let me in. Lord Brandon came to me with a very concerning allegation. I have been listening." His lined face was bright with anger. "Put that thing away before you further dishonor this family."

Canning flushed. "I don't know what he told you but—"

"What the marquess said to me is irrelevant." Blaine spoke sharply. "What does matter is what I have just heard with my own ears."

Canning kept the pistol trained on Brandon. "You planned this. You arranged to bring Grandfather here."

"Guilty as charged." From the corner of his eye, he registered Rose edging closer to Canning. *What the devil is she doing*? "I thought it would be the most expedient way to deal with you."

"And thank goodness he did," Blaine said. "You have behaved most dishonorably. I am ashamed to call you my grandson."

"This is all Brandon's fault. I will shoot him for dis-dishonoring my name." Canning stumbled over his words. "We'll say he attacked me and that I was defending myself. Grandfather, you shall be the witness. Everyone will believe you. Your reputation is exemplary."

"Exactly," his grandfather snapped. "Which is why I will have nothing to do with murder. Put that thing down this instant."

Brandon's heart slammed. Rose had managed to move behind Canning without his noticing. If he noticed her, God only knew what he would do. What if the pistol went off by accident?

Canning shook his head in jerky motions. "I cannot," he pleaded with his grandfather. "You don't understand- "

"I do," Rose said just before she smashed the blue-and-white vase over Canning's head. The villain stumbled backward, a stunned expression on his face. Brandon leaped forward and wrestled the pistol out of Canning's hand as the man staggered, trying to keep his balance.

"I should shoot you myself," he growled, his pulse galloping, "for daring to endanger my wife."

"I would be much obliged if you did not," the earl said, "although my grandson does deserve to be punished."

Brandon set the pistol down and pulled Rose into his arms. "Are you hurt?"

"No." She hugged him tightly. "Are you?"

"I'm the one who's injured," Canning snarled. "She broke a valuable vase."

"I wish I had broken your head for threatening my husband," she snapped.

Canning sank into the nearest chair. "I wouldn't have shot him," he said to his grandfather. "I was just defending myself. I can explain everything about the map."

"I doubt that. This is what will happen next," the earl said in a hard tone. "Lady Brandon will create a new map, one we shall all accept. We will put this matter quietly to rights, if Lord Brandon agrees."

"I have no quarrel with you, my lord." Brandon tried to calm his raging pulse. "But Canning must pay for trying to cheat me and for putting my wife's life at risk."

"I agree." The earl nodded. "What are your terms?"

"I demand that Canning be exiled from London. He is a danger to society."

"Exiled from London!" Canning exclaimed. "Not likely."

"Done." The earl spoke over his grandson's objections. "What else do you require to be satisfied?"

"I want this place."

"Which place?" Canning asked.

"The Willows."

"What? *You want my home*?" Canning's eyes bulged. "Absolutely not. You cannot have it."

"The Willows is not part of the entailment." The earl gave Brandon a considering look. "It was meant for Charles to have."

"*Was*?" Canning beseeched his grandfather. "You know how hard I've worked to transform this property into a showcase."

The earl favored Canning with a disdainful look. "We cannot ask Lord and Lady Brandon to live side by side with a neighbor who not only cheated him, but also threatened to kill him." He met Brandon's gaze. "Will my grandson's exile and the acquisition of The Willows settle this dispute between our houses?"

"I want him guarded at all times by a minder of my choice while he is in exile. His minder will report directly to me. I must be assured that your grandson will pose no further threat to my family."

"Consider it done," the older man said. "Would meeting your conditions mean that my family name will not be touched by dishonor?"

"It would. That will satisfy me."

"You cannot be serious!" Canning sputtered. "I am the fourth son of the fourth son. The Willows is the only property I've ever owned or could hope to own. It is my birthright."

"Perhaps you should have thought of that before you tried to kill my husband," Rose snarled. "I should shoot you right now."

"I understand your sentiments, Lady Brandon." The earl turned to his grandson. "You will sell the house and land to Lord Brandon."

"I will not."

"You dare to defy me?" The earl's eyes blazed. "I should disown you for your impudence and dishonorable behavior."

"It's my land," Canning whimpered. "It's all I have."

The earl ignored him. "We will handle the sale of the property through my solicitor," he said to Brandon. "Charles will obey me."

"Very well." Brandon tipped his head. "I shall have my man of business contact your agent."

"Then the matter is settled. I apologize for the harm my grandson has done you."

"But The Willows is mine," Canning practically wailed. "It means more to me than anything else."

"Which is precisely why I am taking it from you," Brandon said with satisfaction, "so that you will know what it feels like to have your land stolen from you."

Canning shook with rage. "You, sir, are nothing but an Arab thief!"

"Unlike you, I do not steal. I am willing to pay a fair price for The Willows." His smile was cold. "Do not worry. Despite rumors to the contrary, we Arabs do have a deep attachment to our land. I intend to take excellent care of it. In fact, nothing would please me more than to plant a grove of olive trees here at The Willows."

Chapter Twenty-Six

$\mathscr{I}$ never thought I'd see olive trees in England." The earl strolled past the long rows of plants in the glass-house once they returned to Highfield. They'd left Canning under guard and with instructions to pack up and depart The Willows in three days' time.

Relief cascaded through Rose. It was over. Alex was safe, he had his land back and her faulty maps would soon be out of circulation.

Blaine gave her a considering look. "So you are the mapmaker."

Her husband nodded. "Allow me to properly intro-duce my marchioness, Lady Brandon."

"My lord." She executed the curtsy she'd practiced, despite being unsure of whether a marchioness should lower herself before an earl. It was deuced confusing trying to remember who she should bow to and who should bow to her. If she'd erred, both Alex and the earl were too gracious to show it.

"Very pretty." Blaine nodded approvingly. "And not just the curtsy. Your marchioness is a beauty, Brandon."

Alex's warm gaze rested on Rose. "I am very aware of my good fortune."

"Is it true that you created Wallthorne's map?" Blaine asked her.

She lifted her chin. "I did, my lord."

"And you are still making maps, even though you've wed the marquess?"

"I am." She tensed for his censure. Apparently, no one had ever heard of a marchioness who worked.

Alex came to her side. "She is far too talented not to share her gift with the world."

"I agree. What are you currently working on?"

She darted a glance at Alex before responding. "It is a secret project. I am afraid I cannot reveal more."

Alex's brows drew together but he remained silent.

The earl chortled. "I suppose we have to allow our wives to keep their secrets, eh, Brandon?"

Her husband's questioning gaze stayed on Rose's face. "Apparently."

"Perhaps one day your lady will draw a map for me."

Rose tipped her head. "It would be my honor."

"I've no doubt my wife will stay busy, given her enormous talents." Alex cleared his throat before focusing his complete attention on the earl. "This afternoon you learned some things of an extremely sensitive nature regarding my wife's past. I hope we can rely upon your discretion."

"You may," the earl responded, "as I hope I may depend upon yours. Charles's machinations must not be allowed to tarnish my family name."

"Then we are in agreement."

"Indeed." The earl paused to examine a particularly

robust plant. "Will you really install an olive tree orchard at The Willows?"

Alex lifted a shoulder. "Perhaps."

"I should like to see that."

"I will invite you to see the grove once it matures. In the meantime, as a token of our friendship, I shall send that particular olive tree to you as a gift, along with directions for your gardener on how to care for it."

"That is most kind. Once you officially own The Willows, this conflict between our houses will be resolved."

"Absolutely. Among other things, the olive tree is a symbol of peace and tranquility." Alex offered his hand and they shook on it. "Once my gift arrives at your estate, I shall consider all matters between us to be officially settled."

"BRANDON?" ROSE ENTERED the glasshouse.

"Back here," he called, setting down the last of the cushions. After the earl's departure hours ago, Rose had retired to her bedchamber for her afternoon nap and he'd spent that time arranging his surprise.

"You may go," he said to his valet.

Dudley had the audacity to wink at him. "This oughta get her ladyship to open her door to you."

"Yes, thank you for that. As I said, you may go."

"Make sure you don't louse it up this time." Dudley nudged him. "You know, the bed sport part."

Brandon exhaled loudly through his nostrils. "That is none of your business. Nor should a valet speak to his master in that way." Their time as fellow footmen sharing a cramped attic chamber made it enormously challenging to establish the appropriate servant-employer relationship. "And, just to be clear, I have had no complaints *at all* in that area."

Dudley looked dubious. "If you say so, guv." He exited through the side door just as Rose came into view with a rolled map tucked under her arm.

"It's almost time for supper. What are you doing back out here?" Her eyes widened as she took in the scene before her. "What have you done?"

"I've arranged for us to have a little celebration for two."

She surveyed the carpets, blankets and pillows spread out on the floor among the olive trees. Mrs. Waller had laid out trays of food, a feast really, of Rose's favorite treats. Lit lanterns were scattered around the area while the delicious smell of the food mixed with the thick, smoky scent of Brandon's beloved olive trees. Her eyes glittered. "This is beautiful."

He offered his hand. "Will you join me?"

She took it. "I most certainly will."

He closed his fingers around hers, relishing the slide of her skin against his palm. "Are you comfortable?" He settled her among the pillows. "Maybe you shouldn't be on the floor in your delicate condition?"

"I am with child. I'm not an invalid." She laughingly pulled him down beside her. "I will not break."

"Thank goodness for that." He willingly sank down next to her. "Did you rest well during your nap?"

"Very much so." Her face was radiant. "I also have something for you."

"What is it?"

"See for yourself." She reached for the rolled map and opened it, spreading it out before him.

Brandon caught his breath. It was the most spectacular map he'd ever laid eyes on, even more splendid than the first map she'd created for him. "It's Highfield."

She beamed. "Do you like it?"

He tried to absorb the unique features. "The glasshouse."

"Yes."

She'd also drawn the stone fence and the disputed water meadow. His finger glided across the map to the tiny but exquisitely detailed orchard. "You included the olive trees out by the southern property line."

"Those were my last addition. And look behind the kitchen."

"The herb garden." He swallowed. "Including *maramia*." Emotion welled in his chest. All his life he'd stood apart from everyone. Largely alone until Rose swept into his world, offering the lifeline he hadn't realized he needed. Brandon felt seen, truly known, for the first time in his memory. Rose didn't just see a marquess. Or the son of the Arab merchant mother. She saw all of him, all of the extraordinary, all of the mundane, details that make a person who they are. "This was the secret project you hid from me."

"Yes. I wanted to be able to present you with the new accurate map the moment you officially got your land back."

"How did you complete this so quickly?"

"All of those naps I've been taking weren't really naps. At least not all of them."

"You were working on this?" His vision blurred as he stared at her handiwork. Rose had not spoken the words, but she had embedded all of her love for him in each stroke of this map.

"What is it?" Her brows drew together as she watched the changing expressions on his face. "Do you not like the map?"

"I adore it." He lifted his gaze to meet hers. "As I love and adore you. With all of my heart."

"Oh, Alex." Her eyes glistened.

"You called me Alex." His voice was whisper soft. "Does that mean—?"

She cupped his cheek. "I am grateful that you came to New Street to be a footman." Her voice caught. "What if we'd never met? I'd still be alone with nothing to look forward to. And now I have everything—you, this child, the shop and my maps. How did I get so lucky?"

"I am the fortunate one. Without you I'd still be alone and not even realize what I was missing." He put the map aside and took her into his arms. "I hope you bury me."

"What? Why would I do that?"

He kissed her nose. "It's something my mother used to say to my father. But I never truly understood its meaning until now, with you."

"What does it mean?"

"Literally, that I hope you outlive me so that I will never have to know the pain of living in this world without you."

"That is lovely." Tenderness shone in her eyes. "I love you, Alex."

He kissed her long and slow, absorbing the tiniest sensations. The taste of her, the warmth of her skin, the delicate scent of her perfume. "Maybe we should eat first."

She pulled him down over her. "We can eat later."

"But the baby."

"Will be fine. I asked the doctor."

Delight streaked through him. "You did?"

"Yes. The servants aren't coming back, are they? I'm desperate for you."

She was? "No, I told them we'll need our privacy."

"Thank goodness," she said breathlessly as they both struggled out of their clothes. Coming up on his knees, Brandon pulled off his linen shirt and then helped her disrobe. First her gown and then her stays and chemise. Her body was already plusher. Her breasts soft and bountiful. The curve of her hips more generous. She looked like all of his tomorrows. She was his purpose when he hadn't known he lacked one.

He explored the landscape of her body, the tiny details no one else would ever be privy to. He explored the dip of her collarbone, the breasts swollen from his child, the wondrous curve of her belly where their baby grew, parts of them forever intertwined.

"Tell me what you like," he said. "I want to please you."

"I adore everything about how you touch me."

"Still, no one knows the map of your body better than you." He touched a particularly sensitive spot. "How's this?"

"Oh! I guess you could say you've found my olive trees." He smiled and applied himself to tending to that particular spot until she was writhing and moaning beneath him. She directed him to the places on her body and the types of touches that gave her the most pleasure. He loved on her with exquisite tenderness, touching, stroking and arousing, until he felt her readiness.

When he finally settled himself over her, his cock was hard and throbbing. She spread her thighs, welcoming him into her body. He plunged into her in one desperate motion. She sighed and adjusted herself to better accommodate him.

He moved inside her, her body clutching and stroking his cock. "Don't hold back. I want all of you," he whisper-panted in her ear, the pressure welling up in his groin.

"I couldn't subdue myself even if I wanted to." Her voice was strained as she rocked her pelvis to take him deeper. "The times I did almost killed me."

"That's my girl." He kissed her with everything in him, all of the love, the tenderness, the gratitude, that this woman had consented to be his. And he was hers, unreservedly. "Always. My beautiful *Warada*. Forever and always."

SOMETIME LATER THEY covered themselves with the blankets and indulged in the succulent food Mrs. Waller had arranged. Lying side by side on their stomachs, they nibbled *maamoul* and sipped *maramia* tea while poring over the new map together.

"Mrs. Waller learned how to make your favorite cookies?" Rose asked as she bit into the deliciously flaky date-filled treat.

"Apparently, she insisted on having a lesson with *Citi*

before we left. Even though she is the housekeeper, Mrs. Waller wanted to make these for us herself."

"That was good of her." She watched him examine the map. "Are the olive trees your favorite element?"

He shook his head. "They're my second favorite."

"Truly?" Puzzled, she reexamined the map. "What do you like best?"

"This." He trailed a light finger over her signature. "Rose, Marchioness of Brandon. I love the sound of that."

"I felt like an interloper when I signed it. Using my title as my signature sounds awfully lofty."

"I think it's perfect." He shifted over to kiss her. "What is more appropriate than having the mistress of Highfield draw and sign the map of her domain?"

"Hopefully, it will not be my last commission."

"Don't be ridiculous. Of course it won't be."

"We cannot know for certain how people will react once they realize all of R. Fleming's maps were drawn by a woman. Half of my previous customers could very well ask for some of their money back."

Brandon bit back a smile. "That's not going to happen."

"How can you know?" She examined his face. "What aren't you telling me?"

He kissed her long and meaningfully. After giving in for several long and delicious minutes, she broke the kiss. "You are trying to distract me."

"I *am* trying to distract you." He rolled over onto his back and pulled her atop him, his hands sneaking under the blankets to cup her delightfully rounded arse. "Is it working?"

She sat up, straddling him, treating him to a most gratifying view. "It is most definitely working."

"Excellent." And then he set about diverting her even more.

"WHY ARE YOU coming to the shop with me?" Rose asked Alex as they entered the establishment. They'd returned from Highfield the previous day and she was eager to visit the shop after having been away.

"Is it not obvious?" Alex held the door for her. "I cannot bear to be parted from my extraordinary wife."

"We've just spent the last week in extreme togetherness." Very extreme. Rose flushed at the memories. Since becoming husband and wife in truth, they rarely left each other's side. Intimacies happened often, more than once a day, and sometimes in the most unexpected places. It was as if Alex was determined to make love to her in every room at Highfield.

"Welcome back, my lady," Ben greeted them.

"Is all well?" she asked. "Did the new hand towels arrive?"

"Yes, ma'am. Just last week." Ben brought out some of the samples and they spent a few minutes discussing the new products Rose wanted to develop. Ben also caught Rose up on other business matters.

Beside her, Alex was brimming with energy. Or was it anticipation? Whatever was the matter with him, he was distracting her when she needed to attend to business. "Are you all right?"

"Me?" He tapped his foot energetically. "Fine. Excellent."

"Then what is wrong with you?"

He edged back closer to the wall. "With me? Nothing. Nothing at all."

She caught sight of something on the wall behind him that had not been there when she'd departed for Highfield. "What is that?"

Alex's eyes twinkled. "What is what?"

"What's on the wall there behind you?"

Ben beamed. "It arrived just the day before yesterday."

"What did?" Rose moved closer and gently ushered Alex out of the way. "What in the world?" Her mouth dropped open. She blinked. Then turned to her husband's smiling face. "You did this?"

"Your talent did this, but yes, I saw to it."

She stared at the display of the royal arms and the words, *By appointment.* "We cannot display the arms." Alarm trilled through her. "We don't have a royal warrant of appointment."

Alex grinned as he pulled a document from his pocket. "Don't you?"

She read the letter. It took her several moments to absorb its meaning. "We have a royal warrant?" she half whispered.

"*You* have a royal warrant. It appears that the prince regent is very taken by your work. He saw the map you did for Wallthorne."

"It isn't possible . . ."

"Why not? You make the very best maps. And this confirms that your work is fit for royalty. Your place as the finest mapmaker in London is assured."

She could hardly believe it. A royal warrant lent her

maps the ultimate prestige. Her future as a mapmaker, and the future of the shop, would never be in question as long as she held a royal warrant. "I don't know what to say."

Alex took her hand and started pulling her to the stairs. "Come along. There's more to show you." Ben smiled and shook his head as he watched Alex usher Rose up the stairs.

"Why are we going upstairs? It's just an empty apartment."

"Not any longer." He threw the door open, inviting her to step inside. In place of a dusty, empty space, was a fully furnished apartment, decorated for comfort in bold colors. A new drafting table stood by the window.

"Oh, Alex, it's marvelous!"

"I asked for Leela's help. She has a rather artistic friend who excels at home decor."

"I adore it, but how much did you spend on this? I hate to be wasteful."

"Nonsense. This is a place where you can work in peace when you are here at the shop. And once the baby comes, you might want the child and its nurse to visit you here."

"You've thought of everything." She wrapped her arms around his neck. "It's so perfect I might never want to go home."

He pulled her in close. "Then I shall have to live here with you."

"You truly are full of delightful surprises," she said. "Life with you will never be boring."

"So true." He started maneuvering her across the room.

"What are you doing?"

"I also had the bedchamber redone." A devilish glint lit his eyes. "And I am about to show you just how exciting married life can be."

Epilogue

$\mathcal{R}$ose shook out her hands. Brandon took hold of one of them. "You're cold."

"I'm nervous." She adjusted her hat with her free hand. "It is not every day that a tradesperson is introduced to the ton."

"You are now the Marchioness of Brandon and that is what people will see when they look at you." He paused. "That and your hat, of course."

"I feel bad for you that you cannot discern the artistic from the outlandish. There is a difference." She had ordered a particularly fine hat for the occasion, one designed with a tasteful abundance of feathers, tassels and beading.

For her entrance into society, Brandon had arranged an exhibition of Rose's finest maps, which were on loan from their owners. In preparation for the show, she had changed the signature on each of the maps. In place of R. Fleming, all of the maps were now signed by *Rose, Marchioness of Brandon*.

"Brace yourself." He settled her hand on his arm. "Here we go."

Rose took a deep breath as they entered the exhibition

hall. The Duke and Duchess of Huntington were the first to greet them. "You must come and visit us at Eaton Park," the duke said.

Leela's eyes twinkled. "Hunt hopes to convince Rose to draw a map of our country estate."

"He could have a long wait," Brandon informed them. "Ever since she secured a royal warrant, Rose has been busier than ever."

"But surely, family should go to the front of the line," said Viscount Griffin as he approached with his wife, Hanna, on his arm. "I would very much like a map of Ashby, my country estate."

Brandon exchanged a knowing look with Rose. "She will have her hands very full in a few months' time. She cannot take on too much extra work."

Before long Rose was pulled away by admirers, leaving Brandon alone with the two couples. He and Leela strolled about the exhibit, admiring Rose's artistry.

"The maps she created for my volume are also extraordinary," Leela said.

"Everything about Rose is exceptional."

She squeezed his arm. "I cannot tell you how relieved I am that you've found true contentment."

"I enjoy every single moment I get to spend with Rose. I never thought such an attachment was possible."

They paused before Rose's depiction of Highfield. "She did a remarkable job." Leela studied the map. "I daresay this piece demonstrates just how well she knows you. And that's no easy task."

"She does." Being with Rose gave him an inner calm that had eluded Brandon until now. Until her. "I am a most fortunate man."

They resumed strolling the exhibition hall. "It's been a long journey but we both managed to find our way," Leela said.

"I adored our parents but I will not bring up my children the way they raised us. They obviously meant well. But can anyone find true contentment if they're expected to completely ignore a significant part of who they are?"

"No. I don't believe so. Maryam is already learning Arabic, along with French."

Rose joined them, her cheeks flushed with excitement. "Several people have approached me about drawing a map for them."

"That's wonderful!" Leela kissed Rose's cheek. "Congratulations. I'll leave my brother to you while I go and run my husband to ground."

"I am not the least bit surprised by your success." Brandon set his wife's hand on his arm. "Your services are so much in demand that you might consider raising your fees."

She brimmed with energy. "It is a lot to keep track of, in addition to the shop."

"Maybe you should consider hiring an assistant."

"Perhaps I'll start looking for a footman," she teased. "The last one I engaged proved to be enormously helpful."

"Never. The only personal footman you'll ever engage is standing by your side."

"I don't know about that. He isn't very skilled at brushing out my skirts."

"But he *is* excellent at getting under them." He brushed a kiss against her cheek, not caring who saw. "The rest of the chores can be distributed among the staff. From now on I think it's best that only female servants touch your personal things. But I shall still tend to you, especially in the bath."

Her eyes heated. "I might very well need to soak in the tub when we return home."

"Now, that would be my pleasure," he murmured in her ear. "After all, it is a footman's duty to see to his mistress's every need."

Acknowledgments

$\mathcal{A}$lthough Rose is a fictional character, her professional plight is based in reality. Female mapmakers in the 1800s often signed their work with their initials in order to hide the fact that a woman had created the map. As a result, generations of talented women cartographers have likely been lost to history.

And yes, there really were Arabs in England during the Regency era. Arab trading houses located in Manchester exported Lancashire-made cotton goods to the Arab world. There were four Arab trading houses in Manchester in 1798, according to directories from the time.

My deepest gratitude goes to my editor, Carrie Feron, who I am convinced knows more about editing than anyone else in publishing. My thanks also to associate editor Asanté Simons and the entire Avon team.

Natasha Yaqub generously shared her experiences of growing up as the child of parents from two cultures. Her candid insights helped inform the characters of Brandon and his sister, Leela. My dear friend Megann Yaqub's unstinting support for every book, her plotting help and critiques of multiple drafts, means everything to me.

I'm grateful to be in the publishing trenches with Joanna Shupe, who provides equal doses of friendship and writerly support. And Faith Lapidus is often one of the last lines of defense, finding typos and other errors, before I turn in the final draft of the manuscript. Also, I forgot to give a shout-out to Usma Khan for sending me the cover inspiration for *The Viscount Made Me Do It*, so here it is now.

Thank you to the readers, librarians, bloggers and bookstagrammers who lift up my books and spread the word about them. I truly appreciate each and every one of you.

And finally, to my husband Taoufiq, who has had my back for twenty-five years, and who told me I should write books long before I ever imagined I could. This one—and all of them really—is for you, *gleebee*.

Next month, don't miss these exciting new love stories only from Avon Books

A Scot is Not Enough by Gina Conkle

Alexander Sloane is finally a finger's breadth from the government post he's worked toward for years. He has one last step—dig up incriminating evidence on the most captivating woman in London. The coy and clever Cecelia MacDonald has never had any trouble using men to do her bidding. But when a mutual enemy proves deadly, she must rely on Alexander for more than flirtation.

The Cowboy Says Yes by Addison Fox

Hadley Wayne is known all over America as The Cowgirl Gourmet, a beloved star on The Cooking Network. Everyone knows all about her perfect life with Zack Wayne, her perfect rancher husband—but it's not real. They're living separate lives in separate bedrooms. But when their work has them leaving the safety of the ranch, they begin to rediscover why they fell in love all those years ago.

All the Duke I Need by Caroline Linden

Philippa Kirkpatrick has been raised at Carlyle Castle by her doting guardian, the Duchess of Carlyle. Preoccupied with the duke's health, the duchess has left the estate in Philippa's hands. When the handsome, scandalously bold William Montclair arrives as the new estate steward, the horrified duchess wants to sack him on sight. Philippa is just as shocked . . . but also, somehow charmed.

REL 0322

NEW YORK TIMES
BESTSELLING AUTHOR

Cathy Maxwell

If Ever I Should Love You
978-0-06-265574-5

A Match Made in Bed
978-0-06-265576-9

The Duke That I Marry
978-0-06-265578-3

His Secret Mistress
978-0-06-289726-8

Her First Desire
978-0-06-289730-5

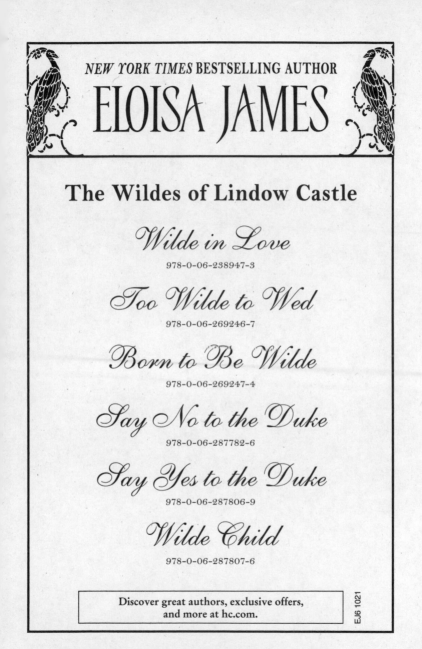

NEW YORK TIMES BESTSELLING AUTHOR

ELOISA JAMES

The Wildes of Lindow Castle

Wilde in Love

978-0-06-238947-3

Too Wilde to Wed

978-0-06-269246-7

Born to Be Wilde

978-0-06-269247-4

Say No to the Duke

978-0-06-287782-6

Say Yes to the Duke

978-0-06-287806-9

Wilde Child

978-0-06-287807-6

EJ6 1021